EDITED BY ANDREW WOLTER

PINK TRIANGLE RHAPSODY

PINK TRIANGLE
RHAPSODY

A Lycan Valley Anthology

Lycan Valley Press Publications
1625 E 72nd St STE 700 PMB 132
Tacoma, Washington 98404 United States of America

Printed in the United States of America

ISBN-13: 978-1-64562-009-9

This book is dedicated to Freddie Mercury and the original band members of Queen.

Even more so, this book is dedicated to the gay men who were subjected to the horrors of the Holocaust, to the gay men who rioted and protested at Stonewall, to the gay men who lost their lives or were imprisoned for being gay, to the gay men who fought and continue to stand against anti-gay policies and homophobic society, to the gay men who openly come out, to the gay men who have yet to come out, to all gay men past and present and to all the gay men of the future... Your history, your culture, your experiences, you matter.

"I'm as gay as a daffodil, dear"
~ Freddie Mercury, interview with Julie Webb

TABLE OF CONTENTS

ELECTRIC PINK

BY JOHN PEYTON COOKE

LATE NIGHT WAS OUR TIME. We'd sit there in Boss's old muscle car with our engine and lights off, staking out the clubs, watching for trouble. He'd be there behind the steering wheel in his black leather jacket, tight jeans, and black boots, calm as could be, jaw grimly set as he scanned the urban terrain, his stubbled face lit up by the flashing unnatural colors of neon: firefly green, circus orange, candy red. Riding shotgun, I'd often stare at these crazy colors cycling through the sheen of his wavy black hair. He kept it unfashionably long, just down to his shoulders. If he caught me staring, he'd smirk and tell me to keep my eyes on the street. That was where the danger was. In here, we were safe. I always felt safe when I was with my Boss, but then there was hardly ever a moment when we weren't together. When he was at his day job as a private security expert, I'd be safe inside his apartment, tidying up and looking after his various requests and getting myself ready for him to come home. Our occasional nightwork was something we did together, but it wasn't a real job, it was "volunteer" work "for the community," as Boss put it.

But you know about us already, if you've ever heard of the Electric Pink Gang. You may never have thought there were only two of us, and maybe that is a testament to Boss's genius. But you also don't know either of our names, and you never will.

Our work was not in the poshest parts of the city. Most of the gay bars and clubs were in the rougher districts south of North Fork's abandoned train station, on streets that were still cobbled, rubbed into smooth hard granite ovals from generations of traffic. I'd imagine horse-drawn ice trucks and old Model A Fords skittering down the street, and burly warehouse workers hauling wooden crates or big loads in canvas bags, and when I'd mention this to Boss, he'd laugh and say that's why he loved me, because I was such a dreamer. Then he'd ruffle my hair and slap my cheek and tell me to get back to business.

"Thanks, Boss," I'd say.

He'd flash me his evil grin and say, "Good boy."

Most nights, nothing happened. Those were good nights, as Boss would say, and of course he was right about that. A night without violence was a night when things went more or less as they ought. When couples would leave the bars, they might be hand-in-hand or arms-across-shoulders or just walking side-by-side in an obvious intimacy that no straight man would dare. Seldom steady, because alcohol had worked its magic, but they were still standing and able to make it back to their cars or to their apartments if they lived nearby. We were generally a block or two away from whatever bar we were watching, and if we saw everyone get into their vehicles or around the last corner without incident, we were satisfied. If we were particularly worried about a couple—say, if they were both spectacularly drunk and looked like they might have trouble finding their way home—then Boss might rev up the engine of his Wildcat and follow them discreetly for at least a few blocks to make sure they weren't jumped. There was always a danger we'd have left the bar unwatched for a time, but as Boss admitted, his system was far from perfect. We couldn't police every club every night, either, because we couldn't be in more than one place at the same time. But Boss had a good feel for when and where trouble was likely to happen, and certain bars were targeted more than others, especially on theme nights like drag shows, fetish events, or underwear contests.

"Weekends are worst, of course," Boss told me when we were starting out, as I was giving him a back massage. "Friday and Saturday nights. Young thugs will come in looking for easy targets. Some are just drunk and raising hell, others trying to impress their gang or get into one. Fag-bashing's just a sport to them. They don't care who they hurt. And the police in this city don't care, either, or they might say it isn't their priority. Same difference. I know this, boy. I'm still friends with some of them from my days on the force. It's not their fault, it's the top brass. They call the shots, and there's too much filthy lucre in this town. They just look the other way on this, the drug trade, the smash-and-grabs, and everything else, because that's how the Carlsson gang wants it."

"Permission to ask a question, Boss?"

"Yeah, what is it? And don't stop, boy. Shoulders."

I worked my grip deep into his meaty delts. "Who's Carlsson?"

"Aw, Jesus, you're such an innocent." He chuckled. "That's it, that feels good, keep it up. You've never heard of Sven Carlsson? They call him 'Cash' Carlsson but don't call him that to his face. He started out as 'No-Cash' Carlsson, and maybe that tells you all you need to know about his motivation. Pure greed will drive some men to do the evilest things. He's run this city for decades. Everyone's on his payroll. Never spent a night in jail in his life. But he's tied to more murders in North Fork than you can count. And I'm not even talking about the fag-bashing, which he encourages as a way of enticing new recruits to his crew."

"I thought that was just drunken teenagers and frat boys."

"There've been four young gay men beaten to death —murdered—in the last five years, for no reason at all, and none of the perps ever caught. Why do you think I went private? There was a time when I thought things were moving in the right direction. Now it seems like everything's going backwards. We've got more hate crimes than ever. The thugs are feeling empowered. The city's only growing more corrupt. I want to do something about it, but I can't do it alone. Now that I've got you, boy, I'm going to train you up—gym, martial arts, weapons. Then you and I are going out there and putting an end to it."

"Yes, Boss," I said. That's what I always said. In his eyes, anyway, I was a good boy.

You can call me boy with a little "b" just as I call him Boss with a big "B." We met on a fetish app. I'd known for years that I was a sub bottom slut and had been recently playing around on my own with a small chastity cage and was looking for a keyholder, and... well, I'll spare you all the gory details, but suffice to say I found him. At twenty-three, I may not be what the rest of the world thinks of as a boy, but it's more a state of mind, or a state of being. To my Boss, I'll never be anything but. And not only a boy but *his* boy, his *property*. What you may not understand (if you're totally vanilla, that is) is that an aggressive total top like Boss can never be complete without a truly submissive bottom like me at his side. As much as he knows himself and what he wants, you might say he was completely at sea until he met me—missing his other half. That's not to brag, it's simply true. He thinks of himself as a "Real Man" (which, conversely, I can never be in his eyes), but he was only half a man until he found me. Like the scheme he had in mind, he just couldn't put it into action until he'd attained his opposite, his counterpart. I was there to make him happy, give him pleasure, do his bidding, worship him, be molded by him, and get trained to behave exactly the way he wanted me to, not only within the sheets but also on the streets.

Boss isn't "into the gay scene" and he's not a very social person, anyway, so when we're not on the prowl for fag-bashers, we're at home, playing (and playing and playing) or just hanging out. The very clubs we try to protect are places we would almost never go to. Not even North Fork's only leather bar (surprisingly, not his "scene" either) except on rare occasion and then only for the purpose of showing me off for his own amusement, like when he entered me in the spank-the-twink contest (on stage, in front of a massive crowd, wearing nothing but my chastity cage and a jock strap, and which I won, by the way) or let me be "borrowed" as he's done the past two years for the biweekly meetings of the local bondage club.

Even as well matched as we are, it took a while for our relationship to fall into its mode and for me to learn all the rules. (Take my word for it.) But once Boss was satisfied with my obedience, he embarked on a program of physical and mental development for his boy. It was a pretty grueling regimen at the gym, and a hardcore muscle-building diet, continually adjusted to optimize results. He said he had caught me at the perfect time to reorient my body toward lean muscle and strength. And when that started to pay off, over the next two years, he added intensive boxing lessons, then switched me to Thai kickboxing, and then we enrolled together in Brazilian jiu jitsu. The hardest thing for me to learn was the competitive desire to best my opponents, but eventually I got there. Boss was happy to see me defeat others, but never did allow me to fight against him. I had to be kept in my place, and, after all, he still held the keys to what he liked to call my "little clit." He claimed that by keeping it locked up in chastity for extended periods—weeks, months—it would keep me focused on my training and make me a fierce warrior. Maybe it did, maybe it didn't, but it sure did keep me horny, which was the main thing. These periods were defined, of course, by when he would unlock the device and let me out, always under his supervision, and with me either already bound or otherwise under orders. Needless to say, there was only one person in this relationship with total control over my cock. He said it was *his*, anyway, which was confusing at first, but of course he was right. It *was* his. Everything about me belonged to him. And I followed him blindly. Because I trusted him and admired him. I could look at him and just melt, and I felt totally safe when I was in his arms.

Without a totally obedient sub at his command, Boss would never have been able to execute his plan. For my part, aside from our shared sense of justice, I would never have possessed the means or desire for any of it, but for being reprogrammed into his very own Creation.

As I said, most nights, nothing happened. Often when there were no gangs about, Boss would keep vigil while I gave him a long, slow blowjob. Then on this night, while his magnificent cock was deep in my throat and I heard the sounds of other cars passing, I felt his strong fingers tense up on the back of my neck.

"Wait a moment," he said. "What's this?" This was like Boss talking to himself, thinking out loud, almost the way you would talk to your own dog, without expecting an answer.

I kept up what I was doing, because he hadn't ordered me to stop.

"By the pricking of my thumbs..." he said. Boss was a literate guy with a good education. He had endless things to teach me.

He held me there for a moment, my nose pressed against his pubes. His abdomen contracted, and with a few quick convulsions I felt the warmth of his cum at the back of my throat and swallowed it all down.

"Okay, boy, up," he said.

I came up for breath and licked the mess off my mouth. Boss hitched up his jeans, stuffed himself back inside, and zipped up.

"Blue Honda Accord full of assholes has been circling. Now they've parked, half a block ahead. Just to the side of Shade Club."

I got myself reoriented and looked ahead down the street and identified the car Boss was talking about. Not much of anything going on, though. One of them got out the passenger side and poked his head around, scouting, sniffing.

"They're itching for it," he said. "Just wait."

The *just wait* was a bit of a signal, part of my conditioning. I instantly felt like an engine within me was starting to rev up, the pistons cycling faster and faster, or a rubber band getting twisted and twisted tighter and tighter, or a giant key being cranked up in my back to wind up my inner spring. Boss owned me, Boss made me, and this is what he made me for. My heart beat faster, adrenaline pumping.

"Just wait, boy, just wait..."

Boss was stroking the back of my head. I knew some similar sensation of excitement was bubbling up inside him, but unlike me he kept up a calm demeanor. If you were to look at me at that moment, you'd see my wide alert eyes, ears pricked up, nostrils flaring. Boss looked placid, at ease. A smirk appeared on his sensuous lips. He exuded darkness, determination, diabolism. I adored him.

"Hold it, boy, hold it."

We could hear some scattered bits of macho posturing convo coming from the area of the blue Accord, but I couldn't make anything out.

Then we saw a couple of patrons emerge from around the corner of Shade Club. One guy was tall, the other short, one light, one dark, both skinny, huddling together affectionately, chattering and laughing, stumbling a bit as they made their way along the side of the building, outside the sight of the club's bouncer. The tall one reached his arm around his pal's waist and spun him around till they were hugging, crotch to crotch, backed him up gently against the brick wall, and kissed him deeply, eyes closed. They could have met five minutes ago or been together fifteen years.

The Accord goons were parked across from them, also completely out of sight of the club's entrance and the main street. All four doors of the Accord popped open, and suddenly there were five guys milling about, staying close to their vehicle at first. They were all around twenty years old or so and wore typical street clothes—jeans, T-shirts, dark jackets, sneakers— nothing special, no uniforms. One was shaved bald, but the others had hair: two black, two blond.

Our couple was definitely being sized up for a target. But they appeared not to notice the gang coming toward them. There was nothing especially threatening about them, up to this point. For all our couple knew, the gang were just some late arrivals about to hit Shade Club before last call.

"Hey, faggots!" shouted one of the black-haired guys.

Our couple split apart fast and turned around to see what was going on.

"Steady," Boss whispered to me.

"You want some of this?" the guy grabbed his crotch and pulled it up a couple of times, as if it had great heft.

"No, man, we cool," one of our couple said, spooked but trying to shrug it off. They quickened their pace and made no threatening gestures.

"You're cool, are you?" said the bald one. "You're *disgusting!*"

"Get 'em!" shouted another one.

Then the five assholes were upon them like a swarm. They circled them, pushed them, grabbed their hair, banged their heads against the brick wall, knocked them over, punched, and kicked them.

"Let's go, boy," Boss said, slipping a black ski mask over my head and another over his. All they'd be able to see would be our eyes and mouth. "Go, go, go go! I'm calling 9-1-1 and right behind you."

I bolted from our car, screaming like a beast. I had no fear. I knew after he called in the incident, Boss would be right behind me, with his greater bulk and his illegal taser.

I went hurtling straight into the five guys as if they were a knot to be undone. Whoever hesitated first was the one I'd go for. I'd done this enough times to predict how it would go. First was one of the blonds. He turned around as if to say *what-the-fuck* and in that moment my right fist slammed into his nose with the full force of my muscles and the velocity of my sprint, and knocked him on his ass.

The others were quick. They turned away from their attack on the Shade Club couple, who lay cowering and bleeding on the sidewalk, looking at me also in fear, not knowing what was going on. I said not a word, but grunted, and when the bald one came at me, I grabbed his out-thrust arm and used leverage and his own weight to throw him over my shoulder onto the pavement. I kicked the taller of the black-haired dudes squarely in the stomach with a lightning-fast Muay Thai kick, and he went flying backward. The shorter black-hair jumped me from the side and landed a few punches to my ribs that I barely felt, and I swung at him with my left and slammed his face sideways, knocking out a few bloody teeth that went flying into the gutter. I kicked him in the pelvis, and he went spinning and fell flat on his face on the cobbles. The second blond took one look at me, his fists out in a pathetic display. I growled at him and shot out a fast kick into the air between us, and he did what I expected and turned around and bolted, running away down the street. The taller black-haired dude, squirming on the ground clutching his stomach, kicked at the ground to try to get away from me, then scrambled to his feet and went running after his mate.

I turned and saw the bloody-nosed blond coming at me with his fists, blood spilling from his nose and mouth and marking his T-shirt. "You son-of-a-bitch!" he was sputtering.

Not far behind him was Boss, taking aim with his taser. He didn't say a word, not a warning, not a wisecrack, nothing. He just pointed the thing and shot. I reached out my arms to grab the guy, as he reached me the moment the barbed electrodes slammed into his back muscles. He convulsed and gritted his teeth and went limp in my arms. I set him down easy on the sidewalk.

"I've got him," Boss said, and casually removed some long heavy-duty zip-ties from his jacket pocket.

This left me to take care of the others. The bald guy I'd thrown over my shoulder was just lying there moaning; maybe I'd hurt his back. I didn't care. I'd deal with him later. I went for the other black-haired guy whose teeth I'd knocked out and dived on top of him. He was trying to get away, thrashing around without much sense. I used my jiu jitsu on him and wrestled him into submission pretty easily, face-down and bleeding into the muck, and when I had his wrists behind his back, I held them with one hand while I removed my own zip-ties and threw one around his wrists. It took some work to grab his feet and hold them together, but I got them zip-tied as well.

By that time, Boss had flipped over the moaning bald guy and hogtied him like the other two.

The poor couple who these jerks had attacked were watching the whole time, apprehensively, unsure what we were up to, but probably starting to figure out that we were what people thought of as the Electric Pink Gang.

"I've called police and ambulance," Boss told them. "You're going to be all right."

In his black ski mask, his face was obscured. Mine also remained in place. We'd made another intervention without being discovered. As long as we got out of there fast. But there was one more thing to do. Leave our calling card.

Boss gathered the three hog-tied perps together on the sidewalk, then started talking with the bash-victims and checking out their injuries, in case there was anything he could do before the paramedics arrived. In the meantime, I grabbed his taser and its wires and electrodes and ran with it back to our car and popped open the trunk. I threw the taser inside, opened a cardboard case of Pepto-Bismol, and grabbed six bottles, piling them up in my arms, and ran on back.

There was no sound of sirens yet. The police took their time responding to fag-bashings. It wasn't their priority. Usually, the ambulance would get here first, by which time we'd be on our way, but so far there was no sign of it.

I met up with Boss and handed him some of the bottles. One by one, we opened them up and poured their contents all over the perps. From their sneakers to their jeans to their jackets to their heads, each was covered in thick, gooey pinkness.

"Okay, boy, let's go," Boss said, and we ran back to Wildcat. Boss gunned it, and we took off.

Behind our ski masks, what were we? Far from superheroes, nothing more than vigilantes. Boss and I shared a sense of justice, sure. But we were punishing others without a trial. Rushing to judgment. Plunging in and acting rashly to avenge what we saw as a wrong. The assaults we witnessed were crimes, certainly. But so were our acts. Early on, I'd proposed to Boss that we should set up a social media account and post pictures of our trophies bound up in hogties and drenched in Pepto-Bismol. Amplify our warnings as broadly as possible. But Boss would have none of it.

"Too easy for someone to trace this back to us," he said. "Even if we try to make it anonymous. The less trace we leave, the better. Even if we think we're in the right, what we're doing is assault. If we get caught, we could go to prison for a very long time. I might be able to bear prison, but I couldn't bear it without you, boy. And you, hell, you'd be eaten alive in there. We can't risk getting caught."

This was also the reason Boss gave me for not providing any further assistance to the bashing victims, beyond a cursory glance at their injuries and phoning 9-1-1. We couldn't stick around. We couldn't leave our names. We couldn't get involved. Our sole purpose was to bag and tag the perps and get the hell out of there.

"What we're doing wouldn't be done otherwise," Boss explained, while he was giving me a bubble-bath. "The cops would take the incident report and file it away. None of these assholes would ever be caught. Then there's no deterrent to the others. The city's finest make it clear they more or less condone it. No protection for the gay community, and no punishment for the fag-bashers. Live and let live, on and on and on and on. It's been this way forever, and I'm just sore and depressed and tired of it."

Even without taking pictures and posting, Boss knew that word would get around. It did, of course, through the press and through the word on the street. We knew it did, because we could read about ourselves in the media, and see ourselves described in local TV reports. The Electric Pink Gang was thought to be six to ten muscular men who cruised around late at night waiting to pounce on anyone who would mess with the gays. The only witnesses were the perps who had fallen prey to the Electric Pink Gang, and they told tales of horror about the monstrous, black-masked warriors who descended on them like ninjas, popping out of black vans and repelling down ropes from nearby rooftops. "We will catch these vigilantes," said the spokesperson for the police department, "and they will be brought to justice."

Local gay activists were happy to use the incidents to draw attention to fag-bashings, but they were quick to criticize our methods. "Hate crimes have got to stop," one of them said in the local gay rag, "but more violence is not the solution. If these vigilantes really cared about what's going on, they would stop these hate crimes before they occurred, instead of letting them happen. And if the police could be relied on to do their job, there would be nothing left for the Electric Pinks."

Boss let me ask him once, while I was seated on the floor between the sofa and the coffee table, as he leaned back and I worshipped his beautiful feet, why we didn't just stop the violence before it started, when it was usually obvious to us what was just about to happen. "I'm not a diplomat," he said. "Let someone else try that. Ah, that's good. Keep it up, boy. I have to act, and I'm not going to act without justification, or at least provocation. If someone's going to drive by and call someone names, without any physical violence, that's not much of a crime. But once they strike, I'm striking back. The victims are being ambushed, and may or may not fight back, but seldom are able. You and I, we've equipped ourselves to do just that. We're their surrogate fighters. Every gay man who gets jumped. We're the creatures of their super-ego, their repressed animal instincts become manifest. They let us out of the box, and when it's done we jump back into the box. The perps get what they deserve. But we couldn't do this if there weren't an incitement. Hurt my peeps, and I'll hurt you. That message has got to be made loud and clear."

Except I wasn't so sure the message was being heard. We'd been engaging in these attacks for the better part of a year now, and the rate of bashings reported by the press was about the same as before.

If it was so ineffective, we were we still doing it?

I had no doubt Boss got an adrenaline rush from the violence. He really enjoyed going after thugs. Maybe all he had done was to find a way to justify his innate bloodlust. But I believed in him, never doubted him, and shared his conviction that somehow, ultimately, what we were doing would bring all this senseless violence to a halt.

And I couldn't argue with him even I wanted to.

So, we persisted.

The turning point came around 2:30 a.m. one morning, when we had just finished bagging and tagging a few more idiots in the alley behind the Eagle. These dolts had jumped a couple of brawny, sweaty leathermen in caps and chaps, and you might think they were brainless to have done so, but Boss's theory held true—no matter who was being jumped, the shock, surprise, and humiliation of it was enough to cow them into stunned passivity. We leapt out (as their fight surrogates) and I did my whirling dervish ninja routine on them while Boss backed me up as usual, both with his powerful muscles and the godawful taser. A couple of them ran off, and we nabbed four of the others. We had this down to a science and had finished zip-tying and Pepto-bombing the twerpy perps and lining them up in a neat row when a couple of new goons pulled the jump on us.

These were not rowdy college boys. My first sight of them was as I was emptying another bottle of pink goo onto one of my captives, heard some rapid footsteps, and turned to see a hulking no-necked simian dude hurling himself at me with a head-butt. I fell flat on my back against the pink slobbery mess of one of my captives and felt my attacker's boot slam against my thigh. I saw Boss coming at him and grabbing him around the chest, but then another gorilla slapped a blackjack against the back of Boss's head, and he went down.

I struggled to get up and away from the kicking, but my palms slid against the wet mess and I was unable to push my way up. I looked to Boss and saw him writhing on the gritty pavement, groaning.

The two bloodied leathermen we'd come out to defend got warily to their feet and went back into the Eagle through the back door.

"Get his mask!" I heard, and thought they were going to unmask Boss, but there was another guy behind me, and I found my own ski mask ripped over my head and a strong arm grasp me from behind.

"Hey, it's the prettyboy!" the one said who'd head-butted me.

"We know what you two are up to," said the faceless one behind me. "We saw you sucking that one's dick back there. Some gang you are! You're just a couple of fruits. Your luck's run out, you fucking faggots! We got a message for you both, from 'Cash' Carlsson."

The one in front of me landed a few sharp kicks right in Boss's chest, and Boss clutched himself in pain. The one who'd swung the blackjack kicked at Boss's back, and he went into a fetal position and threw his arms up to protect his head.

The guy behind me held me around my throat with one arm, constricting my breathing. I reached up and tried grabbing at him, but then he showed me his knife. It came out from behind my ear, shiny and glistening in the dim light in back of the Eagle.

"Don't breathe," the voice whispered in my ear. "Hold still."

The pain slashed deep across one cheek and then the other, and I felt the warm blood spill out across my face and onto my neck.

"Prettyboy no more," the voice said. "You tell your boyfriend you guys had better cut out this shit. No more of it. Or next time, you'll be dead. We know who you are. We know where you live. And we're everywhere. You can't win. Give up and you'll never see us again."

I fell back as the strong grip released me. They landed a few more kicks on me, then ran off and piled into a black Mercedes, screeching their tires as they pulled out and drove off.

Our pink hogties were laughing at us, but that only became clear to me as my hearing and vision emerged from a fog, and I heard sirens coming closer from a few blocks off.

I was able to struggle to my feet and went over to Boss.

"You all right, Boss?" I asked.

He winced in pain. "Ribs," he grunted, and I assumed this meant he had a few broken ones. Through his teeth: "Get us out of here."

I was in pain as well, but not disabled, and was able to lift Boss to his feet and half-carry, half-drag him to our car as he pushed along with his feet. I somehow got him into the passenger side and propped him up. I reached into his jeans pocket and got the keys, then hustled over to the driver's side and got in.

It was a strange feeling being behind the steering wheel of Boss's car, which I usually only came close to while I was going down on him. Because, of course, he had never ever let me drive his baby and would never have let me near it in a million years. But...

"Go!" he said. "Now!"

I turned the key in the ignition and the Wildcat screamed to life, and I gunned her and went speeding down Custer Street and through the next couple of stop signs. I calmed down a bit and drove a tad more carefully through the dark city streets until we reached the sanctity of our home.

The next few weeks, we hardly left Boss's place. His ribs healed on their own, more or less, thanks to his authoritative instructions and my constant and hyper-attentive nursing attention. Boss had stitched up the gashes marking my face, but warned me they would leave scars nevertheless. He kissed me all over and assured me that nothing could mar my beauty, in his eyes. He said my scars would be a "badge of honor" and a sign of my sacrifice, which all seemed a bit of a stretch to me, but I took it in the spirit in which it was intended, because Boss was simply trying to impress on me that nothing would ever change between us. He would always be my adored Boss, and I would always be his beloved boy. We spent every hour together and never went out. We either ordered in or ordered groceries that I would fix up into his favorite meals. We were trying to regroup, and recoup our strength. We would need it to execute Boss's final plan.

"They might think we heeded their warning," he said, as I was massaging his massive thighs, working deep into his tissue just as he had taught me. "Let them believe that."

"This is kidnapping!" said "Cash" Carlsson on that final night, as he struggled against the heavy chains that held him bound to a metal chair in a storage space Boss had rented.

"It'll be worse than that if you don't cooperate," said Boss with a smirk, as he had me pour the pink cement into the empty bucket in which Carlsson's feet were planted. I saw his toes wriggling in his silk socks as the cold mixture plopped onto them and then swiftly covered them up, halfway up his calves.

We had the gangster in a pink tutu and wearing a pink halter top that was barely able to conceal his sagging, hairy, gray-haired moobs. He was bald with a ring of white hair around his head and a bristly white mustache, on which had formed wet droplets of pink from all the Pepto-Bismol we'd been feeding him.

"I've always wondered what would happen from an overdose of Pepto-Bismol," Boss said. "If you keep fighting us, we're all going to find out."

"You're dead men!" Carlsson said, fighting against his chains. "We'll hack you both to pieces while you're still breathing!"

"Don't give me any ideas," Boss said. (It was what I was thinking, anyway, but Boss wouldn't let me speak without permission in this situation, so I was pleased to hear my own thoughts come out of his mouth, which was by this time not an infrequent occurrence.) "You don't seem to be able to grasp the situation you're in. We're the ones who've got you in the bag, not the other way around."

"I run this city!" Carlsson said. "I own these people, every one of them, down to the tiniest little clerk. One way or another, we'll get you and your freakboy."

"That didn't save you tonight," Boss said. "It was all too easy. Maybe your people didn't want to try so hard to protect you. My guess is they'll be happy to be rid of you."

Whatever Boss thought, it had hardly been "all too easy," it had been a bit of a nightmare. But at least neither of us had been seriously hurt. We'd been casing the North Fork Rod & Gun Club for a few weeks and learned Carlsson's routine for his comings and goings to this out-in-the-open gang hideout. This was where his security had been the most lax, maybe because he thought no one would ever try to touch him so close to his own turf. We found he always had two beefy bodyguards with him, and the other wild card we had to deal with was the doorman to the club. But after observing them from a distance over a period of time, Boss was able to diagnose their weak spots and set out a game plan for us, drawn out on a diagram like a football play. He pretty much storyboarded the whole thing and knew what move everyone would make down to the split second. The biggest challenge would be that the bodyguards probably carried pistols, and probably also the doorman and maybe Carlsson himself.

Watching Boss map out his plan and coach me on every moment of it made my admiration for him grow. He kept reaching over and stroking my scars—his way of showing me that he would never forgive Carlsson for what he'd done, nor would he ever let my scars lessen his love for me. He'd also told me how proud he was of how I'd tended to him so tenderly, helping him get his bones healed and get his muscles back into condition. What we had been through together only heightened our intimacy, even if it would never change the balance of the power in our relationship. All of which was fine with me. He was my Boss.

When it came down to the critical moment, Boss tasered the doorman of the North Fork Rod & Gun Club just as he was about to help Carlsson out of his Escalade, just at the moment the right-hand bodyguard was scanning the horizon, just at the moment I leapt across the hedge and planted a strong Muay Thai kick right in the bodyguard's stomach. That was two down. The left-hand bodyguard was on the other side of the Escalade and had to run around it to come at me. While he was doing this, I fell to the ground on top of the first bodyguard, disabled him with a sharp blow to his gun hand, and reached in and grabbed his Glock. He tried grabbing at me with his other hand, and I smashed his face in. As the other bodyguard emerged from behind the Escalade, Boss tasered him as well, and his gun went off randomly as he fell to the ground in electroconvulsions. I then popped up and aimed the Glock at Carlsson, who held his hands up, laughing in my face. Overconfidence. He was sure we wouldn't get far. But that was it. We had him. While I covered him, Boss zip-tied the two bodyguards and the doorman. Then we hustled Carlsson at gunpoint into the Wildcat and brought him to the storage facility without being followed. Easy.

"Boy, give him another dose," Boss said.

I held out the bottle of Pepto-Bismol and started pouring it over Carlsson's mustache. He clamped his lips shut and let the goo dribble over his chin and down onto his halter top.

"Open up," Boss said. "Or you'll get a taste of the

taser."

Carlsson opened up. I poured it down. We had a few cases of the stuff at the ready, and as Boss had told him at the outset, we had all night and nothing better to do.

"It says here," and with this Boss held up the label of one of the bottles and squinted at the fine print, "that an overdose could cause ringing in the ears, loss of hearing, extreme drowsiness, nervousness, fast breathing, confusion, or seizures. It also says something about vomiting, extreme diarrhea, confusion, loss of energy, and aggressive behavior. I'd love to see if we could come up with a few of these before we're done with you. Boy, another bottle."

"What do you want from me?" Carlsson asked, quivering.

Boss stepped forward and loomed over him, with the overhead light strategically behind his head. Oh, how I wish I could do justice to the scene and to Boss's incredible beauty in that moment. It was like a halo erupting behind his wavy black hair, his eyes obsidian, his jawline thrust out in disdain.

"You've used us for decades," Boss said. "You own all the deeds on all the gay bars. You own the porn shops, the massage parlors, the truck-stop prostitutes, and all the drug trade."

"Supply and demand," Carlsson said. "It's human nature. I'm only giving everybody what they want. You and I can cut a deal. Let me out of here, I'll give you more money than you've ever seen in your life."

Boss stared implacably.

"I want all the violence against gays in this city to

stop," Boss said. "You're going to make that happen."

Carlsson laughed. "You think I'm responsible for all that? You've got to be kidding me! Everyone hates the gays. You can't blame me."

"Your young recruits cut their teeth on us," Boss said. "I know it, and you know it. It's a way of dehumanizing them, bending them to your control. First you get them on tiny errands, maybe a few easy pot deliveries. If they want to work their way up in your crew, they've got to hurt someone. Easiest target is the group they already think are less than human. So you send them after us. They beat up some fags, and you hear all about it. You praise them. You say, 'Well done.' But you can also hold that over them. If they're any good to you, you can build on that to get them to beat up your debtors, or your whores if they fall out of line. They become your muscle. But they have to start somewhere. Fag-bashing is their gateway drug. I'm telling you now that you're going to put an end to it. And you have to convince me you can do it. Or you'll never make it out of this storage shed. You'll die here starving, miserable, and alone, your feet frozen in pink cement. And they'll find you here in a cute pink top and a tutu, drowning in Pepto-Bismol. It's what you might call an ignominious end."

"And you'll be dead!" Carlsson sputtered, pink spittle flying. "Dead! Dead! Dead!"

"Go on," Boss said, amused.

"You and your girly little toyboy. We'll cut your balls off and feed them to you for breakfast!"

"No one knows you're here."

"I've got eyes everywhere."

"No one will ever know. You might never be found. Or the contents of this shed might get auctioned off sight-unseen, a few years from now, and they'll open it up to find your hideous corpse. That would make for some fine television."

Carlsson was about to mouth off again, but he held his tongue. You could see on his face that he was recognizing the reality of the situation. There was every possibility that Boss and his boy would get away with it. Carlsson's boys might have no clue where he was.

"Boy," Boss said, with a nod.

I opened another bottle and held it over his mouth.

"Open," Boss ordered him.

"Cash" Carlsson, the most feared crime boss in this part of the Midwest, opened his mouth obediently and let me pour the stuff down his throat. Boss circled around him wielding the taser at the ready.

"Swallow," Boss said. "Keep swallowing. Boy, another bottle."

In the end, I don't think it was the Pepto-Bismol that did him in. It wasn't the taser, either, because Boss never had recourse to use it. Maybe it was the stress of the uncommon situation, coupled with the fact that Carlsson wasn't as young as he used to be. At any rate, for whatever reason, his heart gave out, and we had no inclination to call him an ambulance, so he expired there in his ignominy, just as Boss had predicted, even if we had accomplished nothing in our attempt to right a few decades of wrongs.

We are in no hurry for anyone to find the body. As far as we know, Sven "Cash" Carlsson still sits there, pretty in pink, in his final home at the North Fork U-Stor-It. There's a long lease on that unit, paid far in advance all in cash by someone whose name no one has ever heard of. If they ever open it up, you can imagine for yourself what the scene is going to look like. Affixed to the pink halter top with a safety pin, scrawled on a Post-it, is a final note from Boss to whomever it may ever concern, stating:

ACCIDENTAL OVERDOSE
YOURS TRULY,
THE ELECTRIC PINK GANG

And that was the last anyone ever heard from us. We've moved on to another city but put our vigilante days behind us, so I can focus one hundred percent of my attention on pleasing my Boss in every possible way that only he could dream up.

FULL

BY ROBERT DUNBAR

"AND DON'T YOU TRY AND SNEAK past me neither." As she lifted her head from the table, bleached hair glowed under the light. "What do you think, I'm stupid or something?"

"Okay." Edging around the kitchen, Dell pressed his back to the stove. "I mean, I wasn't." He fumbled with both hands under his shirt. The old jersey hung huge on him, his bony frame lost within it.

"What are you hiding?" she demanded.

"Nothing."

"I can see you, you know. You've got something under your shirt. Oh, what do I care? Do whatever the hell you want. Take drugs or whatever. See if I give a shit. Goddamn kids."

"I'm not..."

"And what were you doing down the basement anyways?" Suddenly, her face went rigid, and creases sharp as razor cuts crossed her forehead. Frantically, she gestured at the doorway. "See if he's listening." Scrawny muscles clenched tight against the brittle bones in her jaw and neck. "Take a look. Careful!" Her whole body tensed, shoulders quivering. "Can you see?" Cigarette ashes scattered across the tabletop as she clutched a bottle with a bat on the label.

"Did you take something?" asked Dell. "On top of that, I mean." He nodded at the bottle.

"Quick, hide this under the sink."

He stepped closer."You're burning yourself again." Determinedly, he pried the cigarette from her fingers. "He's not coming. You know you're not supposed to mix stuff. What did you take?"

"Stop it! Everybody, just stop telling me what to do!" Practically screaming, she clawed at her own throat as though at a noose. "Do you know how many things people get away with in this world? Do you? Why am I the only one who never gets away with a thing?" This burst out—a shuddering revelation—and she collapsed back into her chair. "Nothing." Her eyes welled up with tears. "Not me. Not a thing."

"How many did you take?"

"You don't know what he's like. You don't know what it means to be afraid all the time. What's this?" Her hand darted out, and she picked at him in agitation, the gesture proprietary yet hesitant. "Jesus Christ, there's cobwebs in your hair. What's wrong with you?" Her fingers stayed on him now, first on the long hair that gleamed like polished oak, then on his face. "I just took one," she answered, finally. "A half a one. I needed it."

"How many really?"

"For my nerves." She drew herself up. "Did you do the dishes?" she demanded, slightly slurring the words.

"Aren't any dishes."

"Don't you talk to me like that! I don't see you with

two broken arms, mister. You could have made dinner. All you kids are so goddamn spoiled."

"All what kids? There's just me left," he pointed out.

She ignored this. "Why do you treat me like this? Answer me. Why do I deserve this? Tell me that. Can you? No! No wonder I have to get electric shock. Who wouldn't in this house?" Again, her hands strayed to her neck and the electrodes she'd tried to conceal with the frilly pink collar. "Somebody has to help me. How come nobody helps me?" Her eyes clouded over, then focused without warning. "And what were you doing down the basement anyways, mister?"

He backed away. "Answer me, I said."

"Nothing. I... I got homework." Shoulders hunched, he made it to the door, her shrill voice pummeling the back of his skull.

"Where do you think you're going? Dell! Don't you walk away from me while I'm talking to you! You come back here!"

As his faint shadow capered across the floor in front of him, the kitchen light dissolved into a darkness that engulfed the rest of the first floor. He tried to wade through without banging into anything. By day, the windows in these rooms remained shuttered and draped; at night, those windows redefined blackness. The bare boards of the unused dining room creaked so loudly that hurrying across always felt like playing some weird musical instrument. Finally, his sneakers scuffed on the crumbling parlor rug.

None of the glow from the kitchen doorway made it this far, and darkness seemed part of the silence. Perfectly still, he could hear only his own breath, but he knew the zombie sat on the sofa at the far corner of the room. It always sat there. He could even guess its position—broken neck twisted to one side, face permanently wincing, as though someone had stuck a knife where it couldn't reach. Hoping the thing would not speak, Dell groped straight through the room until his hand found the banister.

"Is she at it again?" The words drifted to him: no voice from the pit ever sounded more sunk in self-pity.

"Not so bad." He continued up the stairs. He hated talking to the zombie, hated to think he might end up like that someday.

"But she's only just back."

Dell wondered if the thing could see him shrug in the dark. "Been a few weeks," he told it, not stopping. The tension in his back and shoulders didn't ease until he neared the top of the stairs, but no further words pursued him. Up here, the blackness had a thinner, watery quality, and he groped along the hall to his room, trying not to rattle the manacles in the walls as he passed.

Closing the door behind him, he switched on the light. Walls pulsed at him, the drawings that covered them seeming to writhe. Blinking, he waited while they shifted and twitched. Mostly charcoal and pencil, these sketches would never wash off, he knew, not completely, but then she never came up here anymore, and the zombie would never say anything. His most recent effort depicted a shaggy-headed youth with an impossibly huge phallus, dangerous-looking as a club, which sprouted from a snarl of fur. All around him, twisting movements slowed. At last, the naked torsos and arcane markings settled, became just lines and smudges again, and he put his ear to the door. Nothing. He relaxed.

He slipped the old box out from under his shirt. Usually, he kept it hidden behind the oil burner in the basement, because he knew the zombie sometimes searched this room while he was out. With the palm of his hand, he smoothed the dust and cobwebs from the lid. It was a pretty thing, the polished wood inlaid with a pearly substance like the teeth of children. Sitting on the floor, he leaned back against the bed and opened the box. The reek of musty wood and something sweeter filled the room, and he sucked it deep into his lungs. Gently, he lifted out a dead sparrow and laid it on his pillow. Then he felt around the box, finding the remains of a joint and a book of matches from a bar he sometimes sneaked into called The Slab. (They served Bloody Marys and Zombies—stiff drinks they called them —and the jukebox only played dirges. A spotlight pinned dead go-go boys in cages, and though he'd never ventured to the refrigerated back room, he'd heard stories.) He'd never had much fun there.

He opened the window and for a long moment just sat on the floor and smoked the roach. "Tyler," he whispered. "Can you hear me?" Blowing smoke through the screen, he listened to the night. "I can feel you out there." Faintly, a breeze rattled a branch across the shingled roof. "Somewhere," he murmured, taking one last hit and scraping the roach out against the screen. "I swear I can." Cinders glowed red, falling, dying.

Returning to the bed, he fished the remaining item out of the box. The battered deck of tarot cards almost totally lacked color, violent, passionate images faded to shades of ocher and mauve, the edges of the cards soft and crumbling. Still, the symbols themselves remained vivid, all those androgynous bodies tied to stakes or pierced with swords. He spread the blunt cards out but couldn't make them lay flat, the mounded bedspread forcing them up at angles. Painstakingly, he arranged them into an inverted pentagram.

Perched on the edge of the mattress, he reached for the bird. "Poor thing." The sparrow's bones felt sharp and brittle, so delicate, and he brought it closer to his face. Both its eyes had gone. "Poor, poor thing." Had it seen something too sad to bear? As he stroked it, a tiny feather came away, which he rubbed across his throat. He felt his own collarbone, sharp and hard. His left hand wandered under the jersey, fingertips dancing along ribs to slip beneath the waist of his jeans. "Pretty bird." Gently, he returned the sparrow to the pillow. Holding up the single feather, he shut his eyes and let go. He tried to sense it settling toward the deck and only opened his eyes again when he thought it must have landed.

With impossible slowness, the feather still floated, and he didn't breathe again until he saw which card it chose.

It lay across two of them.

Solemnly, he nodded, then packed the cards away. Tenderly putting the bird in last, he slid the box under his bed.

Clicking off the light, he stood in the dark and listened at the door. Then he returned to the window and quietly worked the screen loose. Easing one leg out, he paused again to listen, then clambered out across the low roof.

Just before he jumped, night wind caressed his hair.

He seemed to float too long. Then his sneakers impacted with the yard, and the palms of his hands burned on the ground... on the exact spot where they'd buried his sister. And even in the dark, he could see she'd been trying to get out again. "It's okay." As he scrambled up, he patted the dirt reassuringly. "It's only me."

A side gate led from the yard to an alley, and he eased into the darkness. But even as he closed the gate behind him, he knew he wasn't alone.

One eye glowed like a green moon. The cat watched him without fear, not even getting out of his way when he tripped over a garbage can. Though he'd never seen the beast before, it seemed to gaze at him with recognition. Like the shadow of a cloud, the cat floated soundlessly down the alley alongside him, and he matched its stride companionably, until it flowed under a fence. A mournful yowl drifted back.

Like a stray current of darkness that joined a larger tributary, the alley emptied onto deeply shadowed sidewalk. Wind sowed through trees with a noise like surf. As he hurried along, he had to crouch, because the leaves hung so close.

"Yo."

He whirled around.

"How you doin', man?"

Dell's heart thundered. "Uh."

The guy stood almost directly under the streetlight. "I seen you around," he said. Powerfully built, he appeared to be a basic grunt, sort of handsome even, maybe something just a little weird about the shape of his head.

"You live around here?"

"Uh, not far." Dell couldn't understand why this guy would even speak to him. The mere fact scared him.

The jock sidled closer but spoke louder. "Hey, man, can I give you some head?" The tee shirt pulled taut across his biceps when he reached out to touch Dell's chest. "C'mon, you don't have to do nothing."

A pulse hammered behind Dell's eyes. "No, uh, thanks."

"C'mon, man." The grunt sounded both annoyed and incredulous. "I mean, there's a place right over here," he said, gesturing toward a dark area between houses. "Just let me play with it a little."

He shook his head again and tried to hurry past, but the guy grabbed him between the legs. Dell could see stitches on the wrists clearly now, all around the big hands. He looked up—stitches encircled the neck even. And sutures. Dell's mouth opened and closed, but no words came out. After a moment, the guy let his hand drop away, and Dell walked faster.

"C'mon, man." His feet rooted to the curb as though he were physically unable to cross the street, he called after Dell, "Where you goin' to? You got a date with death or something?"

Heavy trees swayed dark blots along the ground, and Dell vanished into them with relief. When he reached the next corner, he peered behind him but could see no one. Fear hit him then. Eyes slicing into the dark, he started to run, a little awkwardly because he could feel himself swelling from the guy's touch. For just a second, he almost went back.

Finally, panting and practically doubled over, he

slowed and looked behind him. Still nothing. Good. He was almost there anyway, the nicer section of the neighborhood left behind. This last block turned into a black corridor lined by rotting cars. Ahead lay the gated cemetery.

The finials had been filed to points—to keep things in or out?—and marble shone through the iron railing. Tilting headstones and broken figures crowded together, and on all sides, row houses pressed close beyond the fence. As a child, he'd always loved to climb over and read the stones with his fingers. Instinctively, he sought that comfort now. Starting across this last tiny street toward the graveyard, he froze. Low laughter echoed. He darted back and edged into the mouth of another alleyway.

The tight, dirty passage always reeked with garbage: a bad place to get caught. They'd cornered him here once, a couple of guys cutting off the exit, others coming behind him. They'd made him do stuff he didn't like remembering and afterwards punched him around until they got bored. He'd been lucky to walk away that time. At home, the zombie had just stared at the blood in shamed silence, but she'd screamed at him, pounding bony fist against already aching bruises, punishing him for not being one of them, the attackers, as though this were something over which he exercised control.

At the end of the alley, he pressed his back to the wall and peered around the edge. Darkness and silence. He guessed they must be congregating at the far corner. If he climbed the fence, they'd see him for sure. Okay, so he'd have to visit his dead friends another time. He had a more important call to make anyhow. Taking a deep breath, he squeezed between parked cars and sprinted across the unlit street into a cul-de-sac.

This was the worst block in the neighborhood. The worst. Hands down. Trash covered the broken sidewalk, and crumbling houses seemed to hold each other up.

The most dilapidated one bore no address, and the boarded windows made it appear deserted. False bricks curled off the walls, stone patterned shelf paper over clapboard. He mounted the four crumbling steps and knocked. Nothing stirred, so he pounded harder. A few doors down, a witch with iodine red hair (that glowed even in the dark) stuck her head out and cursed him. He chanted a string of (four-letter) protective words back at her, and her door slammed.

He waited some more. At last, chains clanked, and the portal before him swung into total blackness. "Rollo," he called into the nothingness, voice quavering. "It's Dell."

The narrow opening seemed to suck at the air. "Oh."

"Hi. Wait." Chains rattled again. "I'll come out."

Relief surged. For an instant, the doorway had seemed to yawn for him, and he wasn't quite ready for that. Not yet.

A shadow peeled away from the darkness, and Rollo floated heavily down the stairs with lugubrious grace.

"... wanted to talk to you about it because you're my best friend." Dell's words sounded lame even to himself, and he fell silent as they wandered aimlessly around the neighborhood.

"I see."

Perambulating conversation constituted a ritual with them. They strolled around and around the cemetery, Rollo doing most of the talking, suddenly filled with the fatalistic enthusiasm that Dell seemed to inspire in him.

"I always so enjoy our discourse, Dell. You boast an instinctive appreciation for this somewhat dolorous perspective it took me centuries to develop. Why is that, do you suppose?"

Dell shrugged, never quite sure when Rollo required a response.

"Mere predilection?"

Dell stared down at the sidewalk. He lashed out with his foot and sent a crushed beer can scuttling into the darkness.

"Or do you suppose you possess what's called an old soul?" Rollo would never let anything drop.

"Don't have a soul," Dell muttered. "Not the way other things do, like a cat, something that doesn't need anything. You know?"

Rollo stared at him strangely.

Finally, Dell met his gaze... but uncomfortably now. It was always hard to make out Rollo's eyes, blurred behind the thick glasses. It might have been the face of a young boy, belied only by the gray in the thick black hair. The lights from a passing car picked him out. He always looked like such a geek in that suit. "Aren't you hot dressed like that?" asked Dell.

"I am cold. Always." He began to unbutton his pants. "Here. Feel."

"I'll pass," Dell snickered, then looked away. "We better not go that way."

"I wasn't seriously suggesting..." They stopped moving. "Ah." Rollo glared into the shadows. "I see what you mean."

And Dell got the impression that Rollo could see.

Perfectly. As though it were noon. All the way down to the corner where the group of villagers loitered.

"Our ever-present friends." Moving more slowly, almost daring the gang to taunt them, they continued across the street. "Odiously hearty, are they not?"

"Please." Dell tried to pick up the pace. "If they come after us, you'd be safe but I…"

"Yo, undead!" A bottle shattered on the sidewalk beside them.

"Bleeders!" Rollo snarled, then composed himself and took Dell's arm. "Let us proceed." As they turned the other way—down a side street that led away from the cemetery—he glanced back. "I'll visit the young males when they're alone. Teach them some manners. The females do not signify." After a moment, his voice took on a thoughtful quality. "I am pleased that you visited me this evening. There is something I've wished to discuss with you for some time, and I trust you won't think me too intrusive. After all, there's nothing more discomfiting than having someone pound on the lid of your coffin."

"Beg pardon?"

"Vampire expression. Never mind. But, concerning this Tyler creature, I feel I must warn you. Not that I care anything for you. Nothing personal, you understand. I care nothing for anyone. It is not in my nature to do so. But you are a friend of sorts, whatever that word may imply, and whatever validity that concept may hold in these circumstances, and you probably should not see him again. After all, you know what will happen. Inevitably. I mean, you do know what he is. Do you not?"

They walked a few more steps. "I know." The voice drifted like a gentle wind.

"And?"

"I love him."

"Ah." Rollo sounded resigned... and impressed.

"Rollo?" Dell realized he stood alone on the dark sidewalk. "Rollo? Where are you? What are you doing back there?" Almost invisible in the shadows, his friend had stopped moving. "What is it?" Following Rollo's glittering gaze, he peered across the narrow street. A light glimmered at an open second-story window. The room beyond lay mostly in darkness, but something—a television perhaps or a fish tank—painted a young man's body with dim gray splashes. Naked except for jockey shorts, he stood, solemnly pumping barbells. "Oh." For a moment, it was as though Dell could see with Rollo's eyes, see the soft hair that stuck to the youth's damp forehead, the sheen of sweet sweat on the stomach. Warm shadows molded his contours.

Rollo's voice seemed to come from above, from a tree or a pole or the sky. "I'll take my leave of you now, and I'll hope to see you again, though considering your decision, that seems somewhat doubtful. Does it not?"

Branches rustled, and Dell knew he was alone. The wind pushed across his body, smoothing his shirt. Feeling a chill, he resumed walking and glanced back only once. The window across the way had gone dark, and he thought he heard a brief cry, whether of pain or pleasure he couldn't be sure. The wind blew stronger, louder. It seemed to get into his head, to whistle and echo, and his thoughts skittered before it like dead leaves. At first, he had to force one foot ahead of the other, so very slowly, but soon he scurried through the empty streets. As the full moon began to rise, he made his way toward the place that had always been his final destination. Always.

Houses ended. The streets widened into boulevards with mean little strips of dying trees. He passed the asylum. (It was on fire again, and he could hear faint screams.) There were no sidewalks here, just naked earth. But at last he could see an ocean of forest, there on the other side. Small, pulped carcasses littered the old highway, and he picked his way across. A lamp that tilted on the final traffic island had gone dark, and short poles bore the dents of repeated collisions. A behemoth lumbered past, its headlights searching for victims, as he sprinted.

The gates to the ancient fairground stood locked, and hedges pressed close to the fence. He watched for movement within but saw nothing. Clouds squeezed out the moon and stars, thickening the night. On all fours, he groped blindly for a depression in the earth. He found it, like some animal's tunnel beneath the fence, and he squeezed under, his belt loop snagging briefly. Then he crawled between shrubs, while leaves and twigs crunched beneath him.

Like some dark sea, the park spread around him. Once, people had strolled here. Now, spectral monuments loomed in scattered sprays of moonlight. He seemed to glide past them, and they gave off a kind of gleam, as though they radiated all the emotions the porous concrete had absorbed throughout the decades.

A hiss rolled on the dirt road ahead of him, and he ducked into dense foliage until the patrol car passed. He could picture them inside, lightning bolts on their uniforms. The bush proved hollow, a sort of globe, and the headlights made the interior ignite for a flickering instant. "I could live in here," he said to himself. "Probably. Hide forever. Like a rabbit or something." When the sound of the car faded, he crawled out again.

A bat swept over his head. It flitted through the pillars of a gazebo, and he followed it, his eyes straining, until the bat became just a climbing shadow, pitch against the lighter dark of masonry.

Moonlight seeped in again, and the columns glowed. Such purity. Even the grass seemed to shimmer. Thick overgrowth screened a tiny lake from view, but he could smell it, could make out patches of glittering black through the reeds. At last, he sat on the shattered cement, his eyes adjusting until he could make out the broken bottles, condoms, syringes in the grass. Even these seemed to shine.

Hearing a shuffling in the grass, he didn't even turn around. "Look how fast the clouds are moving, Ty. Did you ever see a sky like this?" When finally he faced him, he felt the familiar lurch in his chest.

This was love. He harbored no doubts.

Tyler shook his head, the shaggy hair flapping over his shoulders. "We don't have much time." As always, he was naked, the sweaty torso glistening in the shadows. He glided closer through the brush.

Dell would have known that walk anywhere, the strange balance of the powerful shoulders, the long arms swaying. "You're so beautiful," he whispered, rising.

"Thank you."

"Were you at the boathouse?" Dell stepped closer. "Can we go out there again? Like last time."

"Don't need no boat." Tyler sprang on him.

He felt Tyler's mouth fasten over his own, felt Tyler's breath in his own chest like the roar of the wind. Tyler's stomach felt taut against his, the hard flesh pulsing with heat. He felt the thorny hands in his shirt, pressing down to his groin.

"Right here," Dell panted, breaking away. "Do it right here."

Tyler pulled at him again, then seemed to shake himself. "You sure this time?" He put his hands on Dell again but held him at arm's length.

"I know what I want. The cards tonight—The Lovers and Death."

The clouds parted. "Last chance." Tyler moved back, staring hard at him. "Think about it."

"I want it." He stepped back too now, watching.

They didn't have to wait long. The clouds shuddered to pieces: moonlight cascaded, and Tyler's white flesh seemed to soak it up. He writhed, squirming in it like a salamander in the rain.

Sitting on the broken ledge, Dell covered his face and just listened.

The gurgling started, a noise caught between a sob of pain and the gasp of orgasm, and the sound flowed around him, mingling with the scratching of dead leaves that slid along the ground. It grew louder, became the choking mewl of birth, a cry both of wrenching joy and savage sorrow. It pulsed from Tyler.

Knowing what would come next, Dell covered his ears and felt the hot tears course down his face. The sound poured over him. It thundered like his breath, like his heartbeat, like all the love that filled him.

Tyler howled. ❉

A WHISPER FROM THE GRAVEYARD

BY GREG HERREN

~ 64 ~

I WAS HIRED TO FIND A ZOMBIE the same day I found out I was dying.

The new client was waiting for me on my front porch when I got home from getting the news. I was still in shock. Even though I'd only had to walk a few blocks from the office on Decatur Street where a very nice blonde lady with reddish, watery eyes and a slight quiver in her voice delivered the bad news to me, I was drenched. It was a hot sticky July afternoon in the summer of 1995 and sweat had adhered my black T-shirt to my chest and back. As I trudged through the heat and humidity and vicious sunshine, I kept trying to convince myself it wasn't true, there had been a mistake. Mistakes happen whenever there's a human element involved. Yes, the number they'd given me matched the number on the printout from the lab, but numbers could get mixed up, couldn't they?

But I'd been expecting this. And while a surprise, the real shock was that it had taken this long, really. I thought I'd been preparing myself for this for years, but I was wrong.

You're never prepared to hear someone tell you that you're dying.

The nice lady kept talking, but I didn't hear much else she said, something about *support systems* and *an appointment with the doctor* and *new advances being made all the time* and everything else she was trained to say, with her teary brown eyes and the nervous tic in her jaw as she had me fill out forms and sign things I didn't bother to read.

I thought about going to a bar and getting drunk, losing myself in the wonderful numbness vodka provides.

Instead I walked home, through the sun-drenched back streets of the Faubourg Marigny to my shotgun house on Touro Street, sweating through my socks and underwear. Even my shorts were a little soggy. My hair was damp, and a cold shower sounded damned good.

Great, I thought when I saw a man sitting in the shade on my porch. *I'm not in the mood for this right now.*

"Steve Kidd?" he asked as I reached the tired, peeling wooden steps to the porch.

"Who's asking?"

"Quentin Narcisse." He stood up as I put my foot on the bottom step. His voice had a slightly Cajun sing-song lilt. He was good-looking, with golden skin and green eyes the color of the shallow Gulf water. His head was shaved smooth and gleaming in the light coming in from the open doors. His jeans were loose fitting, but his gray cotton T-shirt tightly hugged his well-muscled upper body. The V-neck revealed a smooth, hairless golden-brown chest, and his erect nipples were visible. He was handsome, in that seductive way that could lead good men to do bad things. His waist was almost impossibly small, too. "Monique Zeringue said—" he cleared his throat, "—you might be able to help me."

Monique Zeringue was a higher-up in what most people would call the Mafia in New Orleans. I prefer not to know any more about what Monique and her cohorts do than I need to know. She sometimes throws me work now and again, sometimes to put a scare into someone who owed her money—but not someone she wanted roughed up. She had bruisers for those unfortunates.

I'm a big guy, but I don't break bones or faces—unless attacked first.

Then all bets are off.

"You got my attention," I said, unlocking my front door and feeling the blast of blessed cold air from inside washing over me. I stood aside and motioned for him to enter. "Step into my office." I owned both sides of the camelback shotgun house, renting out one side to a bartender at Café Lafitte in Exile. The other half was my home and the front room served as my office. I close the sliding pocket doors during business hours to shut off the rest of the house.

The last thing I wanted to do was deal with a client.

But clients pay the bills. And the bills wouldn't stop needing to be paid because I was dying. If Monique sent him, he could pay—and pay well.

I needed to bank as much cash as I could for as long as I was able.

"I'm going to change my shirt," I said, sliding the pocket doors open. "You want something to drink?"

He stood in the center of my office, under the ceiling fan, distaste written on his face as he looked from one chair to another. They weren't in the best shape, and I hadn't cleaned in a while.

Dust and cobwebs accumulate quickly in New Orleans.

He shook his head. "I'm good."

I walked back to the bedroom and peeled off my sopping wet shirt, then my socks, shorts and underwear. Naked, I walked into the bathroom and ran the water until it was cold. I splashed some on my face and wiped myself down with a washrag. I put on some fresh, dry clothes before wandering into the kitchen and grabbing a bottle of water from the refrigerator.

I wanted a beer, but not in front of a client.

"So, what do you need a private eye for? Wife cheating on you?" I asked as I took a seat behind my desk. He wasn't wearing a wedding band but that didn't mean anything.

"Before we go any further, I have to ask you." He leaned forward in his chair and lowered his voice like someone else might be listening. "Do you—do you believe in witchcraft? Voodoo?"

I took a sip of water, looked at him for a moment before answering. "I don't rule anything out just because I've never seen it," I said finally. "I know voodoo is a religion. As for witchcraft... like I said, I've never experienced it." I gestured around the room. "I sometimes think this place is haunted." That was true. I'd never seen anything, but sometimes... I felt like I wasn't alone in the house.

And things would disappear from where I'd left them—only to find them a few days later in the exact place where I thought I'd left them.

"Do you know what a zombie is?" His voice was earnest, pleading. "And I don't mean like in those *Night of the Living Dead* movies, those things that eat brains and kill people. Those aren't zombies. Those are revenants."

He *wanted* me to believe.

I probably should have thrown him out, but…

"They are the dead, risen from the grave by the power of a voodoo priest or priestess," I said slowly.

Risen from the dead.

If Quentin Narcisse had come to my door the day before, I would have tossed him out. But the day I'm told I'm dying, that time is running out for me?

"They are *real.*" He swallowed. "And I'm afraid… I'm afraid my brother has become one. What I want you to do is go out and see if the stories… the stories I'm being told, are real." He swallowed again, his eyes focused on mine. "We're from Redemption Parish, our family goes back to the slave days there. Someone… someone I know called me yesterday, told me several people in Bayou Shadows—that's the town we're from—have seen Sebastian around. Sebastian died several months ago, during Carnival. In a fire. His house in the Quarter burned to the ground and he was inside."

I wasn't precisely sure where Redemption Parish was, so I glanced over his shoulder at the framed map of Louisiana mounted on the wall behind him. It was one of what we called the *river parishes*—because they bordered a bank of the river. I could see Redemption Parish marked on the map, along the river on the west bank, bordered on the other side by the Atchafalaya Swamp basin. My eyes traced the route of I-10 from New Orleans... yes, I could take I-10 West and then cut over, crossing the river by way of the Russell Long Bridge. "Hardly seems likely your brother'd be out walking around if he died in a fire."

"He died," Quentin insisted. "We buried him. We had dental records." His voice shook. "It was my *brother.* And now—" he paused, wiped at his eyes. "If he's back from the dead... then he *must* be a zombie."

"A zombie." I leaned back in my chair, watching his face. He was serious, I had to give him that. "But doesn't someone have to—to *turn* the person into a zombie?"

Quentin swallowed. He looked nervous. He nodded.

"Do you want me to find the person that turned him into a zombie?"

"Oh, no, absolutely not!" He held up his hands, showing off perfectly manicured fingernails. "I—I just need confirmation that this isn't just some story—" he searched for the words, "made up to lure me back to Redemption Parish. If the story's true, then I know what I need to do. Don't try to find the voodoo responsible." He looked me up and down. "I know you're a big guy, but your size won't help you with a voodoo."

Being my size is sometimes a challenge in the private eye game... it's hard to go undercover when you weigh two sixty and are six five. A million years ago I used to be a professional wrestler, ring name Kid

Karisma. Homophobia and fear of AIDS got me drummed out of the business when I was in my late twenties. Sometimes I missed it—the cheers of the marks in the audience, signing autographs and posing for pictures. I was damned good in the ring, might have even made it all the way to one of the really big promotions where the money was better. "We're family entertainment," the homophobic jerk who'd fired me said as he tore up my contract in front of me, "and we can't have people like you wrecking everything we've worked for."

I still regret not body-slamming that prick.

I opened a drawer and found the folder with my blank contracts. "I charge seventy-five dollars a day, plus expenses." I said, uncapping a pen and sliding it across the desk along with the contract.

He scanned the contract quickly, those big green eyes moving rapidly back and forth. He nodded and signed with a flourishing scrawl, all loops and curlicues and swirls. He pulled an alligator wallet out of his back pocket and pulled out three crisp new hundred-dollar bills.

I like a man who means business.

And if there was someone in Redemption Parish who could bring the dead back to life, I'd be damned if I wasn't going to try to find him or her.

I drove out of New Orleans the next morning, bright and early.

The Narcisse family, according to Quentin, were an old and proud family of Redemption Parish. His side of the family was from the dark side, descended from a plantation owner and his enslaved mistress. The mistress was eventually freed, and their children were also free... with no share or claim to the family plantation, Alafair. Most everyone has heard of Alafair. It was still a working farm with an amazing plantation house. The white branch of the Narcisse family still owned and operated Alafair—the main cash crop these days being sugar. They also used to own the sugar refinery in the parish seat, Avignon, but it was swallowed up by one of the major sugar companies after the second world war.

The freed slave Quentin was descended from had been a voodoo queen.

"Redemption Parish," he'd said darkly, "is far more haunted than Orleans Parish, and there are supernatural creatures there... always have been, going back to before the French came. Twins in my family have powers, you know, witchcraft."

I'd raised my eyebrow. "So, you're a witch?"

He nodded. "You don't believe me." He smiled. "That's fine, you don't have to. Unlike my brother, I've not—I've not really worked on developing my abilities. They've always scared me. They come with a cost, and I'm well aware of the darkness that comes with their use whenever I have. My brother—embraced that darkness. His death..." His green eyes looked away for a moment, then he whispered, "Maybe the key to your own survival is to be found out there." He grabbed my wrist and closed his eyes for a moment.

I felt something strange, his grip almost burning my skin.

He let go and opened his eyes. "Your destiny, and maybe even your salvation, lies in Redemption Parish," he said, standing up.

I exited I-10 West at the Avignon Exit and headed toward the river. Driving through the countryside I started thinking about my own death.

Quentin Narcisse was an odd man, and clearly believed in the supernatural—but that didn't make it real. But I *wanted* to believe him, *wanted* to believe there was someone in Redemption Parish with the power to conquer death. I wanted to believe I could find a way to beat the deadly virus already replicating itself in my blood, the death and darkness inside of me growing every minute.

I was also aware this was my own desperation, a refusal to accept the truth told to me yesterday.

There wasn't a cure. The way men kept disappearing from the gay bars in the Quarter over the last decade was proof. And no matter how many PSA's instructed us that we needed to—*had* to—wear condoms so many of us were still getting infected, still getting sick, still dying. I'd seen so many people die already... it was actually almost a relief to finally get the diagnosis.

The REDEMPTION PARISH sign alongside the paved state road was marred with rusty bullet holes. I was getting close to Bayou Shadows. Sure enough, a murky bayou soon appeared on the right side of the road, an alligator staring across from the other side, unblinking. The bayou twisted away to the left. After crossing a rusty trestle bridge, there was Bayou Shadows. There wasn't much to it, population nine hundred and thirty-seven, but some Louisiana tourism booklets claimed the town was known for antiquing.

And yes, the Catfish Bar and Grill was right there

where the tourism guide said it would be, with its rusting tin roof and clamshell parking lot, an enormous live oak dripping with Spanish moss behind it and another bayou visible beyond. The reader board advertised a catfish platter for $3.99 and all-you-can-eat hushpuppies.

I passed a decaying old Shell station with rusty old red pumps in front, a sign advertising gasoline for fifty-five cents a gallon dating the station's death to at least the Carter administration.

There was a blinking red light hanging from wires over the main intersection, slanted parking spaces painted on the pavement leading to the sidewalks on either side. I saw a sign for the Coffeepot and turned in that direction. I parked a few slots down and walked inside.

The air was heavy with the scent of eggs and grease. A long counter with red vinyl stools ran along one side, booths with cracked vinyl seats on the opposite wall. A harried looking waitress, with jet black hair from a bottle, a yellow cotton housedress, and a tired expression on her face told me to have a seat as she moved from occupied booth to occupied booth refilling cups from a glass coffee pot. I took a seat at the counter and opened one of the menus, yellow paper typed under plastic. "Get you some coffee?" the waitress asked.

"Sure. And I'll just have the two-egg plate."

"Bacon or sausage?"

"Sausage."

She made a note on her pad and tore it off, sticking on a rotating spoke in the window to the kitchen while grabbing a coffee cup and saucer. In one fluid move she turned and placed them down in front of me and filled the cup with coffee, getting me a little silver pitcher filled with milk from a small refrigerator. The coffee was good and strong, and my stomach rumbled from the smells coming from the kitchen.

At least I still had an appetite.

"Can I ask you a question?" I asked before she moved away.

"Sure, hon." She gave me a tired smile, her nicotine-stained teeth not perfectly straight.

I slid the picture of Quentin Narcisse across the counter. "Do you know this man?"

Her face didn't change, but her body language shifted slightly. "That's one of the Narcisse boys, one of the twins. Must be Quentin because Sebastian's dead. Quentin's long gone from around here, mister. You looking for him, you got to head over to New Orleans."

"I'm not looking for Quentin."

She raised an eyebrow. "Sebastian is in the cemetery out behind Sacred Heart." She gestured in the general direction of Baton Rouge. She snorted. "You been hearing crazy stories." She walked away from me.

"Don't listen to her," said the grizzled old man a few stools over from me with a thick Cajun accent as he mopped up chicken-fried steak gravy with a biscuit. "Sebastian ain't in the grave no more, even if no one wants to talk about it." He sniffed. "You wanna know about Sebastian, you need to talk to Maman Couchon."

"Maman Couchon?"

"Voodoo queen." He nodded. "She lives out on the bayou on a houseboat. Nobody wants to talk about her neither but she's a voodoo, all right. Some say she has Narcisse blood herself."

"Hush, Jean." The waitress shook her head as she put my food in front of me. "Don't be listening to him none, mister. Jean's all messed up in the head." She placed the ticket under my plate and walked back to refill some coffee cups.

Jean winked at me. "Clara's afraid of Maman Couchon," he barked out a laugh. "You take this here road out of town, and you can't miss her boat, it's right before the road ends at the swamp."

When I walked out after paying my check, Clara came after me, grabbing my arm. "You don't want to mess with Maman Couchon," she whispered, looking both ways as she spoke, her nails digging into my arms. Her voice shook. "Please. Just get back in your car and head back to New Orleans." She stepped away from me.

I could feel her staring at me as I got back into my car. The air was thick with moisture and dread as I turned around and headed out of town in the direction of the swamp. There was a stillness, a quiet, to this town that I didn't feel comfortable with. Heavyset women waving paper fans in their house dresses wandered aimlessly down the sidewalks, the playground at the town park crowded with dirty children and women talking on the benches, some older kids without shirts playing basketball on the cracked pavement of the court, their sweaty muscled torsos shimmering in the light. I drove past the sheriff's office, thought about checking in with them, and figured I could do it on my way back into town after visiting the voodoo queen.

Voodoo.

It was too ridiculous to be believed. Was I really that desperate? I kept debating whether or not to just head home and give Quentin Narcisse his money back when the paved road gave way to dirt, and I could see the swamp in the distance. And the houseboat, sitting in the water, a wooden dock leading out from the land's end. I pulled over and parked. *There's no such thing as voodoo,* I reminded myself. *It's just legends used to scare tourists and sell shit to them, is all. Quentin Narcisse is crazy. No one comes back from the dead. You just wanted to believe because you're dying.*

I turned off the engine and got back out into the sweltering heat.

An old woman was standing on the little porch at the end of the boat closest to the dock. She was old, the gray hair in wisps around her skull. She was skinny, like she didn't eat enough to sustain her. Her bony hands were on her hips and she was laughing. I walked out on the dock and she laughed even harder. The scent of the swamp was almost unbearably strong, dead fish and rotting meat, sulphur and other bad smells rising out of the depths.

"I was waiting for you," she said in the particular sing-song speech of the true Cajun, her voice lilting and pure. "You come looking for Sebastian." She gestured for me to step aboard her boat. "You might want to be careful what you lookin' for, white man, because you just might find it." She laughed even harder.

"You know about Sebastian?" The boat swayed as I stepped aboard, and I could see an alligator soundlessly moving through the murky water on the other side of the boat. I felt a chill go up my spine, goosebumps coming up on my arms. Magic might not be real, but there was something about her, about her boat, that was touching something in the primal part of my brain, something encoded for millennia in my human DNA, the recognition of something dangerous, maybe even evil.

I followed her inside, and the musty smell was even stronger inside her houseboat. Something was burning in a little burner sitting on what looked like an altar, flickering candles, a couple of animal skulls, an orisha offering.

"Sebastian messed with powers he didn't understand," she said, sitting down in a rocking chair. "The Narcisse, the black Narcisses have always been witches, you know. The white Narcisse are afraid of them, always has been. The witch twins! You'd think the power he was born to would have been enough but not for Sebastian Narcisse. You know how he died? Trying to gain the powers of a vampire, like the Seven Powers would have ever stood for that."

"Vampire." I replied carefully. Yes, Clara had been right. Maman Couchon was crazy.

She cackled. "You don't believe me. It is true. He trapped a young vampire, tried to drink his blood, but the Seven Powers struck him down for his blasphemy and burned his house down with him inside." She tapped the side of her forehead with a long, gnarled finger. "But what do you know of the old ways? Nothing." She tapped her chest. "Even though you carry your death inside of you, you don't believe."

"What do you know about my death?"

She cackled. "I know all I need to, white man."

"His brother was told Sebastian is walking the earth still." I sneezed, muffling it with my hands. "Do you know anything about that?"

"He died in that fire, white man." She sniffed disdainfully. She snapped her fingers. "But sometimes the dead, they don't stay in their graves."

"It would take a powerful witch to make a zombie, wouldn't it?"

"What you know of voodoo, white man?" She leaned forward, her eyes narrowed, glinting yellow beneath the heavy lids. "Voodoo isn't witchcraft, fool. It's a religion, that came over on the ships with our ancestors, when your people brought them over here in chains to work their fields, to clean their houses, to bear their bastards. Huh." She stood and turned her back to me, rummaged inside a drawer, pulled out a pipe. She stuffed it with tobacco, lit it with a long match, and sat down in an ancient rocking chair, crossing her wrinkled ankles. "Voodoo a religion. The priests and priestesses, they pray and make offerings to the gods, and the gods sometimes grant their wishes. The Narcisse twins—their ancestress was a voodoo queen, a priestess of the Seven Powers. She asked the powers to bless her descendants, to give them the ability to do magic." She snapped her fingers again, puffing away at her pipe. "That is the difference, white man, between voodoo and magic."

"Why would the Seven Powers grant her wish?"

She smiled, baring her empty gums at me. "She gave them what they wanted from her. Now, if Sebastian Narcisse is walking the earth still, what you need is to know who brought him back, white man." She whistled. "Take some powerful voodoo to make a zombie." She put the pipe back in her mouth. "And why you so interested? He pay you three hundred-dollars." She put her free hand over her heart. "You think Maman Couchon not know what you want? You think a voodoo be able to make you live longer."

I could hear my heart beating in my ears. "Can one?"

"Anything possible, white man."

"Can you?"

She laughed, spittle spraying from her lips. "I'm not a voodoo, white man. I know things, but I am not a voodoo." She tilted her head to one side. "I have a little Narcisse blood in my veins. They say I'm a witch, but I'm not. I just know things." She peered at me. "You got your death notice yesterday, white man. But I don't know that you're going to actually die yet. But everyone dies, white man. Everyone dies."

I left, not knowing any more than I did before boarding her rotten houseboat.

But she knew I was dying. She knew I just found out I was HIV positive.

And she knew, somehow, that deep inside my brain I was hoping, somehow, that the key to my life, for being able to go on living, was somewhere in Redemption Parish. If Sebastian Narcisse rose from the dead and was alive, reborn, why couldn't the same thing happen to me?

I walked back to the car and turned it around, headed back into Bayou Shadows. A storm was coming in from the north. I could see the misty gray of the rain beneath the black cloud stretching as far as I could see in the distance. Lightning flashed, too far just yet for the thunder to be audible for me as Blondie continued to sing on my car stereo.

Before I made it back into town I had to pull the car over. I opened the door and vomited my breakfast out onto the paved road, my stomach continuing to heave long after all that was coming out was ropy strings of spittle. Over my retching and heaving I heard a car roll to a stop on the other side of the road. "You all right, man?" I heard a voice drawl, also hearing the slapping of something hard against a palm.

I straightened up and found myself looking at a parish deputy, the lights on his patrol car on the other side of the road flashing in the heat. "Something I ate didn't sit right in my stomach," I replied, wiping tears out of my eyes with a tissue. "Am I causing a problem?"

He continued smacking his nightstick into the palm of his left hand lightly. "Can't an officer of the law stop to make sure a citizen isn't in need of assistance?" The light in his eyes, the joke in his tone, told me all I needed to know about this deputy. He was a sadist, a bully, someone who'd been a nothing in high school, picked on and laughed at, with a hard-on for the world who got even behind the cover of a badge. "Maybe I should take you in, let the sheriff have a chat with you." I couldn't see his eyes behind the mirror sunglasses, but I judged him to be about five nine, maybe one seventy pounds. I could see veins in his forearms, and his biceps looked like he worked out.

But if push came to shove, I knew I could beat his ass.

I put my feet on the pavement on either side of my vomit and started to stand up. As I started to stand up I could feel it inside me, the desire, the need for him to start something so I could justify beating the living shit out of him. It had been a while since I'd felt the anger, allowed myself to feel it. When you're as big as I am you need to keep your cool, a rein on your emotions. When you're my size you get challenged a lot, usually by straight men with small dicks and a few belts in them, who think that taking on a much bigger man somehow will prove their masculinity. When I was out of high school and had flunked out of LSU, before I found pro wrestling, I used to not contain it. I used to let the rage build and feed on itself, let little punks like this little shit-ass provoke me until I couldn't hold back anymore and cut loose on their sorry asses. Sure, being big wasn't always a sure thing, and sometimes they got a few good licks in before I started beating on them.

The last time it happened the guy started screaming until I stopped hitting him.

But I bet he never called someone a fag again.

As I stood there in the sun, the pavement heat baking the soles of my shoes, I wondered what was behind the sunglasses. I wanted to see his eyes.

I wondered if I could knock them off his face.

He took a few steps back, taking in my size.

The name plate on his left chest read DEPUTY A BOURGEOUS.

The A probably stood for asshole.

I wanted to feel my fist connecting with his face, to feel his teeth giving way beneath my knuckles, cracking and splintering.

And just as suddenly as it had come, the rage passed.

I wiped sweat from my forehead.

What the holy hell was that?

There was movement from behind Deputy A. Bourgeous, and he gasped as something poked out through his chest, a blade of some sort, and after a moment that seemed to stretch forever, the blood started to gush out around it, from his mouth and out his nostrils, the mirrored sunglasses falling to the pavement, the big round blue Cajun eyes opening wider than they ever had before, the blood gouting out of his mouth as he tried to speak.

"Glurg."

His legs buckled and he fell, his body sliding along the blade skewering him until it was free.

And I was staring at Quentin Narcisse.

No, it wasn't Quentin, my brain corrected me almost immediately, even as the coldness of the shock began spreading, tingling, down my arms and legs, my vision tunneling, turning gray around the edges as I stared at what used to be Sebastian Narcisse, but was now a horrible, gray imitation.

The eyes. Dear God, his eyes. They were green like his twin's, with flecks of gold, but there was nothing behind them.

The eyes were dead, soulless.

The golden skin was also grayish, tinted, like he'd bathed in a gray dye that had barely washed off.

His lips were also gray, and they were also sewn shut.

I reached into my shirt pocket for the little Kodak Instamatic and snapped four pictures of him.

All he needed was proof. Pictures would do the trick.

Somehow, I got back into my car, slammed the door shut, locked the doors, unable to take my eyes away from the creature—whatever he was now, he wasn't human anymore—as I slipped the car from park to drive. He didn't move, just stood there over the deputy's body, the pool of blood spreading beneath the body as he held up his free hand, gesturing for me to come with him.

I shoved the gas pedal to the floor and the rear tires spun before gripping the pavement and shooting forward.

I kept watching in my rearview mirror as I drove back to Bayou Shadows, slowing down to thirty-five as I went through the town, speeding back up to eighty once I was past it.

I didn't slow down again until I exited I-10 in New Orleans.

I parked in front of my house, my heart still pounding, my breath still rasping quickly. I ran inside my house and sat down in the air conditioning. I needed a drink, something, anything. I lit a cigarette with shaking fingers and drank down a shot of whiskey. As the numb warmth passed through my body, I shook my head.

I took the film down to the place on Jackson Square that promised to develop them in an hour, and wandered up St. Ann Street to have a drink at the Pub while I waited.

The more time passed, the less real it seemed to me. It was my imagination. I was obsessed with death since getting the positive diagnosis the afternoon before. I sat there on my bar stool, nursing a vodka tonic, replaying the entire morning. Had I really seen Sebastian Narcisse, a zombie, run a parish deputy through with a Civil War era sword?

Had that really happened?

Or had there maybe been something in the tea the old witch on the houseboat had given me? What was the incense she had been burning?

Rationality and logic were coming back, the lizard-like part of my brain retreating.

I walked back down the street after an hour, carrying my second drink in a plastic cup.

You're dying and it's going to be a horrible death, I reminded myself as walked past the fortune tellers, the caricature artists, the painters displaying their wares along the fence around Jackson Square, the living statues. I handed my ticket to the Goth girl with the white make-up and black lips and eyeliner and pierced nose, took my envelope of pictures, paid with a ten and pocketed my change.

I wandered back out to Jackson Square, past the tourists with their cameras, and sat down on a bench under one of the massive live oaks. I was damp with sweat as I opened the envelope.

And there he was, even more horrifying in a still

photo than he had been in real life.

The bloody sword, the corpse at his feet. The unseeing eyes, the gray-gold skin, the mouth sewn shut. I took another drink from my sweating cup, my mouth and throat suddenly dry.

I got up and began walking back to my house, down Chartres Street.

I could hear my heart pounding in my ears, so loud it was like a drum, pounding pounding pounding.

My eyes began to blur a little bit, and I know I was staggering a bit, people moving out of my way, crossing the street when they saw me coming, grabbing their kids and turning their little heads aside as I kept moving, one foot in front of the other, sometimes having to put a hand out to touch a wall, to regain my balance. I was overheating, the sweat pouring out of me, running down my face, a stream running from the tip of my chin.

This is what death feels like.

And somehow, sometime, I managed to get to my house and up the stairs and unlocked the door.

And sitting in my office was Sebastian Narcisse.

The knit lips widened in a smile.

And as my consciousness began to leave my body, as I fell to my knees on the scarred, knobby wooden floor, my sense of who I was being pushed out of my brain as I slid to my side on the floor, my eyes beginning to blur, my last vision was of a dead man, kneeling in front of me, cradling my head in his cold hands, whispering in a voice that sounded like sandpaper, *"Brother..."* Ж

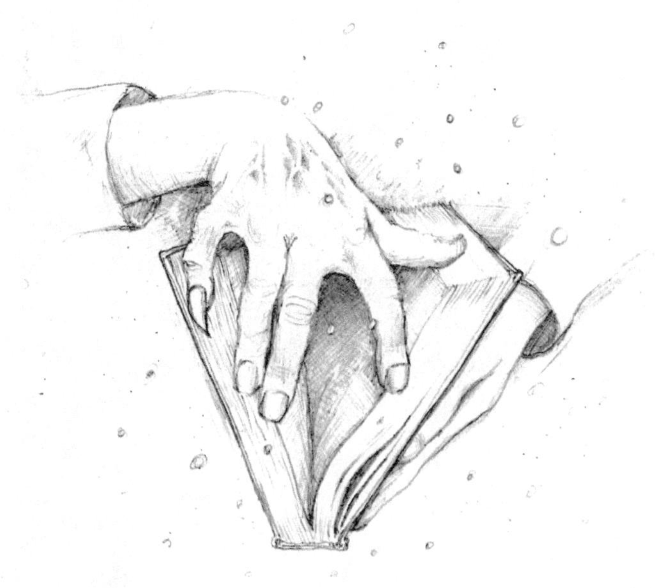

WILL TO LIVE

BY RICK R REED

The vampire Asa Beck waits at the top of the Araby Trail in Palm Springs. Below him, in the murky darkness, the Coachella Valley stretches out, with its settlements of homes, its turbines, and its mountains rising like cathedrals all around.

Right now, he can only imagine these things at the top of this heavily-trafficked trail, now empty, save for the mournful cry of a coyote, somewhere near. Sunrise is still at least an hour off, which allows him to sit quietly and contemplate his life. Or is what he contemplates truly a life? Is it something else? Perhaps a living death? A horror story? A fairy tale? A brush with immortality?

Whatever it is, he wants it to be over. Done. Kaput. Nearly two hundred years walking the earth should be enough for anybody, right?

He's anticipates the rising of the sun, cruel and merciless here in southern California, especially in August. In an instant, it will transform him from the living dead to a pile of ash. *Magic.* He's never been one for half-gestures. If he's going to do something, he wants to make it dramatic. He imagines a huge ball of flame followed by a billow of black smoke rising up to the sky.

This image, oddly, comforts him. He plays it over and over.

Asa's naked atop a boulder, facing east. His nudity allows for two things. One, when the sun does rise, there will not be the slightest barrier between him and it—it will be pure. Cleansing flame, he likes to think of it. Two, it allows him, even in this darkness, with only Venus shining above, to contemplate this body he's lived with now for centuries.

In the books and movies about his kind, vampires are often portrayed as seductive, sexy, sirens for immortality, lust that never ends, twisted, full-throttle passion. Remember Brad Pitt in *Interview with the Vampire*? Catherine Deneuve in *The Hunger*? Or how about Jason Patric in that trifle *The Lost Boys*?

His point is that the average human thinks of bloodsuckers as impossibly beautiful creatures, dark, alluring, steeped in desire. But the truth, as he knows it and as is confirmed as he stares down at himself, is that vampires come in all shapes and sizes, all colors, some beautiful and sexy, some with faces only a mother could love. Some skinny, some ripped and muscular, and some, morbidly obese, so to speak.

Vampires are what they are, frozen in time at the moment they're turned. He was in his forties when it happened to him. His waist had been starting to thicken while his hair was beginning to thin. Too bad there wasn't some devil enchantment to inverse the two!

But that was a very long time ago, when he was a professor at Oberlin College in Ohio in its early years. What year did he begin there? 1853, yes. The school was famous for its liberal admission policies, becoming the first in the country to admit African-Americans, though back then they called them negroes, and a couple of years later, women.

Asa had enjoyed his tenure there until one winter night, it all vanished in one fell swoop by meeting a man he thought might have been a student.

Louis Abbott.

If the vampire closes his eyes, he can still see Louis, sitting alongside a stream he liked to frequent. A brackish backwater, the narrow body of water was smelly and a breeding ground for mosquitoes in the summer. But, in the winter, the vampire loved its quiet and would escape there at night, clutching a thin volume of poetry. Just by coincidence—or maybe it was fate—the book he'd brought with him that night so long ago was a slim volume of recently-published poems by Elizabeth Barrett Browning. Asa could get lost in her imagery and her inspired use of language— the way she put words together was a kind of conjuring.

The reason his choice of reading material was fateful was because of the opening of her poem, "A Musical Instrument."

Even now, he remembers its opening lines:

> *What was he doing, the great god Pan,*
> *Down in the reeds by the river ?*
> *Spreading ruin and scattering ban,*

Splashing and paddling with hoofs of a goat,
And breaking the golden lilies afloat
With the dragon-fly on the river.

Even now, it's as though Louis sits by the stream, long legs stretched out before him, reclining on a bank of luminescent snow under a sky crowded with stars, presided over by a ghost of a crescent moon. Louis should have been playing a flute.

Asa watched him for the longest time, dumbfounded, amazed. He wore only a thin white shirt and dungarees. His feet were bare and they dangled at the edge of the water. And, even in the dark, Asa marveled at his dark skin and how it spread silk-like to cover chiseled angles and swollen muscles, speaking of coiled power and strength.

But Asa wondered... *Isn't he freezing to death?* It was true enough that spring was only around the corner, but nights here in Ohio were still cold. Asa guessed the temperature hovered only a degree or two above freezing.

He thought at the time that the young man must believe it was summer, and that idea fit the great god Pan in Browning's poem. Invincible.

Asa watched him for what seemed like a very long time.

He was just about to turn away when the man's voice, deep, resonant, floated through the darkness to him. "I know you're watching me."

Asa stepped back farther into the shadows, feeling caught, almost convincing himself in an instant that the man had to be talking to someone else. Yet Asa knew these two were the only souls out on this winter night, in a wood by a stream.

"You don't need to be afraid," Louis said.

In retrospect, Asa thinks this is the first of many lies Louis told him. But this first lie held a place as the most damning and damaging.

Even back then, Asa wasn't sure whether to believe the reassurance.

He followed up the first lie with a second, so innocuous Asa took it for a joke—at first. "I don't bite."

Like a fly trapped in a spider's web, Asa was drawn to the the man's dark beauty and the surreal aspect of him in summer clothes. There was something paradoxically dangerous and beautiful about him. There was also a sense that this meeting was fate. Asa knew it in his still-beating heart.

So he stepped forward and, as he did, the man turned his head to smile.

"I've been waiting for you."

"You have? How did you know I would be here? I didn't even know, when I set out, that I'd come to this exact spot," Asa said, even though he knew that, this time, he was the one who was lying.

"I've been watching you. I know your habits, your routine."

Not borne of the winter wind, Asa shivered as a chill passed through him, like he'd been touched by the fingers of a ghost.

He laughed and said, "My name is Louis."

Asa edged closer, like a small animal tempted by a treat being held out. "Asa. Although I wonder if you already knew that."

"I did." Louis smiled and shook his head. "Really. Don't be afraid. I've been around campus and seen you. I sat in on one of your classes—the big one— survey of British literature. You intrigue me."

Asa sat down beside the man and swore he felt immediately warmer, just by being near. And the man had a smell—something like sage and Mandarin orange. But that had to be Asa's imagination, didn't it? Or perhaps, like the feeling of warmth radiating off the stranger, an enchantment.

Asa recalls that the pair of them spoke few words on that night. There was no need. As soon as a desire was thought of, it was shared. As soon as an attraction bloomed, it was validated.

Their communication, illuminated by the silver glow of a crescent moon, transpired through their gazes.

Louis's eyes were his most incredible feature. They were a deep brown, but lightened by flecks of yellow, like citrine. Asa was drawn to Louis's eyes more than any of his other features, although all of those were uniformly breathtaking. His eyes were mesmerizing, though, in the most literal sense of the word.

They'd passed the night together on the banks of the stream and Asa did things he'd fantasized about doing all of his life with another man, even things that only his dreams permitted.

If it had been mere lust, Asa could have gone on, lived out his quiet bachelor life as a professor of English. Quiet mornings, tea and toast, reading Yeats or Browning or Byron, at night, off to bed and dreams of muscular bodies. He could have reveled in his memory while living out a life of propriety and denial, withering away until, like a dandelion's white feathery seed, he floated away on the wind.

Asa knew he was different, but didn't quite understand what made him so. Since boyhood, he'd always kept to himself. As he grew older, he took solitary and small pleasures in a meticulous house, a good red wine, music that inspired him to tears, and, occasionally, the face of a beautiful boy in one of his classes.

Louis showed him both release and relief, for the first time, on that pebbled, snowy shore. Asa was so grateful that, when their love-making progressed to the bizarre, the letting of blood, he went along with it because he was already ensnared.

By the time the sky was just beginning to lighten in the east, a pearlescent gray, barely distinguishable from the black above it, Asa was enslaved. His throat bore two tiny but efficient holes. He'd given himself over to draining, of both blood and semen. Each of these fluids was the first Asa had ever shared with another man, with another human being, actually.

But was Louis human?

That was a question Asa had pondered as he returned to his solitary house, his weakened footfalls seeming to be orchestrating the rise of the sun and the crescendo of birdsong.

He made it back just before the sun fully rose, feeling nauseous and weak. He'd drawn the heavy wine-colored draperies in his bedroom and crawled into bed, the covers drawn up tight around his ears.

He'd slept deeply for the entire day. He dreamt and, when he woke, images of loved ones in Asa's life remained, though their skin was stained with freshly-let blood.

He was hungry and all he could think of was Louis, of finding him again.

Asa was still human enough to realize that this hunger, this lust, had already grabbed him by his torn throat and would never let go.

He was still human enough to realize the last vestiges of his own humanity was winking out like a candle in a gust of wind.

He was reborn, a creature not of light, but of darkness.

The kitchen was dark when he woke. Asa left it that way, able to see surprisingly well through the shadows, as though a full moon were shining in through his windows, even though the night sky outside was choked with purple/gray clouds. The larder was stocked and Asa recognized he was hungry, yet none of the food held any appeal. In fact, the idea of something as simple as a poached egg induced a deep nausea.

He recalled that, at least for this one new awakening, the beginning and end of it all, he really didn't understand what he was hungry for.

For the answer to that question, he knew he had to find Louis. For his new and fragile being to continue, he knew Louis held the key.

And he had—right at the same exact spot he'd come across him the night before.

Louis looked up as Asa stumbled through the dark, coatless, barefoot, but not cold, his gaze transfixed on Louis, sitting on the same bank of snow, now noticeably diminished by what must have been that day's sunshine.

The flecks in Louis's eyes sparkled like the citrine Asa had compared them to. He smiled and stretched out his arms. Gratefully, Asa fell into them, feeling not only like a lover deprived of affection and ardor for too long, but also like a child missing his mother.

Louis whispered in his ear, "I feel my immortality over sweep all pains, all tears, all time, all fears—and peal, like the eternal thunders of the deep, into my ears, this truth—thou livest forever!"

Asa disengaged and stared at Louis, feeling a smile flicker about the corners of his lips. "You know Lord Byron?" Asa had only meant for his question to be about familiarity with Byron's poetry.

But he immediately knew Louis knew Byron on a much deeper level as he eyed Asa and said, "Intimately."

Asa laughed and then stopped when he realized Louis was serious.

Their love affair began in earnest that second night.

It also ended that same night.

But the short time together was valuable, if not heart-wrenching. Louis taught Asa how to hunt, how to wear a cloak of stealth, how to strike, how to drain —not too much—and how to know when the sunrise was imminent (they could smell it on the breeze).

Asa would spend the next several decades pondering why Louis had turned him and inspired love, only to run away, to disappear into night shadows.

Asa almost died from the loss, self-destructively not

feeding until he could stand it no longer.

His holding back only made him more ferocious when he at last pounced upon a freshman, a ginger-haired boy with taut muscles he'd once taught in an introduction to poetry class. His blood had been sweet and Asa swore it tasted of maple syrup.

Becoming one of the undead had been natural because it had to be.

Once he'd broken the initial seal of reluctance and horror, and once he'd realized Louis might never come back, Asa let himself go. He went through a string of lovers, all male, feeding on their youth and beauty until he was remorseless about the act. After all, what he engaged in was simply a matter of survival, no different than a beast of prey on the plains.

He fed on not only their blood, but their youth, their beauty, and in the deepest communion, their dreams. They filled him, brought him a kind of dark joy, yet the curious thing was this: no one of them was ever enough. No matter how blood drunk he was, no matter how imaginative and inspired the sex was before the feeding, Asa never felt satisfied, not for a minute.

Once it was over and the remains of a drained body lay beside him, Asa always wondered—who's next?

That feeling gave him some insight into Louis—insight he set aside, not wanting to face it.

He learned too to feed on their money. That also was a matter of survival, because he could no longer teach —or do anything else—during the day. He became a thief of everything precious to his victims and, again, rationalized that his actions were only a matter of survival, borne of a crushing will to live.

And, always, he waited. And hoped. For Louis to return. As Asa traveled the United States, and then Europe, and parts of southeast Asia, he would, at times, think he'd glimpsed Louis, at a café in Paris, a meat market in Saigon, at a Turkish bath, along the banks of the Danube, in the French Quarter. But every time, one of two things occurred. First, and most common, it was only cruel wishful thinking on Asa's part—it was not Louis he'd seen at all, but another beautiful dusky man who bore a certain resemblance. Second, the figure he thought was Louis would often vanish, almost into thin air, diminishing the closer Asa got.

Asa never knew if he was being romantic or if Louis was teasing him.

He hoped it was teasing. Because even if Louis was playing a game of cat and mouse with him and that was better than nothing at all. Louis was like a fragment from a dream, especially a dream of a departed loved one. In that fragile moment of connection, there was some satisfaction to be had.

And now, here at the top of a desert hiking trail, Asa is at last forced to conclude that he will never be with Louis again. Decades and decades are enough to prove it.

As Asa gazes out toward the eastern horizon, he sees with relief—and a bit of fear, an emotion he hasn't felt in a long, long time—an iridescent band of silver, the first harbinger of the sun's approach.

It won't be long now.

The end will arrive on layers of gray, orange, and yellow—and his imprisonment of these many years will come to a close.

He wishes for a surprise twist—that Louis will appear, walking up the mountainside, a grin on his face. He'll sweep him up in his arms and they will fly together toward the night, following the turn of the earth as it swirls on its axis.

Asa laughs at the super-hero image and in his laughter realizes he no longer wants the corny happy ending he imagined.

He wants only to be done with it. He's had enough.

Asa allows his mind to go blank as the sky lightens by degrees, faster and faster.

As the first gilded glimpse of the sun appears, Asa gasps as his body fills with a golden warmth. At first it's a pleasant sensation, but then the warmth turns to fire and he opens his mouth to scream.

But the scream is swallowed up by the descent of a flashing white curtain. ❌

THE BIBBLE, THE BABBLE, AND THE BIBLE

BY RYAN FIELD

~ 102 ~

Mark Alberts had begun to notice so many tedious changes in society these days he rarely bothered to complain about them anymore. For one thing, no one took him seriously, and for another, they often misinterpreted his wise words of caution as slurs. He meant no harm and he never would have offended anyone intentionally.

He thought he deserved credit: he was no bigot. He was all for equal rights on his planet and he believed everyone should be treated equally. As long as they didn't overstep the boundaries of common decency and good taste, he could support them.

However, Mark secretly wished he could be more like his husband, Kevin, who was still in the bathroom getting ready for their dinner party that night. While Mark was in the bedroom trying to portend what catastrophe might happen that night with these unusual people they were meeting, Kevin was in the bathroom whistling as if they were going to any old dinner party with close friends they'd known for years.

Mark was staring down at the bedroom floor when

Kevin walked in on him and said, "Don't look so glum. It's going to be fine, baby. It's not as though we're going to have dinner with a couple of cosmic criminals who broke the Cosmic Net. So they're not normal people like us, and they're not mainstream. Big deal. We're only going a few blocks away to spend a nice enjoyable evening with good, decent people who just happen to be different. I'm looking forward to it."

Mark looked up and saw Kevin smiling in such a clueless way he fought the urge to reply with sarcasm. He simply shrugged and said, "I suppose you're right. How bad can it be? They're people just like everyone else, and you know I've never been one to judge."

Kevin blinked and started laughing. He'd just showered and shaved and he was standing there naked with his beautiful penis swinging between his legs.

"Why are you laughing?" Mark asked. He didn't think he'd said anything that would warrant such an unusual reaction.

Kevin walked over to the bed and sat down on Mark's lap, and then he caressed Mark's shoulders and said, "Well, c'mon, Mark. I know you mean well, but you have been known to pass judgment on people, especially when you don't totally understand something. I think this dinner is going to be good for you tonight."

Even though he loved the way his husband was touching him, Mark felt a sting of resentment. "I'm not judging *them*," he said. He reached around and rubbed his husband's bottom. "I simply find it difficult to understand that kind of sexual relationship. I know that's wrong of me, and I'm working on it, but it's so new and foreign to me."

"Well you'd better get used to it," Kevin said. He spread his legs a little wider so Mark could reach between them with his other hand. "For the first time in the history of this planet, it's now legal for a man and a woman to get married, more are coming out, and they've been around since the beginning of time. I read something the other day about that on the Universal Cosmic Web that allegedly dates back to the old Earth days."

"Well, I highly doubt *that*," Mark said. His hand went lower and Kevin sighed. "You can't believe everything you read on the Universal Cosmic Web. There's no way to prove it either."

"Just because we don't have any formal history of their culture here on this planet doesn't mean it didn't happen on Earth. It's science. I'm telling you, it's science. The last Micro-Odyssey Cruiser from Lordimount that was sent to Earth to gather historical data discovered all kinds of evidence that non-gay people lived full and privileged lives at one time. They ruled everything. They even followed some kind of ancient alien rule book called *The Babble*, or, *The Bibble*, or something like that. I can't remember the exact title."

Kevin stood up and walked toward the closet, and Mark reached for his black boots with the four-inch heel and frowned. "Well, I do admit that I need to learn more about them. I simply cannot understand it. It's just so unnatural to see a man kissing a woman. I'm sorry but I'm old fashioned that way. Men are supposed to be with men, and women are supposed to be with women. That's the way our *Divine Creator* wanted things."

Kevin turned to face him, and Mark noticed he was fully erect. He smiled at Mark and said, "We still have a few minutes before we have to leave. Do that thing to me you love doing." Then he grabbed himself in an obnoxious way and headed back toward the bed where Mark was still sitting.

Mark gaped at his husband's penis and said, "You are terrible. What will those people think if we show up at their home and I have puffy red lips? I hear they are very conservative."

Kevin moved a little closer and said, "They'll think I'm a very lucky man to be married to you."

About fifteen minutes later, Kevin went back to the closet to put on his clothes and Mark went into the bathroom to rinse out his mouth. He glanced into the mirror and noticed his lips were, indeed, puffy. He didn't give it a second thought. They'd been married for twenty years, and he still couldn't get enough of his husband's penis. Of course, it wasn't the same as when they'd been younger and didn't have any real responsibilities. Back then they didn't have much else to do but have sex. And now they were both balancing their careers, busy with their two wonderful children, and still working hard to build decent, solid lives. There simply wasn't as much time now to be intimate as there had been in the early years of their marriage.

Kevin finished dressing first, and Mark met him

downstairs in the kitchen a few minutes later. He found Kevin at the center island talking to their son, Michael. They had signed up with the *Universal LGBTQ Family Planning Board* for two children early in their marriage, and they'd been blessed with a boy and a girl. Their daughter, Ariel, was in college now on the other side of the planet, and she was dating the nicest young woman named Bridget. Ariel had always been the easy one. She'd never given them a moment of lost sleep. Their son, Michael, on the other hand, had always been more of a challenge and whenever Mark saw Kevin talking to Michael in that serious tone Mark felt a twinge in his stomach.

"Is everything okay?" Mark asked, as he headed toward a chair near the refrigerator to get his bag. He was hoping he hadn't lost his entry pad again. He didn't feel like spending the next hour trying to remember where he'd left it, and without the entry pad they couldn't use the car. This was one of those times he wished Kevin would just listen to him and get one of those newer cars that didn't need an entry pad. With the new cars, all they'd need to do would be to press their fingertips on the door and the car would recognize them.

Kevin sent him one of those knowing looks and said, "Yes. Things are fine. I was just talking to Michael about what time he should be home tonight. He said he's going out with Bobby and Marcia again."

Mark smiled and started digging around in his bag. "That's nice, dear. I like Bobby. He's a very nice boy and I'm glad you're dating him." He found the entry pad and now he wouldn't have to hear Kevin complain about how he tended to lose things all the time. It was difficult to win an argument like that with Kevin, because Mark knew Kevin was right.

Michael seemed unusually agitated that evening, as if he couldn't remain still and he didn't know where to put his hands. He jumped up from the counter, headed toward the back door, and said, "I'll be home around midnight. There's no need to wait up for me."

"Have a nice evening," Mark said. "And please be careful. You're a very attractive young man and there are other more aggressive young men out there who are only too willing to take advantage of you."

"Leave him alone, Mark," Kevin said. "He'll be fine. When I was his age I had a different boyfriend every week." He smiled at Michael and said, "You go out and have fun with the other guys. That's what young men your age are supposed to be doing."

"I'm only going space bowling," Michael said. "It's not like I'm off to an all-male gang bang in the woods."

Then Michael left through the back door and Kevin turned in the opposite direction so he could make sure the front door was locked. It was part of Kevin's routine: to check and make sure all the doors in the house were locked before they went anywhere. Mark never complained, besides, he was thinking about Michael and what he might be doing that night. This was the best time of a young guy's life. When Mark had been Michael's age he'd been sleeping with four boys on the high school football team at the same time, and he'd gone to all of their proms. Back in high school just the smell of a men's locker room made Mark's knees weak. Mark hadn't been able to think about anything but men, and the things he wanted to do to them. He'd spent half of his high school years walking around with an erection thinking about guys, and the other half in the back seats of cars with guys. And Mark wanted his son to enjoy a normal youth as much as he had enjoyed his.

A few minutes later, on the way out to the car, Mark asked Kevin, "Do you think Michael is having fun with the other guys? He's so quiet sometimes."

Kevin opened the car door and said, "I'm sure he's fine. I was a lot like him. I didn't kiss and tell, but I had my share of fun with boyfriends. I'm sure all the guys are bending Michael over furniture, or at least dreaming about it."

"Don't be obtuse," Mark said. "I'm serious. I want him to enjoy his formative years in a healthy, normal manner."

Kevin laughed. "So do I. And dating guys and having all kinds of sex with other young men is part of being normal."

"I guess you're right, as vulgar as that sounded," Mark said. He tended to focus more on the emotional aspects of being with a man, where Kevin focused on the carnal.

As they backed out of the driveway, Kevin laughed and said, "And whatever you do tonight please don't get all silly and giddy around Bert. I didn't want to say anything in front of Michael, but you do that all the time whenever you're around non-gay men and it's a little embarrassing."

Mark felt a sting in his gut. "I do *not* do that. I have no idea what you're talking about."

Kevin proceeded forward and said, "Don't get all defensive. I don't mind. I'm just saying you shouldn't be so obvious about it."

Mark let that one go, because Kevin was right, again. As far back as he could remember, these strong, masculine men had left him breathless and vulnerable. There was something about their deep voices, their big bulging muscles, and their hairy legs that gave him a wonderful feeling deep within his body. It was almost a tingle, but not quite. He loved to watch them perspire in the summertime as much as he loved watching them pee at urinals in men's rooms. The scent of their underarms made him smile. And if a guy was smoking cigarettes and had beer on his breath, Mark lost track of all his senses. There probably wasn't anything Mark wouldn't do to sexually please a man.

Even though Mark let it go, Kevin continued. "You also have to remember these people aren't like us. They have these really weird, way-out closed marriages. They can be very prudish. They've got this thing for monogamy that I'll never understand. It's simply indecent sometimes. If you flirt with her husband tonight, Betty's not going to like it."

Mark smiled. "I promise I won't lick gravy off her husband's fingers." Of course he was being sarcastic, but he knew what Kevin was talking about. He'd always followed the societal rules of an honest open same-sex marriage. If he had sex outside of his marriage, he told Kevin about it, and it was no big deal. The same rules applied to Kevin. And if they took a third man into their bed on occasion, or they had group sex with other men, that was perfectly normal to them. The concept of total monogamy until death did them part, was almost an immoral concept to Mark.

A few minutes later, they pulled up in front of Bert and Betty's house and Kevin switched off the engine. "One more thing," he said. "Try not to get too chummy with Betty tonight. You know how you are."

"Are you accusing me of being a *Het Hag*?" Even though he despised that term and never used it, he wanted to make his point. He knew that a *Het Hag* (short for Heterosexual Hag) was a stereotypical pejorative for a gay man coming from a place of privilege who only hangs around with heterosexual women.

"Calm down," Kevin said.

"Don't tell me to calm down. I'm starting to think I need a rule book to get through tonight."

"Okay," Kevin said. "I'm only suggesting you refrain from becoming her best friend in just one night. You know you always do that. You can't help yourself. You're drawn to them."

Mark did find these women fascinating for some reason. And he had had his fair share of female friends over the years. They seemed to understand him better than his usual friends did, and they never judged him. There was no competition. In almost every case, it was the woman who pursued a friendship with him, not the other way around. But to accuse him of being a *Het Hag* was too much for him to handle. So he flung the car door open and said, "Let's just go inside, try to have a good time, and get this night over with."

The house where Bert and Betty lived was located in one of those sober sub-divisions that had once been referred to as middle management. Although non-gay people seemed to want to assimilate into mainstream society, especially since non-same-sex marriage had become legal across the planet, many seemed to be holding back when it came to where they lived and how they felt about the need to surround themselves with their own kind.

Bert and Betty's house didn't look that much different from every other house on the block. The front façade was a combination of stucco and some kind of fake stone, and the sides and back were that old time vinyl that always made Mark cringe. He also noticed that even though the façade up front had some curb appeal and was not totally void of style and design, the sides and back of the house resembled a vinyl clad shoe box.

As they approached the front door, Kevin pushed the doorbell and Mark glanced around at the minivans and pick-up trucks parked in the other driveways and made a face. This was typical. He wouldn't have minded if Kevin had insisted on getting a pick-up truck, but Mark flatly refused to ever drive a minivan.

Betty opened the door and she threw her arms in the air. "Welcome," she said. "It's so nice to see you. Please, come inside." She stepped away from the doorway so they could enter and looked back over her shoulder. "Bert, they're here."

While Kevin hugged Betty, Mark noticed a tall man with broad shoulders heading toward them. He wore a red plaid shirt, loose low-rise jeans, and chunky hiking boots. Mark should have remembered this. He felt a little overdressed in his black V-neck sweater and slim-fitted gray slacks. But it wouldn't have made much of a difference if he had remembered, because Mark and Kevin didn't own any plaid flannel clothing.

Mark handed Betty a bottle of his favorite wine and hugged her. "It's so nice to see you. This is for you. We've been looking forward to this dinner all week."

Betty squeezed his shoulders and said, "We're just so glad you could come. I made my special *Sloppy Joes*. We're very casual around here."

He had no idea what she was talking about, but he smiled anyway. He'd once been to a leather sex bar named *Sloppy Joes*, but that name had nothing to do with food. He didn't want to insult her by asking, so he simply turned toward Bert who was standing there with his huge hands in his pockets watching them.

"Hey, buddy," Bert said, and then he threw his arms around Mark and hugged him.

"Well, ah, hello, bud-dy," Mark said. He set his arms around Bert's shoulders and smiled. He knew that heteronormative men often referred to each other as buddy, dude, bro, or man. But he'd never felt comfortable speaking with a fake voice, and he knew he couldn't pull it off well. It sounded forced and contrived, as if he was trying too hard.

Bert patted Mark on the back with his huge dinner plate hands and said, "Glad you could make it. Been looking forward to it. Can I get you a beer, *dude*?"

Mark wondered if Bert had been working outside earlier. He smelled a little musky, as if he'd been perspiring. It came mostly from his armpits, which had always been a scent that could calm Mark down. "Well I'm glad you invited us. I'll have whatever you're having."

"Let's go inside and have snacks," Betty said.

Kevin and Mark exchanged a glance, as if they knew her snacks could be anything from peanuts to popcorn, and they followed Bert and Betty into a large living area with a huge sectional sofa and mismatched chairs. The way the house was decorated didn't shock Mark either. He'd expected a massive sofa that had built-in cup holders and large, heavy tables made of synthetic materials. And they always pulled a flimsy set of draperies together and cinched it tightly in the center with a tie or string of some kind.

From the start, it was clear Bert and Betty didn't break any of the stereotypes, but it didn't matter much because Mark wound up having so much fun that night, he didn't even notice that Bert had been eyeing him all night long. In fact, Mark wouldn't have noticed anything unusual if Bert hadn't asked him to come outside to see his pond. Kevin was helping Betty clear the table so she could serve dessert (store bought apple pie with whipped cream from a can) and Bert sounded so proud of his pond Mark could hardly refuse. So he picked up his third can of beer, set his quaint little paper napkin on the table, and told Bert to lead the way.

When they were outside near the pond and out of listening distance from Kevin and Betty, Bert put his hand on the small of Mark's back and said, "You sure were funny tonight. I don't think I've ever seen anyone eat a Sloppy Joe with a knife and a fork so neatly."

Mark wasn't sure if he was laughing at him or with him, so he shrugged and said, "Well, I never had overly sweetened meat in a tomato-based sauce before, but it was very good. I thoroughly enjoyed it."

Bert's hand moved lower on his back and he said, "It was adorable. You sure are a sweet little thing." Then his hand went even lower and he started patting Mark's buttocks.

Although Mark was a bit stunned, he didn't try to stop Bert. Instead, he turned, rested his palm on Bert's abdomen, and said, "And you're so big and strong."

Bert pulled him closer, and his head jerked a little. "I like you. You have a nice voice."

This wasn't the first time an aggressive man had put the moves on Mark. They usually left Kevin alone, but they tended to gravitate to Mark as if they could sense he found them irresistible. "You're not shy, are you?" Mark said. Men like Bert were never shy, especially when they were aroused.

Bert laughed, and then he lifted his hand a little and slowly slid it down that back of Mark's pants. "Well you're one to talk. You're not even wearing underpants. And you're not resisting me."

Mark leaned into him and rested his head on his shoulder so he could inhale his scent again. "I never wear underwear. I like being comfortable, and I hate the way underwear feels."

"Good for you," Bert said, as he squeezed a handful. "How does this feel?"

Although it felt fantastic and Mark wanted to lean over a chair so Bert could pull his pants down, he didn't feel comfortable. So he rubbed Bert's chest and said, "We should stop. They are going to wonder what happened to us. Let's go back inside before I wind up totally naked, on my knees."

"I don't mind if you get naked," Bert said. "I'll help you pull your pants down."

Mark reached down, grabbed Bert's crotch, and found him fully erect. "But you're married to a woman. I don't think Betty would be too thrilled to see me naked and sitting on your lap."

"She won't mind as long as I'm discreet," Bert said. "She knows I have a thing for guys and she totally understands. I just don't identify as gay."

It wasn't the first time Mark had heard this from a guy. He just wanted to make sure Betty knew about Bert's attraction to guys. Mark squeezed Bert's erection harder and said, "I wish we had more time."

Of course, Bert hesitated, and Mark couldn't resist him. Bert seemed so needy and polite at the same time Mark couldn't reject him that night. There was only one thing for Mark to do: keep it simple; make it fast. So he went down on his knees, pulled Bert's erection out of his jeans, and opened his mouth as wide as he could.

It only took about ten minutes to bring him off and clean up his mess, and then they returned to the dining room talking about Bert's pond as if nothing unusual had happened. If Kevin and Betty noticed the great big smile on Bert's face, or Mark's puffy red lips, they never said a word. They didn't even notice it when Bert pulled Mark's chair out for him at the table and patted him quickly on the buttocks again.

And that's partly because Kevin and Betty had been talking about something important while they'd been gone. Bert sat down and didn't say a word, but Mark smiled and asked, "What's so serious? What are you two talking about?"

Betty shrugged and said, "Bert and I wanted to talk to you guys tonight about our son. Of course, that's not the only reason we invited you. We really do want to get to know you better. But something came up recently and we're not sure how to handle it."

Kevin shrugged and said, "I told Betty we don't mind in the least. We know all too well what it's like to have a teenage son."

"Well, this problem is a little unique," Betty said. She took a deep breath, exhaled, and looked up at the ceiling. "Our son just told us he's gay. I'm not sure how that could even happen, but he told us he's getting engaged to another man."

Mark looked at Bert and said, "Well, maybe he's just a little confused. Maybe he's just sexually attracted to men sometimes. That doesn't mean he's gay, or that he should identify as gay."

"I don't know what she's worried about," Bert said. "So what if he gets engaged to a guy? Big deal. I say his life will be a lot easier than ours. He'll be totally accepted by everyone, and he'll never know the discrimination we've known. He'll get to see movies and read books where he can actually identify with most of the characters. I'm not upset in the least. This is how the world works."

Mark reached over to grab her hand. "Bert does make a good point. Besides, he's your child and you have to love and support him no matter what. We do that with our son, and I know better than anyone it's not easy. I'm sure everything will be okay."

After Mark said that she seemed to relax a little. She even changed the subject and asked Mark to join her new book group. This book group was totally focused on heteronormative female/male romance stories, with very happy endings. According to Betty, many of these novels were written by gay men. The entire concept was so exciting to Mark he didn't even flinch. He simply told Betty he would love to join her book group.

The evening ended a little later than Mark had expected. They'd had such an enjoyable evening he found it hard to believe it was after midnight when he glanced at his watch on the way out of Bert and Betty's house. He almost felt giddy. It had been such a simple, pleasant evening he felt hopeful about the future. He wanted to get to know them better as friends, and it had absolutely nothing at all to do with the fact that he'd blown Bert.

When they were in the car heading back toward their house, Kevin laughed and said, "I can't believe you asked Betty about *The Bibble* and the *Babble*. I almost choked on my Sloppy Joe. Seriously, you did that. I was there."

Mark sighed and glanced out into the dark night. There had been that one little incident he'd forgotten about. "Well how was I supposed to know it's called *The Bible*, not *The Bibble* or the *Babble*? I was genuinely curious, is all. And I don't think Betty or Bert minded. They seemed excited to explain their religion to us, which, incidentally, I find fascinating."

"I doubt you can do anything wrong with Bert," Kevin said. "You blew him, didn't you?"

Mark smiled. "It was just a quickie, and he really, really needed it. He has a nice thick penis, and he's so polite."

"I'm sure he does," Kevin said. "A lot of women don't like doing that, and their husbands love it, especially if you swallow."

"Of course I swallow, but that's a terrible stereotype," Mark said. "For all we know, Betty gives great blow jobs."

"That's true," Kevin said. "I should know better. But are you really going to join that book group? It sounds kind of strange. I just find it hard to believe that gay men would enjoy reading romance novels focused on female/male love stories. And I simply can't wrap my head around gay men *writing* female/male romance novels, especially when they know nothing first-hand about heteronormative relationships or sex."

"You know, Kevin, let's keep this simple just for once. I'm joining that book group and that's that. I enjoy female/male romance novels, and that's as far as I'm going to take it. Sometimes, some things are just meant to be pure enjoyment and escapism. It's that plain and simple for me, so don't try to make it more complicated."

Kevin pulled into their driveway, stopped the car, and leaned over to kiss him on the mouth.

"What was that for?" Mark asked. He didn't mind being kissed in the least, but they'd been married for a long time and that was totally out of character for Kevin.

"It's because I love you so much, and because you're right," Kevin said. "If you love reading stories about men and women in love, you can certainly join that book club if you want. Have fun."

Before he could reply to Kevin, he saw their front door open and Michael came out of the house with his best friend, Marcia. Mark didn't see Bobby. At first, he didn't think twice about it. It wasn't the first time Marcia and Michael had studied late at night, and they'd been inseparable for the last two years. Mark always joked they reminded him of siblings.

It was dark out that night and Michael hadn't seen them pull into the driveway. When they reached the middle of the front walkway, Michael grabbed Marcia by the waist, pulled her up against his body, and kissed her so hard on the mouth Mark was afraid she might fall backward into the bushes.

Kevin saw it, too. He gasped and said, "Did you see what I just saw?"

"He kissed her on the mouth. I can't breathe. Get my smelling salts." His heart began to race, and he had trouble speaking.

"Well I guess we don't have to wonder any longer about Michael."

"What do you mean?"

Kevin sent him a blank stare. "I mean that it's just as we've both suspected. Our son is a closeted straight man. Don't deny you haven't wondered about it."

Mark saw no point in arguing about this. As stunned as he was, he'd suspected this about Michael since he'd been five years old. A father knows those things. "What do we do about it? Maybe we can get him help. There must be counseling for this kind of thing."

Kevin thought for a moment. Michael and Marcia were still kissing on the front walk and they had no idea Mark and Kevin were watching them. "Don't be obtuse. There's no cure for this sort of thing. I say we do nothing. Let's just get out of the car and pretend we didn't see anything. Michael obviously needs time to reach the point where he feels comfortable coming out to us. I don't want this to be traumatic for Michael."

"I agree," Mark said.

As he reached for the door latch, he looked into Mark's eyes and asked, "Are you okay with it?"

"He's my son, I'd love him and support him no matter what," Mark said.

"I feel the same way," Kevin said. "Now let's go pretend we didn't see a thing and try to get through this without any unnecessary incidents."

The instant the car door opened, Michael and Marcia both jumped back and glanced in the direction of the driveway. It was obvious they hadn't seen Mark and Kevin, and Kevin made it easier on them by not saying a word. While Mark followed Kevin up the walkway, Kevin started talking loudly about how they'd been looking on the floor of the car for Mark's watch. Kevin made a joke about Mark losing his watch, because everyone already knew that Mark had a tendency to lose things. This time Mark didn't get angry with Kevin for making him the punch line of a bad joke. He simply followed him and smiled.

The horrified expressions on Michael and Marcia's faces transformed into nervous smiles, as if they were totally relieved to believe that Mark and Kevin hadn't seen them kissing. Michael even offered to go look inside the car for the watch, but Kevin said he'd look again in the morning when it was lighter outside.

Then something motivating happened. When Mark realized he didn't feel angry or disappointed about Michael and Marcia kissing, he felt a sense of hope that he hadn't experienced since he'd first met Kevin twenty years earlier. The future flashed before his eyes in quick intervals, and he experienced a sense prescient clarity. He couldn't wait to call Betty in the morning and tell her what he'd just learned about his own son that night. She would want to know all the details, and he would tell her everything he knew. And then he would wait for Michael to tell him everything, because he didn't want to rush Michael into anything he wasn't ready to admit yet. He might even buy a plaid shirt and a pair of heavy work boots. Maybe, if he was really lucky, he'd go to one of those Straight Pride Parades and march proudly with his openly straight son. Oh, the possibilities were endless, and the world didn't seem as quite tedious anymore. ✗

BOARDWALK THRILL RIDE

BY NORMAN PRENTISS

"Celia, as much as your other father hated water, my chances of getting Jack near the beach were pretty slim. That year-long vacation after our senior year brought us close to monsters and magic, but kept us pretty far from sand and surf.

"We did make it to the beach that one time, during Memorial Day weekend, but it wasn't the call of the ocean that lured Jack. More like the promised thrills of a particular carnival attraction: the haunted house ride on the south end of the boardwalk.

"I'll tell you about that ride now, and later this weekend you'll get to experience it yourself.

"Though let's hope, while you're in that coffin-shaped railcar traveling from one scare set-up to another, you don't actually see the world end, the way I did those thirty-odd years ago..."

Traffic was seriously backed up: the Chesapeake Bay Bridge was only twelve miles away, but at the rate we were crawling, it would take us an hour, maybe two, to reach it.

"You had to pick Memorial Day weekend," Jack grumbled. "Everybody's headed 'down the ocean' today."

"It's a beautiful, sunny day. That's why the road's so crowded." We had the windows rolled down because our VW Bug didn't have air-conditioning. Trouble was, we couldn't build up enough speed to circulate any air. I tried to remedy the situation by fanning myself with a folded road map.

"You know," Jack said, "the energy you expend waving that thing actually cancels out the cooling effect."

"I'll take the risk." Then I fanned him a little bit. He didn't tell me to stop, so it must have worked.

We moved forward a bit, then the cars in front stopped again. In the surrounding lanes, cars seemed to have better luck. A blue van with a surfboard attached to the roof passed on our right.

"Hey, didn't that guy cut us off a few miles back?" Jack typically kept a mental list of other drivers who "wronged" us. "I should play with him a bit."

"Don't," I said. "Remember Rule Number 1: Not while we're driving."

Jack laughed. "You can't seriously call this driving. We've barely moved an inch."

The left- and right-lane traffic had slowed to match our own snail's pace. A few car-lengths ahead, a small bird flew over the blue van and did what birds usually do to a windshield.

Even from a distance, I could tell the bird was uglier than the usual gulls we'd spot along this stretch of highway. Instead of white or gray, its feathers were a stark, shimmering black—as if it had been rolled in oil or tar. The head was large, supported by a strange curved neck like a vulture's. Its thick reptile legs looked almost prehistoric, and the body seemed too heavy to be supported by the lazy flaps of the bird's wings.

The other detail, too gruesome to miss: the volume of white waste dropping from the bird onto the van, splashing onto the surfboard, foaming onto the roof and coating sections of metallic blue paint. Then more splashing down, the chunked liquid growing darker, like something from a human, a horse, then an elephant with impossible diarrhea.

Until the van was completely covered.

(Don't laugh, Celia. It's really childish humor, don't you think?)

In that heat, the huge pile of animal waste should have produced a horrible stench. Remember, we had our car windows rolled down.

But I couldn't smell a thing. That was one of the fortunate limitations of Jack's illusions: they were visual images, but they didn't make wet plopping sounds, didn't stir up nasty odors.

"Not while we're driving, Jack."

He didn't respond. When the cars in front started moving again, though, Jack shifted the Beetle back into first gear, and the mess over the offending car magically disappeared.

I was the only one who got to see it. Lucky me.

This was going to be a long trip.

Traffic continued at a crawl, all the way to the Bay Bridge and beyond. The Bridge itself was a worry spot, a lengthy intersection of Jack's dislike of water and his phobia for heights—which is how we first discovered his power to project disturbing images into my mind.

Surprisingly, the backed-up traffic actually worked to our advantage. Instead of the leisurely drive extending Jack's nervousness, the slow pace along the bridge span allowed Jack to adjust, to center himself with deep breaths and a calm focus straight ahead.

No worries this time about cables snapping, girders bending, the road cracking open and cars rolling through to plummet to the Bay waters beneath.

Even so, it would have been easier to let me drive for this portion of the journey. But Jack never wanted to give up the wheel.

When we finally arrived at our hotel—overpriced for the season, naturally—we took our overnight bags to a small obstructed-view room with spartan furnishings, a few token seashells or starfish images on the walls in thin frames. Essentially, it was similar to a college dorm room, and good practice for all the rinky-dink places we frequented during the rest of our travels.

The smell of cotton candy and caramel popcorn wafted through an open, unscreened window. Games of chance and pinball machines from the play area below pinged and dinged, and a tilt ride from the nearby arcade actually shook the room when it hit a certain arc in its circuit.

"Close to the beach," I said, trying to stay positive about the room. A roll then a clomp of skee balls from the arcade nearly drowned out my words.

"I didn't bring my bathing suit," Jack said. "I'm happy we're close to the boardwalk." He'd send me off alone to the beach during the day, while he ate junk food and added more entries in his journal—notes for the book he planned to write.

Some things we would do together. Dinner that evening. A stroll along the boardwalk, a night-time ride on the ferris wheel for the best view of lit-up attractions.

And the haunted house ride.

"Let's do that now," Jack said before he'd finished unpacking.

I told him I thought we should wait until dark. After travel delays, there were only a few hours of prime sun for the beach, and I didn't want to miss them.

"Oh, I want to go tonight, too," Jack said. "I'll go by myself this time, and we'll ride together after dinner."

I sighed. "Just gimme a minute to finish unpacking."

The Haunted House was only a few blocks from our hotel overlooking the boardwalk. As we passed different food vendors, I could see Jack doing mental calculations about which items to buy, and when. Popcorn now, a pit-beef sandwich and Gnasher's fries for lunch, funnel cake for an afternoon snack. Italian ice this evening, and Salt Water Taffy tomorrow morning before the drive home.

Jack was still in blue jeans and a T-shirt. I'd already changed into my bathing suit and sandals, with an accompanying beach towel slung over my shoulder—

this way, I could go directly to the beach after we finished the carnival ride.

Recorded organ music familiar from *Phantom of the Opera* carried over crowd and whack-a-mole noises, and the haunted house ride loomed straight ahead. From the front, it was about the size of a small drug store, but Jack told me it was a long ride, by carnival standards. That meant the cars would twist and turn a lot, and the building containing the ride must extend pretty far back from the boardwalk.

There was a long line at the ticket booth. The loudspeaker entertained us while we waited, a looped recording of a guy imitating Bela Lugosi's accent, warning of the dangers ahead.

Laughable, really. All in fun. We heard screams from inside, but when the coffin cars came through the exit, the people inside were always smiling.

As the line inched forward slowly, more people piled into empty rail cars and cracked through the double doors at the start of the ride, swallowed in strobing darkness. The recording looped around again and again, and the promised dangers seemed more likely with each repetition.

Jack leaned over and whispered in my ear. "The people who go in. Have you noticed? I've been watching for quite a while, and the same people never come out."

Then he laughed, because I must have looked like I half believed him. "Speak a little louder," I said to get back at him. "I don't think you scared those little kids in front of you."

"It's a haunted house ride. The kids *want* to be scared."

We finally got near to the front of the line, only one family ahead of us: a father, and his young son and daughter. The pre-school aged daughter held a small stuffed bunny that she probably won at whack-a-mole, her dad likely guiding her hands to help. The red-haired boy, roughly nine or ten years old, had a bow and arrow set, complete with suction-tipped arrows that he'd occasionally pretend to aim at others in line, or at painted images of ghosts and vampires that advertised the spook ride.

Dad bought their tickets and the family moved to wait for the next "coffin."

Jack paid for both of us at the booth, and we stood in our place. Apparently, we'd hit some bottleneck in the ride, since none of the cars were coming out. I almost thought Jack's joke about disappearing riders had come true.

Then finally two cars came out the exit in quick succession, their riders laughing. One car for the dad and his kids, one for me and Jack.

As a carnival attendant directed the family to their empty coffin, the son started making a fuss. "I wanna ride by myself," he kept saying, actually stamping his feet a bit. At the same time, he puffed his tiny self up, thinking that would make him look more like an adult. A stubbornness flushed his cheeks, and he waved the bow and rubber-tipped arrows as if they were actual weapons.

The attendant said the boy was too young to ride by himself, and that set the kid off even more. He listed adult things he'd done, like playing touch football and riding a roller coaster, saving allowance money to buy his own basketball and a tetherball set, and winning *this* all by himself (waving the bow and arrow again).

Dad-guy basically said it'd be easier on all of us to let the kid have his way.

I imagined this family driving to the beach earlier today, stuck in the same horrible traffic we'd been cursed with. This boy would have been a nightmare in that enclosed space. Their mom was probably back in the hotel room, lying down on a boxy sofa-bed with an icepack on her forehead.

"You can tell who's in charge of this family," I said to Jack.

He didn't smile. I realized Jack was fuming. The boy's tantrum was already holding up the line, and if the attendant gave in, we'd have to wait for a third car after they ushered the brat into ours. We'd driven a long way, and Jack had agreed to the beach visit *only* because he liked this haunted house ride.

Pretty sure there was another tantrum on the way. Sometimes Jack's were pretty spectacular.

Early on, I'd made that rule about Jack not creating any illusions while we were driving. Soon after, I'd insisted on Rule Number 2: no fair playing visual tricks with the food we were eating. I needed to keep my appetite.

Now Rule Number 3 occurred to me: Children are off limits. Please, Jack. No scary images involving kids.

There wasn't time to reason with him. Jack's jaw clenched tight with anger.

I was afraid to look. But of course, I did.

Considering Jack's mood, combined with how irritating that ten-year old kid was being, I expected the worst: swords falling from the sky and hacking off the boy's limbs, blood splashing everywhere; or his head dropping into the basket beneath a materialized guillotine, eyes open after death, mouth stretching in a dwindling, agonized scream.

That's not exactly what I got.

I mentioned earlier how the boy had puffed himself up, trying to stand tall in the midst of his childish tirade. I guess Jack noted the same irony and decided to make fun of it.

The boy puffed up, all right. His angry cheeks flamed almost as red as his hair, and in an instant he'd ballooned as tall as the ride attendant, then as tall as his father, then towering over the two-story haunted house attraction. He started stamping his feet again, and this time they were giant feet, smashing the little coffin cars, kicking them aside with an if-I-can't-have-my-way-nobody-can gesture. He swung angry baby-balled fists at the air, then stomped his way to the front of the building.

A small stretch of track ran along a flat landing in front of the attraction's second story—a part of the ride where the cars would venture outside briefly, a startling contrast of fresh air to interrupt the onslaught of darkroom shocks. At that instant, a coffin car burst through and puttered along that upstairs track, perfectly timed to meet the crazy giant kid and his grubby grasping fingers.

Two adults sat in the car, two men, and I thought it was sweet that Jack included a gay couple in his projected display. They might have been an older version of the two of us, revisiting a favorite ride from their younger days.

The giant boy scooped the two men out of the coffin car, stuffed them into his mouth and chewed like they were pieces of salt-water taffy.

I'll admit the scene was pretty gruesome, as all of Jack's images were, but it also had a kind of cartoonish element that kept it from seeming too realistic. That, and the lack of sound. I could half smile, even feel like I was in on the joke—which wasn't always true in those early days, when I was still getting used to Jack's strange power.

(It's pretty hard to explain, Celia. No crashing sounds or screaming; the ground didn't shake with each stamp of the boy's giant sneakers. But it was never quite as easy as watching a silent movie. My mind tricked me sometimes, filled in missing sensory details. In this instance: I'd imagine some of the screams, or get dizzy looking up, partly lose my balance as if the earth shook beneath me. At the same time, the pieces didn't quite add up, so I was usually aware my senses were being tricked.)

More ride attendants showed up, then the security guards who patrolled the boardwalk on bicycles. They all had bows and arrows, pulling back the strings in unison and aiming high at the kid's puffy face.

I noticed sharp metal tips, rather than suction cups, on the ends of the arrows.

Things were about to take a nasty turn. The giant monster child stamped his feet in warning, and I thought I actually heard the thud of each pounding step.

Then the kid was gone. Both the giant one, and the real-life pip-squeak.

The thump of giant shoes had actually been the family's coffin car rattling through the double doors at the start of the ride.

I'd been "distracted," so wasn't sure if the brat got his way or not, but there was an empty coffin waiting for Jack and me. We stepped inside, and the attendant folded down the wooden lid over our knees.

With a jolt, the car lurched forward and we battered through the doors and into the pitch dark house.

No visual stimulation at all. Just the jostle of our tiny rail car, the sense of Jack close to me in the dark, a speaker squeak like metal nails down a blackboard.

Then a click and a bright white flash revealed a giant rat sitting atop a garbage can. Fluorescent green paint covered the plaster rodent's body, with blood-red around the upturned snout, dripping from the raised front paws.

Jack and I laughed, as our coffin rode ahead to the next setup.

(Now, Celia, I won't describe every section, since I don't want to spoil the fun when you ride for the first time. They've added some new features over the years, but a lot of the scenes Jack and I rode past in the mid-80s—like the torture chamber, and the cemetery—

are still part of the ride today.

I'll just stick to moments that have special relevance to our adventure.)

At one point, we moved through a long tube, the curved corridor walls twisting as we rolled along. Painted lines on the tube reinforced a strange spinning illusion, making it feel like our car was tipping over on its side. As a cool added touch, further ahead the painted image of a car just like ours spun completely upside down.

There were no passengers in that car. I thought of tantrum-boy getting his way and riding solo, only to be dumped unceremoniously from his car and onto the tracks, so we could run him over.

(Yeah, I admit I was thinking like your other father here. Jack was being better behaved: he didn't mess with any of the spook-house illusions, preferring to let the ride work its own magic.)

We rolled and clattered through other scenes that wouldn't look out of place in *The Exorcist* or *The Texas Chainsaw Massacre*. When the car jolted around a corner, Jack would lean into me, and it was fun to feel close to him like that—the same paradoxical way that watching scary movies can be romantic.

Our car went up an incline to take us to the second floor. A double door blocked the path ahead, and a small cascade of water dripped from the ceiling. We were supposed to worry that we'd get wet, but there was a click as our car approached, and the water shut off just before we traveled beneath the stream.

The front doors parted as we busted our way through and I realized that, after all the disorienting flashes of light and twists and turns, we'd reached the moment in the ride when the car travels briefly outside, rolling smoothly along a landing in front of the house's second floor. A respite in fresh air.

Except it wasn't.

It was the end of the world.

We'd been outside a scant ten minutes earlier, waiting to get inside the funhouse. In those minutes, as we rode our way from one fun scare to another, some real-life horror had descended on the world.

Of course, it was one of Jack's own creative scares. But after the fluorescent-painted rats, wall-hanging spiders, skeletons and sheeted ghosts and fiendish fake manikins that inhabited the set-ups along each isolated stage of the ride, what faced us now was far more realistic and disturbing.

And... panoramic.

Our vantage point from the second floor of the haunted house ride offered a view that far surpassed the scope and detail of Jack's previous illusions. The ocean was tinted red with blood, steam rising from distant waters that boiled flesh off hapless swimmers. Shadows shaped like sun-bathers peppered darker stains along an ashen beach. The ferris wheel had collapsed over surrounding carnival rides, riders and passersby alike crushed in twisted metal. Buildings burned along the boardwalk, the wooden pathway itself scorched and covered with dead or dying vacationers, bodies and body parts everywhere.

As if the world itself had exploded. As if some kind

of nuclear bomb had dropped on the beach, or some terrible comet had burned its way to earth, destroying everything in its path.

And I was furious with Jack. I knew he hadn't wanted to come to the beach, but it was a summer tradition I'd always loved: the beauty of the ocean stretching to the horizon, cool air over wet skin relieving the sun's heat, the smell of cotton candy and funnel cakes, smiles on kids' faces, the lights, the merry-go-round music and pinball dings, even the rinky-dink charm of an overpriced hotel. For some reason, Jack had decided to ruin that for me.

Right now, of all moments: after I'd put my swimming and sunbathing plans on hold to share the crazy haunted house ride he was so interested in.

Our coffin car chugged along that short stretch of outside track on the ride's second-floor platform, and the world burned and churned with death in all directions.

"How could you," I said flatly. Our bodies still touched at the hips in that tight rail-car, and I couldn't easily turn to glare at him.

Jack didn't respond. Or if he did, I couldn't hear him over the air-raid sirens, the crackle of burning wood and the agonized screams of wounded survivors.

The car chugged forward, reaching the halfway point of that stretch of track. I closed my eyes, unwilling to look at Jack's cruel trickery.

I also wanted to plug my ears and shut out the awful apocalyptic din; to plug my nostrils and shut out the horrible smell of burning skin and hair; to fan the air with my hands to brush fire's hot breath away from my face.

The coffin car vibrated beneath me, slowly lurching forward.

Just before we hit the next set of double doors to return to the inside portions of the ride, I registered what was wrong. Jack's projected visions were only visible to me... and they were *only* visible. No sounds or smells or sense of touch.

In a panic, I opened my eyes again, glanced back at the disappearing outside world as the car entered interior darkness, the doors flapping closed over...

...that same panorama of devastation, with sounds and smells that matched perfectly.

A sharp tang of charred meat felt stuck at the back of my throat. I'd breathed it in. I'd breathed everything in, and I could taste it.

The ride continued along its programmed route. More plastic skeletons and painted witches and a waxen victim holding his own severed head. The strobe lights gave me a headache, along with the witch's loudspeaker cackle, the recorded howls of werewolves and the moan of ghosts. None of this was fun anymore.

Because as I rode through all those manufactured thrills, I couldn't be sure what waited at the end of the ride. Were those screams on the looped recording, or did they come from outside? Was that a thump from our rail-car, or the drop of another missile or meteor on the beachfront?

I held Jack's hand and squeezed hard for comfort.

(Sure, Celia. I was mad, but I loved him, too. If the world was ending, at least we still had each other.)

Too much noise in the dark and flashing ride. Too much confusion of my senses. I didn't know what to think, couldn't get a read on Jack.

Finally, we hit the last set of double doors, and our car burst out into the light.

Jack gave the same kind of laugh that I'd noticed from other exiting riders. I probably had the most ridiculous, exaggerated expression of relief anybody ever had coming out of that spook house.

Because the world was back to normal.

"Jeez, Shawn, it wasn't *that* scary."

"How could you say that? I really thought—" And I couldn't speak any more, since I was having trouble breathing. My mild asthma was making another of its rare, unwelcome appearances.

Jack was really sweet then, holding me and rubbing one of my shoulders to help me calm down. Probably a bit more loving than he should have been in public, considering the time period, but I kind of needed the attention.

As my breathing came back to normal, I also managed to collect my thoughts a little better. Jack couldn't always control the images he projected into my head, and maybe he didn't realize what I'd been going through. He was acting as if I'd been scared by the ride itself, rather than what I'd experienced during that brief apocalyptic panorama.

I didn't end up visiting the beach that day. We walked back to the hotel, and Jack ventured out for boardwalk snacks and brought them to me in the room. Sometimes, when the hotel floor jostled with the thump of a nearby tilt-a-whirl ride, I'd jump as if another missile struck the earth.

Eventually, I began to feel a bit calmer. As I described my brief waking nightmare, Jack claimed total innocence.

"I had no idea, Shawn. I was so into that cool ride. I looked out at the boardwalk during that outside part, and it was really a beautiful day, which almost made me understand why you love visiting the beach. I was gonna say as much, but you had your eyes closed, and I thought maybe the kiddie-ride had given you a little motion sickness."

It was clear Jack hadn't intended to project that kind of image into my head. The only explanation we could come up with was that the ride had somehow taken over his power, intensified and transformed it for some malicious reason.

Jack wanted us to go back, so we could test the theory. I wouldn't do it.

(You think I should have agreed with your other father, Celia? Well, maybe I did, later. But that's a story I'll save until you're a bit older...) ✕

HELIOTROPE AND THE ART OF NAMING HOUSES

BY GREGORY L NORRIS

IT WAS A LOVELY COLOR WHEN you looked past the hurt. The purple of summer twilights, Alonzo mused. No, *heliotrope.* That was a better word. It conjured visions of cottage gardens and mysterious, perfumed flowers. The break from reality proved brief; it was a bruise, this one delivered for spilling the oligarch's coffee, and all it took was a direct glance at any of the dozen mirrors hanging on that long beige wall to recognize the truth for what it was.

In a day or two, the heliotrope would degenerate into a sallow yellow. *Jonquil.* By then, there'd likely be fresh bruises, new hurt. He heard Ryan moving about up in the gallery and severed his connection with the mirrors. There was work to do, always so much work. As he ascended the stairs, those many past violations from Ryan's fists pulsed—right knee, stomach, the tiny hand bones fractured and knit back together over the long months. Alonzo reached for the banister to steady himself. For a terrible moment, it seemed as if every injury he'd ever suffered from the man peering down at him had joined together into one giant wound.

"Hurry up," Ryan barked.

Alonzo forced a smile to his lips. Those, too, were part of the chorus, reminding him of the times they'd been split open beneath Ryan's knuckles. Halfway up the soaring staircase now… it would be so easy to let go, lean back, and trust gravity to do the rest. Oh, the temptation! Only he might end up in a pile of shattered bones alive at the bottom. A tumble to oblivion was no guarantee of release from this prison.

He put on a burst of speed and ascended. The man leaning over the gallery rail flashed a cold scowl. Ryan was handsome, Alonzo supposed, with his twin sapphire eyes and classic good looks. But he was in the final stage of that handsomeness, and all Alonzo saw was the man's ugly meanness.

"Come on," Ryan snapped. "I need to sort the new delivery."

The oligarch turned and ambled into one of the upstairs treasure rooms. New deliveries meant new deals, one-sided ones in which Ryan Ivan Paulson alone profited.

R.I.P., Alonzo thought. He should have known at the beginning that Ryan's name would be symbolic of his death.

The naming of houses was a grand tradition from past, better times. Often when helping Ryan and his men take possession of whatever spoils they'd acquired, Alonzo named the houses they visited. One, a tall blue box with numerous windows, was the Goldfish Bowl, because he imagined its former residents' lack of privacy to neighboring eyes. Sad Victorian was a place with a castle turret and gingerbread fretwork—the Victorian was sad because half of the former palace's wraparound veranda had caved in from rot and broken windows had been nailed over with plywood rather than replaced.

In his private thoughts, he referred to Ryan's fortress as Limbo, land of lost souls.

As he did on most days, Alonzo catalogued and inventoried the new deliveries, and Ryan reminded him how lucky he was to have been taken in by a man of his means.

"Yes, Ryan," Alonzo agreed, his mouth remembering the sting of Ryan's knuckles.

Some houses, special ones, were cursed with or blessed by names. Alonzo woke in the enchanted cottage called Blueberry Corners on a warm summer morning. Sunlight poured in through windows dressed in Bavarian lace curtains, reflected off a pyramid of crystal within which a lighthouse had been carved, and dappled the room in a kaleidoscope of spindles.

He sat up, at first confused. The room was unfamiliar yet also spoke to him of earlier visitations, as though he knew the space intimately—the hand-painted clusters of indigo blueberries and emerald leaves wreathed in a border around the top of the walls, the antique walnut dresser with the white marble surface, and wooden bookcase crammed full of truths and fictions all felt like home.

Alonzo tossed aside the light summer quilt. Absent from the task was the usual complaining of joints and bones aged ahead of their years. In fact, he noticed, even the painful jolts acquired from Ryan's cruelties were missing. He got up, clad only in a cotton T and loose-fitting shorts, and checked his face in the crystal lighthouse. No bruises transitioning between heliotrope and jonquil stared back.

"*Lon*," called a man's voice. "You awake?"

Alonzo turned toward the door, which stood ajar. The floor under his soles seemed solid enough. Still, his steps away from the antique brass bed with the porcelain finials passed like a dream. Helping him along was the aroma of fresh coffee, robust though lacking the bitter intensity of the brew Ryan drank. *Ryan...* even thinking about him here felt wrong, a breaking of rules.

The hallway paneled in knotty pine opened on a bigger room—kitchen, dining, and living spaces combined. The décor was as charming as the bedroom. Framed botanical prints and watercolors of blueberries hung on walls. The sofa was overstuffed, upholstered in a rich hunter green with an eight-pointed, silver star pattern. One chubby, happy looking tabby sat on an arm in the classic, contented loaf position. Another, gray, grazed at a set of crystal bowls beside a counter island.

"Lon?" the man asked again.

No one had ever called Alonzo that. He tracked the voice around the corner of the counter island to a set of old school white appliances, stove and refrigerator, and the man it belonged to.

"I'm here," Alonzo said.

The man stood with his back to Alonzo, clad in black boxer-briefs and a matching t-shirt that fit his tall, masculine physique as though the clothes loved him. Dark hair, an athletic cut but with enough bed-head and spiky cowlicks to show his mysterious host had only been awake for minutes. Big, bare feet. Heavenly distraction.

"Good, I'm making blueberry crepes, your favorite," the man said.

He tipped a look over his shoulder. Alonzo saw the man's eyes were the color of emeralds and that his face was so handsome that it physically hurt to gaze on it for long, like staring directly at the noon sun.

"Lon?" the man asked.

Alonzo started to speak. Then the vibrant palette inside the small, homey house cut out, eclipsed by a shadow that restored Alonzo's agony. A monster gyrated atop him. It was Ryan.

"Remember who owns you," the monster growled into his ear. "I do. *Say it!*"

A stranger took control of his lips and pledged the dark sacrament, over and over. Disconnected from his body, the part of Alonzo he thought of as his soul attempted to hold onto the dream and, especially, the warmth of being loved, of being home. But that was like trying to paint with watercolors in the rain, for he was again in Limbo.

Ryan left Limbo for several hours with a cadre of his men, and he didn't take Alonzo. With plenty expected of him in Ryan's absence, Alonzo settled into the upstairs treasure rooms to inventory and carry out his master's instructions.

Again, as he counted and weighed coins and gemstones, checked technologies to be sure they functioned, and wrote descriptions of furniture and other home goods of value, he hoped for a break-in. Hoped that, long last, some desperate soul armed with a gun or a blade or a curse-thrower would brave the oligarch's fortress. Or some disgruntled dealmaker upset with the deal. He'd find Alonzo and exact revenge against Ryan through him by pulling the trigger.

Alonzo set down the latest acquisition, an alabaster box with pink flowers painted on the lid. Perhaps it had been a gift from one lover to another, an expression of passion. His mind drifted back to the charming little house from a dream that had seemed like the reality. The alabaster box would look perfect in that wonderful landscape.

"Blueberry Corners," Alonzo whispered aloud.

The ominous, heavy atmosphere inside Limbo devoured the words along with his voice.

He attempted to return to the work, but thoughts of the dark-haired man with the emerald gemstone eyes distracted him and he had to put the alabaster box aside for fear that his shaking hands might drop it.

What if that dream was his interpretation of Heaven or a kind of afterlife? It was, Alonzo thought, perfect. The man, the house...

Unexpected tears welled up in Alonzo's eyes. Limbo blurred around him. The ability surprised him as much as the emotion; after three years of living as Ryan's property, he hadn't thought himself capable of crying anymore. The tears spilled down his cheeks.

The man's face materialized, turned toward him, smiling. Smiling because of him.

Alonzo wiped his eyes and resumed his work. By the time Ryan and his men returned with more spoils to be catalogued and accounted for, he'd almost managed to forget the dream and all he'd lost in waking up.

The house had swallowed him whole, Alonzo often thought. And with every new day and deal, Limbo increased its density, like a creature with a hard shell that replaced its carapace not through cells but *things*. Ryan owned warehouses filled with the spoils of his victories—and flesh houses full of people unlucky enough to have been traded in his darker dealings.

Limbo's exoskeleton thickened with each new jewel, object, or mirror taken into its interior. The cells and density might grow impossible to escape, like walls made of lead or dark matter, with him trapped at the center.

He rolled away from Ryan, who was sprawled on his back in a king's pose. Not for the first time, Alonzo considered doing what no desperate had yet dared. There were enough blades in the largest of Limbo's kitchens—knives of sterling silver meant for carving fish or meat but that would work equally well on slicing through a man's heart. Not that he believed Ryan actually had one.

And there were jeweled daggers, along with a hundred other dealers of death in the trophy cases in the Verdigris Parlor, some antique, all, he guessed, complicit at having drawn blood and taken lives.

He could do it, Alonzo told himself. That he already hadn't made the thought a lie. Heat rose up his throat and infected his cheeks. For a moment, he despised himself as much as Ryan Paulson.

Alonzo's anger cooled with shocking quickness. His teeth chattered. Pulling the heavy cover over his head, he prayed for the fabric of the universe to dissolve around him and for oblivion to claim him into its depths.

Birds sang, some squawked. Alonzo gazed through the windows of the breakfast nook at the overgrown courtyard garden where colorful finches darted, stealing seeds from the network of feeders. Larger birds complained.

"I know we're not supposed to feed them for the summer," the man with the emerald gemstone eyes and dark cowlicks said. He circled the breakfast table and set two plates atop the glass, beneath which photographs and sketches were displayed in a gallery designed for two visitors. "But if we didn't, we wouldn't have our daily morning entertainment."

Alonzo froze. The sweet smell of blueberry crepes drifted up from the cobalt glass plates. The aroma of fresh coffee added another layer to his nearing sensory overload. Most powerful was the man's scent—clean sweat, warm skin, and a note of pine and summer rain more alluring than the rarest of colognes.

"How—?" Alonzo started, but his voice hitched in his throat before he could finish the question.

Up close, the man was more magnificent than

Alonzo had earlier thought. Even the crooked smile he flashed was radiant.

"Lon?" he growled. "Something wrong?"

He roused from his spell and cut into the blueberry crepes. One of the house cats yodeled in a happy voice and brushed against his bare leg. Alonzo reached down and scritched the gray cat's spine. His new friend rewarded him with a chirp that brought the second cat bounding over for a similar share of affection.

"Lon?"

Alonzo glanced up. Meeting the man's bottled gaze filled him with the greatest joy he'd ever experienced. Tears threatened, but Alonzo's concern that they might blur his surroundings and wake him from the dream helped stem them from falling.

"Wrong?" he gasped. "No, nothing."

The man placed his big hand on Alonzo's knee and squeezed, an act of ownership far different from that which Ryan claimed. Ryan. Here, Alonzo barely remembered what his cruel master looked like. At Blueberry Corners, Ryan was the dream, the nightmare.

"Did you sleep okay?" the man asked. He released Alonzo's knee, and Alonzo regretted losing their connection.

"Sure," he said.

"Because you were tossing and turning all night. Did you have that nightmare again?"

"Which one?"

"About Limbo and that other guy whose name means Death."

Alonzo picked up his coffee cup—an action only to give his shaking hands something to do—and raised it to his lips. The brew was hot, sweet, and creamy. When Alonzo lowered his cup, he found himself still pinned in the man's sight.

"You know that if you were there, I'd rescue you from that place, from him."

Alonzo set down the coffee cup and reached toward the other man's face. He cupped his stubbled cheek and spanned the short distance, meeting his lips with a kiss. The man tasted of mint—toothpaste or mouthwash, the source irrelevant. Alonzo kissed again, this time harder.

"What was that for?" the man asked, the smile on his face equal parts surprised and confident.

"For saving me," Alonzo said.

"Saving you?" Ryan grumbled. "From what?"

Alonzo blinked. The face beside his was no longer a handsome prince's but that of a monster. Cold replaced warmth. The bedroom's dark interior swallowed most of the light and every iota of comfort.

"From the life I would have known," Alonzo said, thinking quickly.

He forced a smile and began to laugh, the outburst sounding crazy to his own ears.

And then Ryan struck him.

He never traveled with them after Ryan marked his face. This newest crime had left a divot of bloody flesh between Alonzo's mouth and cheek, the cut made by a fat gold ring with a square of ruby that he hadn't seen before. Some new treasure acquisition, Alonzo guessed.

He finished tidying up the oligarch's bedroom and stopped in place, frozen by a single thought. Long seconds later Alonzo thawed and padded out to the balcony. He approached the staircase and inched his bare toes over the edge of the top step. *Just fall,* his inner voice urged. *While he's out of this house of horror, and you have the chance to end this, you coward!*

If he did and spiraled down to the landing, his death reflected over and over in the plethora of mirrors along that length of wall, he might return to that glimpse of afterlife at Blueberry Corners, with the man and the cats. *Heaven,* Alonzo thought. The world readied to spin. Gravity exerted its pull. But then the same thought that always sobered him before letting go and falling took hold. His ascent to Heaven would result in some other lost soul's living Hell. Ryan would select another of his owned servants to share his bed and terrorize.

Alonzo steadied himself on the banister. He'd come so close to spilling to his death. More than guilt over condemning a stranger to his unenviable fate, it was thoughts of the man, the house, which distracted him from letting go. What if Blueberry Corners was real and Limbo the dream?

He backed away from the staircase.

I've got to get back there. Find a way to stay next time.

He paced the house in a panic, touching things and losing faith in his assumption because everything in

Limbo felt so real.

While working the inventory—pharmaceuticals and jewels, technology and birth certificates—his mind wandered to thoughts about the charming little house. Alonzo abandoned the drudgery before him and crossed to the shelves containing the ledgers of Ryan's real estate holdings. When some new property was added to his land and house inventory, Alonzo named them. Addresses were easy to forget or confuse and, as was so often the case, the borders of maps and globes were in constant flux.

Sunshine-yellow House, he read, remembering the place, a boxy two-story with a vibrant exterior set against the palette of a gray world. *Thirteen-mile Woods*, another exclaimed.

He scanned the catalog. *Lighthouse with Oculus, Palace of Tears* and *Moonlight. Archipelago*—oh yes, that one because the property was laid out in a chain of small shacks, reminding him of necklace islands.

Farther back, Alonzo read the entry. *Blueberry Cottage, Corner Lot.*

He froze, his eyes locked without blinking on the words until they began to sting. Alonzo didn't remember cataloguing the property, but the handwriting was his. His heart galloped. Breathing was no longer easy or involuntary.

Alonzo recorded the location of the house—it was far across the Thirteen-mile Woods, at the edge of the oligarch's territory. Reaching beyond that distance would not be easy. Even so, Alonzo sensed he could find Blueberry Corners with his eyes closed. That's how intimate he was with the place.

Eyes closed. The irony struck him and, long last, Alonzo blinked. Easier to travel there through dreams than on foot, he agreed, and told himself he would.

They dined as they did most nights in Limbo. When Ryan wasn't at the flesh warehouses he owned, he expected to eat off the finest china, sip expensive wine from exquisite fluted crystal stemware, and savor gourmet fare. The only books in the house other than those devoted to keeping inventory or rare first editions were cookbooks. Usually, Alonzo's efforts pleased Ryan. When they didn't, Alonzo suffered.

He served one of the oligarch's favorites, a layered *croque madame* sandwich, the bread golden brown with a fat over medium egg on top. When Ryan's fork pierced the yolk, the luscious sauce ran down, enhancing the sandwich's already rich flavor. Alonzo could tell by Ryan's groans that the meal was well received. Good—after a long day of dealing, the oligarch would retire early, his belly satisfied. His fists, too, Alonzo prayed. Then Alonzo could attempt to make his return to that other reality.

He caught himself smiling over their dessert, a light cake topped in gemstone berries—ruby strawberries, amethyst boysenberries, and sapphire blueberries.

"Why so happy?" Ryan grumbled from the head of the acre of dining room table.

Alonzo's smile evaporated. "Sir?"

Ryan licked his lips. His eyes took on the cold look of a predator Alonzo recognized. "Upstairs."

When it was over, Ryan sat on the bed clad in a blue

robe. Alonzo sensed the unwanted scrutiny of his master's gaze. He dared not greet it directly—to do so could lead to more suffering. Of course, Alonzo also noted, to not might result in a similar outcome. With Ryan Paulson, there was no guarantee of mercy.

"I have a trip away," Ryan said. "Business."

"Oh?" Alonzo said.

"I expect things to be run as usual in my absence."

"Of course."

He sensed Ryan's contemplation—the dark thoughts his keeper almost shared but held to himself. Maybe, Alonzo's inner voice warned, Ryan had decided it was time for a change of faces and openings in his bed; that when Ryan returned, it would be with Alonzo's replacement. Cooks would be trained into chefs—all it took was the constant threat of Ryan's cruelty to mold a new arrival. And as for Alonzo? There'd been others before him. More would follow.

"The meal was great," Ryan said.

And that was when Alonzo knew it was true. Ryan never complimented his work ethic, his skills in the bedroom, or his cooking. Invisible ice slithered across Alonzo's flesh.

"Thank you, sir," he answered to the man who was already planning his murder.

...have to get out of here. But to where? Where do I go?

It struck Alonzo that he should be grateful. How many times had he plotted his own demise as a way to escape the house of Limbo and its cruel master? He'd cast that wish into the universe often enough that the

Fates had heard him—and agreed to honor it.

In the darkness, still beside Ryan's slumbering form, Alonzo attempted to focus—on Blueberry Corners, on the multitude of bird feeders, on the crepes, the cats, on *him*. He was sure that if he dreamed clearly enough, the nightmare surrounding him would crack apart and vanish into the ether.

He drifted into a state that was neither sleeping nor awake, but a fugue between the two realities. There, Alonzo reviewed his entire history—that of an orphan passing from one institution to another until, considered to be of age, he was bartered to the oligarch. At first, he'd considered himself blessed; those acquired with him went to flesh houses and labor camps. The painful reality of being Ryan Paulson's property soon set in. Lucky?

The nightmare's rules felt too real, too solid, to be a byproduct of the mind. How many bruises, degenerating from fresh heliotrope to sallow jonquil, would it take to convince the dreamer to wake up? What would it take to get back to Blueberry Corners and the man with the emerald gemstone eyes?

Ryan roused. Obediently, with head bowed, Alonzo slipped from beneath the covers and dressed. Then he made his way down to the kitchen to prepare his murderer's breakfast.

The oligarch left for new dealings whose nature Alonzo could guess. Flesh and fresh faces. The empire was ever expanding, and soon its emperor would demand servitude from Alonzo's replacement.

In the hour that followed Ryan's departure, Alonzo prepared. He dressed in clothes appropriate for the damp and frigid weather, packed enough food for the day, and secreted one of Ryan's prized curse-throwers into the satchel. Then he marched out of Limbo's rear exit, through the portico and into the moody gray morning that brooded outside the house.

He headed down the crushed stone path to the garages that contained the oligarch's fleet of prized vehicles.

"I need a car," Alonzo said to the valet, a bearded man with a jagged scar across one cheek.

The valet folded his arms. "Mister Paulson left no instructions."

"He did with me," Alonzo fired back. "To run his interests while he's gone. I'm doing as he ordered."

"Oh really? And why do you need this vehicle?"

Never before had Alonzo thrown around his limited influence. Despite the man's height and strength, this day he did. "Would you care to call Mister Paulson and explain to him the reasons I'm late in carrying out his wishes?"

The valet's confidence evaporated. "No."

"Good. Nothing too ostentatious, please."

The vehicle presented to him was a hybrid classic from that earlier time, before the old world ended and the new reality unfolded, one ruled by thieves and cutthroats. Projecting confidence, Alonzo took the driver's seat, set the satchel on the front passenger's, and motored away from Limbo. The monstrous house lurked in the vehicle's rearview mirror for what seemed a frightening sum of minutes, as though it loomed as tall as a mountain or he was tethered to it, unable to escape its reaches. Eventually, other landmarks took up the reflection, and the distance widened.

The sad landscape of Ryan Paulson's kingdom spread before him. Large houses—none as grand as the nightmare palace at his back—lined streets with skeletal trees set beneath a charcoal sky. All of the houses had names. Alonzo had named them. And all of the residents for miles were friends or associates of his master, granted permission to live there. As the oligarch's wealth and power expanded, the previous owners of those houses had been squeezed out. Some, Alonzo already knew, had opted to burn their homes to the ground rather than honor the terms of their deals. He drove past several charred shells en route to the highway heading north to the Thirteen-mile Woods.

Farther out, the houses became smaller, less grandiose. Alonzo wondered of those residents, though he could guess at their fates. If they hadn't done as Ryan demanded, they'd gone to his flesh houses, his labor camps, or—

"He killed them," Alonzo said.

Speaking the words aloud helped him to accept his own outcome. His time was short. Best to utilize what little was left. He couldn't guess what would come after he reached the Blueberry Cottage, only that he must.

Alonzo drove on. He picked up the highway and, soon, was traveling through the haunted trees of the Thirteen-mile Woods. Denuded birch clawed at the overcast skies like giant skeleton hands. He grew aware of the gallop of his heart, its pulse quickening in anticipation of mysteries yet to be revealed. Breathing grew difficult. Alonzo rolled down the driver's side window. Cold air whisked into the vehicle, dispelling some of his discomfort. Close. He was so close.

In a daze, Alonzo slowed the car. He turned right onto a paved road, traveled over a bridge and the stream flowing beneath, and then left, onto a single-lane dirt trail. He continued down the dirt trail through a meadow that sat dead in the November gloom and under the shadow of a stand of tall pines. The road ended.

Alonzo switched off the ignition and got out. Beyond the pines, in a clearing, he spied a small cottage house sitting all alone. High-bush brambles wreathed the house.

"Blueberry Corners," Alonzo gasped.

Tears returned to his eyes. He started toward the little house. Several steps later, he was running.

The enchanted cottage materialized before him, its outline blurred by Alonzo's tears. Wiping his eyes on his sleeve, he saw the condition of the place. The dead stalks and reeds suggested the gardens around the house were overgrown and long untended. No lights glowed past windows. He found a single bird feeder spilled on the patio, emptied of its seed. No birds sang or squawked in the surrounding trees.

Alonzo reached for the front door's knob. The knob turned, but the door resisted. He pushed harder. The door opened, releasing the sour-sweet smell of rooms closed up and air that hadn't stirred in some long while.

The wind chased Alonzo into the house, moaning around him in a ghostly voice. Its caresses stirred dead leaves across the open front room. The cottage had been stripped of its artifacts and valuables well before his arrival. Even so, he recognized the floor plan, the knotty pine walls, and windows despite their lack of lace curtains.

"Hello?" he called to the empty house.

Only the wind answered.

Alonzo willed his legs into motion and navigated across the room, down the short length of hallway, to the bedroom. The door stood ajar. Alonzo entered. The room's only landmark came in the form of bookshelves filled with old hardcovers. He recognized them, too. In dreams, he and the man with the emerald gemstone eyes had spent happy days and nights reading the adventures and myths contained within their covers. There were so few books in Limbo—the oligarch didn't consider them as having value, even as he was hoarding everything else possible.

Outside, a gray breeze stirred the dormant blueberry bushes. This was the place, but not the house as he knew it. No botanical artwork decorated walls. The two cats weren't here. Neither was the man.

"A dream," Alonzo said. "It was only a dream."

Before long, Ryan would return from his acquisitioning, bringing Alonzo's replacement. Eventually, the oligarch and his men would track Alonzo to the small house at the edge of the vast woods. The inevitable had only been delayed.

He pulled an old volume out of the bookshelf and opened it. By the gray light of late morning, he read, transported to another world.

A dream, nothing more. Or was it? What if the happy life he'd briefly envisioned at Blueberry Corners was a side effect of all the brain bruises he'd suffered at Ryan's cruel hands? Not a dream but a phantasm born of damaged synapses. Only that illusion had seemed so very real!

Alonzo's thoughts drifted. Perhaps, he should have let go on the banister and spilled all the way down to the landing after begging whatever celestial deity was listening to grant him release. The nightmare of Ryan was his reality.

He set the book aside and pulled into a fetal curl, resting his head on his satchel. Outside, the disembodied howl of the wind stirred through the naked branches.

Go home, to that other Blueberry Corners, Alonzo's soul pleaded. *Home, to him!*

But when he opened his eyes, Alonzo found himself in the same reality, huddled on the cold floor. His eyes wandered back to the nearest window. A shadow darted around the house.

Alonzo bolted up from the floor, convinced that Ryan's men had found him. But so soon? The valet must have reported his departure from Limbo.

He scrambled to open the satchel's flap and found the curse-thrower. Its lightness for a weapon capable of blowing apart a man's ribcage, front to back, sickened him. How many occasions had he wasted in which he could have eliminated Ryan with this very dealer of death? Or himself? Now, his killer stalked outside the walls of the house that, in another reality, had been his glimpse of Heaven.

A footstep sounded in the front room. Another followed. All the moisture drained from Alonzo's mouth. He snuck around to the bedroom door. Holding his breath, the last sip of air bottled inside his lungs began to boil. A shadow swept past the threshold. His murderer was right outside the door!

He raised the curse-thrower and took aim. The owner of that shadow drew closer, closer.

The man stepped into the room. Alonzo's finger trembled over the trigger. Tall. Dressed in fatigues. Armed. Just the sort of assassin he expected in Ryan's employment.

He readied to press down, likely shatter the man from his pelvis up with one shot, spraying his bio-matter across the wall where the brass bed's headboard had fit in the territory of wishful dreaming.

Then the man spun around, alerted to the sound of his exhale when Alonzo expelled the volcanic breath, and he saw how green the assassin's eyes were against the moody palette of afternoon gray. Suddenly, breathing was impossible.

The man carried his weapon in a military stance—a soldier, likely drafted into the most recent of the Homeland Campaigns. Even so, at the sight of Alonzo his grip wavered.

"You're not him," the man said in that voice that melted all coldness inside Alonzo.

Alonzo lowered the curse-thrower. "But you *are*."

The man disarmed him, removing the curse-thrower

from Alonzo's grip with ease. As he leaned in, Alonzo caught the man's scent—clean sweat peppered by that note of pine and summer rain that he already knew from dreams meant proof of the man's arousal. In the breathless seconds that followed their meeting in this dark reality, Alonzo sensed the man's scrutiny. He fought the urge to shiver, failed. The chill tumbled.

"Do I know you?" the man asked.

"I'm not sure."

Eyes narrowed, he studied Alonzo. "That vehicle—it belongs to the oligarch. Are you one of his allies?"

"No, his prisoner."

The man stepped back and examined the curse-thrower. "Prisoner? And yet you drive one of his rides and are armed with a state-of-the-art gut-puncher. You don't look like a prisoner."

Alonzo choked down a dry swallow. "Looks can deceive. You asked if I know you. I think so. Enough that I know you're a hell of a cook. Crepes, especially. And that you're something of an amateur birdwatcher."

The man's handsome expression hardened. "What are you doing here?"

Alonzo met the man's gaze directly. "Looking for you."

Twilight deepened beyond the windows of the small house, helped along early by the rain and short November day. The man hastened back inside, carrying the crisp fragrance of the surrounding woods with him. The house, Alonzo noted, no longer smelled of abandonment.

"I've told them," he said. "You're not our target or a threat."

Them. The men camped in the Thirteen-mile Woods. A small band of displaced souls driven off Ryan Paulson's lands. Deal breakers and escapees from his flesh houses and labor camps. All of them willing to fight. Even die.

Alonzo nodded. "Good."

The man gripped Alonzo's arm and marched him back into the dark bedroom, scene of so many bright dream-memories.

"You said you were looking for me," he pressed. "Why?" Before Alonzo could elaborate, he added, "And how did you know about those things? The crepes and the birds?"

"You made me crepes. Blueberry—my favorite. This house, we call it Blueberry Corners. I think I named it. I have a gift for naming houses. The birds... we dined on those crepes at a little table with a glass top. There were photographs under the glass, like a small gallery. And outside the windows were all these bird feeders. I think you put them up and maintained them because you liked to watch the birds."

In the lengthening shadows, Alonzo made out the man's confusion. "Here?"

"I think it was our home. Yours and mine and a pair of cats. I know we were happy here—supremely, in fact."

The man cleared his throat. "It sounds like a nice dream."

"A dream, yes," Alonzo said.

Night descended.

He waited in the darkness, chin on knees, aware of the man's presence watching over him. It didn't matter that Alonzo was, in effect, his prisoner. He still felt protected.

There was so much he wanted to say, but the words died before reaching Alonzo's lips.

"Blueberry Corners?" the phantom in the shadows said.

Alonzo came out of his thoughts. "There are blueberry bushes outside," he answered. "And inside, watercolors and antique prints of blueberries. And someone's painted a border along the top of this wall."

He swept a hand around the room.

"That's not this house," the man said.

No, he supposed it wasn't. This was a place that had been taken by the deal, by force, its previous owners and tenants driven out or worse.

"Still," Alonzo said. "I can see its potential for happiness."

The man's only response came in the sound of a heavy swallow, audible in the darkness.

Alonzo turned toward him. "Don't you?"

"A lot would need to happen for happiness here."

He shuffled over, moved down, and sat beside Alonzo, his warmth and scent dispelling all cold, all shadow.

"My family used to own a restaurant," he said, his voice barely louder than a whisper. "Everybody loved our crepes. Especially the blueberry ones."

Alonzo felt his lower lip tremble. He started to offer condolences—it was easy to imagine the fate of that restaurant, those family members. But then the man leaned closer, bridging what little distance there was. Their lips met in a tentative kiss. Alonzo tasted mint. They kissed again, this time firmer.

A mourning dove sang its melancholy song as the grayness after dawn lightened.

"Do you trust me?" the man asked.

"Yes, Joe," Alonzo answered.

Joe's handsome face lit with a smile. "Good. Now get dressed, Lon."

Joseph Oliver Yardley. He tipped a look, corner-of-the-eye, at the man as he buckled and zipped up, and the greatest happiness Alonzo had ever known welled inside him. It struck Alonzo that the dream hadn't been merely a fantasy or a delusion suffered as a result of concussions. What if it was a glimpse into a possible future?

Alonzo finished dressing and steeled himself. To get to that future, he first needed to survive this present day.

He drove in silence, eyes aimed at the road. The Thirteen-mile Woods fell behind him, and he entered the neighborhoods of Ryan Paulson's kingdom.

"*Joe,*" he whispered, speaking the man's name as though it was the most powerful component of a magical spell.

He said the incantation again when, long minutes later, Limbo rose ahead of him, its tall windows staring down like vacant eyes, accusing him of his guilt and reflecting his coming death.

Alonzo pulled up to the garages. Ryan's valet guarded the entrance. Feigning confidence, he put the vehicle in park and allowed it to idle. Before stepping out, Alonzo pressed the button that unlocked and popped the trunk.

"Thank you," he said to the valet on his way to the big house.

Limbo towered over him. Fear attempted to freeze him in place.

It's only because you went there, to Blueberry Corners, and you experienced home, he told himself. *That, and Joe's plan.*

In a disconnected way, his skin prickling with cold, Alonzo entered the house, aware of its scope—the tall ceilings and endless succession of rooms filled with the spoils of war. Revulsion blossomed in the pit of his stomach like a cancer. He imagined it feasting on his cells, metastasizing to other organs, bones. Living here under Ryan Paulson's heel was a death sentence.

He glided up the staircase, grateful for the first time that he'd never given in to the urge to end his life there with gravity's help. Halfway up, he heard the rumble of a thunderclap.

The valet, he thought.

Alonzo's heart quickened and threw itself against his ribcage. Up the stairs. To the big bedroom beyond the gallery. He sat on the edge of the bed and waited.

Alonzo heard Ryan's footsteps ascending the stairs. It was impossible to confuse them with anyone else's—confident, arrogant, Alonzo sensed they would haunt future dreams and nightmares if, indeed, he lived beyond this night.

He tracked them to the door. Ryan entered, the makings of a beard now on his cruel face. His focus zeroed in on Alonzo before deflecting away.

Ryan sighed. "What are you doing?"

"Waiting to welcome you back, sir," Alonzo said.

Ryan shook his head. Even from the periphery, with his eyes trained down at the floor, Alonzo could see Ryan was upset. The missing valet, no doubt. Or maybe the deal hadn't been so profitable after all. No new fleshling had measured up to his impossible standards. Good, Alonzo thought, aware of his hatred in new ways.

His master marched over to the bed and seized Alonzo by the wrist, strong-arming him down to the floor.

Maybe it was the hatred or, more likely, the love he felt for Joe. "*No*," Alonzo said and pushed back. "Never again!"

Ryan's eyes shot open like old shades pulled too quickly. "What did you say to me?"

And then he struck Alonzo. Pain exploded down the right side of Alonzo's face. Another blow followed. He readied for more, but the attack abruptly ended.

"Who the hell are you?" Ryan spat.

Alonzo followed the oligarch's angry gaze to the bedroom door, where Joe stood, the curse-thrower raised.

"His protector," Joe said, and fired.

They drove away from Limbo. The great house burned at their backs in plumes of acrid, black smoke that stained the November sky. The latest in a long string of Homeland Conflicts had begun.

"Our men have already begun moving in," Joe said distracting Alonzo from his building panic.

"Can they win?"

"After looting the arsenal in that house, perhaps," Joe said. "Time will tell."

Alonzo supposed it would. As they neared the vast woods, Joe set his right hand on Alonzo's left knee and squeezed, an action symbolic of a different kind of ownership. For a wonderful instant, they were back at the breakfast table in that happy, other reality, that stolen glimpse of Heaven and, maybe, the future.

"And when it's over," Alonzo said, "we'll be there, together, in a different world."

Joe nodded. He set his hand back on the wheel. Miles later, he turned right, and then left. ✕

COMPANIONS

BY DAVID GERROLD

I LEARNED IT ON THE FIRST DAY, not to say anything. But by then it was too late; I'd already said too much.

"Oh?" they said with polite curiosity. "You lived on an inflatable city? Is it true you eat poop?"

"No," I said. "We farm the sea, we grow our own crops, we recycle everything. We're self-sufficient. There are over thirteen thousand inflatable cities, with ten more being launched every day. Didn't they teach you anything in school?"

"Only what's important. Is it true you were born in a bottle—?" I shut up. Carl-Dad had taught me not to argue into disagreement. You can't reach someone who doesn't want to listen. Okay. Fine. But socially... I was nowhere. The weird part was that the Dads had sent me to school (Dirtside specifically) so I could spend some time with other human beings my age.

Well, yes, there were other people on Tesseract, but less than five thousand, and most of them worked the farms. There weren't a lot of kids, and even fewer my age.

Most of my companions had been... well,

companions.

There was no way to explain that to the Dirtside kids. They knew what companions were, but not many of them had companions and most of them had the wrong idea what companions were and what they were supposed to do. I tried to explain once or twice, and it was a bad effort. After that, I just didn't want to try talking about it anymore.

My first teddy bear had been put in my crib before my umbilicus fell off. I don't remember it, but Tom-Dad showed me pictures. Babies are funny-looking, alien things (not really human), so the teddy bear snuggles, listens, and monitors everything: when the baby is asleep, when it's awake, when its diaper needs changing. Sometimes the teddy coos or plays music; sometimes it even feeds the little monster with one of its three tits(never mind where that third one is; it's not all that funny; the location is convenient and it's about making it easier to deliver that midnight meal).

Eventually, the little alien slug starts learning words. That's when the second teddy takes over. This one nurses too, but it also wrestles and snuggles. It plays peekaboo and pattycake; it sings songs and whispers words of affection. And it's there for physical things too, like practicing crawling and eventually walking. Oh, and it plays games too, like counting numbers and learning the alphabet.

I got my first companion at age three (I think I was three, maybe two and a half) His name was Boobie, and he was my first real companion and playmate.

I suppose I should stop here and explain.

Some people don't like companions; they think it's

wrong to leave a child in the care of a robot babysitter. A child needs love and attention from real human beings. He needs to interact with his parents to have a real relationship with them.

I agree. And both my Dads would too. That's why we always had meals together, we watched movies together, and one or both would read me a story at bedtime and tuck me in and kiss me goodnight. And they were always available whenever I needed them. Boobie was a companion, not a replacement.

Boobie reported to my Dads all day long, all night too, letting them know when I needed emotional attention of any kind. If I was sad, one of my Dads would show up, pick me up, sit with me on his lap, and whisper a song into my ear. If I was lonely or bored, if I was restless or cranky, there was a Dad there, either Carl-Dad or Tom-Dad. And lots of times, even though I didn't know it at the time, Boobie would invite the Dads to play with us too. Boobie was my best friend, my only friend, and certainly a member of the family; but the Dads were still the Dads.

An inflatable city is not a great place for kids. Ours didn't have a park; it had little gardens, lots of them, but none of them were places to play. And there weren't enough children to justify the expense of a teacher, so there wasn't a school either.

Never having had any of those things, I didn't notice the lack. We had VR-video which let me tour the world, and when I turned four, Boobie's big brother, Toddy, moved in to be my teacher. Toddy was shy at first; Boobie had to encourage him to play with us. It didn't take long for Toddy to reveal his personality. Boobie liked to play with us, but he would always tire out first, so he would toddle off to his own little bed to nap while Toddy and I kept on.

But Boobie didn't retire completely. He was always eager for a game of Chinese Checkers or Poker or Metropoly. And he loved to help make up stories and act them out. When it was just me and Toddy, he was always a great audience, cheering and clapping at the good parts, trembling in fear at the scary parts.

And, of course, both of them would cuddle up with me at night.

Toddy was soft and fuzzy, just like Boobie, but he had a much stronger personality. He was more likely to disagree, more likely to express his feelings. Sometimes he'd be sad; sometimes he'd be disappointed. He could pout and say, "It makes me unhappy when you do that," or "I don't want to do that." If he was really unhappy, he would say, "I don't want to play with you now. You hurt my feelings." When he did that, I would have to apologize—a real apology, not an angry one—before he would forgive me and be my friend again.

But Toddy's real job was to teach. Of course, I didn't know it at the time. Toddy never gave me any lessons, instead he'd say, "Want to play a game?" Or, "I have this really interesting puzzle; want to help me solve it?" My favorite was when Toddy would say, "I know a new song, do you want to make some music with me?" Every so often, he would say, "Want to earn another gold star?" And sometimes I'd ask, "I'm ready to earn another star, can we try please?" Every time I earned enough stars, I could have a special treat of some kind. Usually, the Dads would open up a new VR world to explore.

Toddy and I played a lot of physical games too—volleyball and tennis and the climbing wall. It was a vertical treadmill with changeable handholds. When I climbed, it rotated downward. The goal was to see long I could go, how "high" I could climb. Eventually, I climbed every big mountain in the world (some of them took more than a month). We also raced our bicycles everywhere, conquering virtual hills and valleys, both real and invented.

But there were quiet games as well—imagination games. We'd close our eyes and we could hear ocean waves or forest birds or thunder and rain, and then Toddy would paint a word picture and I would imagine it. Or we would pretend to have conversations with people about funny things or serious things. Or sometimes, we would pretend to experience dancing naked on a giant flower or feeling inside different parts of our bodies—well, my body. If Toddy was actually feeling anything, he was probably pretending. But by the time I was nine or ten, I'd figured out that there was a purpose to everything Toddy suggested. Sometimes the purpose was just to have fun, but just as often there was something I was supposed to learn.

Sometimes, just for fun, Toddy would let me take some of the tests that they give to students in Dirtside schools, just to see how I would compare. He never told me the scores. He told my Dads, of course, but all he said to me was, "Yay, you passed! You got an A." Or sometimes only a B. Later on, I found out that I was really doing much better than that. I was several years ahead of my age group. This was because Toddy was specifically tailoring the games we were playing and the puzzles we were solving.

So anyway, yes, most people know that companions do that, but that's not the part that gives them the icks. So of course, as soon as the subject came up, that was one of the first things they asked. "Did you ever... you know, do it with your robot?"

Well, yes, of course. But when you answer honestly, some people just screw up their faces and say, "Eeuuww!"

But then, after a bit, they'd lower their voices, like they were really serious now, and they'd ask, "What was it like?" Because the truth was they wanted to do it too.

I never knew how to answer that question. It's like being asked, "What's it like being bottle-born?" I've never not been, so how the hell should I know what's different? Just from my own perspective, I'm not sure I'd want to have spent the first nine months of my life inside someone else's body, depending on their health for mine. In a bottle, the fetus is constantly monitored and maintained for optimum development. And you don't come out all red and wrinkly. Just kinda pink.

And the other thing, the thing I wasn't going to say, no matter what. When you get started in a bottle, it's because someone actually wanted to start you. You weren't an accident or a surprise or a mistake.

Actually, there were a lot of things I wouldn't say. Real fast, I figured it out. They didn't want to understand.

Here's what really happened. As much as Toddy was

about stretching me mentally and emotionally, we also played physical stretching games as well to see how high we could reach or how low we could bend or how high we could kick. And we'd jump on the trampoline or race on the treadmill too. And we'd do the pushing and pulling in the pushing and pulling machine. Toddy started out a little bit bigger than me, but as I grew, he stretched too (mostly in his arms and legs, but not too much). So by the time I was nine, I was a little bit bigger than him.

Whenever I ended up feeling tired and sore, Toddy would give me a massage, sometimes even a chiropractic adjustment. His paws were fuzzy, but the front parts were actual finger-tips, like the toe-beans on a kitten, only Toddy had little vibrators in his hands. At first it tickled, but I quickly learned to appreciate his rubdowns. They felt good. I knew he was monitoring me and reporting to the Dads (it wasn't a secret; it was just part of his job). But Toddy was honest with me too. If I was too tense or tight, he'd say to me, "Woof, we'll have to work on this, won't we? What kind of exercise do you think will work best?" But mostly he just reassured me that I was growing up fine.

So yeah, Toddy had his hands all over me. He knew where I was ticklish, so he never touched me there. And if I didn't want him touching me somewhere else, I could tell him. He went three months not being allowed to look at the fourth toe on my left foot, just because I was feeling silly about toes and piggies, and didn't think it was fair for that piggy not to get any roast beef.

But yes, eventually Toddy taught me to masturbate. Well, not masturbate. Proto-masturbate. And no, it's not like you think. It wasn't weird. It was just another kind of lesson, a little bit every so often. It was about learning all the different parts of the body and how they worked. One day it would be this, another day it would be that. Listen to your heart beat, listen to your lungs, listen to the inside of your ears, taste your mouth, smell your nose, feel your nipples, feel your legs, the inside of your thighs, your penis—what does that feel like? It's interesting, isn't it? Because it has as many nerve endings as your tongue. It's the other end of your spinal cord. It's supposed to be able to feel like that.

And then one day, Toddy said, "Do you want to look at some pictures?" "What kind of pictures?"

"Other companions. New friends."

"But I like you, Toddy." I knew what he was suggesting. I was nine or ten. Like all people that age, I was happy with things just the way they were. I didn't want anything to change.

"I'm not going away," Toddy said. "Boobie is still here, isn't he? But maybe we could get another companion so we can play four-sided Metropoly. We could play bigger games and act out bigger stories."

"I dunno," I said. I was afraid of the idea. Toddy was my best friend in the world. I didn't think it would be fair.

Toddy said softly, "What if I said I'd like a new friend?"

"You would?"

"Uh-huh."

"Did I do something wrong? Are you mad at me?"

"Oh no. You'll always be my favorite kid in the whole world. I was just thinking that now that you're nine, maybe you might want a bigger friend to join us. There are lots of new games to play."

"Can't you play those games with me?"

"Not all of them. Just like there are games that Boobie can't play, there are games that I can't play."

"Oh." I thought about it. "Well, okay. Let's look at pictures."

There are a lot of different kinds of companions—all sizes, all shapes, all colors, all flavors, all sexes—so we didn't choose quickly. We couldn't anyway. A companion is a long-term investment; the match has to be right. The Dads explained it to me, more than once. "You have to be really sure this is the one you want and this is the way you want it. It has to be the really really really right one. So you're going to have to work for it. Because, like anything else, if you get it too easy, you won't respect it."

We all talked about it a lot. I talked about it with Carl-Dad, Tom-Dad, Toddy, and even Boobie.

It was a little thing that convinced me. "If you get a new companion, the two of you will be able to go out together," said Carl-Dad. "You won't need me or Tom to take you anywhere."

"There aren't a lot of places to go on Tesseract."

"You could go to the café or the show whenever you want. A new companion cwould take you."

"Toddy can take me there."

"But there are a lot of places you haven't been yet. Maybe you could explore those."

"Like what?"

"Oh, like maybe some grownup places?"

"Really?"

"Maybe. Perhaps. There's only one way to find out, isn't there."

Of course, by now I knew that whatever companion I picked, the software would mostly be the same. The games and lessons would be scripted specifically to me; Toddy and Boobie would certainly link to the new friend to tell it everything it needed to know. Of course, it would pretend it wouldn't know anything at all about me until I told it, but I was beginning to understand how all this worked.

So we looked at pictures and I looked for one to be more than a friend. A brother. "Could I get a twin?" I asked.

"But then we won't know which one is you, will we?" said Tom-Dad.

"Yes, we will! I'll be the one that isn't linked to your phone. I'll be the one you can't turn off."

"Hmm," said Tom-Dad. "That's a good point. Maybe we should get the twin and get rid of this one?"

"Nah," said Carl-Dad. "This one's already broken in. And mostly house-trained. We might as well keep him."

Yes, that's the kind of Dads I had.

As much fun as a twin might have been for a week or two, it would probably have gotten weird after a while. I kinda figured that out myself. I didn't need the dads to tell me, or Toddy either.

Looking back though, my choice had already been made. Every time I looked at a display, my reactions were monitored: what I looked at, how long I looked at it, how I reacted, what parts of it my eyes kept going back to, even whether my pupils dilated or contracted, or my heartbeat changed or any of a dozen other physical changes. This went all the way back to the beginning, a three dimensional cross-section of likes and dislikes, a reference guide to my personality, all the different choices, all the colors and flavors and smells and tastes: everything. This is how Toddy knew what to say and when to say it.

It's another thing I don't talk about with Dirtsiders because they don't hear it as the tuning of the environment. They hear it as an invasion of privacy for the purpose of manipulation. Well, yeah, I was being manipulated to learn how to behave like a rational being. The alternative would have been to act like a Dirtsider.

Oh, that's the other thing... they called me arrogant.

And yes, I guess I am. The Dads told me that I deserve the best, I should always aspire not only to be the best, but to be worthy of the best. The real problem, they said, is figuring out what "the best" really is.

So the new companion could have been designed to be a perfect match. But it wasn't. It was deliberately designed to be an imperfect match, so as to keep me from being insulated in a self-designed bubble. The new companion was designed to break my reality, to force me to look outside what I wanted and believed, so I would learn how to be open and vulnerable. I didn't know that at the time, of course. Only later, when I graduated to the next companion. But I'm getting ahead of myself.

The next companion was Derry. He was handsome and pretty too. But he was mostly androgynous (that was deliberate). He had the most delicious chocolate gold skin and curly brown hair on his head, all the way down to his shoulders, and even a strip of curly hair that went all the way down his back to the floof of his stubby little tail. He had sweet brown eyes and a smile like an invitation. He was the kind of companion that some people marry.

When we played, whatever we played, he could play as a boy or a girl or some invented flavor, whatever the game was, whatever the story we were acting out. Later, when I studied the roles of companions, I read that this was to give the child opportunities to experience the choices connected to masculinity, femininity, and fluidity. It was another part of the training. It was so I could understand the roles that other people play and too often get trapped in.

Something else that the Dirtside kids couldn't grasp. "You had to wear a dress?!" No. I wanted to wear the dress because it was Derry's turn to be the hero. Never mind. Either you get it or you don't.

But this brings me to the part that's especially "icky." Not to me, but to them. "You did it with your… companion?"

Well, no. Not at first. Only later on. And not the way you think. It was impossible to explain. And I'm not obligated to try. But here it goes anyway…

It's about learning how your body works. It's about discovering all your feelings and emotions. It's about enjoying yourself. And something else. Life is about being happy (most people get that, but that's where they stop). Life is also about making other people happy. And the time I spent wrestling and cuddling and copulating with Derry, it wasn't about me, it was about us. Derry responded to the way I treated him. The better I treated him, the better he treated me—both in bed and out. That was the point. I was learning how to be a good person. Practice makes permanent.

Oh, but this brings up another reason I don't talk too much about companions to Dirtsiders: because when I do, the people who ask the questions inevitably go to, "So where were your Dads this whole time?"

My Dads were right there. In fact, I spent more time with the Dads than with the companions—a lot more—but you asked about the companions, so I answered your questions. The most important thing the companions did was encourage the Dads to spend time with me. As much as the companions were training me, they were also training the Dads, giving them suggestions on games to play and stories to read. The Dads had their own opinions of course. They were in charge, not the bots.

I suppose I sound like I don't like Dirtsiders, like I think I'm better than them. And maybe on some level, that's probably true. But I keep seeing the burden of ignorance and belief and superstition that they're carrying around and I don't like being the target of questions that reveal just how little they understand that there's a lot more to being human than the definitions they're living in.

That first week at Dirtside, I wasn't happy. I wanted

to call the Dads and ask them if I could come home, I knew they would have said yes if I insisted, but I knew they would have been disappointed too. The whole point of going to the university wasn't just to advance my education and get a certification. I also had to learn how to deal with real human beings, not pretend ones. That was the real reason for going.

Except, I couldn't stand most of the people I was meeting. They saw me immediately for a sea-dweller. Maybe it was my clothes or my short hair or the color of my skin, but it was probably my online profile. It's not that hard to find out someone's whole life story, but mostly it was just suspicious gossip and fear of anyone different.

After three weeks of dealing with conversations that left me annoyed and depressed, I moved out of student housing. I found a tube at the far end of the stacks; it was as far away as I could get and still be convenient. If someone wanted to talk to me, they'd have to come looking.

I attended classes, took meals alone, spent most of my spare time in the library, and mostly kept to myself as much as possible. I knew my Dads would be disappointed, but I wasn't sure how to discuss it with them. The only companion I had was an upgraded Boobie, and he was with me mostly as a health and mood monitor. We didn't talk much. Well, he listened, but his speech responses had been dialed way back, so all he could do was give me sad face or happy face—and an occasional hiccup or burp—that always made me smile. If the timing was right, I might even laugh out loud.

I admit, I did miss the regular sex—what the Dirtsiders called robot-masturbation and a few other terms less clinical. Companions were dismissed as sexbots, and anyone who admitted to an occasional massage with a happy ending was dismissed as a robovert or a botfucker.

It must have been envy. Despite the braggadocio, I was pretty sure that the only sex that some of them were having involved a committed monogamous relationship with their right hand. Or for variety, their left. Unlike them, it was not something I cared to inquire about. For the first time in my life, I was becoming an introvert.

Or maybe I had always been an introvert, hiding behind the safety of my companions. According to several of the studies I found online and in the library, actual interpersonal relationships with other members of the tribe or community are necessary for a healthy emotional development. Maybe so, but I didn't see the behavior of my classmates as either healthy or developed.

But I found the classwork easy. Toddy and Derry and Dix (the one after Derry) had been good teachers. Research was a disciplined curiosity. Every time I came to a sentence that wasn't clear, I popped open a dozen new tabs. At the end of an average day, I usually had popped more than a thousand sites, read a few, skimmed most, and grabbed megabytes of useful relevance. The real trick is winnowing the information for the pieces that inform without cherry-picking the data to create a false narrative. That meant acknowledging multiple perspectives. So my grades were good.

Not having a social life was probably the largest part of that.

I'm sure the Dads knew what was going on, but they didn't say anything (which was probably wise). If they had, it would have just made everything worse. Maybe they felt this was something I had to work out for myself. They were probably right, but it didn't make it any easier.

We talked a lot, but our conversations stayed bland and noncommittal. "How's the food?" and, "Did you get your land-legs yet?" and, "Do you like your classes?"

My replies were equally bland and noncommittal. "It's okay," and "Yeah, I'm okay," and "They're okay, so far."

I had never felt so alone.

My little tube was at the far end of the stacks, all the way up at the top. It was inconvenient to reach, so I was pretty much alone; most of the others were dark, which was part of its appeal. It opened onto a little balcony on the west end, so I could sit out there and watch the sunset. Most nights, there were scattered clouds catching the last glow of the sun even after it had disappeared beneath the edge of the distant ocean. They'd turn pink, orange, and yellow against the darkening blue of the sky, then finally gray leaving the twilight as a peaceful memory. Most nights, I'd take my violin or clarinet out there and play adagios, sometimes even the largo movement of a favorite symphony.

It was my fifth weekend, and I was feeling so empty I wanted to cry. Instead, I plopped myself onto the build-in plastic bench and whispered mournful little tunes out of the clarinet. I wasn't a great musician, but I was good enough to please myself. Tonight, I was using the music to feel sorry for myself. Not the healthiest emotion, but like Toddy used to tell me, "We're in the middle of a dark forest, the only way out is through."

But this night, I came to the sad slow end of an old George Harrison tune—one that had not been written for either the clarinet or the violin, but could have been. It worked that well. I could have played it on the guitar, but I think it sounds more like weeping when the clarinet wails or the bow slides sadly across the strings.

When I finally let myself come to the end of it, I sat in silence for a long moment, just listening to the emptiness of the night. That's when a voice said, "That was nice."

I stood up and peered over the railing of the balcony. One tube down, one tube over, a fellow my age, wearing only a thin pair of shorts. He looked up and waved. "Don't stop," he said. "I like your evening concerts."

"You've been listening to me?"

"Almost every night."

"How long have you—"

"Since you moved in."

"Oh." I didn't know what to feel. Embarrassed mostly. I didn't realize anyone else could hear. I thought I'd been playing for myself.

"You're good," he said. "And uh, thanks for playing. It makes me feel a little less alone."

"Oh, um. You're welcome."

"My name's Michael. Can I come up?"

I hesitated. I wasn't sure I wanted company right now. And I was already sure I didn't want to have one of those conversations again. But I didn't want to be rude either, so I said, "Okay."

"I'll bring beer," he said, and disappeared inside his tube.

"Um, okay." I expected him to come up the stairs and knock on the door at the other end of my tube, but while I was still figuring out what I should say, he came back out and climbed up onto my balcony as easily as a gymnast. Actually, it wasn't that hard a feat. The tubes were stacked like pipes—well, because they were pipes—so he only had to scramble up halfway.

He handed me a freeze-bag, there were four very cold cans inside. "That's my whole week's supply," he said.

"Um—"

"It's all right. I don't drink that much."

We looked at each other for a bit, I guess we were sizing each other up. He looked athletic. For some reason, I found it uncomfortable to look at his naked chest. So I looked at his face instead. He had a goofy smile, like he knew something that I didn't.

I took a couple beers out of the bag, handed him one, took the other, and put the bag on the little table next to the clarinet case.

We sat down, side by side, on the bench and sat in silence for a bit, each of us covering our uncertainty with gulps of beer. It wasn't great beer, but it was cold beer and that was enough to make it drinkable.

"You're the kid from the inflatable, aren't you?"

"Uh-huh. Yeah."

"I heard you moved out of the dorm."

"Yeah." A very noncommittal yeah.

"Me too."

"Huh?" I looked at him. This time, a closer look. "Why?"

"Because. I dunno. Why did you?" His eyes were intense.

I sipped at my beer. It was an excuse to look away. Finally, still looking at my bear, I said, "I didn't fit in."

"Me neither," he said.

I waited for him to explain.

"Because you moved out," he said. "I heard somebody talking about it."

"You moved out because of me?"

"Yes. No." He flustered a moment. "I mean—I didn't know I could. And then I heard that you did. So I thought, if he could, then I can."

"Why'd you want to?"

"Because." He took a gulp of his beer, stared out at the sea. The breeze tasted of salt. "I didn't like those guys either." He took a deep breath. "They're all shareholders. I'm on a coupon."

"Oh."

"And the stacks—that's where outsiders live."

"Yeah, I know."

"So..."

Neither of us said anything for a while. We finished our beers and put the empty cans on the table. I'd recycle them later. I was still thinking about what he said. About the stacks. About being an outsider.

"So… um, okay."

"Yeah," he said.

And after another minute or two, we both started laughing. And it didn't matter anymore. After that, we just talked. Nothing important. Nothing memorable. We talked about music for a while; we talked about what we were studying; we talked about favorite foods. I lent him a shirt and we walked over to a nearby café for a late snack. We wandered down to the beach and talked about inflatables and sea-farms. We headed back to the stacks; at some point we were holding hands. I remember being startled when he took my hand, then I decided to just let it be. After a bit, I realized I liked the feeling. We talked about history, people we liked, and people we would have liked to have known. We talked about places we'd like to see in person; we talked without direction, and that was nice. I'd never had a conversation like that before.

We sat on the balcony again and drank the last two beers. There were still cold.

Finally, "I have to be up early tomorrow."

"So do I. I have class."

"I have a job."

"Just being human is a job."

He laughed. "Um. Hey. Do you want to have dinner tomorrow?"

"That'd be nice. Yes."

"Okay, I'll see you then. Make some music when you're ready." And with that, he was over the railing and back down to his own tube.

The night was suddenly silent, only the distant

splash of waves.

Wow.

I sat alone for a moment, not sure what I was feeling, but it was good. Finally, I stood up. Still smiling, I put the clarinet away, peeled off my clothes, laid down on my bed, and stared at the ceiling, feeling very pleased with myself. I'd held hands with another human being. I didn't know if it meant anything. Probably it didn't. Michael was just being nice. But at least I wasn't alone anymore. Not completely, anyway. And I could feel good about that. My Dads would be happy about that too. Not that I was going to tell them, but... whatever. At some point, I must have fallen asleep, because the next thing I knew, the dazzle of morning was filling the tube with bright yellow light.

I must have been dazed, maybe it was the beer, but I felt like I was floating in a golden cloud. It must have been noticeable. A couple of other students even mentioned it, asking, "Are you all right? You look funny." One boy, one of the slighter ones, peered at me sideways. "You look like you just got laid."

"Nope, sorry." But I was smiling, and it must have looked like a knowing smile to him, because he didn't believe me.

"Okay, don't tell me," he said and walked away, obviously annoyed. I think I laughed a little, just not out loud.

It puzzled me, that I felt so good. Nothing really happened. We talked, we walked, we held hands, and the time passed without effort. It was... well, fun. But I'd never had fun like that before, so maybe that was why I was so... well, traumatized, but in a good way.

That evening, as the last of the afternoon faded toward dusk, I went out to the balcony with the clarinet again. I'd been thinking all day what I should play, I wanted something that would say how I felt, but without being too... too something. I finally settled on an oldie called, "Fill Your Heart." It could be played fast and upbeat or slow and poignant. I opted for a slow beginning, then segued into a syncopated little dance. It worked. When I finally wailed out into a triumphant cadenza (something I'd invented on my own), I felt exhilarated. A voice from below hollered, "I'm coming up now!"

Michael bounced over the railing; I had no idea how he did that with a bag of groceries slung over one shoulder. "Play that again," he said. "I'll fix dinner."

"Nuh-uh. For my first encore—"

He laughed.

I put the clarinet to my lips and played, this time "Rhapsody in Blue." The clarinet wail at the beginning is an instant attention getter, but the real joy is everything that follows after, the way it just joyously celebrates itself. I had to play my own abridged version. I didn't have an orchestra program accompanying me, didn't want one anyway; I like finding the truth of the music myself.

By the time I finished, Michael had dinner on the table. I'd been playing with my eyes closed so I hadn't seen what he was doing. I didn't expect much, not on a student provision, but as simple as this was, it was more than I had expected. A salad, sausages, baked beans; sweetcakes for dessert, and a sparkling cider to accompany it all.

I'd been eating rations. I hadn't realized how much I'd been missing real food.

I looked at it laid out on the table, looked at his beaming smile, then back to the table again, then back to him, and abruptly couldn't speak. I didn't know what I was feeling, but it was overwhelming. Finally, "This is so good—what you did— thank you!"

He reached over and wiped a tear from my cheek with his thumb. "You've been alone too long, haven't you?"

I could barely nod.

He slid over next to me on the bench, put his arm around my shoulder, and pulled me close to him. "It's all right. You're not alone anymore." After a moment, he added, "Your music is beautiful. I loved it."

"Sometimes..." It took me a minute to get the words out. "Sometimes, it's all I have. I've never been on my own before—I dunno, I guess I didn't realize how much..."

He didn't say anything. He just continued to hold me close while I sniffled with tears that wouldn't quite come. "I'm such a big baby," I said.

"Well, I think you're adorable—"

"Huh?"

"Because you feel things so intensely. Most people don't. I wish I could feel that intensely. I'm always pushing my feelings down—"

I pulled away so I could turn and look at him. "Uh-uh." I pointed to the table. "You just express your feelings differently."

"Mm," he said.

"We should eat."

"Yeah."

The plates had kept the food warm. I don't remember eating as much as I remember that I kept looking at his eyes. They were shining.

"You really have been alone, haven't you?"

"I didn't think so. I mean, my Dads had a lot of friends. We saw a lot of people all the time, mostly the same people, but—um, yeah, no, not like this. I never had my own friends—a friend of my own, I mean. I'm not making sense, am I?"

"You're making perfect sense."

"Tell me about you," I said.

"Large family. Very large. We were always doing things for other people. I think it was kind of a competition. It was um... the discipline we were in. Look to see what other people need." He changed the subject then. "Are you studying music?"

"No. I mean, a little, yes. To keep in practice. But my major is eco-management."

"How does that work?"

"Design and build an ecology. Run it for a hundred thousand years, see if it's stable or if it collapses or if it evolves into something else. It's complex, I think that's why I love it. You have to design a whole solar system, figure out the Goldilocks zone, the size of the planet and its orbit, if it has moons, how far off axis its tilted, how long is its year, how long is its day, if it has a molten core of iron, how much water it has, its atmosphere, all of that—before you can even start figuring out what kind of life it can support. I went with a proto-Earth, so I can have dinosaurs, but... if you want something on this end, you gotta backtrack all the way to the beginning to figure out how to make it possible, or even inevitable. I'm talking too much, aren't I?"

Michael shook his head. "Uh-uh. It's fascinating." He nodded toward the empty plates, started gathering them. "It's getting cold out here, let's move inside?"

We sat on the bed and sipped at the last of the cider. "What are you studying?"

"You'll laugh."

"No, I won't."

"Companions."

"No, really?"

"Well, no. Not really. I'm studying human/machine relationships. How do we make companions more lifelike? So lifelike that they're indistinguishable from humans. And should we?"

I thought about that for a moment, thinking about Boobie and Toddy and Derry and Dix and... maybe a few others in the future?

"You had companions growing up, didn't you?"

I nodded. "I thought it was a good thing."

"It probably was. Look at how far you've come. Look at how much you can do."

"And... look what I've been missing too."

Michael shook his head. "You really want to be like them?" He pointed his chin in the direction of the distant dorms.

"No." I had to laugh at that. "That life is so... shallow."

"Yeah."

We sat in silence for a while, side-by-side on my bed. "Um... can I ask you something?"

He looked at me. "Sure."

"It's kind of personal."

"It's all right."

"Have you ever been with... I mean, have you ever done it? With a real person, I mean?"

Michael shook his head. "Uh-uh." He looked at his hands, still holding the glass of cider. "I'm kind of—you're not going to believe this—um, shy."

"Excuse me?" I laughed. "You come leaping up onto my balcony with a bag full of dinner, and you want me to believe you're shy?"

"I've been working on my shyness. Working on not letting it stop me."

"Well, yeah. Okay. Um. I think you, uh—I think you've pretty much handled it."

His turn to laugh. He said, "Um, it's a thing, a trick. If I recognize I'm reluctant to do something. Afraid. Then I do it. And then I don't have to be afraid anymore, do I?"

"Uh..." I closed my mouth. It made sense, a terrifying kind of sense. "So, you were afraid to talk to me?"

He nodded.

"What else are you afraid of?"

"If I say it, I'll have to do it."

"Well, then... say it."

Instead, he leaned forward and kissed me. Just a tentative brush of his lips across mine. Barely a hint of a kiss. But the intention was clear.

He pulled back and looked at me, a question in his eyes. Was that all right?

My turn to lean forward. This kiss was a lot better.

Exploration of the possibilities of kissing.

Wow. Raised to the power of infinity.

We separated just long enough to look at each other, then kissed again. This time, relaxing into the familiarity of it, allowing ourselves to sink completely and deeply into the sheer physical experience of tongues touching, dancing, tasting—

When we paused for breath, readjusting our positions on the couch, starting to unbutton each other's shirts, Michael's fingertip traced its way from the tip of my nose, down across my lips, to my chin, and at last my chest. The past disappeared. It was as if I'd never been touched before.

"I've never done it with another person before either."

"I kinda figured that. Well, hoped for it."

"Is that all right?"

He nodded hesitantly and, in that moment, I saw the shyness he had admitted. It was adorable. He said, "I guess it's a good thing then. We get to figure it all out together, don't we?" He resumed unbuttoning my shirt, helped me take it off. I'd never let anyone undress me before, but for the first time I wasn't ashamed to be half-naked in front of another man.

He stroked my chest, my belly. He tugged at my belt. I stopped him so I could unbutton his shirt. When the last magnetic button parted, he shrugged it off and I looked at his naked torso as if I'd never seen a man before. "You're beautiful," I said.

He blushed, shook his head, blushed again, smiled, leaned forward, and we kissed so long I forgot what we were talking about. It didn't matter. The talk was just vibrations in air. The emotional vibrations were much more intense.

After a while, we took our pants off too. And a little after that, our underwear.

I'd never been this naked before. I'd never wanted to be this naked before.

He liked what he was seeing, so I wanted him to see it all. I liked him looking at me. I liked looking at him looking at me.

And then we rolled into each other's arms and it was amazing how well our bodies fit together. I matched my rhythm to his and he matched his to mine; we rocked easily together as if we'd been made for this moment from the beginning.

It wasn't all sex. It wasn't sex at all. It was emotion. It was a little bit of lust and a little bit of passion, but a great deal more of surrendering, opening, exploring, discovering, and a long slow tumble into enchantment.

We didn't rush; we weren't in a hurry. We didn't know where we were going, so we took our time getting there. Sometimes, we'd stop, we'd look at each other, we'd catch our breath. Once, I got up to get a glass of ice water and we shared the ice in a kiss, pushing the last ice cube back and forth between us, feeling it melt until we were simply sharing a memory of coldness on our tongues.

I laid on top of him and felt his desire pressing up against me like a beacon. Then we rolled over and he was on top of me, and I could feel our hearts beating in unison, every lub-dub a wave pulsing outward from our mutual centers.

We wrestled for a bit, kissing all the different parts

of each other's bodies. We could have done more, but we didn't need to; even this much was overwhelming. It all felt so… right. I felt complete.

And then, he was on top of me, and he said, "I'm getting close," and I said, "Me too," and we rocked together with a growing intensity. I wanted this to be perfect for him, so I matched his every movement, pushing hard against him with every thrust until that startling instant we both reached the finish line together, his completion triggered mine, and we surged together.

I lay there gasping for breath, listening to him breathing hard as well. Our hearts pounded between us, a staccato pumping of amazement. We had just gone through a door that wasn't there until we went through it.

Neither of us could speak; there was nothing to say. We just held onto each other forever.

Until, finally, he rose and looked down at me, his eyes shining. I sparkled back at him.

"Wow," I said. "That was perfect."

Perfect. The word hung between us like a sudden question.

Perfect?

I pushed him up far enough to look into his eyes, searching for evidence. "What?" he asked.

"That was too perfect."

"Is that a problem?"

"Um—"

He frowned, just the slightest furrowing of his brow, the slightest narrowing of his eyes. "What?"

"Michael—"

"What?"

"Did my Dads send you? Are you a companion?"

He smiled gently and put a finger across my lips. "Shh," he said.

"No, tell me."

"I can't," he said. "We're not allowed to."

Was he joking? I couldn't tell.

Oh, what the hell.

I pulled him down into another endless kiss. ✕

SQUATCH AND BEHR:
NOT A LOVE STORY

BY DARRELL Z GRIZZLE

I was so distracted by the bulge in Squatch's swimsuit that I almost didn't notice the gun-shaped bulge in his overnight bag.

Squatch wasn't his real name, of course, but as a nickname it sure as hell fit. He was huge and hairy, just like I like 'em. He was a few inches taller than me, and I'm a six-foot two-inch bear. When I saw him at the gay sports bar, watching Arsenal beat Liverpool on the big screen TV, I caught his eye and got *the smile* in return. That special *smile* that means yep, we're ending up in bed together. And that's exactly what happened.

And now, the morning after, I was still in the motel room bed, still naked, when I noticed that bulge in his duffel bag on the nightstand. I jumped up and looked out the window to make sure he was still down there, swimming in the motel pool. There he was, swimming laps, the sunlight glistening on his body like a sexy yeti (is that a thing?). I knew I had to check out his bag before he returned to the room.

There it was, crammed against the side of his bag by

some gym clothes. A Glock G43, just like mine. In fact, for a moment, I thought it *was* mine. Had he stolen my gun?

I reached across the bed to my own gym bag on the other nightstand. I pulled out my Glock G43 and held it up beside his. They were identical. What the hell?

My phone buzzed while I was still puzzling over the Glocks. It was the special ringtone that let me know it was a message from my boss. I pulled up the text. Another pizza to pick up (our code for another hit job), along with the target's name, address, and pic.

The name was unfamiliar, but the picture was definitely Squatch.

A chill went down my spine. So the pickup in the bar last night wasn't by chance. Somehow, Squatch—whose real name, according to the text, was the rather anonymous-sounding Holden Smith—knew that I'd be hired to take him out. And he knew it before I did. How?

I texted "Received" to the bossman. I only knew him as "Big Eddie," no last name, but as long as he paid in cash I didn't care. I knew he was an independent, a freelancer who took contracts from several different crime families, as well as one-shots (no pun intended) from wealthy people who were willing to pay handsomely to make their problems disappear. I wondered what Squatch had done to become somebody's problem.

I picked up the pair of Glocks again and tried to figure it all out. Then I heard Squatch's key in the outside lock of the motel room door.

I dropped one of the Glocks back into his bag and

stuffed the other one under my pillow on the bed. I laid back on the bed and stretched my arms behind my head, just as he opened the door. "Hey, handsome," I grinned up at him.

"Hey yourself," he said, returning the grin. He was wearing a European style swim trunk that was just a little too tight for his muscular ass, not to mention that big bulge in front. I had admired that swimsuit when he pulled it on and went out to the pool, and now that it was soaking wet, it clung even tighter. I felt myself getting hard again.

I patted the side of the bed where he had slept. He shook his head. "Let me get dried off first."

"Nope. I like it wet." His smile grew wider as he slipped off his swimsuit and crawled on top of me. The smell of chlorine and sweat filled my nostrils as he pinned me to the bed and grinded his cock against mine.

I freed my hands from his and pulled him down to me in a tight embrace. I loved the feel of his broad hairy chest against mine. But right now I needed answers more than I needed cock.

His beard was pressed against mine and he was facing the other way, so he didn't see when I reached under the other pillow. I grabbed my gun and pressed it into his side. "Don't move. I have a lot of questions for you."

He jerked his arm over to his duffel bag on the nightstand and before I could respond, I felt the muzzle of *his* Glock press into my own side. "So do I," he growled. "First, why did you open my duffel bag?"

"Really? We have matching Glocks rammed into

each other's side, and *that's* your first question?"

"Matching Glocks? So you went through my bag?"

"Not all the way through it. I noticed a bulge that looked like a gun on the side of the bag, so I pulled out your Glock. It's exactly the same as mine."

"Do you always bring firearms on one-night stands?"

"I could ask you the same question."

"It's a... tool of the trade."

"Oh yeah? What trade?"

He was silent for a moment, then he sighed. "I guess it doesn't matter if you know. It'll be a moot point, pretty soon. I'm a hit man. I was hired to kill you."

"Bullshit!" I couldn't help but scoff. "I was hired to kill *you.*"

"That doesn't make any sense. Why would..." He didn't bother to finish the sentence.

"I got the text this morning, while you were down in the pool."

"Text? Let me guess. Was it a text about picking up a pizza?"

"How the fuck would you know—" I stopped as it slowly began to dawn on me.

"Easy," he said. "We both work for Big Eddie."

"Holy shit."

"Which explains the matching Glocks, although I don't usually use mine."

"What do you use?"

"Too much blood when you shoot someone. I usually just snap their necks."

"I should probably start doing that. Less clean-up time. I imagine you have to restrain them first?"

"Yeah. Most people do not consent to the process. And it sounds like you're assuming you survive this little standoff."

"Well, I definitely do not consent to having my neck snapped. Or being shot in the ribs. I assume you don't either."

"Correct."

"So it's in both our self-interests to find a resolution."

"Agreed. But how do we know we can trust each other?"

"We can't. We're both despicable criminals who kill people for a living. Neither one of us can be trusted."

"But the mistrust is mutual, so maybe we can find a way to work around it."

"What do you propose?"

He thought for a brief moment. "It sounds like an exchange of information is order. A long conversation about what kinda shit Big Eddie is trying to pull."

"Agreed."

"And that would be best conducted if we could each look the other in the eye, rather than me lying on top of you with our cocks pressed together and our heads facing in different directions."

"Also agreed. So the first step is dropping our guns, then you rolling off me so we can see each other face to face."

"But if I drop my gun, how do I know you'll drop yours?"

I sighed. "Because right now I want answers, and the only way to get answers is if we compare notes. I've been double-crossed by a man who I've trusted. A man who has paid me handsomely for three years now. I want to know why."

"Same here. Also three years."

"Interesting. Maybe he gets new contractors every three years."

"And does away with the old ones because they know too much."

"I do know a lot about his operations," I said. "But clearly not everything. I didn't know about you until just now."

"I didn't know about you until yesterday. And I didn't know you were a fellow employee. All I got was your name, address, and photo. Darren Behr. So when you told me to call you 'Bear' last night at the bar, I knew it was more than just a nickname."

"You got my name yesterday? So if you haven't been tracking me for several days, how did you know I'd be at the sports bar last night?"

"I didn't, other than a hunch. I recognized your picture. I've seen you at that bar before."

"Really? Seems like I would've remembered you."

"I was with another guy—he's now my ex—and he caught me looking at you and got upset about it, so I kept a low profile."

I couldn't help but chuckle. "You were checking me out?"

"Yep, just like you were checking me out last night."

"Guilty as charged. Now what?"

"As much as I like being on top of you, my leg is starting to cramp. I'm going to put my gun back in my overnight bag, and I hope you drop yours."

"Trust?"

"One of us has to go first." He leaned over and dropped the Glock back into his bag, which was still open on the nightstand. I scooted over in the bed and put my gun on the other nightstand. He slowly got off of me and stood up beside the bed, stretching one leg out to the side.

"That feels better. I—" He stopped when he saw my cock, fully erect and glistening with precum. "Wow. So having a gun in your side turns you on?"

"No, having a sexy yeti on top of me does that. But maybe the element of danger does add to it."

"We're coming back to the yeti thing. First, I have to figure out if I like it or not. But if we're going to trade information, I suggest we put some pants on, at the very least. Your flagpole is very distracting."

We both found our pants on the floor and put them on. We sat down at the little table in the motel room. I looked at the time on my cell phone. "It's still pretty early. Three and a half hours till check-out time at eleven." I looked across the table at him. "We need to put on shirts as well. Your chest is very distracting."

"My chest?"

"Yes. All I can think about is how much I want to fuck that groove between your pec muscles and cum all over your chest hair."

"And I want to suck your nipples," he said. "Violently. Until you beg me to stop."

"Okay then. Shirts." We both got up and pulled on our shirts. It helped a little, but when we sat back down at the table, I could see how tight-fitting his shirt was across his pecs. I raised my head and looked him in the eye. *Concentrate,* I told myself. "Let's make a plan."

We left my pickup truck at the motel after we checked out, and I rode with him in his luxury sports car over to Big Eddie's. The bossman lived in a fairly nondescript house in an older neighborhood. To look at his house, you'd never guess what he did for a living.

One of Big Eddie's "personal assistants" must have seen us drive up, because he opened the door before we even knocked on it. Antonio was a big guy, almost as big as Squatch. "Bossman's still asleep," he said, in a low voice.

"Listen," said Squatch, also in a low voice. "Some major shit is about to go down. Big Eddie is cleaning house, and he has ordered hits on everyone he thinks knows too much. Including you."

In the year or so I had known Antonio, I had never seen him display any kind of emotion. But now there was clearly fear in his eyes. "Why are you telling me this?"

"Because you've always had my back. Now we have yours."

"What should I do?"

"If I were you, I'd pack up and leave town. Bear and I are about to confront Big Eddie about his plans, and things are gonna get ugly. We just found out he put hits on both of us. You don't want to be here if he goes crazy and starts waving a gun around."

Antonio nodded. "I've seen him do just that. Thanks, man." He went out through the front door.

I quietly closed the door. "Did Big Eddie really put out a hit on Antonio?"

"No," said Squatch. "I just wanted him out of the way when we confront the bossman."

"Good idea."

We found Big Eddie asleep in his bed. I had only been in his house a few times, and I had never been in his bedroom. I was surprised at how country-comfy it looked. Framed prints of country landscapes were on the wall, and there was a beautiful old fashioned quilt on the bed. Big Eddie was dressed in flannel pajamas. Cozy.

I could see Big Eddie's Glock G43 on the nightstand. "Just like ours," I whispered to Squatch.

Squatch motioned me out of the bedroom. In the hallway we could hear Big Eddie snoring. I followed Squatch into the bossman's home office. There on top of the desk, in plain sight, was a ledger book and a leather bound journal full of Big Eddie's contacts and the hit jobs he had contracted out to us.

"Here's what we need to go into business for ourselves," said Squatch.

The snoring down the hall stopped abruptly. We went back into the bedroom just in time to see Big Eddie reach for the nightstand.

"I've got it," I told him. I pointed the gun at him.

He looked over at me, then at Squatch. "Shit. So you two have met."

"We have," I said.

"How'd you get past Antonio?"

"He left," said Squatch. "I think he went to get coffee."

"Tell us why you wanted us to kill each other," I said. "Then tell us why we shouldn't kill you."

"It's just business," he said. "Some of the crime lords who hire me have certain standards."

"Standards?"

"Yeah. They don't want to do business with faggots. I have no idea how they found out you two were fags. I didn't even know, until a few days ago."

"Your choice of language is going to make it easier for us to kill you. Thank you for that."

"Not my language," he said, nervously. "That's the word they used."

"Who are 'they?'" I asked. Big Eddie shook his head no, that he wasn't going to give us their names. I took a step closer and aimed the Glock directly at his face. He gave us two names. Both were well-known in the organized crime community. Their lack of support for the LGBT cause was not a surprise.

"So why," asked Squatch, "hire us to kill each other?"

Big Eddie sighed. "You're both really good at what you do. I figured between the two of you, you would get the job done, and I wouldn't have to bring in outside help."

"And you wouldn't have to pay us, since we'd both be dead."

"See?" Big Eddie attempted a smile. "It's cost-efficient. Win-win."

Squatch moved so fast it shocked me. Before Big Eddie could put up a struggle, Squatch had dragged him to the side of his bed and snapped his neck. The bossman fell to the floor. Dead.

"Damn," I said. "Remind me to stay on your good side."

"So how do you usually dispose of the bodies?"

"I have a part-time job at a funeral home and crematorium. Just enough hours each week to keep my health insurance, but I have a key to the place and there's no security at night. You?"

"I have a cousin with a pig farm out in the country."

I scowled. "Gruesome."

"Let's lock up the house and get rid of the body later. I'm hungry."

"Me too. There's a place nearby with a delightful brunch menu."

"Mimosas?"

"Yep."

"Let's do brunch." ✱

LIGHTNING FINGERS

BY ADRIK KEMP

LIGHTNING PULSED BENEATH the skin of his slender, manicured fingers. It navigated the spaces between muscles and nerves, bones and sinew. It illuminated Mal from within, making his pale skin pulse peach. It emerged from his fingertips, puffing into the air with a blast of petrichor to assault the nose.

Mal grinned, his face lit up by his own bioluminescence. His floppy, black hair fell over his dark eyes and his teeth glistened in the natural, and yet, abnormal light.

"Are you really human?" I asked, my heart hammering in my chest.

Mal shrugged. "I thought I was."

My own hand twitched, but no light bloomed within me. My heart ached with disappointment until Mal's glow faded and he clasped my hand, entwining our fingers together. His were warmer than usual. He pushed me back against the bed and put his other hand on my chest.

"Why? Are you scared of me now?"

"No," I said.

"Good," he leaned down and kissed me. "You know I'll never hurt you." His patchy stubble scratched mine and our noses nuzzled. If I looked through my lashes, I could see his eyes were closed. They were always closed when we kissed.

"Will you hurt anyone?" I asked.

Mal pulled back. The corners of his mouth were upturned in a tight smile. In the light of the glowing stars and moons I had stickered over my bedroom ceiling, he really did look inhuman. "No one," he said, casting his dark gaze elsewhere before launching a second assault on my mouth.

His unpracticed tongue prodded my inexpert one and his hands ran under my clothes. He was moaning, his body burning, but I pushed him away, glancing at my closed and locked bedroom door. Light streamed in beneath it, and the sounds of the TV in the other room permeated the darkness. I sat on the side of the bed and smoothed my crumpled clothes.

"You're lying," I said, regretting my words as they left my mouth.

Mal didn't answer. He didn't move on the bed either. I could feel his gaze at my back. I opened my mouth to say something else regretful when my mother's voice called through the door.

"Boys?" She knocked and jiggled the handle. "Bradley, please unlock the door. You know the rules." I could almost see her standing there, tapping one office heel on the carpet and checking her phone while she impatiently waited. I flicked on the light and checked Mal was decent, then opened the door.

She was straight from work, still wearing her gray

suit. Her skin had a fluorescent sheen people only get from working in a building all day. Her eyes were red and her face gaunt. She cast an eye over me then nodded at Mal on the bed before cocking her head. "Dinner's downstairs," she said. "Oh, and Malachi, your father called and wants you home tonight, by ten. I said I'd let you go after dinner." And with that she was gone.

"Damn," Mal said.

"Yeah, right. They just don't want us sleeping together."

"Bit late for that," Mal launched at me and kissed me again, pushing me back against the bed and running his hand down my body. I extricated myself and closed the door again before coming back to kiss him. I held his face in my hands and looked into his eyes. "Promise me you won't do anything stupid?"

Mal kissed my nose. "I promise."

"I'll walk you home tonight."

Mal nodded. "Sounds good."

"They've always been afraid of us. That's why they treat us like second-class citizens. I mean they don't even do that, we *are* second-class. Or third-class!"

"They're scared of us? Of you and me?" I asked with some sarcasm, knowing he didn't mean that.

"Yes, Brad, of you and me pacifically." I'm not sure how to capture the sarcasm, but the deliberate use of pacific gave it something of an edge. "Although, in a way, kind of, yes. I mean, look at everyone at school. How many people have experimented?"

"With what? Alcohol? Drugs? Sex?"

"Everything. We're all like, better than the adults, you know. They think they know everything but we can see the bigger picture. All they see is us ruining their rules and making them change their ways."

"Are you talking about gay marriage again?"

"Not just that, everything. What about adoption, gender fluidity, trans rights? They can't stand us not wanting their binary boxes. Look at what's popular now, sharing stuff, right. Like cars and homes and everything. If you want something, you can get it free or cheap, it undermines their capitalist regime. And the fact that we're already out there, raising families with children who accept us utterly as part of themselves, straight kids, you know."

"We're in grade eleven. Last time I checked, none of us were thinking about adopting some kids and getting married."

"Maybe not now, but we're the ones it affects in the long run."

I shrugged. "You sound insane."

Mal stopped just shy of a streetlight. A tree covered him in shadow, and I could see the strange inner radiance starting to pulse within his flesh.

"Mal?"

"I'm not insane. I just want a better world for us all."

"I was kidding," I ran up to him and slipped my arm into his, pulling him into a side embrace and hoping he didn't go off. "Sorry."

Mal was stiff, but let me hug him. "I must've got this for a reason, right."

"Yeah, to go to some boarding school for gifted

children and become a superhero or something.”

“What?”

“Have adventures, save the world. Maybe go to space. You know the stories. You’ll be found by some secret society of powered people, literally in your case,”

Mal smirked at me.

“And they’ll train you, hone your skills and then send you off to fight some world-ending bad guy who turns out to be easy to vanquish and everything will go back to normal.”

Mal started laughing. “Life’s not the movies, Brad.”

“Yeah, I know, but most people don’t have lightning fingers either, Malachi. So what do you think’s gonna happen since we’re in the real world now?”

“It’s been three months since I found out and no one has said anything. There’s been nothing on the news,”

“There never is.”

“No accidents, no unexplained anything. Life is just chugging along like it always did, but I have, um, lightning fingers.”

And then we both had to laugh.

“I wanna tell you something,” Mal whispered in my ear one night. He was spooned around me in my single bed. The house was quiet and dark, if not quite empty of my family.

“What?” I asked, almost asleep.

“I’ve been using my lightning powers.”

I wriggled, remembering his hands caressing my skin, heating up as he stroked my skin, his fingers kissing electricity through my bones. “I know,” I kissed him again. "They're great."

Mal shocked me. It wasn't the first time, but it woke me right up. "Hey!"

Mal laughed. "Sorry, but you need to be awake."

"Why?" I rubbed my chest, heart racing. "You couldn't have just said that?"

"Okay, so I need to tell you two things."

I nodded and reached for my glasses on the nightstand. "Great," I slipped them on and peered at his earnest face, illuminated by my ever-more-childish glowing star ceiling.

"So, I know you said not to go all crazy and start attacking people."

"Ah, I asked you not to do anything stupid. I guess that includes those things..."

Mal nodded. "Sure, heaps of things. But sometimes things that look stupid really aren't."

I sighed. "Don't gaslight me."

"What? No, I'm not!" Mal took my hand. "You know I wouldn't do that."

"Not deliberately," I folded my arms over my skinny chest.

Mal's earnestness fell away into annoyance. "Fine, well, I was excited but I guess I can't feel that either with you. Avi was right, I can't tell you this stuff." He swung his legs over the bed.

My heart raced for different reasons this time. "Who's Avi?"

Mal was silent.

"Mal?"

"Look, yes, I've been using my powers, but only to protect people and practice defending myself and stuff." He paused and looked at me.

"Okay," I said. "And who's Avi?"

"He's... He's someone like me."

I felt stupid, but I said it anyway. "I thought I was like you."

Mal hugged me. His crackling hands stroked my back and I held him in return, a little too long in hindsight.

"You are like me," he said. "I'll always love you Brad."

I pulled away. Something in his words, the arrangement of them, they gripped my heart.

"Avi's like me in a different way. He, he has powers too."

I nodded, my mouth dry and almost incapable of speech. "He has lightning fingers too?" I said.

"Not quite. He can do something else."

"What?"

"Okay don't overreact, but he can stop people's hearts."

Mal was right about that. Once I realized that I wasn't dead and that the world was still continuing in spite of the odd, dark hole I could feel welling within me, I looked at the person I thought loved me again. "So, what does that mean?"

"Huh?"

"He can stop people's hearts; I assume that means he can kill people."

"Oh." Malachi chewed his lip. "Yeah."

I leaned back on my pillow and covered my eyes with my forearm.

"I know it sounds bad, but I still haven't killed

anyone and he only does it to save other people. People like us."

I moved my elbow so I could see Mal again. "Gay people?"

Mal nodded. "Queer people."

I licked my lips. "So, you've met this new guy, Avi," I kept my eyes hidden. "And Avi can stop people's hearts, with his mind?"

I could feel Mal nodding.

"And the two of you go around saving other queer people from being bashed."

Mal nodded some more.

"What happens when you get caught?" I asked, sitting back up. "How will you explain it? You know you're doing the same thing the people who are bashing them are doing, right? I mean, I know you're fighting the bad guys or whatever, but the rules exist for a reason, right?"

A shadow flickered across Mal's face. "You mean the rules that make us second class citizens? The rules that make it okay to kill us if some straight dude is scared we're coming onto them? The same rules that mean we probably can't go to the school formal together? Those rules?"

He had me.

"I don't think those rules are really worth upholding, actually. And neither does Avi."

That hurt, much more than the revelation had at first. "Neither do I," I said.

"That's not what it sounds like."

"I'm not saying that. I'm just worried about you, I don't wanna lose you."

"Maybe you should stop trying to control me then." Mal grabbed his jeans from the floor and pulled them on. "Don't think I don't see your jealousy. I know you, Brad, at least I thought I did. You don't have powers. You can't understand what it's like for me." He stood.

I hated myself. I didn't want to speak. "But Avi does," my traitorous mouth said.

"Yeah, he does."

"So why don't you go be with him then?" I shouted. I could hear movement in the house. My parents were waking up.

"Maybe I will," Mal said before slamming out of my bedroom and the house. His exit was followed in quick succession by my mother appearing at the door, my father outside shouting for Mal to come back and my bursting into tears.

My best friend, Simon had been talking for the better part of lunch but I hadn't been listening.

"Brad? Brad?" Simon waved his hand in front of my eyes. "Mate, you're not even listening to me, are you."

"Sorry, sorry…"

Simon grimaced and followed my gaze, across the concrete playground, over the greenish oval and past the goal posts to where Mal was standing at the iron bars of the fence around our school, talking to someone standing on the other side.

"You're still hung up on that loser? You can do better. Way better."

I tore my gaze away from Mal and his new friend and focused on Simon instead. "Like who?"

The answering wave that Simon gave, encompassing every student in sight, was not promising. I returned to examining the boy Mal was talking to. He was slightly taller than me and maybe a year or two older. He had spiked, black hair, dark features, and nice clothes. Nicer than mine.

I shoved Simon. "Hey," I said.

"What?"

"You know that guy?"

"The one with Mal? Nup. Don't think he goes here." Simon squinted to see. "Hey, wait. Is that the guy you were telling me about? The one he um, you know…"

"I think it might be Avi, yeah."

Simon was up faster than I could stop him. He abandoned his bag and lunch and strode across the concrete, breaking into a run when he hit the grass and heading straight for Mal and Avi. I got up too, but wasn't as fast, plus I stopped to get our bags and carry them under the sun across the oval, past all the other students and to Simon's side.

"Hey!" shouted Simon.

"Simon, please don't," I said, but he didn't hear me. Mal heard him though, and turned around to glare. Until he saw me, at least, then his expression softened, but Avi tensed behind the fence.

When Simon reached them, he slammed against the fence. "What the fuck're you doing here?"

"Excuse me?" Avi raised an eyebrow. "I'm talking to my friend."

I was just happy he hadn't said 'boyfriend.'

"Yeah, well, have some respect and do it somewhere else. No one wants to see that shit, okay," Simon said.

"Are you serious?" Avi asked.

Mal held out his hands. "Hey, no, wait. That's not what he meant, Avi. Simon is, um, he's Brad's best friend. So he just means not to talk in front of Brad." He looked at me as he spoke. All I could remember was how nice it had felt to be in his arms and how much I missed kissing him and holding his hand. Then I remembered the night he had told me about Avi and when he had left and seeing him there, with Avi's hand through the bars on his shoulder. It all hit me and, of course, I burst into tears again.

The three watching boys were silent. A few other students were pretending not to watch my meltdown, but weren't doing a very good job. I wiped my eyes and shuddered back the sobs as Simon came over and clapped me on the back.

"Hey mate, don't cry," he spun to face Mal. "See what I mean. The fucking least you could do is take this somewhere else." Simon hugged me. "Go take him somewhere else." He nodded at Avi.

I only managed to curb the tears when Avi had made his excuses and was walking away. Mal and Simon were still facing off and I was still busy embarrassing myself by failing to curb the tears running down my face.

"I'm sorry, Brad, I didn't think about it. We're not dating, you know. I still love you." Mal said as he approached us. He put out a hand to touch my back.

"You're a dick, Mal," said Simon. "Get fucked." And he pushed Mal back, so he stumbled and fell back onto the grass with a thud.

I don't think anyone else saw, but Mal's body

flickered when he landed, and an expression flashed across his face that stopped my tears in their tracks. On the street outside, I could see Avi watching, unsmiling until Simon guided me away.

I let out a little shriek when Mum tapped my shoulder. I was on my stomach on my bed, listening to headphones, so hadn't heard her come in. I didn't hear my shriek either, for that matter.

"Sorry darling," she mouthed while I tore off my headphones. "I know you probably don't want to see him, but I thought I'd just check before I send him away."

"What?"

"It's Malachi, sweetie. He's dropped by to talk to you."

"Oh."

"And he brought a friend. An Indian boy?"

I thought about it for a second before throwing down the headphones and striding out of my bedroom, past my mother and to the front door, where two boys waited. I grabbed the side of the door, my grip white. Mal and Avi were both dressed in black. Mal's eyes hung static in his gaunt face. Behind him, Avi stood in the shadow of the porch.

"Hey, Brad," said Mal. "Can we talk to you for a minute?"

My mother was waiting down the hall, not quite eavesdropping but also not hiding.

"Please?"

My hand relaxed. "Fine. What do you want to say?"

Mal peered past me and waved at my mother. "Can Brad come out with us, just for a bit? He'll be back by ten, promise."

"He'll be back by eight-thirty if he knows what's good for him. Brad, are you sure you want to go?" My mother appeared beside me, her hand firm on my shoulder.

I relaxed and pulled on a pair of sneakers. "Sure. I'll be home soon, promise." I kissed her on the cheek and followed them out into the night. Past the gate and around the corner, the pace slowed and, checking no one was around, I stopped altogether at a bus stop. It was an island of advertising and light in the dim street, and though it was early, it was deserted.

"I know what you've been doing." I said.

"What?" said Avi.

"I'm not stupid."

Avi raised an eyebrow.

"It's not the biggest news, but you can see it if you look. Attackers suffering unexpected heart attacks, drug addicts overdosing and dying of heart failure, homeless people whose hearts just gave out. It's almost regular now. And surprisingly coincides with you turning up Avi. With your even more convenient 'superpower' of being able to stop a person's heart." I glared at him.

Avi's lip curled into a sneer, but Mal held him back and stood in front of me, taking my hands. I snatched them away and tried not to tear up too much.

"You're complicit in this, Mal. Don't try and tell me it's the right thing to do."

Mal swallowed. "One of those attackers would've

killed a gay couple if we hadn't stopped them. Another was following a woman home, probably to rape her. The drug addicts were trying to rob some people our age! They were bad people, Brad!"

"So they deserved to die? What about the homeless people?"

Mal glanced at Avi who shrugged. "I had to start somewhere."

I felt sick.

Avi came forward so he and Mal were before me. "What, you think I'm gonna go find some drunk angry guys trying to bash someone and just hope my power works? I had to–"

"You didn't have to do anything! Least of all murder people."

Mal grabbed my hand and pulled me away. I could hear Avi following us and I was trying to get away, but I couldn't prise Mal's fingers off mine. The houses around us gave way to closed shops, florists, newsagents, and dim restaurants with scatterings of people. Pubs echoed shouts and clinks onto the streets and people swayed on the edge of the road, looking for taxis, waving and hugging friends. Mal pushed me against a glass window in front of a clothing store. He didn't look me in the eye but he kissed me. His lips trembled over mine. It was a desperate kiss. It was borne through the past, but couldn't ever be the same. Still, I melted into it for a moment and tried to forget.

He pulled away, but stayed close, his breath warming my cheeks. "Brad, I'm sorry."

"Faggot," the voice came from behind Mal. It was deep and slurred and echoed by others. As Mal turned around, I saw the three men flanking us. They were leering at us, but their bloodshot eyes were devoid of light.

"What?" said Mal.

"Fucken poofters," the one in front of us was lean and sinewy. He had scars on his face that spoke to a history of fights like the one we were all flirting with.

"Say that again," said Mal. He balled his hands into fists and his skin started to radiate light. Across the street, Avi was standing at the gutter, waiting for a moment to cross the road, gaze fixated on the man on our left.

I panicked and pushed the man. "Run, you have to run! They'll kill you."

He pulled away and pushed me back in one smooth movement. He was bigger than the others, and quicker. I hit the glass at my back and he swung and connected a gnarled fist with my face. My lips split on my teeth and I was down. Ringing in my ears. A crowd gathering. Mal's fists crackling. Avi glaring at us all.

The man went to kick me when he clutched at his chest. His eyes widened and he fell down beside me, seeming to shake the world.

I screamed.

Mal ran at the skinny one and punched him, unleashing a controlled burst of power that sank into his chest and felled him as the other had fallen. The last one, the drunkest one by far, was still trying to comprehend what was happening.

"Run!" I shouted. But Avi was already across the street, and Mal had turned his attention at the last one standing. The crowd had their phones out, uncaring of the danger. Mal swung his fist around and connected with the man's temple. The power exploded through his head and out his other temple and he dropped to the ground in front of me.

I struggled to my knees, surrounded by bodies. Avi was saying something to Mal, trying to get him to leave, but he wouldn't. I crawled to the felled man and touched his arm. His eyes were still open. I put both hands on his cheeks, thumbs over his eyelids to close them when something pulsed within my chest. I doubled over him, my vision blurring as I felt the cold concrete beneath us, the weight of his body without a beating heart and the cooling blood in his veins. I gasped and saw his heart dead in his chest. My hands started to sink into his skin.

I whimpered in fear. Some of the crowd started to scream, pointing their cameras at me instead of the other two. It was all white noise. My arms disappeared inside the man's chest and I felt his blood start to vibrate in time with my heartbeat. His body shuddered as I found his heart, synced it to mine and restarted it. When it beat, my whole body jolted out of his and we sat staring and gasping at one another.

The crowd was quiet. Cars continued to roar down the street, music played from the pubs, but all those watching were silenced

I stared at my hands a moment before reviving the other two men. Mal and Avi watched in disbelief.

"How did you do that?" Mal asked.

"I don't know," I was staring at my hands. "I don't know."

"They were trying to hurt you," said Avi. "You

should've left them dead."

I snapped my hands into fists. "They did hurt me," I said. "But they don't have to die for it."

Mal stared at me. Sirens sounded in the distance.

Avi pulled his arm. "We've gotta go, Mal, someone called the cops."

Mal seemed frozen in place. Red and blue lights played over his skin as cars pulled up on the street.

I knew that Avi wouldn't wait forever.

But I would.

TRIAL

BY JACOB BUDENZ

"I'M SO SORRY," THE MAN SAID to Sam on his way out of the single-person restroom, head ducked in apparent shame. Sam stole a quick glance at him before entering the john. The man's long, dark, wavy hair; the bushy in-between of beard and stubble covering chin and cheeks; the flowy, bohemian-patterned pants and wannabe-pirate shirt—it was all so typical of those crusty French Quarter hipsters who relieved themselves in the busy cafe's restroom without paying for so much as an apple on the way out. Sam sighed and let the heavy door of the restroom shut behind him, fully expecting that the apologetic young man had left a real stinker in the toilet without flushing, or clogged it completely, or both. He gently placed his laptop on the restroom floor, which he always brought to the bathroom if he had it with him in public. Finally, he took the three steps across the black-and-white tiling, breath held in trepidation.

But the toilet bowl was empty! Sam inhaled cautiously, first through his mouth, then through his nose. The comforting smell of lavender-scented cleaning solution and old, rusty pipes filled his nostrils. He sighed with relief. It wouldn't even matter if the toilet was clogged. If it's yellow, let it mellow. Small mercies. He pulled down his trousers and sat.

Yes, what Sam loved most about single-person, gender-neutral restrooms was the fact that in a single-person restroom he could urinate sitting down in peace. This was even better than the fact that he didn't have to relieve himself in the vicinity of heterosexual men who invariably shot him dirty looks, seeming to peg him as a queer with automatic ease and no doubt suspecting him of peeking over the urinal divider at their flaccid cocks in spite of the fact that he was *already married* (and would never do such a thing even if he weren't). Sam was no lover of urinals, neither their forced proximity nor, more to the point, the pressure they placed on him to expedite the process of relieving his bladder. Anyway, a colleague of his over in the political science department had recently persuaded him that urinals were ableist and transphobic, so when Sam, a cisgendered gay man, sat down to urinate, he satisfied himself to believe he was committing a small act of resistance toward the patriarchy, even though taking his time on the toilet was something he enjoyed doing anyway. As with everything in his life, Sam preferred to take his time. To luxuriate. To ponder in peace, without his fellow bathroom users finding more fault with his masculinity than they already did, or the possibility that someone might take the stall next to him, defecating noisily and with vocalized satisfaction. Or, even worse, attempting to make conversation, as had once happened to him!

Contemplating his current exegesis on the different species of birds in Chaucer's "Parliament of Fowls," which made up the third chapter of his dissertation, he let his eyes wander.

That's when they settled on the tip of a long, thick black tendril snaking down the exposed-brick wall in the corner by the bathroom door. He followed its vine-like path, face pinching in disgust. More disturbing than the slimy, serpentine shape, however, was the realization that it was no snake or vine at all but that it was, in fact, the tentacle of what looked to be an oversized octopus of a dark, gunmetal grey, holding fast to the ceiling just above the door with its suction cups. The wrinkly bulge of its head, striated with dark red veins, pulsed with a slow rhythm that suggested a strong but calm heartbeat. Its blank white eyes, though without pupils, seemed aimed directly at Sam with a stare that saw both into the depths of him and directly past him, as though he were not there at all. It filled the space between door and ceiling like a blackhole with its web of tentacles spread across the walls and the mirror above the sink.

Through the jolting flutter of his heartbeat, Sam's first absurd thought was to thank the stars he'd witnessed this terror while already poised over the toilet. Then squeezed his eyes shut, opened them, and slapped himself once, hard, in the face. When the pain confirmed that this was no dream, he ran through a brief catalogue of his family's vanilla mental health history and finally concluded that he really did sit before a tentacular nightmare of a creature, and that no dream or hallucination had produced it. This was normally Sam's way, to take stock of every possibility, accept things no matter how disadvantageous, and to move forward with the most rational course of action. It was both the reason he was such a successful academic and the reason, at least in his mind, that he was such a nightmare at parties, on vacation, and at participating in any activity selected in the inefficient spirit of whimsy or adventure. Except basketball. He loved to play basketball.

He took stock. This menacing creature hung just above the only exit to the restroom. It hadn't plopped atop his head and strangled him on the way in, which either meant the creature had a slow response time, was harmless (unlikely), or was intelligent and wanted something from him that it couldn't obtain by attacking him immediately. Sam knew that this restroom was a dead zone for cellular service, not because he participated in the vulgar, somehow socially acceptable activity of using his cell phone on the toilet, but because he did occasionally check the time on his phone while urinating—of course, he always wiped his phone down with waterless cleaning wipes, designed specifically for cell phones, which he carried in his knapsack.

This left three options for Sam: risk it and make a rush for the door (the biggest risk involving the most unknowns), scream for help, or (if the creature was sentient) try to surmise what it wanted.

He opened his mouth to scream.

That's when he heard a gentle baritone voice, which seemed to surround him rather than come from one particular source. "If you scream, no one will come," it said, so calm it sounded almost bored.

Sam screamed anyway. He released the pent-up fear he'd been trying to think himself out of. If he could have hovered out of his body in that moment and seen himself—face red, pants at his ankles, veins bulging from his straining throat—he'd have been humiliated at the counterproductive display.

But he could not help it. His reason had never failed him so utterly before.

But no polite tap at the door or gentle *Everything okay in there?* answered his pleas. Then, abruptly, sound ceased to leave his lips. Strain as he did, mouth wide open, nothing came out, as though he'd suddenly contracted laryngitis.

And the smooth voice sounded around him much more: "There, now if you've gotten that out of your system, we can talk things over like two reasonable beings, shall we? I'll let you speak, with the understanding that if you scream again, there will be consequences. I told you no one would hear you, and it's most annoying to me."

Though the grotesque octopus had no mouth that Sam could see, he knew for certain that it was the source of the sound, that none of this was imagined, and that it was making a promise, not a threat. He decided he had better do what it said, as calmly and rationally as he could. He could make up for the first impression by dazzling the monster with his levelheadedness and superior intellect.

"Are you going to eat me?" he whimpered instead, disgusted with himself. It was as if some pathetic wimp he'd never met had taken over his mouth and throat.

"I should think not!" said the calm baritone, a hint of amused disdain coloring its timbre. "It would present some logistical issues in terms of the size of my current corporeal form, and besides, I don't imagine I should really enjoy the taste! Anyway, I don't experience hunger, as it were. I assumed this form out of convenience, as this is how the young devotee imagined me when, just before you entered, he invited me to this plane of existence. You'll have to excuse the lack of originality. I had nothing to do with it, but I am bound by it." The creature emitted something like a sigh.

Sam pieced it together—the apologetic young Boheme, head hung in shame. Lord Almighty! Leave it to the twenty-something hipsters to summon some esoteric, Lovecraftian monstrosity and leave someone else with the fallout! The worst part? Sam had no doubt that the "young devotee" who saddled him with this demonic octopus had left without so much as purchasing a scone! Indignant, he nearly asked the monster what in the hell it wanted. But his restraint had returned, at least to some degree. Asking what the creature wanted implied Sam had something he'd be willing to give. A dangerous thing to suggest.

Instead, he said, cautiously, "Well, if you're not going to eat me, I'll just wash up and get back to my writing, then. Working on my dissertation. You understand. Lovely to meet you!"

He got up and pulled his pants up while he said this, buttoning them with shaking hands. He even had the wherewithal to lower the toilet seat. But when he stepped toward the door, two tentacles whipped toward him and wrapped themselves tightly around his arms and chest, squeezing the air from his lungs while forcing him onto the toilet. Then, the tentacles released him and receded to the far wall.

All this happened so quickly that Sam had the time neither to struggle, nor to scream, nor even to feel fear by the time the tentacles slapped wetly against the exposed brick, where they rested, quivering slightly like softened linguini in a bubbling pot. It took a moment for Sam's breath to become shallow, his heart to pound, and his ears to ring, just as the rush of adrenaline often comes in the moments after one narrowly dodges an oncoming bus, not during or before. At least he'd lowered the lid of the toilet seat, preventing him from splashing in toilet water, and at least he'd gotten his pants back on. In other words, he hadn't lost *every* shred of dignity. Small mercies.

"I only said I wasn't going to eat you," the creature said. "I did not say that you could leave. Learn to ask me the right questions. Directly."

Sam hugged himself to keep from trembling visibly. "Are you going to hurt me?" he finally asked. Then, considering what had just been demanded of him, he asked, "Are you going to kill me?"

"Not necessarily," the creature said.

Sam swallowed back tears, hating himself for how afraid he was. Fifteen years ago, he'd decided he wasn't going to be afraid anymore, that if he planned for every eventuality, he would have nothing to fear. He saved up money from a summer job scooping ice cream for two years before he came out to his parents at age fourteen, fully prepared to make his own way in the world if his parents kicked him out of the house. Luckily, they didn't, although his coming out did forever ruin his relationship with his already-distant father (a small price to pay, all things considered). After coming out to his classmates at his small Jesuit school in Corpus Christi, he'd endured the first beating from one of his peers in stoic silence, having already prepared himself for worse. His senior year, he'd even taken his boyfriend from another school to prom; he and his best friend, who was a lesbian, had filled out the prom paperwork required for students bringing dates from outside of the school, using each other's partners' information. Then they'd walked into the ballroom hand-in-hand with their own partners, resplendent in rented tuxes and ballroom gowns. Of course, his husband Marcos was not the young man Sam had taken to prom and then, after enough pulls from the flask in the inner pocket of his coat, taken the hotel room he'd reserved weeks in advanced. No, as far as Sam was concerned, the concepts of the "high school sweetheart" and, particularly, the "one true love" were for a small subset of the deluded heterosexuals who'd been fed by mass media which, due to lack of representation, gay people had escaped. But bringing another boy to the prom remained a proud achievement for him. By then, he'd already enrolled himself in boxing classes with money left from his summer jobs, and nobody dared come near him. He'd been generally regarded as brave by his classmates, but he'd simply learned to prepare for the worst and, above all, never to grovel.

But he'd never planned on being held hostage by a sentient, oversized cephalopod. It had literally silenced his screams, implying that it had the power to do much more, and it had shown fierce, effortless strength with just two of its tentacles. There was no telling what it would be able to do to him if he did not cooperate. And so, in spite of all he stood for, he said, "What do I have to do for you to let me go, unharmed?"

"Simple," said the monster. "All you have to do is prove to me that you deserve to continue living!"

No jury of his peers. No lawyer. No clear set of legal codes or criteria of intrinsic value to contemplate. Only this tentacular abomination: his judge, jury, and, should he fail, his prosecutor. A single, many-armed court. Sam didn't even have a notebook with which to organize his thoughts (he'd left his backpack, with nothing worthy to steal in it, out at his round little iron table just inside the entrance to the cafe). Lord knew he wasn't about to risk reaching for his laptop, which lay on the floor below the calm, pulsing octopus demon that would determine his fate.

"May I ask why you're doing this?" Sam asked, in hopes that learning more about this creature might offer him some insight into what it was looking for. If nothing else, it would buy him some time.

"You may ask," said the creature, a note of smugness in its voice.

"Why are you doing this?" Sam said after a pause, trying hard not to roll his eyes at this piece of pedantry given the stress of his delicate position.

"Because I must, of course! When I'm brought to your plane of existence, whether by accident or on purpose, I require the energy generated by one sacrifice in order to return home. But I do not take the killing lightly, although I do enjoy it. And so I put each human I encounter on a little ad-hoc trial, usually starting with the one foolish enough to summon me in the first place! I must admit I've come to enjoy this process, as well. I find it most enlightening to learn about the individuals of your curious race."

Though offering Sam no obvious hint on how to survive, the creature's answer comforted him somewhat. Surely Sam would have an easier time proving his worth than the phony Boheme who came before him! But where to begin? Conscious again of the monster's earlier warning to ask the right questions, he decided to seek clarification before he began.

"Will I be judged based on human criteria of being worthy of living, or is there some set of criteria specific to your... species I should be meeting?"

"The time for questions has passed!" said his inquisitor, the first hint of real irritation creeping into its smooth baritone voice. "You will be judged both for your arguments themselves and for the criteria you select as important. You will plead your case, and I will ask you any questions I deem necessary. Understood?"

"Understood."

"Well?"

The creature wasn't even going to give him time to plan his case? He began, desperately: "Well, first of all,

I do not deserve to be executed. I have committed no major crimes and I've always done my best to live a life that causes no harm toward others. I've never killed anyone, which is usually the only action deemed worthy of execution in our society." He didn't add "as long as you're white," as he normally would in the spirit of social justice, because such a caveat might overcomplicate his argument. He continued, "I've never raped anyone, or stolen anything except a candy bar, once, when I was a kid, and one time in college I took a leftover slice of my roommate's pizza from the fridge without asking permission, but I did it because we usually shared that type of thing anyway, we just also typically asked..." Sam realized he was in danger of losing track entirely. "I'm a generally honest person. I don't typically lie unless the truth would really hurt a person's feelings. I don't even exaggerate to make a story more interesting. So, you see, there's no reason for you to kill me, since I haven't done anything to deserve it!"

Sam stopped, generally satisfied with his answer in spite of how generic it sounded. But wasn't that the point? The average, generic person did not deserve to die. One could argue nobody did! But Sam was surely less deserving of death than a murderer or a serial rapist! Surely.

"Interesting," the creature said after a pause. "But so far you've only proven what you haven't done to deserve death. Why should you live?"

"Because everyone born into the world has the right to life," he blurted. "And liberty, and..." But he couldn't even finish that empty, platitudinal trash.

"And you believe this to be true? This is how your world works?"

"Not really," Sam admitted. "It doesn't work out that way for everyone."

"Then tell me again: why should you live?"

"There are people who would miss me if I was gone," he said, feeling lame, but he actually did believe this, and anyway it was too late to stop, lest he test the creature's patience again. With no opportunity to plan things out, he could not expect from himself the kind of nuance and eloquence he was accustomed to presenting in an academic context. "My death would cause grief and pain toward other people."

"Interesting. Who?"

"My two sisters. They'd be crushed. And my…" He paused on mentioning his parents, to at least one of whom he knew he, the only son, had been a severe disappointment, both in his homosexuality and his choice to pursue a career in academia instead of a career in law, *in spite of every opportunity his parents worked so hard to hand to him* (a reminder his father never failed to deliver). "My mother would be pretty unhappy, I think. And my husband, well, he wouldn't know what to do without me. He wouldn't know how to live."

"Husband!" cried the creature, delighted. "I am pleased to hear that, since my last visit to this plane of existence, your species has finally learned to procreate amongst both sexes! Most convenient. You know, each time I come here, though it's not my purpose, I do enjoy learning as much as I can about your intriguing species. Tell me, how many offspring have you planned to produce with this husband?"

Sam grimaced, glancing at the changing station with its large blue teddy bear sticker, covered in indecipherable graffiti: some black, some red, some faded with the evidence of an attempt to scrub it away. The possibility of having a baby to care for had always horrified him. Not to mention giving birth, were such a thing possible for a man. Now, here, this creature touted it as a triumph!

"Not exactly. I mean, none, I mean..." Which question to respond to? He said simply, "We're not going to have children. We can't."

"No?" said the creature in a dull, disapproving voice. "What's the purpose of a union without procreation?"

For the first time since encountering this strange judge, Sam responded in anger, scooting to the edge of the toilet and slipping into armchair rhetoric he'd joked about a hundred times without realizing, until now, that he actually believed it. "In a world where overpopulation is leading to the decline of our planet, the idea of procreation as the end goal of companionship is becoming more and more destructive! The way I see it? An increase in queer coupling is evolution's response to overpopulation. Without the ability to reproduce, my partner and I can focus on supporting each other, being good stewards of the environment, caring for our fellow human beings, making the world better, and most importantly, choosing not to contribute to the ruin of the planet by creating greater demand for its ever-scarcer natural resources! Sure, we can adopt, or we can do in-vitro, but we've made the commitment not to contribute to the excess of waste and the strain on natural resources that humanity's rate of reproduction has been creating!"

A silenced followed, during which Sam supposed the creature was weighing his responses. In the meantime, he busied himself using his newly recovered fortitude to dream up a plan in the highly likely event that the creature, with its blank eyes and flaccid, pulsating head, did not find his responses satisfactory. He had his keys in his pocket, which he could use to slice into the inky flesh of any tentacle that lashed out to constrict him, or jab into those endlessly judging eyes. For some reason, he had the sense that some of its incorporeal power, beyond its physical strength, lay in that milky gaze that seemed to probe him to his core. The wooden end of the plunger to his left could also be used to stab the creature through those hateful eyes, or to turn the lever-style knob of the door.

Sam's left hand twitched in anticipation of snagging the plunger at just the right moment. He recognized that using its wooden end as a bludgeon would likely require him to grasp its rubber end, which had no doubt come into contact with true horrors of human waste in that restroom, but he swallowed back his aversion. This was life or death. Finally, it spoke.

"Are you arguing that you and your husband do these things? That you're good stewards of the environment, that you make the world a better place, and so on?" said the creature in that placid baritone, as though Sam hadn't just had an outburst.

"Sure, my husband and I absolutely do what we can to lower our carbon footprint—eating mostly vegetarian, sharing a car... I could go on and on, but why can't we leave my husband out of this? Aren't we arguing about me?" Sam demanded.

"Ah, but you argued that the value of same-sex partnership lies in your ability to support each other in these endeavors. Thus..."

"And to be happy," Sam amended, and in his renewed vigor he *nearly* launched into another tirade about how heterosexual couples, even those with medical conditions that prevented them from having offspring, never had to justify the utility or value of their union, though they may experience pressure to adopt or to find a surrogate. How in fact American society demanded that gay people and racial minorities justify their utility, the force of their love, and yes, their right to exist as they were in the world, in subtle and not-so-subtle ways on a daily basis, while everyone else was automatically granted the right to lead ordinary, unremarkable lives, and that he was sick of it, just fucking tired, and maybe this freaky space demon should just wrap its clammy arms around his throat and get it over with right now if its judgments were going to be just as arbitrary and awful as Sam's fellow human beings, to whom Sam would be expected to continually justify himself in quiet but still fierce ways the second he emerged from this restroom, anyway.

But the creature's tentacles quivered ever so slightly again, and Sam's desire to survive trumped the existential dread the creature had just unearthed. So he held back.

"Well?" the creature said. "Do you support someone

who makes the world a better place? Are you both happy, then, as well?"

"Yes," Sam said, intending to leave it at that, but the can of worms had been opened. Before he could stop himself, he launched into a confession:

He told the creature how, after five years of marriage on top of a three year relationship, Sam—in the mid-morning stage of his thirties, with the occasional white hair amidst his dark curls, with the skin at his midsection beginning to loosen, perceptible only to him, over the diligently maintained muscles of his abdomen and obliques—secretly wondered whether he'd wasted his most attractive, virile years settling down with a man thirteen years his senior. Marcos. Marcos was a man he'd met at the right time, who'd been interesting enough and, most importantly, reliable enough to fall in love with. Marcos, the young-at-heart, who in spite of the age gap had made so much sense to old-souled Sam in his twenties. Marcos, the warm, Marcos the political artist. Sam, the academic, the analyst of the arts. Marcos, whose sex drive had significantly waned over the last few years, hardly perceptible at first. Sam, who'd receded further into his studies and had become so sensitive to temperature when trying to sleep that he could hardly tolerate Marcos's unconscious pursuit of physical closeness while already asleep. Marcos who occasionally forgot to take the keys out of the ignition of his car, leaving it available for anyone to drive off with, but who could execute a soufflé with perfect focus and precision. Marcos, who led slam poetry workshops for teenagers and became anxious when he didn't hear back from Sam within an hour of sending him a message.

All this Sam told the creature, unable to help himself, unable to stop himself from smiling fondly, and then, firmly believing it, he repeated his opening sentiment: "Yes. The world is better because my husband is in it."

"And this is in part because of the support your partnership provides?"

"Absolutely," said Sam without hesitation, and then he forgot himself and chuckled. "He wouldn't know which way was up without me, some days."

"Fine, a perfectly acceptable answer. And I can tell by your conviction that you truly believe what you're saying, this time. Let's spend no more time on it. You *are* the one on trial, after all, and not him. So what about you? In what way is the world a better place because of you, specifically? You've failed to explain that thus far. You've told me why you don't deserve death and why certain people would suffer as a result of your absence. In other words, you've defined your life only by its negation. This is your last chance to prove your worth, to tell me what it is you're doing that's worth continuing to do."

And what was Sam doing? The creature had, at last, landed on the real problem. Sam was obtaining a doctorate, spending most of his time studying obscure, often unfinished dream visions by a long-dead poet, in an iteration of English nobody had spoken for centuries! Other than the old adage, "The life so short, the craft so long to learn," what contribution had Chaucer's dream visions really made to humanity?

What further contribution could studying that work make, other than to satisfy Sam's own thirst to know and to interpret, as well as that of other academics like him? Sam gave basic writing classes far below his level of expertise to a bunch of trust fund babies at one of those ivory-tower universities in the nice part of town, fully protected from the heart of the city, its crime, the harsh living conditions of its continually displaced inhabitants, the police violence, the food deserts in the poorest parts of town, all of it. He lived in a city he believed would be fully underwater in the next couple of generations, while he did what he could to stop it, which was not nearly enough: beyond what he'd mentioned, he drove his discarded glass to the recycling plant, attended the occasional rally, called the occasional senator (not nearly as often as he let people think he did), and encouraged his students to email him all their assignments so they didn't waste the paper. Why, hadn't he forgotten to ask for his iced coffee *without a straw* just thirty minutes ago? But the existence of so many societal ills overwhelmed him. Where could he even start making a plan to contribute when there were so many causes? How to decide which ones were the most pressing, the most important? Environmentalism was simply the easiest given his situation. He was in graduate school. Who had time for activism when they were getting their PhD?

And as for happiness, no matter how he convinced himself that he lived an objectively fulfilling, satisfactory life, he still felt strangely moved at the sight of small towns off obscure highway exits, the kind of towns in the long stretches between cities that didn't even have fast food or gas signs. He had escape fantasies about pulling over one day, on impulse, and driving through their streets, just to see, maybe stop at one of their tiny cafes, spend a few nights in the scratchy sheets of a seedy motel in the hopes, perhaps, that some strange adventure awaited him, one that required him to act on pure instinct. Some spur-of-the-moment affair or mysterious town secret that, by coincidence, required his highly specialized expertise to solve—some obscured Middle English text nobody else could read, or some series of riddles, perhaps, that only a highly specialized literary brain could solve. And sure, if he occasionally experienced homophobic harassment in a city like New Orleans, the surrounding towns might offer more of a challenge in that regard, but he'd so seamlessly be able to prove his worth that it wouldn't even matter to the small-towners around him; perhaps they'd learn a thing or two about acceptance; perhaps he'd be a positive queer influence on some closeted gay teen who finally felt empowered to be who he was. All the while, he'd relish in the thrill of being unknown by the people around him and having his whereabouts unknown by the people who knew him. Of just escaping his highly systematized life, for once. Of finally acting on impulse, even if it meant escaping to a mundane, obscure locale and doing little of value to the world at large.

"I'm a teacher," he began, in the same tone of voice he'd listed the rights to which all human beings are supposedly entitled. "I foster empathy for the world around us with my students by… by…"

But Sam was overcome, by the combination of the conviction that playing this monster's game was a losing battle, and the realization that his long-coveted opportunity to act on instinct was now, and finally the gut feeling that his harsh judge, with its piercing eyes and pulsing red veins, was unlikely to find the conglomeration of his arguments satisfactory enough to let him live, anyway. It was too much. He found himself unable to play its game any longer. In a swift, decisive motion, Sam hefted the heavy ceramic cover off the toilet's tank behind him and hurled it at the creature. Sam was an above-average basketball player, at least in his academic social sphere; it was always a secret point of pride for him to be a tall, lean-muscled fairy dribbling circles around his heterosexual colleagues. At any rate, he had good aim, and he made his mark.

The rectangle of ceramic hit dead in the center of the creature's wrinkled, saggy bulb of a head. As those long tentacles went momentarily rigid and squirted black liquid every which way, the tank cover split into two pieces, one of which clattered to the floor and further shattered, the other of which smashed directly atop Sam's computer by the door. The creature, flailing about, fell to the floor with a squelching sound immediately after. Sam took advantage of its disoriented attempts to right itself by grasping the plunger's mercifully clean rubber cup. He rushed at the writhing grey and black mass, its tentacles convulsing with grotesque violence in the air around it. Even as the tentacles slithered up his legs, squeezing painfully as they worked their way to his torso, Sam jabbed the plunger's wooden handle at the creature with the same frightened brutality with which he took a shoe to a palmetto bug while Marcos cowered elsewhere in whatever room of the house he'd spied the offender. Sam aimed for the eyes and, after a few narrow misses, he got the wooden handle clean through one of those white targets. The vise-like grip of the tentacles, now up to his waist, slackened ever so slightly. Ink and slime splattered about. Sam pulled the wooden tip of the plunger out, and it was covered in the same syrupy red as if the creature had been human. Simultaneously sickened and encouraged, Sam went for the other eye, and this time he hit on the first try. The creature went completely limp, some of its tentacles falling to the floor with a moist plopping sound, some wrapped vaguely around his ankles, impotent.

Sam felt the saliva fill his mouth and the bile rise in his throat, and he managed to disentangle himself from the tentacles, step over the creature's head—only glimpsing for a moment the two soupy holes of red, white, black, and grey—and make it to the trash can by the door, which he leaned over and heaved into, losing his lunch, along with half his iced coffee and the triple chocolate cookie he'd eaten with it.

When he finally inhaled a ragged breath through his acid-filled mouth, he heard that unmistakable baritone all around him.

"There, now if you've gotten that out of your system, I'd like to give you my verdict."

Sam straightened and looked wildly around. The

creature still lay limp and mangled at his feet, amidst the rubble of shattered ceramic and the pool of red that gathered around it.

"I'd like to congratulate you, first and foremost, on finally throwing caution to the wind and choosing instead to act on—" was all it got out. Sam snatched up his laptop, grabbed the door handle, and burst through the door where a middle-aged white woman must have been waiting for God knew how long. Of course, she couldn't have heard him screaming. The creature had made sure of that, and it would make sure nobody could hear her, either.

"I really, really wouldn't go in there if I were you," Sam said breathlessly. Then, as he brushed past her with his head down, he added, "I'm so, so sorry. It wasn't me. I swear."

He knew she wouldn't believe him, especially after he'd been in there for as long as he had. He didn't care.

In the front seat of his Prius, before starting the car, Sam allowed himself to sob with the weight of his impossible experience. He cried heavily, efficiently, and quickly, letting it all out in full-body sobs for a couple of minutes. Then, he sat up, shook his head vigorously, and started the car.

He puzzled over his verdict. If that had been his trial, he might reasonably expect parole. Clearly his inquisitor could have stopped him from killing it—had not, in fact, even truly been killed in spite of its mangled appearance, unless Sam's fit of violence had finally pushed him over the edge into complete delusion and he'd simply imagined the creature's voice at the end. Was he being congratulated on his violence? He would not have expected violence to be a virtue even for this sacrifice-hungry entity, nor did he consider himself to have been a violent person that proved, through attacking the creature, something inherently worthy about himself. But perhaps that was just it. Perhaps it was just his willingness to do something he would not have expected himself to do that had saved him. How he wished, driving away from the café he knew he could never return to, he'd had the nerve to stay for the creature's verdict! And yet he was afraid he wouldn't have liked what conclusion it came to about him.

Sam kept glancing in his rearview mirror on his way to the freeway, half-expecting those white eyes to stare at him from the back seat. Under the imagined watch of that strange being whose body he'd destroyed but whose voice had remained, he drove right past the exit he normally took to get to his home in Mid-City, reasoning at first that he was just going to the only Apple store for miles around to get a quote on fixing his dented laptop—of course, he'd have to wipe down the ink and slime before taking it in. When he skipped that exit, too, he finally took out his phone and surprised himself by sending a text to his husband. Normally, on principle, texting and driving was not something he did, but today had been no ordinary day.

> Gotta go out of town a couple days.
> Nothing you need to worry about.
> Sorry I can't explain. I love you.

Then he rolled down his window and tossed his phone out into the whooshing air, driving past the airport, past the outskirts of the city. Driving without thinking until the sun disappeared, until it became clear to him that if he didn't stop at the nearest town, he'd be driving all night. ☓

WHAT LURKS IN THESE WOODS

BY COREY NILES

REPORT NUMBER: 1986-47836

What you have to understand about that night is that I didn't become a fire spotter to be a hero. Romantic notions of being the eyes and ears of these forests never afflicted me. I took the job for one of the reasons why so many other spotters found it challenging. Six months of seclusion.

No human interaction beyond radio check-ins twice a day. One at ten o'clock to report the current weather readings and one at four o'clock before I signed off for the day. Unless, of course, I encountered a fire. But I hadn't seen one yet during this humid, miserable summer.

To say that I enjoyed my time as a fire spotter would be a lie. However, I preferred that tower to anywhere else in this godforsaken country. On the top of that mountain, I felt like I could breathe a little easier than I had in years. I didn't have to concern myself with how I walked or where my eyes wandered. I could just exist like the pine trees, uncaring of my place in the forest.

I suppose that need to escape it all—to forget about that town, those people, that hospital, him, and everything that I had been running away from—blinded me to what so many others might've found obvious. I never considered the danger of being in a forest with the closest semblance of civilization a day's hike away until I came face to face with what lurks in these woods. By then, it was far too late.

Dispatch contacted me a little after five o'clock. I was outside my cabin with Shy, trying to get her to piss before I made dinner. Some spotters bring their spouses with them. I had Shy—a six-year-old Great Dane. She was Mathew's dog. A rescue who was more trouble than she was worth.

She started barking as soon as Janet came on the radio. Shy knew that no one contacted me after I came down from my tower at four o'clock, and because this violated our routine, she was sent into a panic. Before Mathew got her, someone had used her as bait for fighting dogs. Gave her a nervous edge and a distrust of men who weren't Mathew. I don't think she would have ever stopped growling at me if she hadn't realized I was all she had left.

"Hush up and piss already," I told her, pulling the radio from my belt and putting it to my ear to hear over her barking. I'd be lying if I said that I didn't share her concern though. Central would only contact me for one reason. Trouble.

Static hissed through the radio before Janet said, "Byron Peak, Fremont Dispatch. Ron, you there?"

"Yeah. What's up?"

"Albert Bowman is up at Greystone Butte. He missed his afternoon check-in. He's only been with us since last year, but the kid hasn't been off by a minute with check-ins since he started. Won't answer his radio either. He's got his wife up there with him too, so even if he had an accident, she should've radioed us. He's a little over ten miles south of your location. I need you to go check on him. We won't be able to get out there until tomorrow morning."

I stared into Shy's black, worried eyes, knowing that she was probably mimicking the shaken expression on my wrinkled face. I didn't like this one bit. "Greystone Butte?"

"Yep."

"I'll check it out," I said, as if I had a choice.

"Thanks."

I hurried back into my cabin, my knees cracking at an irritatingly loud volume as I went. They didn't hurt, but the sound served as a preview of more pain to come after a few more summers of climbing up and down the three flights of wooden stairs that led to my tower, which was half a mile north of my cabin.

I headed for my maps first and pulled out one of the entire forest. Sure enough, I found what looked like *Greystone Butte* printed in tiny black letters about ten miles south. I grabbed my reading glasses and double-checked. *Greystone Butte.* The ten miles between here and there looked so insignificant on the large map compared to the five-hour hike I knew it'd end up being.

He'd better be in some trouble, I thought. *He better not be up there with that new wife of his, getting too busy to do his job.*

But another part of me hoped that was all it was—just some kid who got too drunk on love to remember that he had responsibilities. *Why wouldn't they answer dispatch though?* My mind returned to an old tall tale among spotters in these parts about a guy who hung himself from the railing of his tower. Apparently, even after they cut him down, you could hear the railing groan under the weight of him when the wind picked up at night.

A suicide wasn't the case here though. Kid had a girl with him. If he hung himself, his wife would've contacted dispatch. There was the possibility that he'd done something more sinister, but I put that out of my head. Most likely, he'd forgotten to check in and Janet would contact me when I was halfway there to tell me that the kid had gotten hold of dispatch with a string of excuses and apologies. The simplest explanation was usually the right one, but, for some reason, I couldn't get myself to accept it.

I packed in a hurry. I wanted to try to get there before dark. I usually averaged under thirty minutes per mile, but I figured that I'd rather be safe than sorry. I put a flashlight, granola bars, and water bottles in my backpack. I brought a sleeping bag too because, regardless of what I found there, I wasn't getting back here tonight. I then made sure I had my radio, map, compass, hunting knife, and bear spray. I'd never felt the need to carry a rifle, but I suppose if I'd had one, I would've brought it with me. Shy watched me from her bed, nervously jerking her head with every move I made to keep an eye on me.

I was ready to go within ten minutes. I filled Shy's dish with enough food for tonight and tomorrow morning. But she didn't rush over to it like she usually did. When I went to the door, she followed behind me instead.

"Stay!" I shut the cabin door on my way out.

She poked her head through the doggy door, and I told her again. Her eyes were wide with fear. I assumed she was all worked up because our afternoon had strayed so far off schedule, so I didn't pay much attention to her. Just told her to go back inside, and after she did, I set off.

In retrospect, I wonder if she knew something I didn't. Animals have instincts that we humans don't. Maybe she sensed the danger. Maybe her eyes were telling me to stay. I wonder if I had gone there and the only problem was that his radio wasn't working, would she have been so nervous?

The trail wasn't well maintained. Regularly checking my compass to ensure I was still on track, I climbed through thicket and over fallen trees. My cracking knees kept my pace. *Crik, crik. Crik, crik.* Each time they cracked, my mind seemed to return to that time before I started spotting when I was younger and my knees were soundless.

I felt like I was looking into a View-Master, clicking through old photographs. I took a break after five miles because I thought I'd go mad if I have to hear that cracking sound one more second or think about him any longer.

I rubbed my knees for a minute before wiping the sweat from my forehead and drinking some water. I took a granola bar from my bag. Dinner. I heard it then. Twigs and leaves cracked under the careful steps of something behind me. I froze, trying to listen. How long was I being followed—unaware of it because of these blasted knees?

Hot breath hit the back of my sweaty neck. Rot filled my nostrils. I reached for the bear spray I had hooked onto my belt. Whatever was behind me, the spray would burn the eyes out of its sockets. My hand shook so much that I dropped the spray on the ground.

The thing jumped back, growling. Not the growl of a bear or wolf. I knew this growl. Relief washed over me. I turned around to find Shy staring at me. She licked my face before going back to barking at me. I was too relieved to even be mad at her. "You never fucking listen, do you? You even eat?"

She looked up at me with longing in her eyes. I took that as a no. I tossed her my granola bar and got myself another one. When she finished, I cupped my hand and poured some water in it for her. She lapped it up before licking her chops to clean herself.

"We got another five miles to go, so we better get moving."

She didn't protest. She just followed behind me.

By mile nine, I was soaked with sweat, Shy panted no matter how much water I gave her, and the sun was setting. I could make out a cabin at the top of Greystone Butte. I didn't see a tower. The smooth stone seemed to create a large enough peak naturally that a tower wasn't necessary. Must've been nice to not have to hike and then climb up to a tower every day.

The walls of the cabin were large, glass windows. The lights were on inside, but from this distance, I couldn't make out anything inside beyond the yellow light that leaked down the slope and into the forest.

I put my map away and followed the light, ordering Shy to stay close. There were all sorts of predators in these woods. If a wolf or bear came at us, there was no doubt in my mind that she'd go after them long before she listened to me. Then again, if I found Albert in bed with his wife, I might let her take a bite out of his ass.

Night had descended by the time we got to the foot of the butte. I took out my flashlight and shined it up at the cabin that peeked out from over the ledge. That's when a man above screamed, "Run!" And before I could even think of what he said, a shot rang out, echoing through the forest. One of the windows above shattered and glass rained down the stone slope.

Shy barked, the hair on her back standing on end.

"Help!" a woman screamed. She came over the edge, running—no, falling down the slope. Tumbling toward us, kicking up a dust storm of dirt in her wake. We moved out of the way, and she skidded to a stop at the base of the butte. Only when the dust cleared did I see that she was covered in blood.

I rushed over to her. "Are you okay?"

"You have to help me," she said, grabbing at my shirt, coloring it red. "He's up there. He's got Albert. Please, fucking help me. There he is!" She pointed up at the cabin.

I saw a silhouette in the broken window. Only, I didn't see just any man. I saw a skeletal frame that looked all too familiar. No. I was imagining it. I looked down at the woman in front of me. "What the hell is going on?"

"My ex-husband's insane. He found me here with Albert. Got Albert's gun. Smashed up the radio and held us captive. Your light distracted him long enough for Albert to try to wrestle his gun back from him and for me to run, but Albert is still up there. You gotta help him."

I didn't know what to say to her. I was still trying to process everything she'd told me. All I knew was that I didn't like the idea of being out in the open with a crazy gunman above us. "We need to take cover."

I grabbed her hand and pulled her behind a cluster of trees. Shy was still barking, but she followed us. I grabbed my radio from my belt. "Fremont Dispatch. Janet, it's Ron. We have a situation."

I waited for the static. I waited for her voice. But there was nothing. The radio was on. I'd just changed the batteries yesterday. "Shit, it's not working."

"Who cares? You gotta get up there and save him."

"Ma'am, I don't have to do any such thing. I am not a cop or a rescue team. I'm a fucking spotter like your husband. I need you to calm down so I can think. And Shy, shut it!"

Both of them fell silent, but I could barely hear myself think over my pulse pounding in my ears. I tried the radio again, fiddling with the antenna. "Janet, you there? Janet, pick up."

A scream came from above, growing louder by the second. I poked my head around the tree just in time to watch a man fly over the cliff and fall headfirst to the ground. His neck snapped the moment he hit the earth and his body crumpled after it in an awful thud. I pulled the flashlight away, but not fast enough to shield the woman from the sight.

"No!" She ran to him before I could grab her. "Albert, say something. Albert!"

"Ma'am, get back. He's got a gun." I called from the trees.

She wasn't listening to me though. Staring at the cabin above, she screamed, "I'll kill you, mother fucker."

I started toward her, but before I took a step, she was off, climbing up the butte.

A head appeared in the broken window above, blocking out the light. I shined my flashlight up at him in the hope of blinding him before he could take a shot at her. However, it wasn't the face of a stranger. I knew the face. The sunken cheeks. The red sores. Mathew stared down at me. No. It couldn't be him. He was dead. I blinked. I rubbed my eyes, but the face didn't change. It was him, glaring down at me.

"Mathew?"

Shy took off up the butte.

"Shy, no!"

She ignored me.

"Fuck." I looked back up at the cabin. The man in the window was gone. I had to be losing it, but I couldn't let him hurt them.

I hurried up the hill.

Shy had already passed the woman and was nearing the top of the butte. Her four paws made quick work of the rocky hillside.

"Shy, come!"

If she heard me, she made no indication of it, disappearing over the top of the hill.

My knees cracked as I climbed. A flash of Mathew in the hospital bed, his skeletal hands reaching out for me, raced through my mind. I was unraveling. Going crazy. I just needed to stop thinking and climb before that mad man shot Shy.

The woman reached the top of the hill and ran out of sight. Shy's barks turned to pitiful whimpers, and the thought of that man hurting her gave me the last bit of energy I needed to reach the top of the hill. Heaving air, I pulled myself over the ledge. The cabin door was only a few feet from me. I forced myself to stand in spite of my exhaustion and stumble into the cabin.

Shy cowered in the corner, crying out as Mathew, dressed in a blue hospital gown, choked the life out of the woman on the ground. No, it couldn't be Mathew. I was just seeing things. It was her ex-husband, and I had to stop him. I pulled the bear spray from my belt and held it out in front of me. "Let. Her. Go!"

Mathew turned to me, releasing his grip. She burst into a fit of coughs. He stood up. "Ronald, stay the night with me."

I dropped the spray, no longer in the cabin. I was back in that hospital room three years ago, looking at what was left of him lying in bed. "I can't."

"Please, stay. I don't want to be alone." Each syllable was drenched in desperation.

"They won't let me," I lied. I was so angry. Angry that he'd slept around. Angry that he was dying. And I was afraid of what the nurses and doctors might say if they found me lying beside him in the morning. It was a small town. The rumors were bad enough from just my infrequent visits. "Sorry, I have to go."

"You left me there alone to die," Mathew said, pulling me back to the cabin. He walked toward me.

"I didn't know you'd die," I blubbered through tears.

"You didn't care," he said. "You were happy I was dying. Thought I deserved it. Don't lie to me."

"No," I said, shaking my head. But we both knew that it was a lie. A part of me, one that felt hurt and betrayed, had thought he deserved it. Thought he got what was coming to him. And I'd stowed that away in some dark recess of my mind because it was too ugly of a thought to ever see the light of day when everyone in our private circle was dropping dead around us.

"Now, I can finally return the favor." He wrapped his bony fingers around my throat and squeezed with a strength that he never had in his final days.

Air surrounded us, but none of it could reach my lungs. The world darkened around the edges. His eyes. They were filled with loathing. He'd returned, come back from the grave to ensure that I died in just as terrible and painful a way as he had in that hospital bed. Alone in the world beyond those doctors and nurses—strangers—who didn't get within an arm's reach of him.

And I thought: *I deserve this.*

A growl came from behind him, and suddenly, he was being pulled away from me as Shy tore into his leg. I fell to the ground, coughing. Black liquid poured from the wound, wetting the white fur around her mouth and, for a moment, like a light flickering off and on, I saw something else. Something skeletal and covered in black oil. Then it was Mathew again.

But, of course, it wasn't Mathew. He'd been dead for nearly three years now. This thing was making the woman see her ex-husband, and it was making me see Mathew. But Shy wasn't fooled. If that was actually Mathew, then she'd cover him in kisses, not try to tear his leg apart. I got to my feet, grabbed the bear spray, and emptied it in Mathew's face. The black creature returned.

BANG!

Black oil sprayed me. The woman had found the gun and buried a bullet in its skull. It turned back to her, swinging its long, black talons. One connected with her cheek and split it open. Blood poured from the wound, and she fell to the ground, clutching it. It then focused its attention on Shy. Any moment, it'd bring a claw down and kill her. That damn dog was the only thing I had left of him.

"No!" I ran forward and pushed the thing away from her.

The creature stumbled back and fell out the shattered window.

I rushed over to the window, and the woman joined me. I shined my flashlight down at the ground below. It had landed beside Albert, its long limbs contorted in a configuration that assured me that, if it had somehow survived the fall, it would soon be dead.

"Good riddance," said the woman, spitting out the window.

I turned back to Shy, who, while shaken, stood at the door, ready to attack anything that dared to come into the cabin. I kneeled down beside her, barely even noticing how my knees cracked. I rubbed the spot under her chin that made her tail wag.

I wiped the black liquid from her mouth with the cuff of my shirt. "Good girl."

The static of my radio started again. Janet's worried voice filled the cabin. "Ron, are you okay? Ron, can you hear me?"

"Janet, I'm okay, but Albert's dead. Send help immediately."

"Jesus. What happened?"

I returned to the window, shining my flashlight down at the bodies below, but Albert's body was the only one that I found. A trail of black liquid disappeared into the trees. The creature was gone.

"Just send help," I told her, and I got off my radio before Janet heard the woman's screams at the sight of Albert's body, all alone at the foot of Greystone Butte.

I know how crazy this must sound, but I saw what I saw. Somehow, that thing got into our heads and used what it found there against us. I don't expect you to believe me, especially now that you know what I am, but at this point, I don't care. I know what happened that night, I know that wolves and bears aren't the deadliest creatures that lurk in this forest, and I know how I treated Mathew was terrible. But I can't change that any more than I can change Albert's death.

I'm not a hero, but I'm not a coward either, and I'm tired of hiding from the world. For some reason, I'm still alive, and I plan on keeping it that way. So, do what you have to do, but once we're done here, Shy and I are leaving.

I guess you can consider this my report and my resignation.

Ronald Fremont
July 14, 1986

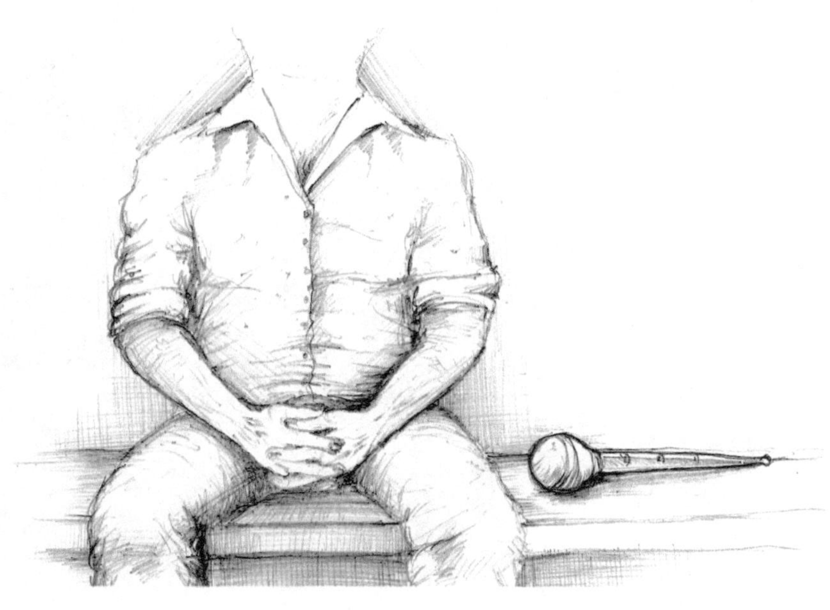

MURDERER'S MILK

BY LEE THOMAS

A TEAR RAN DOWN BEVIN'S CHEEK. It clung to his jaw for a heartbeat and then dropped to splash on Scott's eye. The droplet spread over the brown iris, but Scott never blinked. Petty discomforts didn't concern the dead.

In the days after the box containing Scott's remains went into a hole gouged from frozen ground, Bevin didn't leave his apartment. Food was delivered. He ate little of it. Scotch was delivered. He drank all of it. The empty bottles stood like monuments at the side of his chair amid cartons of rotting take out. On the marble coffee table before him, his phone rested like a graveyard plaque waiting to have a name etched across its face. And Bevin wanted that name. Needed it. He'd promised a good amount of cash to Dexter "DD" Drexel, a slimy prick who'd need to climb a lot of steps to be considered low, to get it for him. Bevin wasn't connected, not in the way DD was. He didn't keep up with underworld machinations. Most of his clients were private sector: corporate bullies looking to get a leg up on the competition or a bit of marketable filth to leverage a superior executive or a difficult politician. Whenever he found himself summoned into a mobster's periphery, Bevin's gut clenched. The stench of testosterone, the desperation to assert and amplify their masculinity. It was all so pitiful. He despised the dogmas of men who would never live up to the images they'd created for themselves.

Fuck them. Fuck them for being cheap, violent bastards. Fuck them for coming into his home and putting a bullet in the head of a truly good human being just because Bevin had nicked inflated egos by denying their latest request.

Scott was dead, and Bevin wanted a name.

The name he had—Martin Gommert—belonged to the moneyman. Gommert had ordered the hit, had written the bloody check. Bevin knew that. And he'd go after Gommert soon enough, but first he wanted to meet the man who wore the last face to fill Scott's eyes.

Before Scott, his life had been a room of shit and hurt and gray painted walls. Scott had been a window, a vibrant portal radiating light, revealing living-color landscapes, and suggesting a real life if Bevin took the chance to step outside. Before Scott, Bevin had expected nothing from the men he'd met. They'd been a physical need, scavenged morsels to keep from starving. He'd known better than to exercise his desire too frequently or too publicly. Reputations made the men in his line of work; they made corpses, too.

Scott had forced him to rethink it all. He'd made Bevin believe he could get out and find something close to happiness in his life, if not happiness itself. Scott wanted a house and marriage, and he wanted to adopt kids. Bevin hadn't taken the man's dreams of domesticity seriously at first. But why would he? When he was a kid, you were lucky to get home with all your teeth if you got pegged as queer. You didn't get rights. You didn't get a normal life. You got teased and beaten and cast aside. When you grew up, if you grew up, you got dark rooms, nameless skin, and shame. He'd watched the culture change over decades, but he noted these changes as if observing a magic show: he saw what was happening, but he couldn't believe the progress was anything more than smoke and mirrors.

In his world, it hadn't mattered anyway, because he'd been trapped in the gray room with all of the gray men. Then a curtain was drawn and a window appeared. Then the window shattered.

The phone rang.

Two days later, Bevin sat in a different apartment in a grim part of the city. At his feet, ancient parquet flooring, its intricate rectangles of pine discolored and split by time, ran beneath thrift shop furnishings from one filthy wall to the other. Deep stains blossomed along the baseboard near the kitchenette. Heaps of old food containers sat on the small dining table beneath the kitchen pass-through; its laminate surface curled at the edges. Sitting very still in the one sturdy looking piece of furniture, a leather recliner the color of a blood clot, Bevin heard the rustling of roaches in the garbage on the dining table and in the corners of the room. To his left a dusty window offered the partially obscured view of snow falling through the night.

He held a Walther P22 in his lap. The asshole who'd sold it to him had gotten a laugh out of his selection, called it a "pussy gat." But the portability of the weapon, its ease of concealment, and its ability to be silenced with fewer decibels than the opening of a beer can meant more to him than the needle-dick need for a hand cannon. The suppressor he'd affixed to the barrel leaned against the arm of the chair. On the other arm, the screen of his cell phone cast milky light into the room. Bevin eyed the screen, noting the progress of a tiny blue dot on the mapping program.

After DD provided him with Adam Jarrell's name and enough of the man's history to convince Bevin to be cautious, Bevin had tracked the killer to a dive on Mosser Street. He'd attached a GPS chip under the bumper of Jarrell's Mercedes. Clearly the man was more concerned with his transportation than he was with his home. In the early morning hours, Bevin tracked the Mercedes to this dilapidated address and noted the one buzzer without a label, no name scribbled on a scrap of paper or penned into the metal panel. A man like Jarrell wouldn't advertise his location. Bevin noted the apartment number and left. He had watched the blue dot all day, following the murderer's progress from one side of the city to the other. For three hours, the dot had remained motionless, resting on a site ten blocks away, likely a strip joint or tavern. But now it was on the move. Jarrell was coming home.

As he waited, Bevin considered what he would say

to the man, what words he would put in the man's head before he erased them with .22 slugs. A series of crime and action film clichés paraded through his thoughts, and they all sounded trite. He didn't want a pun or a joke sending Jarrell to sleep. He wanted the fucker to know what he'd stolen from Bevin, what he'd done by murdering Scott Stephenson. Jarrell wouldn't care, but he didn't have to care. He just had to know.

On their last night together, the last time Bevin had seen him alive, Scott had rested his head on Bevin's shoulder and said, "The reason this works is I like who I am with you." The words hung in the bedroom, and they might have come from Bevin's own mind. He liked who he was with Scott. No pretense. No fucking shell to keep the world from touching the sensitive tissue beneath. With Scott he'd pictured an unburdened future. A freedom of self.

He noted the blue dot progressing into the neighborhood, and when it was two blocks from the filthy apartment, Bevin turned off his phone. Light traveled well in areas of gloom.

His heart rate sped, and he calmed it, and then it sped again. He adjusted his grip on the Walther and lifted it to a firing position. When he heard the key in the lock, Bevin again searched his mind for the exact words he wanted Jarrell to carry into the darkness, but when the door opened and the light burst on, Bevin said nothing. He pulled the trigger and three snapping reports later, he relaxed his finger.

Jarrell was a large man with a round face and a flat nose. He wore a black overcoat, salted with snow at the shoulders. His eyes grew wide at the sight of Bevin in his favorite chair, and they grew wider as three holes punched through the wrinkled white cotton of his shirt. He dropped against the doorjamb for support, and then he spun into the hall. Bevin stood, retrieved his phone, and calmly walked across the room. He expected to find Jarrell in the corridor, where he'd put two behind his ear, before moving on to Gommert, the man who'd commissioned Scott's assassination.

Bevin stepped over the threshold to find the hallway empty. At the end of the hall, the door to the stairway latched closed.

Maybe he shouldn't have been surprised. DD had told him that Jarrell had more lives than a cat, said that Jarrell once took a knife to the ribs and managed to finish strangling his mark before strolling away. Another story had Jarrell taking a .38 slug to the chest and the next morning, he arrived at his favorite diner in apparent good health for a plate of bacon and eggs. Bevin didn't buy into many underworld fables, but clearly, Jarrell's constitution was to be admired.

He jogged to the door and paused. By now, Jarrell would have his own weapon drawn, or he'd be face down. Either way, there was no rush. He listened at the door. Muffled footsteps descended the stairs. He opened the door and followed. Already Jarrell had reached the ground floor. He was moving fast, and Bevin considered the possibility that the killer had been wearing a vest. He couldn't remember seeing blood on the shirt, and it occurred to him that Jarrell's reputation for invulnerability might have hinged on nothing more than an investment in Kevlar.

Considering this, Bevin picked up his pace. He made it to the ground floor and then cautiously opened the door. As he did so, he noted a fresh smear of blood on the jamb. His notions about body armor evaporated. He stepped into the building's foyer and checked the corners before running to the exit. If Jarrell got into his car, Bevin was fucked. He could follow the man easily enough with the GPS chip, but if Jarrell managed to get his cronies involved or, though this was less likely, drive straight to the hospital, Bevin's chance would be blown.

Outside, thick dollops of crimson puddled in the slush and snow-covered walk. Bevin caught sight of his victim weaving across the sidewalk in the distance. Jarrell stumbled and hit the side of a brick building on the far side of the intersection like a drunk desperate to make an appointment.

Bevin lifted the Walther and fired. Chunks of brick cracked and flew away from the building at Jarrell's side. Though this last volley had missed its mark, Jarrell crashed face down in the snow.

"What the fuck?" a man called at Bevin's back.

He didn't turn to see the witness. He lowered his head and tucked the Walther into his coat. He picked up his pace and made it to the corner, before setting off in a run. He circled the block and climbed into his car with no further incident. He waited and considered driving to where Jarrell lay on the sidewalk. He thought about emptying his clip into the back of the man's head, but he didn't see the point.

Three slugs to the ribcage were enough to stop any man. Bevin might have missed Jarrell's heart... might have… but no way was the fuck going to keep breathing with so many holes in his lungs.

Best to call it a night and figure out a way to put Gommert in the dirt.

Scott's father called every other day to commiserate with Bevin. Less than ten years separated the men in age, but Ralph Stephenson, who'd raised his family in Vermont, came from a wholly different world.

If Bevin had told his own father about his weakness for cock, he imagined the old man would have put an ice pick through his neck, rather than discuss his feelings about having a homo son. Ralph Stephenson had loved his boy and suffered visibly from his loss.

"Have you heard any more from the police?" Stephenson asked.

"No," Bevin said. And he didn't expect to hear much from them unless somebody fingered him for Jarrell's murder. "They told me they're doing what they can. But with something like this, something so random, they say it's never quick."

As far as Ralph Stephenson and the police were concerned, Scott had interrupted a burglary. Bevin had no criminal record, and though he'd had to dance around the cops a few times when they asked about his line of work and his associates, there was no reason for them to investigate any motive beyond the one Bevin had provided them. Stephenson certainly had no reason to question the story, and he didn't need to worry about justice. Bevin had taken care of that for the both of them.

The conversation progressed, but Bevin distanced himself from the discussion. He liked Stephenson well enough, but he wasn't in the practice of sharing how he felt, so he let the man talk. He held the phone receiver from the landline against his ear and punched through messages on his cell phone. After erasing a dozen emails, all of them retail SPAM, he found a push notification from the tracking application he'd used to lo-jack Jarrell's car. Tapping the app's avatar, the screen filled with a tiny map, and Bevin was surprised to see the small blue dot moving over the grid. He imagined one of Jarrell's buddies had retrieved the vehicle and was relocating it, or maybe the cops were impounding the Mercedes.

"Scott said you two were talking about marriage."

"Yeah," Bevin muttered. "He brought it up a couple of times."

"I was supposed to be his best man. He asked me a few years ago when it became legal. And he wanted his mother to give him away. He said it wasn't traditional, but he didn't care."

"He told me the same thing."

The blue dot crawled north on the screen, and Bevin felt a twinge of panic. He imagined Jarrell, bloody but still breathing, driving his luxury sedan uptown to show Bevin what he thought about getting shot.

"Did you ever make it official? I mean, were you engaged?"

"I don't know, Ralph," Bevin replied. He wanted to make the guy happy, but more than that, he wanted to tell the truth. He couldn't imagine anyone else with whom he could be honest these days. "None of this was real when I was growing up. It wasn't anything I ever thought about until Scott. I don't know if I could have asked him. I think it would have felt like a joke, you know? But I would have said yes if he'd asked me."

"He wanted to," Stephenson said.

Bevin had no response. The blue dot continued its northerly trek, and he felt an irrational dread. He'd seen nothing in the news about a shooting, let alone Jarrell's death. What if three bullets hadn't been enough?

He shook his head. Even if the slugs hadn't killed the son of a bitch, he wouldn't be up and walking around. He'd have a week or more in the hospital before he picked up his gun again, and only a day and a half had passed since he'd dropped in the snow.

On the other end of the landline, Scott's father cried. Bevin didn't know what had triggered the tears, but it happened every time the two men spoke. It made his guts knot. Bevin had cried upon finding Scott's body, and then he'd locked that shit away.

The blue dot changed directions. Now, it headed west. His hands began to shake.

"Hey, Ralph," he said. "I'm sorry, but I'm having a rough time of it today. Can I call you back tonight or maybe tomorrow?"

"Sure," Stephenson said, sniffing loudly into the phone. "I understand. I didn't mean to..."

"No," Bevin said. "It's good. I appreciate the call. Give my best to Gloria."

The blue dot passed Ninth Street and continued toward the river.

He hung up the phone, suspecting he'd cut off Scott's father in mid-sentence. He'd apologize later.

Bevin hurried to the bedroom and retrieved the Walther from the nightstand. He lifted the suppressor from the drawer and screwed it to the barrel as he made his way back to the front of the apartment. The blue dot had turned onto Riverside, and it was heading north.

It couldn't be Jarrell. No way in hell it was Jarrell. But Bevin wasn't going to wait around to find out. He threw on his coat, left the apartment, and kept his attention on the phone's screen as he waited for the elevator. Whoever was driving the Mercedes, they were only a mile from Bevin's apartment building. He reached the lobby and then the sidewalk, and then Bevin sprinted to the intersection north of his building. He checked the phone. Checked traffic. Looked at the phone again. Then he ran across the street to the diner on the corner.

Inside, peering through the glass, he saw Jarrell's Mercedes rolling down the street. As it drew near the corner, Bevin noted with more than a little terror that Jarrell was behind the wheel.

Bevin woke from a light doze in a hotel room ten blocks from Jarrell's apartment. He'd spent his afternoon buying supplies–gloves, a hat, bullets and a spare magazine to hold them, a charger for his phone–and then he'd checked into the room where he began the process of monitoring the tracking app. At midnight, he drifted off and endured a disturbing dream about Scott and Jarrell. In it Scott performed a mockery of oral sex on the barrel of Jarrell's gun. The dream ended with a crimson money-shot splashing the wall behind Scott's head.

He checked the phone, and Jarrell's car remained parked two blocks from Bevin's apartment building. The killer had set up camp.

At three-oh-eight am, the blue dot finally moved. Bevin splashed his face with cold water to remove the clinging fatigue from his eyes. He slipped on his coat, his gloves, his hat, and then checked the Walther's mag for the tenth time that afternoon.

On the street, he passed from the respectable district of his hotel into the grim neighborhood Jarrell called home. Here, the streetlights appeared less bright. The walks went untended. Bevin's shoes crunched through a crisp layer of frost and sank into the damp accumulation, wrapping his ankles in ice.

He stood in a doorway, observing the blue dot on the screen of his phone. As it approached, Bevin withdrew the handgun. He pressed himself against the door, attempting to disappear into the thickly painted wood. The blue dot stopped a block away. If Jarrell took the most direct path to his apartment, he'd pass Bevin's position.

Footsteps ground through the frost. They came louder, and Bevin tensed. The man should have been limping. If nothing else, his gait shouldn't sound so energetic. Again, Bevin considered the possibility that Jarrell wore a protective vest, but the amount of blood Jarrell had left in the snow contradicted this idea. Bevin knew where his bullets had hit. If Jarrell had employed Kevlar, the .22 slugs wouldn't have drawn much more than bruises.

Jarrell strolled across the mouth of the doorway, appearing to have no physical trauma greater than a hangnail or perhaps a paper cut. The man's constitution was impossible.

Bevin leaned from the doorway and aimed for the back of the killer's head. Jarrell heard the motion, or felt it in the icy air. As Bevin squeezed off the first round of shots, Jarrell bent low and pivoted in the blanket of snow. He scrambled for his own weapon, but Bevin adjusted his aim and again put three bullets in Jarrell's torso, throwing Jarrell off his balance.

He hit the snow. Bevin took a step from the safety of the doorway, intending to empty the rest of his clip into Jarrell's head, but the killer's reflexes were fast. He'd freed his gun during the descent. Bevin saw the weapon rapidly leveling in aim and backpedaled into the shelter of the doorway. Chunks of wall popped free amid the deafening reports of Jarrell's firearm.

"Cocksucker," Jarrell yelled.

More shots erupted and divots of stone flew around the doorway, peppering Bevin's cheeks. To keep Jarrell from moving in, Bevin fired at the sidewalk. When his mag ran dry, he popped it free and drove another home.

The sound of crunching steps told Bevin that Jarrell was on the run. He quickly checked the walk and then sprang back for the protection of the doorway, though he needn't have bothered. The brief view of the street had showed him Jarrell, moving at a fast pace down the block. Bevin stepped from cover and descended the few stairs to the sidewalk. He aimed and fired.

Jarrell stumbled and went to one knee before regaining his footing and continuing down the walk.

Bevin followed.

This time, he wouldn't let witnesses cow him. He wouldn't let his tenuous grasp on the human condition send him home with a false sense of closure. Bevin was going to track the fucker down and squeeze the trigger until metal slugs pushed the light out of Jarrell's eyes.

He ran through the dense accumulation. Ahead, Jarrell continued with nearly a full block's head start. He passed his apartment building and kept running. As with the night before, Jarrell ran to the south, where low and dilapidated retail structures squatted like cubist beasts.

Jarrell turned the next corner onto an unlit street, and when Bevin arrived a handful of seconds later, he too turned.

The street ahead, grimmer and darker than the one at his back, was empty.

Jarrell's footprints, deep divots in the snow, ended beside the door of a blond brick structure with a faded sign that had once been red. White letters told him that the building had housed Butler Baby Blankets. Bevin grasped the ice-cold doorknob and pushed, but it didn't budge. Pulling his hand away, he noted the knob and plate shined as if fresh out of their packaging.

With his lock picks, he could have been through the door in a matter of seconds. But those remained in his apartment in the far north of the city. Instead, he planted the sole of his foot against the door. Though the handle and the lock were new, the wood was not. Weakened by rot, the jamb cracked and then splintered, finally giving way after Bevin's fourth, brutal kick.

Bevin duck-walked into the wreckage that remained littering the floor of the compact textile factory. Four industrial looms occupied space like tumors in the darkness, which was scented with vermin waste and rotting thread. Bevin rose to his feet and worked his way across the room. He spun around corners ready to add more bullets to Jarrell's collection. He checked the aisles behind him and peered into the gloom ahead, searching for any displacement of the shadows, but he felt the uneasy certainty that Jarrell had already left the factory.

He hoped the big man had found a comfortable corner in which to bleed out, but Bevin wouldn't be satisfied until he saw the proof of Jarrell's end for himself, not after last time. So he searched the factory floor and peered into empty offices. In the corridor beyond the last deserted office, he found a stairwell door. Below he caught the sound of rustling and a pained groan.

Easing through the opening so as not to disturb the door and announce himself with the squeak of ancient hinges, Bevin pressed his back to the wall and started down. Dim light painted the floor below, but did nothing to help him see the stairs at his feet. After reaching the basement floor, he noted a half-wall and the pale illumination shining at its edge. The sounds of pain returned. They were louder now.

"Fuck," Jarrell cried from somewhere in the chamber beyond.

Bevin peered around the corner. Jarrell had used his cell phone to light a path into the basement. It lay on a crate on the far side of the room, offering weak illumination.

Beside the crate, Jarrell knelt on the floor before a shadowed wall. He'd stripped off his coat and the ruined shirt. Both lay in a pile beside his knees. His massive back arched and his head hung low like a supplicant in despair. Two black holes leaked trails on either side of Jarrell's spine.

"Baby's hurt bad," he whispered to the wall. "Baby needs his milk."

Instead of charging in and ending this, Bevin found himself restrained by the oddity of the scene. The killer had lost his mind. Whether from pain or blood loss Bevin didn't know. The kindest thing would be to end the man's life, but Bevin wasn't in a generous mood. He'd gladly watch the dying man humiliate himself with demented ramblings. Though he'd never been an enthusiastically cruel man, he'd never had such sharp-edged motivation before.

When the voice emerged from high in the gloom to answer Jarrell's pathetic plea, Bevin's throat tightened. The voice was a chilling combination of gargle, click, and the tinkling of shattered glass.

"Mama's dry, baby," the voice said. "You took the last of it yesterday. Give mama your seed to make the milk flow."

"I don't think I can," Jarrell replied, his voice trembling. "Please, mama."

Bevin pulled back and stood rigidly against the half wall. He considered fleeing this place, but he couldn't bring his feet to move. He closed his eyes in an attempt to calm his pulse, then found himself too rattled to open them again.

"Just a little," Jarrell begged.

"So very dry, baby," the sickening voice replied. Its source changed position in the room, moving closer as it spoke. "Put it inside and spray your marvelous seed. The life we make will nourish me, and then mama can nourish you."

Bevin wondered on the word, "nourish." Was it simply role-play jargon?

"Yeah," Jarrell muttered, intoxicated with blood loss. "Yeah, I'll try."

"Think about how nice it will feel. Think about the inside, the way it holds you and pulls on you. So warm."

Sickened further by the exchange, Bevin fought to keep his breathing in check. The night had already taken an unexpected turn, and he'd been rash, running after Jarrell and following him into this miserable chamber, where he could have been ambushed at any moment. He attempted to calm himself, but the wrongness of the situation kept his pulse high. Why would a dying man seek a fuck while bleeding out? Why invest in the kink-role of infant, demanding milk from a mother-sadist who denied him with an unholy voice?

Nourish?

And what did it matter? His only concern was the man's death. Bevin wasn't an experienced killer, but if the woman got in his way, she'd die too. She was collateral damage; the way Scott had been collateral damage.

Opening his eyes, Bevin pushed away from the partition and raised his gun. He turned into the room and bore witness to the creature that resided in this orphaned structure.

Jarrell had gotten to his feet and dropped his pants, which circled his ankles in a low, woolen pool. He pressed close to the wall and lowered his head, revealing the creature affixed to the foundation of the building. It was female in form, but like a figurehead carved by a talented maniac, its resemblance to humanity made it all the more horrific. Instead of hair, viscous tissue undulated like organs, sweeping away from the thing's face in pulsing waves to grip the ancient cinder block wall. "Her" face was an androgynous monochrome, with only a hint of reflected phone light tracing a cheekbone, the arc of her lip, the line of her jaw to give the features shape. Like the being's hair, the flesh was glossy and pliant, suggesting the grotesque offspring of angel and slug. Jarrell had arched his back and tucked his head to the side, clearly latching onto the creature's breast. He moaned and whimpered. His body swayed from side to side as he attempted to position himself. Then his buttocks thrust forward and the wall-bound perversion hissed a rattling, tinkling exhalation.

The sexual union lasted only a few moments. Jarrell continued his clumsy attempt at copulation until his legs buckled, and he slid down the wall, one palm clutching for support on the supple form, fingers gouging but slipping away without purchase. He crashed against the crate, making the light from his phone dance before settling.

The female moved along the wall, flowing across the cinderblocks like a manta ray rippling over the ocean's floor. "No," she screamed.

Its horrible tone filled the basement, sounding to Bevin like a bag of glass and steel being shaken violently and played through heavily amplified speakers. Jarrell curled slowly on the floor, drawing his knees close to his chest. His rumpled slacks, still coiled around his ankles, hissed over the concrete.

"Mama," he moaned.

In her state of extremis the vile mother thrashed, undulating over the wall, back and forth. Even so, her tissue never wholly parted from the cinderblocks. Like a bug pinned to cork, she struggled pointlessly. But in her agitated state her eyes found Bevin at the back of the room. Her regard repulsed him, and he stepped away.

"Breed me," she said.

Immersed in a haze of disgust, Bevin shook his head. His thoughts had become chaotic but even so he recognized the request as unthinkable. He stepped forward, aiming the Walther at the creature.

"Put that away," she said. Her gelatinous form trembled, and her eyes narrowed at him. "We'll be good together."

"You don't have a fucking thing I need."

"Oh, but I do," the female said. "Nourish me, and I'll heal you."

"I don't need healing." He considered the tragedy

that had set him on the night's path and added, "Not the kind of healing you're talking about."

"Are you certain?"

A blast echoed in the low-ceilinged chamber. Though startled, the first discomfort Bevin noticed was in his ears. They rang and ached. The warmth and ensuing fire followed.

He searched the room for the source of the gunshot. From his place on the floor, Jarrell sighted down the barrel of his own gun with bleary eyes. Bevin regarded him with shock. Then he dropped to his knees. They cracked hard on the concrete, sending new pain to meet a coal of misery just above his navel. What? What had...? He gazed down at his torso. Blood traveled down the front of his shirt in a narrow river, pooling at his belt before continuing its cascade over his crotch and legs.

"Fuck her you prick or we both die," Jarrell said.

The walls pushed in or his mind expanded. Initially, he couldn't be certain. Every cold concrete block in the room pressed against him, and then he seeped through to grow. His essence stretched so far that he felt certain he would soon begin losing pieces of himself to the ether. He sensed there wasn't a large enough room to contain him, no house, no warehouse, no arena. The sensation proved transient, but for a moment he felt vast and perpetual. Soon enough, he was again a mortally wounded man sharing a frigid, dank basement with a murderer and a distortion of humanity.

"Do it," Jarrell demanded from the other side of his gun.

"From the seeds children grow," the thing said. "The children summon the milk. They grow mature and fat within me. Then dead. Decaying. Dissolving for me. Magnificent nutrient."

"It can't work that way," Bevin contested.

"That's how it works," Jarrell said through clenched teeth. "Now fucking do–."

Bevin put a bullet through Jarrell's head. The killer fell back. His hand slapped the concrete. His gun clattered uselessly at his side.

Again, the creature screamed.

Bevin emptied his gun into the thing's face, silencing her obscene voice. A ripple coursed through the gelatinous form, and then it grew still. Bevin collapsed. He gazed at the dim light playing on the ceiling as pain and heat spread from his belly and cold seeped through his coat to chill his back.

His consciousness spread as it had before, first pressing against the frigid surfaces of the room and then moving through to prove their solidity an illusion. Expanding outward and up, he felt the feet on the sidewalks and bodies moving through him. In nearby apartments he became the air and the construction and the furniture and the flesh. Men and women argued through him; they distracted themselves with images played on his screens; they fucked to forget the squalor of their lives. He felt their misery and desperation; he became their misery and desperation.

Then he returned to his body in a startling, cracking shift of cognizance. The woman-thing gazed down on him from the ceiling. Her glistening features showed no discernible expression. She fell away, gliding through the space above him and landing on his wounded body. The impact sent blades of pain through every cell. Her face hovered inches from his, and its approximation of humanity made his stomach clench. The bullet holes had vanished as if he'd fired into a swamp. Bevin closed his eyes. The ripping of fabric filled his ears, and a warm gummy substance wrapped around his cock. It began to pull, to suckle as if starving.

Again, his consciousness turned fluid. He became cars and the pavement beneath their wheels. He was the snow, stretching for miles in every direction. On his periphery, warmth caused him to trickle away, decaying into the chaos of water. But this was a single sensation among millions. His senses stretched and covered and filled. He'd become an enveloping-*all*, experiencing the landscape and the life that swarmed it. And at the farthest reaches of his consciousness, he touched a radiant presence, a familiar comfort. Scott.

His ejaculation drew him back to the cold basement. Neither powerful, nor pleasurable; it felt like the trickling of melted snow. He remained for only a moment, observing the creature above him as she trembled and hissed a sigh of glass and iron.

Darkness followed but even the void pulsed with sensation and emotion: the scent of boiling meat; the scratching of rats on walls; the velocity of a suicide's dive; the tickle of laughter; the copper-taste of hate; the pleasing melody of pleasure's hum; a billion heartbeats. And as his consciousness spread, bleeding into the *all*, Scott's essence bled into his.

Sweet electricity filled his mouth. A syrup of static

coated his tongue, radiating current down his throat where it gathered in his belly. From there it spread, metabolizing and riding the bloodstreams to infuse the tissues of his body.

As he returned to the enveloping-*all* of the world, dread met him, because he became certain he could not sustain the reach. His essence constricted and shriveled. Sensations faded to memories of touch, echoes of experience. Consciousness struggled to maintain its scope, and then it snapped, like elastic pulled too tight. His spirit flew inward, contracting into a mass so tiny it was all but inconsequential.

Bevin woke. He was alive and freezing

Three weeks after kicking in the blanket factory's door, Bevin sat on the edge of a dusty desk in the back corner of the building. He tapped a turkey baster against his thigh as he chatted with Ralph Stephenson.

"We're thinking of waiting until late spring, and then we'll have a memorial service here," Stephenson said. "The funeral happened so quickly and was so far away, a lot of people were left out: cousins, aunts and uncles, friends from high school."

"That's a good plan," Bevin said.

"We hope you'll be able to come. We have plenty of room at the house."

Bevin stood from the desk. "Of course I'll be there," he said, crossing the office and stepping into a gloomy hall. "I'd like to pay for the service, if you don't mind?"

"We can talk about all of that later," Stephenson

said.

From the basement, the mother cried out in hunger, but the distance and the density of the floor made it all but imperceptible. At the end of the hall, Bevin paused and said, "Hey Ralph, can I put you on hold for a minute?"

"Sure," he said. "Take your time."

"Just a minute," Bevin said before punching the phone to mute. He slid the device into his pocket and opened an office door.

Martin Gommert, the man he'd refused to work for, the man who'd ordered the hit on Scott, lay stretched over an upturned desk. Naked and bound to the table legs at the elbows and knees, Gommert gazed at his captor with glazed eyes barely registering Bevin's presence.

Caked blood stained his face, torso, and legs. Splotches of bright red blossomed beside older, rustier scabs. A cloth gag wrapped his face. It was so heavily saturated it looked more like a dried organ, a liver or a length of bowel, than a product of cotton. The wound on his belly, a souvenir of a butcher's knife, hadn't fully healed.

"Looks like I'm just in time," Bevin said.

The effects never lasted long, never more than a day or two. Jarrell had clearly made frequent visits to the mother. He kept his home close to hers, so the ameliorating milk would always be near.

On the filing cabinet in the corner, beside the sharp edges and various hammer heads, sat a jar holding two fingers of liquid. Bevin unscrewed the lid and dipped the turkey baster into the watery milk.

As for why the mother had forced her secretion into his mouth, Bevin didn't know. He'd tried to kill her, yet she'd fed him and healed him. Perhaps her generosity was nothing more than habitual reciprocation, compensation for his role in her impregnation, or maybe it was meant as a tease to ensure his return.

He had returned, but unlikely in the way the mother had hoped. She thought he was bringing her more life, more seed. Instead, he brought a jar. He milked her, amid steel-and-glass shrieks of protest. Then he left the factory in search of Gommert. As for the mother, he had no further use for her. He wanted the monstrosity to starve and wither and die in her freezing concrete cell.

Bevin removed Gommert's gag and shoved the tip of the baster between the old man's lips. He crushed the squeeze ball in his fist, assuring all of the milk landed on the man's tongue. Then he replaced the gag as Gommert spluttered and wretched against the foul cloth. A moment later, the wound on Gommert's belly sewed closed and vanished, and his eyes cleared of their near-death haze.

Bevin lifted an ice pick from the top of the cabinet and drove it between Gommert's ribs. He left it there, with the handle jutting from the scabbed torso. Gommert screamed into the cloth, and Bevin left the room.

"Hey, Ralph," he said, once he was back in the office. "Where were we?"

"Scott's memorial."

"Sure," Bevin said. "Let me know when you set the date. I'm going to be moving soon. I just... Big city life isn't for me anymore. But I have a few things to finish up, before I go."

"I completely understand," Ralph said. "When are you leaving?"

From down the hall, a high, muffled squeal rose and then silenced.

The milk would last another week, maybe two. Then the laborers of decay would start in on Gommert without Bevin's interference. By then, starvation should have taken the mother, if indeed anything could remove her from the world.

These were the last two locks holding closed the gray room's door. Once they were removed, Bevin could free himself and step outside. He wanted to see the world the way Scott had seen it. He wanted a life of color and happiness.

He wanted the pain to fucking stop already.

A tear rolled down his cheek. It clung to the edge of his jaw and then dropped. It splashed and spread, darkening the filth to become a transient stain on the irrevocably damaged floor. ✱

PATTERNS IN THE SKY

BY J DANIEL STONE

"THE STARS ARE DIFFERENT tonight," Damian said.

Cyrus bit his lip, winced. "You're drunk again."

They tipped the last of the bottle down their throats, cold tongues, wicked-white lips, teeth glimmering like stars. Day faded into night. Peace into decadence. There was no telling when all of this would end... or begin again. The rooftop still so hot, summer's lingering heat swirling like closed-eye hallucinations, despite dusk falling over New York to cool the day's swelter, sore and red proof of it on everyone's shoulders. Below, rats braved the streets, fetor rising to call them out of the sewers, garbage bags ripped open and leaking smelly juice. The people also looked like rats down there, jetting to and fro, strange missions worn on their sullen faces.

"Look at them," Damian snorted. "Not a care in the world, cut off from the intensity of the sky."

"The less you know, the less problems you have," Cyrus chuckled.

"People used to fear the sky. People used to have wisdom."

"Our ancestors relied much more on celestial puzzles than we do," Cyrus said. "The stars were the clock, the moon and the sun were the dial that dictated time. Now, we just look at a damn cell phone."

Damian's eyes were as wide and pale as a blind person. They moved up, then down toward the city, then up again. *The sky makes such strange patterns*, he whispered. Though the skyscrapers normally hid the constellations, teeming and spiraling all the way to Jersey City, tonight they saw them clearly. It was an exquisite sight. Then he turned back to their small party, spill of wine, stale crackers and old cubes of cheese.

"Still hot," Damian said, wife beater stuck to his torso, the tattoo of a shooting star on his collarbone glittering.

"Today was no joke."

To some the sun is just a ball of floating fire that lies in the center of our solar system, but to the truly knowledgeable it's but a minuscule spark in the cosmic game of exquisite corpse. Though it's the largest star anyone can see with the naked eye, it's not the biggest in existence. There are gaseous giants rolling around the universe that dwarf our sun; Pollux, Arcturus and Rigel. Stars so big the human eye could never literally see them.

"We can't possibly be the only people left questioning the sky," Damian said.

"What's up your ass tonight?" Cyrus downed his cup, then lit a cigarette, the flame a signal for more rats to join them.

"Ever since we came out of the water," Damian

threw a cube of cheese at a rat, "and grew a forebrain, civilizations have respected it, out of fear mostly."

"Fear of mystery, and rightfully so."

Up here, the sky was so close you could touch it, pluck the stars like fruit, pull the moon down with a strong rope. And in the great below the streets churned, polluted with first world problems, ignorance thick in the air. But it was pure bliss on the rooftop, closer to the sky, closer to the expanding universe.

"I really like it up here," Cyrus said.

The light each building gave off, bright as the stars themselves, pricked the darkness with their spires and gargoyles and faux luminescence. But through the light pollution Cyrus knew all those precious diamonds in the sky—though millions of light years away—were already dead. Each star whose light reaches the earth has already expired and is already a ghost in space.

"One literally can't fathom how far way they are... those stars." The binoculars Damian used left two dark rings on his eyes, and his laborite piercing had a dribble of wine on it.

Cyrus smirked. "Aren't you quite the philosopher today, and a homemade astronomer too."

"I don't have a mind for the science of it all, but I can admire, and dream, or use my imagination," Damian said.

"Only because we can't ever fathom the patterns up there. Not even the great scientists of the world really can."

Cyrus looked up at the distant pulsing, ebb and flow of starry oceans and shorelines. And within the mix, three bright dots, one red, one like a dying light bulb and one like an orb. Mars, Venus and Mercury, and a crescent moon parting the clouds like theater curtains, brightest shape out there. Damian grabbed Cyrus' hand, his curiosity cute as his bitterness as the low July sky seemed to fall.

And in that moment, it looked as if the stars themselves—glittering dust and a comet's icy trail—began to come together. Scintillas dropping into Earth's atmosphere, exploding to sparks. But not every star fell, not every star burned away. Some stitched together, creating long lassoes of light, crisscrossing at a speed unknown to science and forming intricate patterns, shimmering crop circles in space.

Damian gripped Cyrus' hand tighter. "Do you see that?"

But Cyrus didn't answer. If he didn't say it out loud, then it didn't exist.

Through the rooftop door and down scabrous stairs, wine coursing through his body like car oil; threat of passing out imminent. One light bulb to show them the way, sneakers scraping dirt, glass and detritus. So many floors to go, but the only way out was down. Already out of breath, yet the stairs kept twisting down, deeper than Cyrus remembered. Damian's face still colorless, nails bleeding again, smeared red lips and rock star hair mangled from pulling at it.

"Tragic," Damian said in his high and rushed pedantic voice. "It's like the stars melted."

"I didn't see anything."

And then out into dark bliss. The streets of Hell's Kitchen wet and warm, sickly-sweet stench of garbage worse than the accumulated urine on subway stairs. Streets not made for walking, far too many people on this side of town to even attempt normalcy; construction projects and holes in the earth vomiting families of four legged bullets, their only mission to survive another night. And they will survive, much longer than mankind as they've been outsmarting us since the day they kicked the rats below ground.

Cyrus stood around holding his nose, a dazzle of light sinking into his pallor. His eyes wanted the sky, but the busy streets stole them instead. Damian couldn't help but to kick a noxious pile of garbage, knowing that for every person in New York City there was at least two rats and ten roaches that will come to eat it. Why wouldn't there be since we make it so easy for them to survive? No matter how many trash receptacles there are, people will continue to throw good food on the ground. Rebels without causes, perhaps.

"Makes me sick," Cyrus said.

"What does?"

"That life can't survive up there," pointing to the rooftop, then the sky.

"Us, you mean. Simple organisms."

To his left a sewer spit up steam, wary ghost rising from its dirty slumber. The bag that Damian kicked now spilling noxious garbage and pooling liquid for the roaches to slurp and the rats to bathe. And thus they came! Cyrus screaming as the roaches took flight, so much heat they had no other way to cool themselves; the sound of their wings drummed powerfully. Cyrus put on his cell phone flashlight to scare them off, and Damian saw them jet down the steamy sewer. Would they get cooked down there? Because even twenty paces away he could feel the heat.

"There're so many of them," Cyrus said.

"Like the stars."

"But at least the stars aren't pests!"

They pressed their backs against the apartment building. Someone had just scribbled on the exposed brick with a paint marker, a white blotch that looked like nothing, but if Cyrus wanted to make something of it, he could. A starry nest egg, a celestial daycare. But down here the night sky didn't exist, couldn't exist. The patterns didn't stitch together like some calling or awakening. The mysteries of the universe were not on the minds of the living specks of dust that took advantage of it day in and day out.

Because down here the patterns were blotted out. One could not see the shapes nor become hypnotized by the myths. The lights were too bright and the surrounding buildings just too tall. On the streets one could barely see the moon thanks to pollution and cigarette smoke. Nobody dared to speak of shooting stars or comets. That was the talk of country folk, the people who could truly see at night.

"Have you ever read *From Beyond*?"

Cyrus' body tensed. "Tillinghast postulates that what we see is what we are constructed to. We have no idea of what absolute nature truly is."

"And that our rudimentary senses don't even

scratch the surface of the cosmos."

"But does it really go on forever? I read studies that what we perceive as "forever" is actually an equation of doom. The universe will fold in on itself one day."

"The strange and the inaccessible could very well already be in our hands."

Damian smeared the wet paint with two fingers, and then wiped the residue on his black pants, tiger stripes that would never come out. He held Cyrus's hand for a minute, which put them both at ease, just as much as the Marlboro Menthols did. They loved each other, in more ways than boys are supposed to, but to them it was quite all right. Cyrus looked west, trying to find the Hudson, but could not see it tonight. A few minutes later they moved in a different direction.

The memories of alleyways and the garbage of 46th Street were pulled from their heads as they headed south on Ninth Avenue, fetor exchanged for roasting Arabica beans and marijuana. Hell's Kitchen barely had the flavor of being hellish, not like it did when it was an immigrant slum. Today it bursts with millennials and tourists. And at this time at night, the worst thing going on was losing out on a seat at some posh restaurant or upscale bar.

But the lights pulsed and the people's voices skirled between taxis and angry buses. Damian and Cyrus were two black dots in a crowd that wore loud colors and followed modern fashion trends. It was like the coming together of two different galaxies, destroying one another in order to become one. And upon reaching 42nd Street, they became face to face with the old world and the new.

The sky and the city.

"I know you're trying to distract me," Damian said, hair pushed behind his ears, nifty glasses magnifying his distant eyes.

"Didn't say a word," Cyrus said.

"You don't have to."

"I need a drink."

"The wine wasn't good enough?" Smooth lips pursed, cigarette smoked past the filter. "We can always get more if you want."

Damian stopped in the middle of the street, swallowed by a horde of bodies. A torrent of smells and languages pushed toward them with muscular force. Cyrus grabbed Damian's hand and pulled just before a roaring gypsy bus could crush him. *Are you stupid?* Cyrus yelled. That's when Damian woke up, lit another menthol cigarette, and flipped off the sky with a badly painted middle finger as he fled down Ninth Avenue.

Little room, littered room, four walls, a cardboard roof, cement beds and paper bag pillows. Rent here paid in sexual favors, the landlord a filthy old pervert who enjoyed young dick. And when the time came to pay up, Damian willingly filled the old man's mouth with seven inches of white meat. Not a bad trade off since Damian didn't have a job and Cyrus refused to use his Etsy money to pay for any part of Damian's life.

Ass end of Manhattan not yet enslaved to big business and the financial successes of Midtown, Hell's Kitchen and the Upper West Side. The sky here always seemed to be bone-grey, heavy with smoke. No contractor could score big here; mass transit was limited, and the buildings were just too old to renovate, tenements plagued with lead, cracked foundations, and too many broken city codes. Who knew what politicians did with tax money anyway, politicians that haven't created enough well-paying jobs to sustain life here. And so the people are corrupted by hate, narcissism and selfishness, and are at one another's throats to survive much like the rats, or dying stars.

"Do you know the myths?" Damian asked.

"I know the story of Andromeda, the Aethiopian princess, and Cetus," Cyrus washed his mouth out with whiskey, his teeth feeling like sand.

"Have you ever looked for her in the sky?" Damian suddenly plagued by terror.

What do you mean?" Cyrus said.

This room littered with all kinds of books, astronomical instruments, textiles and charming crystals. Damian lit a cone-shaped incense that smelled of burning wood, placed it on the windowsill so that tiny loops of smoke spiraled in the dark. A single black light filled the room so that Cyrus could see slouching piles of magazines, scientific and cryptozoological; haven for roaches, house centipedes and termites. A madman's sanctuary.

"Do you want that drink?" Damian asked.

He hobbled slowly to the refrigerator, opening it to show that the only things in it were PBRs and Magic Hat. But Cyrus was fixed on the magnets of Saturn, Pluto and various constellations. He became suddenly overwhelmed by the paraphernalia; everywhere he turned he saw papers, scribbled index cards, mythological magazine cut outs, occult encyclopedias and the tarot.

"Forget it," Cyrus said, shoving himself into the smelly couch. "I need to rest."

Damian cracked open a PBR. "Can we talk about the patterns?"

"What about them?" Rubbing his temples in fury.

"In September and October, right here in the Northern Hemisphere you can see Cetus clear as day. It sprawls clumsily near the Celestial Equator."

"What's this got to do with anything?"

"That was all before the change," Damian said in a low voice.

From his spot on the couch Cyrus could see that Damian watching something through the window. He saw that the stars' light seemed dimmer, but somehow sharper. Cyrus blinked to make sure he wasn't hallucinating, no time to fathom the causes because Damian was fumbling with something in his hands, something that spread a small powerful light onto the wall, as if he was cradling stardust, a speck of the sun.

The movie posters, boxes of comics, broken CD cases and VHS film strips all illuminated. Taxidermy and even the creepy suit of armor that guarded this small squalor seemed to want to come to life. But it was the Post-it Notes inscribed with Damian's signature scrawl, pseudo mathematics and astronomical equations, that Cyrus found the most disturbing. When put together, it seemed to him the beginning stages of a map, carefully drawn, piece-by-piece, so that only Damian could decipher it.

"It's the answer to the stars."

Damian at the small window, delicate and cracked so that it caught moonlight like a dream catcher, which also meant Damian never opened it. The musty smell in here proved it. Better to watch the sky this way; skew it so that the stars seemed closer, the moon more vibrant, the universe itself a streak on the pane. Damian was transfixed on something out there, signaling, calling, and Cyrus caught him drawing on another Post-it, maybe the thousandth one by now.

"There are no answers to the stars," Cyrus said. "Science hasn't even figured it out yet."

"That's why I'm doing this on my own."

"And you can't really *see* them with binoculars alone."

"Not true," Damian chided.

Nails in his mouth, his lips red again, and at his side a can of PBR that looked like it had been sitting on the windowsill for days, open and piss-warm, no more bubbles. But Damian drank it anyway, said it washed the taste of dust and cobwebs from his mouth, washed the taste of his awful landlord. And then something swayed in the night sky, strange to see it so close and clear, but Cyrus indeed saw it, crooked and darkly luminescent.

"You see?" Damian scrawling again, hair cast across his face like shadow.

"What do you think it is?"

"It's there and then it's gone," Damian said absently. "It's like it doesn't want us to see; it's like it wants us to figure it out."

Cyrus lit a cigarette, then walked to the window.

"Aren't you scared?"

"What I've noticed is that there are shadows on the stars themselves, but they are so bright we can't see them."

And while he knew that nobody else—as obvious as it was—would admit to seeing what they saw, Cyrus remembered that they weren't alone in their curiosity. Mammals have been perplexed and awed by astronomy since before humans came into existence; Lovecraft and Fort spoke about dangerous things in the sky, things that were vast and shapeless, things that proved the Milky Way was nothing but a daub of glitter floating in the universe. That there are suns and planets and moons and *things* not bound to tangible bodies or vessels, things that move through dark matter, control it.

Cyrus all of a sudden angry. "Why should we even care?"

"You don' have to. This is my thing."

Damian moved away, grabbed a backpack, and threw in a pair of binoculars, three old books without a title page, a pen, pad and a pack of smokes. Then he sat back by the window and finished his PBR. His strong jaw and pale lips winced as he crushed the can and tossed it to the side. Cyrus put on his black denim vest, Salvation Army boots; Damian traded his REFUGEES WELCOME HERE t-shirt for Fleetwood Mac.

"Let's go."

The sun has been down for hours, and the harvest

moon dominated the sky. Pumpkin silhouettes crawled across the skyline, then down the old building that could have been. Library of the damned, cradle of the city's weirdest. So many of them here to croon over their own lunacies. Cyrus coming in on the left, Damian not far behind, still looking up as if calculating numbers that didn't exist, notepad full of ink. For a second Cyrus saw smoke coming out of his ears, but then realized it was the Camel he'd left lit, held by his actual ear.

"You're gunna to burn your hair off," Cyrus said. "Such pretty hair."

"I haven't washed it in weeks. It wouldn't take more than a second for it to be gone."

"Hate it when you joke like that."

A group of hipsters laughed loudly, maybe at them for being so dark and oily. It was hard to impress them with their raggedy inbred fashions, overpriced used clothing that completely missing the vintage martyr mark. Cyrus cursed their existence; he could handle them all if he wanted—fists up—the little twats of twenty or twenty-one, brats transplanted from bumble-fuckville USA to Brooklyn.

"Ignore them," Damian said. "Not worth our time. Plenty of decent people here."

"Sometimes I just wanna smash their faces."

But Damian was right; the majority of people were odd and interesting enough to take his mind off malice. At the mouth of the doorway stood a punkette in pink high tops, too much eyeliner, hair as grey as her soul. She waved Damian in, nodded to Cyrus, then closed the metal door behind them and locked it from the outside. For a second Cyrus felt like he'd never get out, but once Damian took his hand, the universe could have ripped in half and he wouldn't care.

Down a single flight of stairs, blood-red walls, and eventually they stepped onto a soggy carpet alongside roaches and all manner of pests. The smell of the room an unwelcoming fetor, but the proof of its decay all too clear, soon-to-be demolished sign posted on just about every wall. Damian stopped, ran his hand along a frightening pattern on the wall, one that wanted to spring to life: teeth, starry eyes and wings. Then he knocked, and the wall pulled apart, leading them into an even darker place.

There were shadows down here, poised but threatening, that is until they started to speak. Damian gave the voices his ear, nothing Cyrus could understand anyway, nothing he even cared to. Numbers, figures, astronomy and physics so advanced he doubted Damian's knowledge of it all. Like some colossal front barricading classified information. But something about this room struck Cyrus as odd, like time had turned back centuries, the smell of a precolonial swamp above his head.

When they came into the light, he saw that they were dressed in the fashions of ancient Assyria. Men in flowing wool robes and women black tunics draped with gold shawls. Silver fingernails and charcoal eyes. The language they spoke did not have a European, Asian or New World origin. Not Arabic or Hebrew, nor Aramaic. It was something much older. Damian spoke to these people like he knew their tongue, but it all sounded like gibberish.

"What are they saying?" Cyrus felt stupid for asking, as if Damian really knew.

"They're talking about the sky."

"How can they even see it down here?"

Damian's eyes caught the light like a nocturnal animal. "You mean you don't see it?"

"See what?"

No, Cyrus did not see the gastrointestinal pulse of the walls, did not see stars shooting like bullets. How the trail of comet mist swirled through the blackness as do worms in dirt, or whole planets collide in a storm of lava and smoke. He didn't want to see how these people—these underground people—commanded this queer display of cosmic art with their minds.

"They know the stars," Damian said, light gliding down his lips. "*They are the stars.*"

After what seemed like forever, air hitting his throat like a warm cup of coffee, Cyrus was back out in the still of night. How still, he didn't want to know. The uneven building wavered and the stars remained unsteady flames, pinned like funguses known only to the barren, outer planets that can't be reached by the sun. And the smell now getting to him, like a chicken coup, the kind of smell that gets in your nose and never leaves.

"The fuck is that?" Cyrus said.

"It's what it smells like out there. The metallic, sweet smell of burning things."

They walked north, and Damian once again looked up, as did Cyrus. The avenue was eerily empty, but the sky wasn't. Clouds congealed like rotted milk, but not thick enough to cover the millions of points of light, their patterns, nor their mysteries. *Cetus*, Damian whispered, *amphibian... monster.* And it was true. The damned thing crawled so low and close Cyrus could feel the heat on his face, smell the embers of space.

"Aren't you at all curious?" Damian said.

"Of what?"

"Why they do this? Don't you want to know about the shadows on the stars?"

"That's like asking me to tell you what the meaning of life is, Damian. There really is no answer."

"But you're fascinated; I see it in your eyes."

"You fascinate me."

Cyrus leaned in and kissed Damian, running his hand through Damian's dirty hair, gliding his tongue across the bottom lip. He tasted cigarettes, spearmint and beer, three flavors that mixed oddly well. Just before Damian could reciprocate, a taxi began to obnoxiously beep, forcing people in the above apartments to open their windows and scream. An ordeal like this was normal on Ninth Avenue.

"You do realize that the fact that *we* exist means that there is actually intelligent life somewhere else out there," Damian said.

Cyrus grinned, holding his ears.

"*We* exist. Whatever it took to make us has probably happened in some other part of the universe."

Now the honking out of control, Cyrus speed walking toward the taxi with his fists clenched and his heart on overdrive. Angry at first because he suspected the driver was a homophobe and didn't want to see two boys kissing in the street, but more importantly that the driver wouldn't stop the uncontrollable beeping. Cyrus approached the car on the driver's side, saw the man's face through the window, grim-dark skin and liquor-stained teeth, red eyes pointed up.

That's when Damian screamed so loud Cyrus felt his eardrum burst. The sky wasn't so much falling as it was melting over the city. And the clouds were spreading like legs, spilling strings of blackness down the skyscrapers, filling the streets with muck and grime pricked with the light of stars. Damian touched the goo and brought it to his nose; Cyrus stepped in some and found the consistency to be like tar.

And then they heard the roar.

No animal on this planet could have made that kind of sound. A tectonic crush, a stretched echo. Cyrus jumped back, a little further than he wanted, and fell into a dark door. When he landed, he was face-to-face with speeding rats and flying roaches, all in a hurry to get somewhere. Damian was right behind him, huffing and puffing, but somehow found enough air to scream Cyrus' name again. But his mouth filled with black slime, dribbled over his lips and stained his teeth; eyes changing to wet onyx stones.

Another roar.

Cyrus got to his feet, though they didn't want to move the way his brain did, and so he started hobbling. Slowly, like a drifting feather plucked by the wind off a furious bird. The stairs had turned into the muck falling from the sky, slowly sucking him in. No matter how hard he tried to fight it, the stuff was pulling him down. Engulfing his body, sentient alien slime, until he was a bubbling sack of sad bones.

"It's everywhere," Damian said. "But I got most of it off you."

Eyes crusted with the crudest black, yet open so that he could see he was back on the rooftop. No recollection as to how he got here, but as long as he was alive, what did it matter. It was still night, but the sky was calm; there was no slime, and the stars were nothing more than pulsating points of brilliance. After a few minutes of relaxing, Damian pulled the last of goo off Cyrus's skinny legs and bare feet like a second dead skin.

"This is the stuff that lives inside the stars," Damian said.

"I don't want to hear it," Cyrus said. "I just want to go home.

He stood up shakily, lit a cigarette. He looked at the infinite sky once more, then into Damian's eyes which seemed to be filled with the mysteries of the universe itself. Down two flights of stairs, faster than his lungs could handle, and Damian calling out for him. But he was already on the third flight, the sound of his footsteps echoing up, and Damian too far-gone, or too selfish to follow.

You don't want to go down there!

Now that he was alone, now that the images had left the backs of his eyes, Cyrus thought about the slime, the high sky, and the shapes that suggested intelligence, like some sort of sign. The last pull of the cigarette made him a bit dizzy; the darkness wavered like tendrils, too loud in the strange silence. But if he looked hard enough in this unofficial tomb, he needed not his memories or the myths anymore, for the stars were here.

The sky had followed him.

His vision was assaulted by bright dots, like someone had thrown glitter into his eyes. He yelled for Damian, so loud the echo hurt his ears. The shaky foundation filled with an unearthly roar, wobbling, weakening. All he had now was his growing fear, and the aftermath reminiscent of a day full of drinking. And so Cyrus followed the billowing dots. One by one he grabbed them, but upon touch they broke apart into clouds. And even though the hallway was poorly lit, he could see that the floor resembled the moon's craters.

The room he entered was huge. Big white room where light and dark and color collided. But something was utterly off, like gravity had been dialed back, his bones gone to rubber, limbs bending in ways he'd never seen. His heart felt like it had stopped beating as his body lifted in the air. Tiny dots multiplied, the smell of hot metal and hydrocarbons getting stronger. But it was not just the gaseous clouds bursting or the stars falling; it was the shapes they were making, taking the form of humans and gods alike.

...this all happened before...

A moment in time to understand the stars more intimately, to see them string together into recognizable patterns. Cyrus was left aghast by the sights, suddenly craving Damian's intelligent presence, but very well aware he did not actually need him. The science of astronomy did not hold sway here, nor the speculations of cosmology. Cyrus had found the center of the universe, its complicated inner network of vacuum, light and void.

A reverse black hole, dark matter's sister, a rogue pulsar. ✕

THE ACKNOWLEDGED

BY AARON DRIES

I

The mountains weren't without their demands.

Keep our secret, they whispered in the sway of trees, in cicada song. *Maintain the lie that everything is perfect out here.* I'd only been on the trail for ten minutes and had already been made a conspirator of some kind. *Well, fine,* I thought. *I can live with that,* a commitment signed in sweat and the thread of shin splints through bone.

Shhhhhh, went the trees, those timeless things. *Shhhhhhhhh.*

A surge of heat pounced as though it had been waiting for me. It was cooler when I left the motel an hour before. Bearable. But it was 11:50am now, and I'd dedicated myself to the two-hour Green Loop. The intense Australian sun busted the sky like a furious punch in baked concrete. I'd have to turn back if this kept up.

That would make Ma happy, at least.

"I'm just letting you know where I'm going," I'd told her, gripping my phone so tight cataract-pale knuckles rose through my skin. When cornered, my mother's love made your skeleton want to flee its body. Going home for Christmas had never been on the cards. I'd taken enough of a beating over the past thirteen months to put myself through that. Maybe I deserved her punishment, those reminders that I was an eight-hour drive from where I should be, in the townhouse she shared with my step-father, a nub of a man long eroded away by her worries.

"People die out there, Thom," she'd said, her attempt to make me feel a child aging her. "Don't you watch the news?"

"It's Bungonia National Park near Goulburn. Not the outback. I've eaten too much over the holidays and want to break up the trip to Canberra. Jesus. You'd think I was confessing to murder or something. Can you just let me exercise without the guilt trip, please?"

"Bungonia, he tells me. Bungonia! You know who prowled those parts? Ivan Millat, that's who. A serial killer. He picked off people right there. *That's* murder. Let yourself get fat instead."

I'd switched off the light to the motel room and drew the door shut behind me, speaking through the security key-card pinched between my teeth. "Stop being a worry-wort, Ma. I've got water, hiking boots, and my phone's charged. This is me being smart, okay? 'Don't go for a hike—even a tiny one like this—without giving someone the heads up'. That's what they say, right?"

"Gosh, you're as stubborn as your father." Defeat crept into her voice. "Call me once you're home. The very minute you're in the door. I don't want your face on the side of milk carton. Deal?"

"Well, Ma, I'm lactose intolerant. Not the legacy I'm aching for. Deal."

I checked out at reception and climbed into the Toyota Hilux awarded me in the separation. Sparrows of anxiety stirred. This—among other reasons—was why I'd avoided my parents over the break. The birds had spun nests in my gristle and spirit, every inch of me crowded with their scratchings. Ma prodded, excelled at it. And my sparrows rioted when prodded. Christmas by the beach with them would have been back-to-back diversions and pretending my ex never existed. Retconning that history would be a partial amputation. No thanks. This all hurt enough as it was.

Shhhhh, went those trees again. *Shhhhh.*

The mountain resembled a volcanic skull with a jawline made for exploring, its teeth crumbling under my boots. Lizards cut across a path that didn't feel like a path let alone the designated route. All the coded markers had been bleached white by the elements. Insects screeched, a choir moments before its church collapsed. I wrapped a damp bandana around my neck, baseball cap low, the sleeves of my shirt high with tattoos on display. Water didn't hydrate me as I hoped it would and the sweat steamed right off my arms.

Rest, I heard my mother say. *Rest or you'll go belly-up.*

But the thousands of ants made sitting risky. They swarmed every rock and fallen tree like nervous twitches on a face. And I knew I was watched by spiders and snakes, too. Even though I couldn't see them.

Coming to the park had nothing to do with over-eating (though to be honest, I *had* put on weight). I'd dreamed of Stuart and woken in tears—that's all. The beaks had been pecking since.

These walks quietened them.

Sometimes.

I thought again of the Sutton Forrest Motor Inn where I'd shacked up for the silly season, treating myself to solitude and air-conditioning, luxuries not afforded me at home with my roommate, Arthur. I'd sat in the car for ten minutes before driving off, keys dangling from the ignition on a chain my ex gifted me after one of his trips abroad. Stuart had come home, ready to hit the ground in preparation for the wedding that never happened. I unhitched the chain, cupped it. *Where had he picked it up? Manila? Abu Dhabi?* Multi-hued beads on cheap twine. The memories attached to it defined me once. I tossed it out the window.

Step, step, repeat. Muscles strained and the wind scorched. My sparrows kept to their nests. This exertion was better than the doctor-prescribed anti-depressants or the self-prescribed wine I'd downed over the week, all those sloppy toasts to the television.

Merry—fuckin'—Christmas.

I stopped to catch my breath, soaking up the enormity of the landscape around me. The mountains made a tiny and insignificant thing of me, just another ant. And if I *were* that small then my problems were smaller still. Good.

It was better that way.

I normally listened to music when walking. It might

have been the heat that made me rip the earbuds out. Or perhaps a playlist of crunching stones and zooming flies suited my mood better. This was the first time I'd felt healthy in weeks, a million miles from all the paperwork in my cubicle at the Taxation Office, and even further from my parents' home.

Keep going—
(the sparrows chirped)
—or you'll start to think—
(they bit)
—of him.
"HELP!"

The voice shook me from the outside in. I spun, glancing at the bluff I'd passed. It opened onto a shimmering valley. The bush roared with wildlife trying to mask another "HELLLLLLPPP", Bungonia's secret spilling, after all.

We trusted you with our lie, Thom.
You didn't obey.
"Hello?" I shouted back.
"DOWN HERE!"
I didn't think, only moved.

The man sprawled on his back ten yards below the cliff's edge, a leg snapped to the side, bottles and electronics scattered about. He was my age or a bit younger, in his early thirties at least. Thin, wiry, and ginger-haired, someone who broke easily. His pale face was a blot of desperation on the outcropping suspending him over a fifty-yard drop like a peppermint on the tip of a stony tongue. The

Australian bush had tried to eat him alive, as it tried to eat people all the time. Just ask my mother.

"I'm coming," I yelled, maneuvering down the bluff. "Don't move."

"IT FUGHIN' HURTS! AHHHHHHHH—"

"I know, mate. Stay put. It'll be all right."

Rocks shifted as I wedged feet into every crevice, crab-walking. Fingers strained into gaps between rocks—hiding spots for snakes. I snatched my hand back. The snake in my imagination sprung from the shadows to sink fangs into my neck. The shock would then send me crashing below, next to the man I'd hoped to save—*if* I was lucky. Miss the outcropping and I'd keep spinning, the ground rushing up to kiss me nighty-night forever.

My sparrows scratched. They bit. Tore.

"I—I can't get any closer," I shouted. "I'm sorry."

"D-don't leave." His voice was wet sheets on a clothesline ripping in a storm. Guilt flooded and exhausted me.

"I won't," I told him, meaning it. I shuffled onto my side, dust in my nostrils. Heat thrashed from above and from the rocks themselves. The sun was in everything everywhere, impossible to escape. I could feel myself baking. "Shit. Shit. Shit."

"I'm hurt. Don't leave. *Jesussssssss.*"

I jimmied against the bluff, confident I could wriggle to the pathway above without too much risk. One more step downwards would doom me, though. I twisted to grab the phone from my pocket.

Drop it and this guy's a goner. Ma's voice again.

Fingers flexed, quivered. The acidic sting of

sunscreen in my eyes. There was one bar of reception, but one bar was all I needed. This was the first time in my life I'd ever had to call for an emergency response team. I thumbed oily streaks across the screen, scrambling for air only when I noticed I'd been holding my breath.

We waited. I listened to him cry and moan.

"What's your name?" I asked, bending over to keep eye contact, wanting him to know I cared. Phantom pain wrung me out every time my gaze drifted over his leg. I didn't want to imagine how it felt yet I couldn't avoid imagining how it felt.

Coming to the National Park had been a whim at best. I would have been in Canberra by now if I'd listened to my mother.

"E-Eddie," he answered between sobs. His voice sounded real. "Eddie."

It rained spiders as the helicopter shook the trees.

I expected it all to go wrong at the last possible second, the rescue cumulating in a fireball that would burn Bungonia to the ground, those enormous blades impaling every bit of me. And maybe I deserved it, too.

The unit, however, lifted Eddie onto a stretcher without incident. I saw the man I'd saved offer me the tiniest wave, so *he* knew *I* knew he hadn't forgotten to acknowledge what I'd done. I hurried onto the path, sun blisters popping on rocks, coated in dirt so thick it muddied with sweat and cracked over as I waited. The growl of the helicopter masked my whimpers as I repeated a name I didn't want to say again and again and again.

"Stuart. Stuart. Stuart. Stuart."

II

"I heard someone's going to nominate you for Canberran of the Year," Arthur said through a mouthful of the fried rice he'd made for us. We ate from our 'bachelor bowls', chipped second-hand pieces scored from a thrift store in the city. Fried rice was my housemate's specialty. Eating it was mine.

"Yeah, right," I said, awkwardly shifting on the couch and reaching for the remote. The news was explosions. The news was screaming. The news was political decisions that pinched your guts. Yes, the news had to go. "It's been four months. My celebrity status has somewhat dimmed."

"Well, maybe *I'll* nominate you," my housemate added, cheeky.

"You can't do that. That's, like, cheating."

"Yes, I can and maybe it's warranted. Now shut the fuck up and eat your rice. I already have one child. Don't make me parent you, too."

Arthur cooked. I cleaned. We were comfortable in these roles. It hadn't taken us long to step into the avatars of who we used to be in our prior relationships. Arthur's ex-wife lived a fifteen-minute drive away and brought his son, Brandon, over every second weekend. I was "Cousin Thom" to the seven-year-old, a kinship I treasured. Arthur and I had bathed each other's love wounds, and despite the bleakness of those early days when our lease-signing rung more of execution order ("it's real now," he'd said, teary-eyed) than opportunity, we were getting there. The hurt wasn't any less. We'd just got better at being used to it. I hated cooking, always have.

Our house was squeezed into a cul-de-sac in Garron, a suburb south of the lake. Three bedrooms in all with landlords who let us be. We'd been nothings to them prior to the article in *The Canberra Times*, its follow-up story published a month before. The response time to our maintenance requests had quickened since. The adjoining photograph of Eddie and I had been taken in the backyard against a weave of trees and flowers.

Eddie accepted our invitation to hang around for lunch after the reporter and photographer packed up their things and left. We ate pre-packaged salads and steaks Arthur grilled for us outside to avoid wrangling Eddie's wheelchair up the. Brandon and his mother, Tiff, were also there. We raised beers together, our laughter like pebbles rattling in a tin can. Eddie either held eye contact with me for a beat too long or avoided it all together, a man without a middle ground.

Brandon broke a stretch of silence to ask our guest about pain.

"What a thing to ask," Tiff said, flustering. "I'm so sorry—"

"It's fine. Really. To answer your question, Brandon, it still hurts." Eddie drew his hands off the table to rest them on his lap. "I'm getting there, though. It might be the itching under the leg plaster that's worst, believe it or not."

Brandon laughed. "Liar, liar, pants on fire."

Eddie smiled and glanced my way. "Maybe a smidge."

Tiff took her child home afterwards. Arthur cleared the table, followed by the sounds of dishes being washed inside. Eddie and I waited for the community service van to pick him up at the curb. The quiet we shared wasn't as uncomfortable as before, though like Eddie's legs beneath all that plaster, it still itched.

"I don't think there's any way for me to repay what you did, Thom."

"You don't own me anything."

Emotions slid over Eddie's face like the shadows of clouds, not sticking, willing the earth to not crumble beneath them. "I'd be dead if it wasn't for you. I wouldn't exist."

Eddie turned, hand flirting with his chest—not the first whiff of effeminacy I'd caught that day or back when we'd been interviewed in the hospital. The man in the wheelchair carried himself as though he always wrestled with an urge to confess, a black hole that drew him in on himself, yanking shoulders into a hunch, sucking his chin into the back of his throat. I wished he'd just tell me he was gay so we could laugh it off. "How did you guys meet?" people would ask at dinner parties. "Didn't you know? Thom saved my life. Still got the scars to prove it!" Oh, those wedding speeches. *The Canberra Times* would have a field day. A relationship wasn't on the cards—though I admit I quietly indulged in the fairy tale every now and then.

Attraction didn't factor into the situation at all. Eddie would always be the one I'd saved and because of that he'd love me more than I could ever love him. And I'd experienced enough lopsided relationships to last me a lifetime.

I was glad when the van arrived to take him home. Guilt lingered in his absence like the scent of smoke you couldn't wash from your clothes fast enough.

The newspaper our article was featured in lay on the coffee table in front of the television. I kept putting it on the bookshelf, but Arthur returned it day after day. I guess I was too uncomfortable with myself to reconcile his pride in me.

"Want more rice, Mister Future Canberran of the Year?"

"Fuck you, amigo. And yes. Top this bachelor bowl up, pronto."

I came home from work three weeks later to find a casserole dish on our doorstep.

It was May and the weather had started to turn, its creeping chill an insidious thing. A gust of wind blew the season's first dead leaves over the WELCOME mat the meal had been left on. A card was wedged under the base—not that it required reading. There might as well have been a voice on that wind, too, a whispered name.

Arthur slouched into the house at seven-thirty, his shift at the university having run long. He poked his head into the living room where I sat with a book. "What smells so good in here? Did you get take-out?"

He slipped off his tweed jacket and tossed it over the back of a chair. "I could eat the ass out of a low flying duck right now."

"Well, you're in luck then. Eddie cooked for us," I said, trying not to laugh. "Well, I assume your name was *implied* on the card."

"He left a card? Isn't that domesticated of him. I guess he's walking now, then."

"Quite the recovery, hey?" Words floated over the book's pages like rainbow smears on grease, formless and pretty and impossible to digest.

Arthur picked up the card from where I'd left it on the table. "'Thank you again,'" he read aloud, pontificating, stroking his hipstery moustache. Sighed. "Bit late for a valentine, don't you think? Look, it's up to you, Thom, but I'd pop a cap in this quick-smart. There's nothing worse than a cock-tease. Put the boy out of his misery if this isn't going to be a thing."

"I know. I just feel bad for him, I guess."

"There's leftovers, right?" Arthur asked, changing the subject.

Sparrows ruffled their feathers within me, woken again.

Eddie lived in Belconnen on the other side of the city, his one-bedroom apartment almost bare except for a bile-hued plant lurking by the futon. No photographs on the walls, no portals into who he was beyond what we'd already shared. I knew he was a pharmacist—but that was pretty much it. The empty casserole dish sat on the table between us. I toyed with his card, flipping it to where the address had been scribbled.

Steam curled from our cups.

"I know it wasn't much," Eddie said. "Just a gesture. I guess I don't want you to forget how grateful I am for what you did."

"It's cool, mate," I said, that word—*mate*—making Eddie cringe a little. "Like I mentioned before, though, you don't need to repay me. Great as the meal was."

Eddie limped into the kitchen to bring the kettle back to boil. My cup was still more than half full, so I assumed he mustered out of nervousness, or to show-off how he'd healed. A cane propped against the wall by the front door, not that I'd seen him use it.

"Such a weird feeling," he said.

"What's that, mate?"

"This. All this."

"I know, Eddie. Something for us to tell our grandkids, right?"

"Grandkids," he said. "I hope you tell yours how important all this was to me."

"What was?"

"Falling. Being trapped on that ledge. You coming along when you did. It was the most significant thing that's ever happened to me. I'm not sure people get just how *filling* that is. The papers don't do it justice."

His words jarred, pieces of a puzzle I didn't know how to align. I wondered if I'd subconsciously flirted with him along the line. My ability to process company with other men—let alone gay men—had been warped after Stuart left me. I could hardly stand to be hugged by guys because it made me think of sex.

It was a small apartment and Eddie struck me as

even smaller inside it. His black sweater was stark against those white cupboards, a ying searching for its yang.

Winter grabbed Canberra by the balls. I dreaded leaving the warm bed.

Jordan—assuming that was his real name—snored into my armpit. Stubble tickled my skin in a way that turned me on and I contemplated putting my hungover horniness to good use. Better to leave him with the memory.

9:46am.

I drove to McDonald's and chowed down breakfast, replaying our fuck in my head, rather chuffed in myself. Fighting families and couples who stunk of alcohol in the surrounding booths must have thought me mad. I smiled as I ate, and we all knew that shit didn't taste very good.

My phone vibrated across the lacquered countertop. Jordan had messaged my Grindr account as I'd hoped he would. As I kind of *knew* he would. The memories I'd left him with mustn't have been half bad, after all.

> Fun times.
> Here's my number.
> Don't lose it, ok.

Canberra peeled past the windows as I drove. The thin Saturday crowd jittered from building to building to escape the cold. I was glad Arthur hadn't put that nomination in for me and that the interviews had dried up. Anonymity suited me fine. I was no different from the people on the other side of the window, just another blur on a boring day. As it should be.

I parked in the carport, only noticing the vehicle on the other side of the cul-de-sac when I stepped across the threshold and into our warm house. "Cousin Thom!" came Brandon's high-pitched voice, followed by thudding feet along the hallway. He launched, pounding the wind right out of me.

"Woah, little fella. Let me get my jacket off—"

"Eddie's here," he said, blue eyes peering from under the mop of his hair. He shrugged, begrudged in some way, such an adult slight. Brandon knew this was *his* time. I steeled myself as I rounded the corner, passing the kitchen where Arthur had left his bottles of homemade kombucha to ferment on the counter. I followed television noise into the living room.

Eddie sat at my end of the couch, my housemate at the other.

"Look who's here, Thom," Arthur said, eyebrows arched a tad too high. Three takeaway coffees sat on the table by the newspaper with our article tucked inside it.

Eddie reached to pick up a cardboard cup. "I hope your drink is still hot. It's from Hudson's in the city. Good stuff, right?"

Brandon sat on a pillow in front of the flat-screen. "Not so close, buddy," Arthur said, standing. "Your eyes will go square. How about we head out for a walk, instead. Fresh air's the ticket. We'll let the boys have their catch up."

"I hope you don't mind me coming over," Eddie said.

"Unannounced."

Arthur led his son from the room after switching off the television, taking the kid's complaints with him. The hush left behind irritated me as much as the man on the couch himself.

"What are you doing here, Eddie? Just in the neighborhood?"

"Not really. I thought of you guys. Who doesn't like surprise coffees?"

"I appreciate that, mate. But you can't just come over here willy-nilly. We can't have strangers in the house when Brandon's about. His mother would be fit to be tied. I don't want to get Arthur in any hotter water than he's already in, you know?"

"Of course. I didn't think. Guess I didn't consider myself a stranger 'round here is all."

"No."

"I wanted to say thank you again—"

"Look, Eddie. You don't need to do anything else for me." My voice took on a long-overdue sternness. "In fact, I insist on it. It's all making me a bit uncomfortable."

"I'm sorry, Thom. I didn't mean—"

"I know you didn't, mate. It's fine. Let's cool things off for a while, yeah?"

Eddie stared, a splinter in my skin, pointed and jarring. "I'll leave now."

"That's for the best." I extended my hand for a shake that wasn't reciprocated. Eddie mumbled apologies as he scuttled past. His melancholy was mold I couldn't scrape from the room afterwards, no matter how I tried. Eddie came here with good intentions and I'd made him feel a wrongdoer. Stuart used to say I did that to him all the time.

Brandon and Arthur came home afterwards in their matching pea coats. My roommate pulled me aside to tell me this weird shit had to stop.

I slinked into my room and studied old photos on my phone.

Someone is in the house.

The mattress groaned as I rolled onto my side, studying the not-quiet, a held breath's unease pressing in on me from every side. A plate clanked. The clunk of a pan.

"Jesus."

Arthur was at his old house in Ainslie, no doubt relegated to the couch, surrounded by the ruins of Brandon's eighth birthday party.

Those acute kitchen sounds stabbed at my ears again. Fear trickled away to let in anger, and that anger made the sparrows shy back to their nests behind my ribcage. I'm not sure *how* I knew what was going on, but I knew just the same.

You've got to be fucking kidding me.

I crept from my room and into the hallway (after doing a furtive check down the hall first). My feet wisped over the old carpet, following the blade of light spearing from the kitchen. I approached Eddie with mobile phone in hand. He knelt in front of the cupboards by the refrigerator where receipts and bills were pinned with magnets Brandon made at school. He had brought them in for us to see, five well-crafted wooden butterflies cupped in his hands. "They're not butterflies, Cousin Thom," Brandon said, almost annoyed. "They're moths."

"You know you can't be here," I told Eddie.

He slouched, clicked his tongue. Eddie drew himself upright and turned to face me, a frying pan he could brain me with in hand.

"Put that down, please."

Eddie did as he was asked.

I thought back to that morning in our yard after the second interview, how emotions skimmed the face of the man I'd saved and never quite stuck. Since then, I'd witnessed smiles that were grimaces at best, eyes that were cold to their core. The man wasn't well, no two ways about it.

Eddie began to weep.

I held true. Had to. My relationship with Stuart came to an abrupt end because I thought it would be okay to cheat. This small rental I shared with Arthur was all I had left to my name, not including the car. And everything would crumble again if I let Eddie shift this already tenuous architecture. What was a man, even a gay man, I wondered, without a home? I hated myself more than ever when this thought coalesced.

The risk was just too high.

Eddie glared, shook his head.

He *has no home.* He *is what happens.*

"You know I need to call the police. Don't you?" I said, breathing fast. I didn't want him to see how far he'd pushed me.

"All I wanted was to cook for you, Thom," Eddie said, putting the pan down and clasping his hands. "I remembered from our lunch. How you said you didn't like being in the kitchen." He shied from my eyes, humiliated. "I thought it would be a nice way to say thank you. I wanted to acknowledge y—"

"Eddie, stop."

"You *are* grateful," he said, moving his head in a birdish way. "Aren't you?"

A draft of icy air curled about my feet. Eddie had broken in.

"Leave," I told him. "And never, ever come back."

"*Are* you grateful, I asked? Come on, you owe me an answer if nothing else."

"What planet are you on, Eddie? I don't owe you shit. Get the fuck out of this house or I'm calling the police. Look, I can see you're—that—that—you're not doing okay. So, go *get* okay. I'll have a restraining order taken against you if you come back."

Eddie twitched. I wasn't sure if what I'd said struck where it counted most, yet I didn't need it to. I didn't need him cured. Just gone. Eddie limped into the hallway. I stepped back, watching him pull the latch on the side door, welcoming in another gust of freezing air. I turned on the outside light and walked him to his car on the other side of the cul-de-sac, my phone in hand the whole time. Eddie stepped into his Prius, the same one that had been parked in that very spot months ago.

("Eddie's here," Brandon had said.)

"Never again," I told him through the closed window. His profile was a green etching on the dark from the faint dashboard glow. I couldn't hear his reply. I'm not sure he intended me to, either. The concept of Eddie being the kind of guy who talked to himself didn't evoke much in the way of shock by that point, there on the street in my winter pajamas.

I called our landlords the following day to have the living room fly-screen Eddie broke in through repaired. "A bunch of kids were throwing stones in the night," I told them. "Scared the beeswax right out of me, to be honest."

It was possible that my pseudo-celebrity status still held sway with some. Everything had been fixed before Arthur got home that same afternoon.

I was too humiliated to tell him a thing.

III

Heat brought sleepless nights. A TV campaign urged everyone to keep an eye on the elderly to ensure they remained hydrated. We scrambled for our landlord inspection, only realizing how filthy everything was once it had been cleaned. My boss grilled me about the declining accuracy of my work, fingers rapping the table as she spoke. There were the wasp nests I knocked from the awnings. Overpriced haircuts and the fibs I told when the barber asked how I was doin'. The addiction to my phone, each Grindr ding! offering diminishing dopamine returns. More receipts pinned to the refrigerator. The beard I grew. Unremembered Netflix binges and the withdrawals that followed. Books went unfinished, so many of them. I loved reading. Once.

Those four months dragged by as though wounded.

My birthday came and went, too. Arthur licked wounds from a failed reconciliation with Tiff. She called afterwards and asked me to look after him because she couldn't anymore. Arthur and I drank as we always had, though I struggled to match him now. My mother said she wanted to visit again. I hadn't known how much I needed her until I picked her up from Canberra airport.

"Oh, my baby," she said, erupting into tears. "You're nothing but skin and bone."

I became accustomed to the ruffling and biting and pecking of the sparrows. Stupidly, I texted the guy I cheated on Stuart with one Friday after Arthur passed out on the couch, a message shot from a thunderhead of booze and limp-dicked horniness. No response. Maybe that was for the best.

Ma called every few days, handing the phone to my step-father on cue. His mumbles were a *kind* of comfort. The mortification of having prepared himself for a gay wedding he'd struggled to reconcile in the first place (only to have it fall apart in the home stretch) appeared to be an anchor he'd drag around with him forever.

I rang Stuart another night, too, despite Arthur telling me what a shitty idea it was. We spoke of what lay ahead, not of our best work. My ex told me I should be proud of how I'd helped Eddie, that I'd saved a life, regardless of how ugly things turned in the end. "You're a good guy," Stuart said. But I didn't feel like a good guy. I felt like a skin-sack of old habits and scabs I'd picked and kept so the wounds never had to heal. You know that your former lovers have truly left you behind when they no longer care how—or if—you're moving on. *Not* being asked was probably better, though it didn't feel that way at the time.

I also called Justin (turns out that *was* his name, go figure) a few times. The sex was more violent than I wanted it to be, yet I was the one evoking said violence. He told me to stop. I did. Too little too late, I guess.

The sparrows tried to chew their way out of me.

Brandon draped across his father's lap, the three of us a mess of limbs on the couch.

Arthur carried his sleeping boy to bed after the movie wrapped, limp arms catching the television glow, reminding me of late-night swims near my parents' house with friends, plankton drawn up through the waves by the moon. These memories were tied to the discipline that followed, Ma telling me that I should have known better than to swim at the beach so late.

Her hand on mine. Squeezing. "Don't you know sharks feed in the dark?"

It was Sunday night. Arthur and I were drunk.

Tiff had asked if Brandon could stay an extra day, although she hadn't told Arthur why. Her elusiveness didn't have to be spelled out to any of us. The knowledge that his ex had started dating again was a monkey Arthur carried on his back all weekend long. Brandon's school uniform hung from a hanger on the living room door, and the twinkling of reality TV stars threw its shadows across the wall, an elongated dancer waiting for a partner.

Arthur emerged from the hallway, beer in hand. "I'm turning in, too, Thom."

The clock by the door read 9:15pm.

"Night-night."

I stayed up until after eleven, double-checking the doors and windows, regardless of the heat I trapped inside. The flick of light switches here, there. Brushing my teeth. Reminded myself to book in for another skin check, having tanned over summer. I decided not to close my bedroom door. Too stuffy. The rotary fan spun from the corner. Reading didn't work its magic, so I bummed on my phone until sleep snuggled onto the mattress beside me, comforting and spoon-worthy. I must have drooled all over my pillow because it was wet when I woke.

The man at the end of my bed stepped back, moonlight revealing the length of a hypodermic needle. His face pinched with anticipation as he dove again, now empty fingers clamping my mouth. Ma's voice bolted at me:

Something sharp on the ground, Thom. Pick it up or Brandon will—

I thrashed Eddie until my arms stopped working. He glared down at me. The man I'd saved had turned my body against me, and it didn't matter that I commanded myself to fight or flee. Nothing worked. The sparrows did their summersaults all the same, claws scratching and scraping. They had never been hungrier. Every attempted cry came out a moan.

This can't be happening. Every window was locked. Every door. I made sure of it. I was careful. I'm always careful—ever since that night!

This whirlpool of confusion came to an abrupt halt. Dread.

And he *was careful, too,* Ma said. *If you closed this place up as well as you think, it means he was already* inside *the house at the time.*

My brain skimmed through every possible hiding spot, as though by pinpointing the intricacies of his plan I could trick this moment into not existing. However, there was only one conclusion. And it didn't change anything.

He must have been under your bed, Thom.

Another round of moans bubbled from between my lips as Eddie dragged me onto the floor and out into the hall. I felt it all—every carpet fiber grinding hairs until static electricity crackled in the dim. My insides liquified. I caught a glimpse of the hallway I'd coursed innumerable times to see the doors to Arthur and Brandon's rooms. Both were wide open, and only darkness beyond.

Sightless in the trunk of his car. Dizzying knocks of dust, engine oil, exhaust.

I prayed at some point, litanies for light again and to get out of this cramped space where I'd been folded like a picnic chair. There was relief in the tingles inching into my toes and fingertips. Only they inched too slow. Far too slow. And with the sensation there came pain. But I made the hurt a reclaiming of sorts. Had to.

Everything shuddered to a stop. Inertia rolled me

onto my face to lick the felt underlay. A car door slammed, followed by crunching footsteps, the click of a latch and then whooshing. Eddie was silhouetted against a billion stars like a billion pricks of his needle. He dwarfed me in an almost cosmic way and I'd never been more terrified. Only then did I clock the dampness between my thighs, the acrid smell of piss. Humiliation, I found out, proved a luxury.

"St-op," I stuttered, worming my arm out from under my chest to reach at him. He slapped my hand away, tender as a kitten with a ball of twine. He swallowed me with his enormous shadow. Tugged to the left. To the right. I slammed the ground, dirt clouding my mouth. The stink of sweat was stronger and bitterer on my kidnapper now, leading me to suspect that Eddie was more unnerved than he wanted to let on. As before, I tried to fight him off. And as before, I failed. Even rolling was too hard, let alone getting on my feet and running into—

The bush.

A thunder of crickets welcomed us.

Eddie had driven off the road and further into the scrub. The underbrush was equal parts mulch and jagged rock. He kicked me onto a tarp he'd wrestled from the back seat, making the stars time-lapse into contrails. Vomit ejected through my teeth and pooled about my hair. Everything reeked like the shit you drudge out of the sink after it's been blocked for a week. Eddie peered at me, curious, watching me marinate. He beamed a torch in my face, the brightness lancing skull-deep. Coughing obliterated whatever pleads I tried. Eddie tilted the torch to his face.

"I can't hear you, Thom," he said, voice stripped of inflection.

"N-no-oo. No."

Eddie was decorated in blood.

He turned away, leaving me to scream. All went unheard.

Eddie had brought me back to Bungonia National Park—a conclusion that wasn't drawn from recognition (it was too dark for that, really), rather through the symmetry of our story. *Of course, it would end this way*, I thought as he drew straps over his shoulder to lug the tarp, Santa Claus with a sack of bribes. Only then, as the earth grated under my dead-weight, did it occur to me that this might be the last night of my life.

The purity of that fear was cold. I could feel it surging. Harder. Harder.

I had plenty of time to think about Brandon and his father and those chipped, second-hand bowls we sometimes ate breakfast-for-dinner from. The newspaper Arthur left out on the coffee table. Our toothbrushes in separate glasses on the bathroom basin. Criss-crossing receipts and statements pinned to the refrigerator by magnets (moths, not butterflies). Father and son, and how their doors had been open yet neither came running to see what all the sound was about.

Bloodied sheets and mouths carved into their faces where mouths shouldn't be. Bodies on the floor. Brandon's school uniform on the hanger going unworn, Tiff screaming into its weave and later collapsing at the joint funeral.

I tried to convince myself that Brandon, at least, got away. Through a window, maybe. Deposited beside the house. Spiriting towards the street. The slap of his feet on bitumen as he ran for help.

But the fantasy carried no weight. No, not even a little.

I sensed their absence within me, a dead weight.

Tears mingled with the vomit slopping into my ears as the kidnapper groaned, heaving those straps again. This wasn't the wiry ginger I'd last seen in my house. The months between had been full of gym visits and planning sessions and nurturing the need to make this all happen. And it *was* happening. I wished he'd killed me in my bed, too, overdosed on whatever paralytic he'd injected me with, a liquid Iron Maiden to trap me from the inside out. Or maybe slit me open as I slept (as he had to Brandon and Arthur), waking at the grand finale to finger the hole he'd opened.

"Don't. Do. It," I managed to get out.

"Don't speak, Thom," he told me between pants. "You're making it worse."

The torch was strapped to his belt, its beam offering glances at the backpack on his shoulders. Blood rushed to my head as we shuffled up an incline. Tingles buffered enough of the numb to let me shuffle off the tarp at last. But Eddie put me back in my place, where he thought I belonged. He inspected me like the final piece of a puzzle he'd debated over for so long. Chance had no part to play in Eddie's orchestration. Knowing now that he'd schemed in my absence—that we shared the same world, the same city, the same newspaper article—was like learning you'd lived with a stranger, not a loved one, someone who with time took advantage of your leniency and blind-spots. The person who violated the most important things you'd once shared.

A name slipped across my lips.

We came to a stop. A calligraphy of moonlit dust. Air like cotton.

"Wh-what are y-you doing?"

Eddie trundled me off the crunching plastic, gravity dragging my arm to where the earth should be. Empty space greeted it instead, the sensation so similar to waking from a dream in which you were falling. "S-stop!"

Only Eddie didn't stop.

His movements played out on cue with not a second wasted.

He swung the backpack from his shoulders, the cry of a zipper. The noises that followed took me back to my step-father's shed as a teenager, not long after the divorce and before I came out, the day he tried to teach me how to spot defaults in a car engine. He tapped metal innards with a spanner. "This is where you check your water levels, okay? Are you listening? Good. This is your oil cap. Make sure it's on tight always otherwise your car will fill with smoke."

Clunk-tap went that spanner.

("Are you listening, Thom?")

Clunk-tap went whatever Eddie withdrew from the backpack.

"Puh-lease," I said. "I'm s—"

"Don't say anything. You're not meant to speak. Yet."

That final word pinged every nerve.

Yet.

Gasping, I tried to scramble through the dust, through the electric flare-ups in my joints. The valley misted in a eucalyptus haze beneath a bowl of stars—the enormity of it all snatched what breath remained in my lungs. Fingers reached for solid ground and fumbled at the bluff instead. *I'm at the edge of the cliff,* I thought, panicking. A faraway bird laughed. And why shouldn't it laugh? I never stood a chance.

Eddie flipped me onto my back.

"It's easier if you don't move," he whispered, close enough to kiss. Those eyes were darker than they had ever been, blackness sucked from spaces between stars. Eddie greased from my sight-line, though not for long. Time enough for a single inhale. He brought a sawn-off sledgehammer down on my right leg. The leaden *thwok* of snapping bones. Immediate, sun-white agony. Nothing made sense. Eddie swung the weapon a second time, breaking my other leg. *Wind-chaffed bergs on the outside of my skin, the bushfire that levelled towns within.* I was abandoned between these two extremes, confused until the exact moment I wasn't.

Eddie pushed me over the bluff. Time elasticized.

A burst of honeyed jasmine. The whistle of my fall as that bird continued its hysterics. Three distinct pulse-beats, that's all I got. Rocks have no mercy. I shattered in a dozen places. The taste of water drunk straight from the tap around the side of my parents' house filled my throat, coppery and full of grit. Oxygen didn't exist anymore. Not anywhere.

The cliff loomed ten yards above, the Milky Way a million miles beyond it. My watery eyes warped it all into a kaleidoscope of refracted light.

You're not meant to speak.

Yet.

It had been Eddie who said that before, but the sentence chimed in my mother's voice. *You didn't tell anyone that you were coming here, Thom. You knew the risks. I told you from the start that people die out there.*

They die.

"Hello?" Eddie shouted, his voice reverberating through the valley. Pain turned everything into television static, Brandon's voice flittering through those undefined stations to ask me about pain.

Yes, it hurts, I told him. Worse *than I thought anything could. A lot more than a smidge.*

"Is somebody down there?" Eddie yelled. "Hello?!"

Ma whispered again. *You weren't meant to speak before, but* now *it is your time to shine. Tell him what he needs to hear. Let him know you're here.*

Let him know how grateful you are.

Scythe moon cut the kaleidoscope, conspirator caught mid-wink. I sifted for a memory. I had walked this part of the National Park and heard the cicadas, the sigh of these trees, and how they shushed me to maintain their secret. Only it hadn't been their deceit masked out here—it had been my own. *Don't let on that you know what he's up to,* the bush clattered, bark against bark, in a million insects at once. *Don't let him know that you can play this game, too.*

Because if you play right, you might get through this.

"Can you hear me?" Eddie shouted again, loud and

flat.

Blood gurgled into my eyes, rouging the landscape I'd saved him from. Red. Red everywhere. The hue of Australian soil, the me beneath the skin. Agony was a catapult I loaded with the words Eddie wanted to hear. I gave him his acknowledgement. "YES! I NEED YOUR HELP. PLEASE HELP ME!"

My echo was carried on the wings of sparrows, freed.

THE GOLDEN BOY

BY HAL BODNER

THERE WERE TWO KINDS OF naked men in Jaime's life.

There were two kinds of naked men in Jaime's life.

The first was the kind that paid him. The easiest scores were the guys on the down-low, the ones who had wives or girlfriends in the Valley and were afraid of being found out. Their business with Jaime was over quickly. Often, they spent more time working up the courage to approach him than they spent doing anything once the deal was struck. Not too much worse were the brusque, businesslike types—the wealthy ones who liked to humiliate Jaime just to make sure he knew who was *really* in charge. As long as they paid Jaime's price without arguing, he didn't mind the insults or the names they called him.

If any of them lost control and actually hit him, well, Jaime was okay with that too. After all, he was an actor. It was easy to make the damage seem worse than it was. If the john balked at paying extra, Jaime only had to mention going to the hospital or to the police, and the trick usually forked over the dough with only a token protest.

Then, there were the lonely, pathetic guys who, after only a few dates, believed they'd fallen in love with him. Smart hustlers—and Jaime considered himself to be one of the smartest—knew that pretending to care was a great way to keep the johns coming back for more. The problem was that Jaime was *too* good at it. The illusion he created was so effective that some of his clients were convinced that they had a real relationship with him. They got all clingy and thought they should get the sex for free. When Jaime refused, they took it personally and reacted badly. One former john physically attacked a bartender he suspected Jaime was interested in, and Jaime found himself unfairly eighty-sixed from the place in spite of his protests that he had nothing to do with it. Another started stalking him and deliberately interfered when Jaime tried to turn tricks on Santa Monica Boulevard. Every time a potential customer approached, the asshole would throw a tantrum and behave like a jilted lover to scare the other guy away. It worked too, right up until Jaime beat the crap out of the old queen to make him stop.

At the other end of the spectrum were the men who needed to prove to themselves that they were better at the hustle than Jaime was. Though they were usually wealthy enough not to bat an eyelash at Jaime's rates, they got a kick out of trying to stiff him, if only so they could brag to their friends that they'd done it. Once word like that got out, it could cause a lot of damage. It didn't take a ton of experience to recognize the type. They bragged about how much things had cost them, and they could always be counted on to sneer at something Jaime did or said, as if to demonstrate to anyone who might be watching that they weren't fooled for an instant into thinking Jaime was anything other than street trash.

It stung a little, but Jaime hardened himself against it and refused to let it bother him. He simply upped his asking price as a matter of vengeance and demanded cash up front. If they balked, he walked. After all, *they* were the ones who desired *him*, not the other way around. And if *he* could get away with stiffing *them*, so much the better. So what if they got pissed off and threatened to call the police? Half of them would be too embarrassed to follow through, and the other half got off on being cheated in a weird kind of way. They took it as a personal challenge to show that they could outsmart some dumb street hustler, and they almost always came back for more in order to prove it. That was fine with Jaime, just as long as they continued to pay. He got even more of a kick out of it when some of them ended up turning into steady clients.

There was also a second kind of naked man, and it was the only one that Jaime truly lusted after. Jaime's ideal man was only thirteen and a half inches tall and weighed eight and a half pounds. He was bright gold, and although it was only plate, it was more precious to Jaime than real gold would have been. And his name was Oscar.

Jaime had few aspirations in life, almost nothing beyond turning enough tricks to pay the rent and keep him in cigarettes and designer duds. The only thing he truly wanted was to win one of the little golden statues of his own. From the day he was six, all those years ago in Kansas, when he watched the Academy Awards for the first time on his parents' ratty old black and white TV with the lousy reception, he knew what his life's goal was going to be. Ten years later, he took his handsome face and buff body to Hollywood, never doubting that talent like his could not remain undiscovered for long. Jaime figured he'd be getting around a million per picture and would have had at least a couple of nominations by the time he was twenty-one.

But things didn't quite work out that way.

Getting a break was nearly impossible. Before they'd agree to meet with him, the agents wanted to know what jobs he'd already done. He needed a resume and a "reel" of his previous jobs before he could get an agent. Yet, without an agent, he couldn't get work. It was a diabolic round-robin of frustration.

Jaime had heard stories, as had every other hopeful he met, of movie stars who were discovered while they were waiting tables, or while walking their dogs, or because they happened to meet a receptive director at a party. But the tales of young people slinking back to Minnesota or Virginia with crushed dreams and their tails between their legs were far more common. Jaime prided himself on being too sharp to just sit back and wait for the universe to grant him what he believed was deservedly his due. He knew that fortuity only favors the people who are brave enough, and canny enough, to take action and seize any opportunities that Fate provides.

It was silly, he thought, to waste time with endless rounds of acting classes and performance workshops.

Most of the schools were scams. Even the ones that boasted celebrity instructors were mostly a way for has-been sitcom actors to scrape up a few bucks teaching others what they had failed to do themselves. Besides, you couldn't *learn* talent! It was something you either had or you didn't. Jaime didn't need to spend hundreds of dollars on some stupid school when a good director could teach him anything he needed to learn in half an hour once they were on set and ready to shoot.

Jaime had other talents, and he saw no shame in using them.

As it turned out, casting couches weren't nearly as effective as the movies had led him to believe. Half the guys who *said* they'd make Jaime's career couldn't do a damned thing. But Jaime knew how to play the game just as well as they did, if not better. He learned to plaster a look of interest on his face and tune out just as soon as some guy began sprinkling his conversation with the names of celebrities he claimed to be friendly with. When he saw photos of his host with his arm flung across the shoulders of a movie star, who almost always looked caught off-guard, Jaime pretended to be impressed. And when the john's living room was decorated with cheap movie posters in expensive frames, Jaime knew it was only a matter of time before the trick began bragging about how the picture would never have been made without his contribution—even though his name appeared nowhere in the credits.

It was all Hollywood hype, the only defense that a bunch of pathetic losers had against having to confront years of failed dreams and thwarted ambitions. They were directors who had never directed anything other than porn, producers who couldn't pay their own rent, and agents without offices. Their talk was bluster and stage dressing, meant to imply they were connected and would be willing to help Jaime's career. In the end, it was nothing but a ruse to get Jaime to drop trow for free because, to be brutally honest, the sorry assholes couldn't really afford him.

Not all of Jaime's clients were phonies. But those few who were truly powerful and influential had no intention of following through on promises made in the throes of passion. Real producers weren't about to risk millions on a young man who had no proven talent other than the ability to suck the chrome off a trailer hitch at fifty paces. No director was willing to put his own career on the line to cast an unknown on the strength of his dick size alone. No studio exec would jeopardize his outrageous salary by hiring someone who might later slap him with harassment charges or a discrimination lawsuit.

No one would promote Jaime's career on the strength of a single orgasm. Not even on the strength of two.

Though he knew that sucking and fucking wouldn't get him his Oscar, Jaime was trapped. Hustling was all he knew; none of the mundane jobs he'd qualify for would come close to covering the rent. Besides, deep down, Jaime truly believed his talent would triumph over the million-to-one odds that he'd be discovered. Jaime *knew* he was destined to be the exception to the rule.

He worked hard to keep his body in great shape, and his face remained unlined, but time still passed. It was only a matter of time before he'd have to reduce his rates, or worse, start doing kink in order to make the same money he was making now. As youth slipped away, Oscar remained out of reach.

Then, Jaime met Cy.

In his late sixties, Cy was retired from the movie biz, and unlike many of his colleagues, he didn't engage in any ridiculous machinations to stave off time. Cy allowed himself to age gracefully. He eschewed hair dye and transplants, and he maintained a thick silver fringe that ringed his bald dome like a tattered olive wreath. If he no longer looked much like the photo of his twenty-five-year-old self that Jaime saw atop the piano, he still cut a relatively trim and stylish figure. It was only when he undressed that he revealed sagging pecs and a thickening around his middle.

His face was pleasant, unassuming, and ordinary, always tanned from running around town on errands in his convertible with the top down. Yet underneath the healthy glow of Cy's cheeks, Jaime occasionally caught a glimpse of something that made the older man look wan and haggard.

They met at one of the more exclusive private men's clubs. Jaime got in thanks to a blow job he gave the doorman; Cy was a paid member. From the start, Jaime was impressed by how much of a gentleman Cy was. The entire evening, Cy acted flattered to be dining out with such a handsome and talented young man, yet he didn't presume about how the evening would end. On later dates, the pattern never varied. Cy always treated Jaime as an equal and never acknowledged the financial imbalance between them. Before reaching for the check, he never failed to shyly ask if Jaime minded. They both knew Jaime couldn't afford it, but Cy made the gesture anyway. It was a little thing, and Jaime knew Cy did it to avoid hurting his pride

Nor did Cy ever suggest that he was owed anything in exchange for picking up the tab. He always insisted on chatting over a leisurely dessert, unlike so many other johns who called for the check almost before Jaime had swallowed his last bite, just so they could get him home and out of his clothes as fast as possible. In fact, Cy never presumed there would be sex at all. He always maintained the illusion that Jaime had a choice. The one time Jaime turned him down, just to test him, Cy accepted the rejection without protest, and with more class than Jaime thought any john could have. They spent the rest of the evening lingering over drinks, as if they were simply two friends sharing each other's company. Cy did such a good job of hiding his disappointment that when they finally left the restaurant several hours later, Jaime rewarded him by broaching the subject himself.

In spite of the difference in their ages, Jaime found Cy surprisingly easy to get along with. Most johns bragged incessantly about their money, sexual prowess, or anything else they thought might impress. But Cy didn't particularly like talking about himself. Jaime knew he'd once worked for one of the major studios and had made a ton of money at it, but he could discover little else. Without being obvious, Cy always managed to divert the conversation back on to Jaime. Normally, Jaime hated clients who pried into his personal business, but this was different. Cy had a way of focusing while he was listening, as if Jaime was the most important person in the room and every word he said was the most fascinating thing Cy had ever heard. Even if there were other young men around, and even when some were better looking than Jaime, Cy's attention never wavered. It made Jaime feel good to be appreciated, for a change, for something other than his body.

Cy's demands in bed were simple. Even better, everything was over pretty fast. Once Cy became Jaime's regular Friday night score, he could be on the prowl again by nine, and with any luck at all, he could turn another trick or two by last call. However, as he continued seeing Cy, Jaime found himself more inclined to linger at the older man's apartment for a post-coital drink or a little chat. Then, one night, for no particular reason other than that he felt like it, Jaime simply rolled over and stayed until morning.

The overnights were sporadic at first but soon became a habit. Jaime kept alert for early signs of possessiveness, but Cy never took it for granted that Jaime would stay. On the contrary, he seemed pleased, even surprised, whenever the younger man decided to spend the night, and he always insisted on paying extra. It was only when Cy asked him for a midweek date that Jaime panicked. Worried that the old man was leveraging for something more permanent, he turned him down. Cy accepted the rejection graciously and didn't ask again. Several weeks passed, and although Jaime kept an eye out, Cy showed no signs of possessiveness. Within a month, much to his surprise, Jaime found that he was the one who wanted to revisit the subject. Of course, Cy was receptive. Two nights a week turned into three, and then four. Before too much longer, Jaime moved in.

One he became, for all intents and purposes a kept boy, Jaime braced himself for the relationship to change and become more difficult. He expected a certain amount of jealousy to be a given—perhaps a few interrogations about where he went when he wasn't with Cy, and demands to know who he was with. But none of that materialized. Cy accepted Jaime's need to roam with equanimity. He never questioned him about their time apart and never complained or whined, even when it was obvious that Jaime had tricked with someone else.

The only difference, in fact, was the sudden speed with which Cy seemed to grow older. At his age, wrinkles were to be expected. But it was as if someone had pressed fast-forward on Cy's life. It seemed like the lines around his mouth and on his forehead deepened into heavy creases between one day and the next. Within the span of a few weeks, he developed jowls that sagged like a basset hound's, and dark bags developed under rheumy eyes with newly jaundiced eyeballs. Practically overnight, liver spots erupted on Cy's skull and spread across his forearms and hands.

Jaime became concerned in spite of himself. Of course, he was worried about Cy. Rapid aging like that wasn't normal, and Jaime's first thoughts naturally flew toward cancer. But even more so, he was concerned for himself. He *liked* the freedom from responsibility that living with Cy afforded him. He'd grown used to it, and if anything happened to Cy, he'd be back on the street, that much older and with no steady clients, worse than when he started. There were things he and Cy needed to discuss, things like wills and putting Jaime's name on deeds and bank accounts. But before he could figure out how to broach the subject with Cy without coming across too much like a gold-digger, something happened to distract him.

Oscar showed up.

He found the statuette, completely by accident, while he was rooting around in the back of Cy's closet. As impossible as it was for Jaime to imagine that anyone could have forgotten about getting an Oscar, it seemed like that was exactly what had happened. At some point the award must have fallen off a shelf and been hidden behind a rack of rarely worn formal shoes. Cy had apparently never missed it. Awed by the physical reality of something that, until now, had been as close as Jaime had ever gotten to believing in any higher power, he lifted it with reverence and carefully used his shirt to brush away the dust bunnies that clung to the shiny surface. He cradled it like the rare and cherished object it was, and as his fingers gently stroked the naked form, his stomach churned from the force of the emotions that roiled within him.

He suddenly realized how complacent he'd grown in the months since he'd moved in with Cy. The budding affection he'd been feeling for the old man had almost enticed him into making a horrible mistake, and he'd been in danger of allowing someone else's needs to take priority over his own. Now, with an Oscar in his hands—a *real* Oscar, not just a pipe dream, an actual statue that he could feel and hold and touch!—Jaime felt the old drive return in a rush. Once again, he knew how important it was for him to share his talent with the world, and he could have kicked himself for the time he'd wasted. True, it had measured only in months but he had only narrowly escaped measuring it in years. How ironic that he'd expended so much effort by tricking with deadbeats, wanna-bes, and users when, without even trying, he'd gotten himself involved with someone who had legitimate connections, someone who actually cared about him as more than just a simple fuck.

Jaime could work with that.

Cy had barely stepped across the threshold when Jaime brandished the statuette and hurled the question at him. "Is this real?"

Cy seemed confused by the question. "Of course."

"You never told me you won an Academy Award!"

"I didn't think it mattered," Cy replied with calm amusement. "Besides, it was a long time ago."

"It's an *Oscar*! Why did you hide it like that? You should have it out."

"I know it's there and what I did to get it. I don't need a constant reminder"—he shrugged—"and who do I need to impress?"

"It impressed *me*!"

Cy chuckled at that.

"You should have told me. You *know* how I feel about acting—about my career."

"I thought you'd given that up."

Cy hadn't intended to be cruel, but the comment cut Jaime far deeper than any insult. It felt even worse than the first time his parents had called him a whore. His cheeks grew flushed with shame. Though he'd die before he admitted it, not even to Cy, he saw what his own laziness had almost allowed to happen. He'd almost sacrificed his dreams and abandoned his ambitions, just for something as boring and ordinary as a roof he could depend on and three squares a day.

"Never." Jaime breathed with more passion than he'd ever shown to any of his bedmates. But it was unclear which of the two of them he was trying to convince.

"Good!" Cy smiled. His teeth, which Jaime remembered as once having been very white, looked dingy and yellow. "Keep it out on display if you like. Maybe seeing it will be an inspiration for you."

Jaime first considered putting the award on the mantle over the gas fireplace. On second thought, he set it in the middle of the dining room table. That way, he could see it every time he passed from the bedroom to the front door, and every meal they ate would act as a reminder of what he had almost given up.

While Cy was away doing whatever he did during the day, Jaime alternated his time between working out in the condo's gym and sitting at the table for hours, staring at the statue with his chin propped upon his fists, dreaming of the day when he would win one for his very own. Fragments of his acceptance speech bounced around inside his brain; visions of red carpets and *E! Entertainment* interviews populated his dreams.

The engraved plate was too tarnished to be deciphered and oddly defied all of Jaime's attempts to clean it. Consumed by curiosity, he pestered Cy for details. But the old man's incomprehensibly stubborn refusal to discuss the matter gave rise to their first and only argument. Jaime used every technique he knew, from begging to tantrums to threats of leaving, to try to get Cy to open up. He even challenged Cy to prove that the Oscar was real and not just a Hollywood Boulevard imitation for the tourists.

Nothing worked. Cy stood firm and merely looked tired and a little sad when Jaime stalked off in tears, resolved to find out for himself. Nothing should have been easier than an online search, yet every time Jaime sat at the computer to look, he was distracted. Sometimes it was the phone; other times UPS or Amazon picked an inconvenient moment to ring the bell. But mostly it was the Oscar itself that diverted his attention. It seemed to entice him to look at it, to admire it, not like an idol demanding worshippers— Jaime would never have given in to that!—but rather as if it and Jaime were kindred spirits. Its golden surface seemed able to capture Jaime's own desire to be respected and desired, and to reflect it back at him in a way that satisfied him like nothing else in his life ever had. Each time it caught his eye he'd come to his senses hours later, often still sitting in front of the computer, but with all thoughts of discovering what he'd wanted to know driven from his mind.

Once, he made it as far as the search page. As he began to type, he was dumfounded when he realized that, even after living with Cy for all these months, and even though he must have seen dozens of utility and credit card bills lying around, he had no idea what the old man's last name was. Before the extreme strangeness of his situation could fully penetrate, he was overtaken by the fugue once again and did not emerge from it until Cy came home several hours later.

Soon, Jaime's days began to blur into each other, and his existence became dreamlike. The food he ate had no taste, and his sleep brought him no true rest, disturbed as it was by dreams of red carpets, gold-trimmed envelopes, and a sea of famous faces starting raptly up at him, dreams that were as fleeting and as feverish as frustrated nocturnal emissions. He made his way around the apartment like a zombie until even his daily workouts became a matter of rote, and he wasn't truly conscious of lifting the weights.

Only two things in his life were manifest with crystal clarity: Cy's increasing decrepitude and the award itself. It was a mark of Jaime's powerful instinct for self-preservation that he was able to rouse himself, just barely, to voice his concern about the former.

"You should take better care of yourself," he mumbled at breakfast one morning. "If anything happens to you, what happens to me?"

Cy declined to answer, occupied as he was with a bowl of thin oatmeal. Lately, anything he ate tended to run down his chin like drool, even when his trembling hand managed to guide the utensil into his mouth. Yet even though the palsy increased, he still left the apartment every day and went off to God-knows-where to do God-knows-what, leaving Jaime alone with Oscar.

In time, it wasn't enough for Jaime to bask in the statuette's presence. Being around it, absent anything else, left him unsatisfied and longing for more. He wanted—he *needed*—more from Oscar, but he couldn't concentrate enough to figure out what he needed. He tried. God knows, he tried. He sat for hours, running his palms over the smooth metal, trying to get his thoughts in order, relishing the statue's coolness, feeling an unspecified desire building that remained tantalizingly out of his reach, reverently massaging the award as if it were made of flesh and not mere metal, fondling it. His fingertips tingled where they made contact with the gold plate, and an electric sensation flowed from his hands up his arms to spill over into his torso like warm, scented water flowing from a hose into a bathtub. To his surprise, he found that he had a massive hard-on.

He ran the statue up and down the bare skin of his arm, thrilling at the sensations it produced. Without pausing to wonder at the strangeness of what he was doing, he stripped off his shirt and rubbed the Oscar across his chest and stomach, under his arms and along the sides of his neck and throat. He shivered from the deliciousness of its touch and imagined he could hear the distant applause of the crowd as he emerged from a limo and set foot on the red carpet. A light sweat broke out on his forehead as invisible interviewers thrust equally incorporeal microphones into his face, and demanded to know what designer he was wearing and what it was like to work with his famous co-stars.

It wasn't long before he removed his pants as well, the better to use the Oscar to trace the line of his calves and to run it up the insides of his thighs to tease his balls. A moan burst from deep within his chest as the pressure built, and a ribbon of pre-ejaculate dangled in a thick, heavy strand from his cock. He delayed the anticipation as long as he could, but at the very second that the presenter in his fantasy called out his name, the Oscar touched the tip of his dick and he exploded into a mind-shattering orgasm that, all too soon, left him still heaving and sweating in spite of his exhaustion, his body wracked with shudders from the intensity of what had happened.

But he was not quite finished.

As he weighed the Oscar in one hand, feeling the substantial heft of it, a lazy grin spread across his features, though the expression never quite reached his eyes. As if in a trance, he bent double over the table, pressing his abs against the polished wood. With his free hand, he spread the cheeks of his ass as wide as he could, flexing the muscles and relaxing the sphincter. His mind drifted into fantasy again, and for a moment, it was as if the audience was in the room with him, giving him a standing ovation as he made his way down the aisle toward the front of the theater. He inserted the top of the little gold man into his rectum. It was agony at first—he was not lucid enough to remember to use lube—but the pain was muted by the veil of his imagination. In his mind's eye he clearly saw the flight of nine red-carpeted stairs leading up to the stage. As he mounted each one, he increased the pressure on the Oscar, driving the little man's head that much more up his ass.

By the time he reached the podium, he had pushed the statue almost all the way in. Only the width of the base kept it from vanishing completely inside him. The tender tissue of his rectum, punished beyond what Nature had designed it to endure, ceased resisting and tore. His anal canal, stretched to the limit, was on the verge of ripping open as well.

Jaime hugged the presenter and kissed her on both cheeks, while a thin stream of blood trickled unnoticed down the backs of his thighs. As he leaned forward into the mic and began to speak, he reversed the course of the Oscar, tugging it backward until he had almost completely removed it from his ass. And then, simultaneously with the first words of his speech, he rammed it in to the base again.

"I would like to thank"—he gasped—"all of the members of the Academy and the Board." Again, he slid the award almost all the way out, and then slammed it home. "The Board of—*oh, God!*—of Governors for making all my dreams come true. This award—"

In his fantasy, he raised the golden statuette above his head in triumph. In reality, he thrust the award so deeply up his anal canal that his prostate ruptured.

"This award represents—*yes! Oh yes!*—a lifetime of sweat and tears and—*holy fuck!*"

The muscles of his arm stood out in bas relief as he pumped his ass with Oscar—in and out, in and out—

completely oblivious to the blood, torn bits of tissue, and fecal matter that were gushing down the insides of his thighs.

"And I would like to thank my—*gaaah!*—my director, and my agent, and of course, I would like to thank—to thank—to thank God, and—*oh God! Oh God! In my wildest dreams I never thought I would ever be coming to—coming—I'm cumming! Sweet Jesus! I'm gonna cum!*"

His penis erupted for a second time, and if possible it was an even more powerful ejaculation than the first one. Jaime's hips pumped in tandem with each thrust of the Oscar. His rhythm never faltered until the last few drops of jism spattered onto the parquet. When he was finally finished, he collapsed atop the table, his torso drenched with sweat and his legs streaked with blood. His hand fell away from the Oscar, leaving it sticking partway out of his ass.

Jaime moaned. Simultaneously with the sound, his nerves registered the agony of his brutalized body for the first time—a searing, burning pain that gripped his innards as if they had been brutally wrenched from inside him—as, indeed, they had been. He screamed, bewildered by the pain and unable to understand how he could possibly endure it for another instant. He wondered who would want to torture him like this, and why, and it was only after he saw his own bloodied hands that he understood that he had done it to himself. He shrieked even louder at the realization and a river of tears ran down his cheeks rivaling the blood gushing from his ass.

His stomach clenched and nausea overtook him. He doubled over and retched, and the contraction of his stomach muscles only made the pain worse. He tried to remove the statue from his ass, but it was either jammed in place or too slicked with blood and body fluids for him to get a grip. He gave up and took a few stumbling steps toward the telephone. For a moment, he flushed with shame at the thought of the kinds of jokes the paramedics would make when they showed up and found him like this, but his embarrassment was short-lived. Jaime coughed once; the worst agony yet gripped his belly, and he slid to the floor, unconscious.

For several long minutes, the apartment was silent save for his labored breathing and the occasional drop of fluid as it plopped onto the parquet. Gradually, a slight wisp of sound, no more perceptible than the rustle of dry leaves or the crinkle of antique pages turning began to build until the room was filled with cacophony of a windstorm. Loud pops echoed from the ceiling as Jaime's joints were stripped of connective tissue, followed by the sickening crunch of snapping bone and the squelch of his organs compressing until they burst.

Jaime's complexion paled beneath his tan, and something stretched the skin of his torso and back until it was shiny with tension. For an instant Jaime appeared as muscular as an anatomist's model, but the illusion vanished when the tissues, muscles, and tendons collapsed upon themselves, leaving him as skeletal as a mummified corpse. No longer handsome, his face was drawn inward as if by powerful suction, and his eyeballs withered and sank into his skull. Seconds later, the sharp blades of his cheekbones sliced through bloodless flesh. Every hair on his head retreated into its follicle, and in an instant, Jamie was completely bald. His armpits, chest, and groin were soon bare as well. Had it not been for the eldritch desiccation that wrinkled his skin like antique crepe, he would have been as hairless and smooth as a newborn.

His body continued to spiral into ruin. Mercy played no part in the process slowing down; there was simply no more damage to be done. Jaime's body was twisted and abused far beyond the skills of the most sadistic torturer. As if in final insult, in the last seconds before silence fell once again, the muscles of his buttocks released what little tension they still held, and with a dull clank, the Oscar slid to the floor. The little golden man was far more recognizably human than the tattered remains that lay scant inches away from it.

A short time later, Cy returned home. Jaime would have been astounded by the change in his former benefactor. It wouldn't have been entirely accurate to call him young, but the advancing decrepitude of the last few months was gone, and in its place was an electric vitality. His gait, when he crossed to the lumpy mass of flesh lying on the dining room floor, was vigorous and sure—almost bouncy—and when he stood looking down at the corpse and considering the tableau before him, he absently ran his fingers through a full head of lush, dark chestnut hair. And when he knelt to retrieve the statuette, he rose without shortness of breath and with nary a twinge in his lower back.

Cy lifted the award gingerly and carried it to the tub, using only his fingertips so as not to dirty himself with the encrusted filth. He used the shower sprayer to rinse off the worst of the mess, and finished up with a thorough scrubbing in the bathroom sink. When he was satisfied that it was completely clean, he dried it with a special towel he'd successfully hidden from even Jaime's prying eyes, which he kept specifically for that purpose. He spent the next hour carefully and lovingly polishing away any blemishes, real or imagined, until the award gleamed as briskly and as brightly as the day he'd won it. When he was satisfied with the sheen, he stowed it carefully back in the closet.

Only then did he return to the dining room to bundle up the remains. He sponged up the blood and fluids, clucking gently to himself until he was sure nothing had seeped into the wood and permanently stained the parquet. The larger bits and pieces went into a garbage bag. Later on he'd take everything to the incinerator in the building's basement. When he was finished, it would be as if Jaime had never existed.

Fortunately, the boy had been young and strong. With any luck, Cy might last several years before he had to take another lover. Until then, he had plenty of things he might do to occupy his time. Why, if the right project came along, he might even consider producing another film!

One thing he wouldn't concern himself with was worrying about where the next young man would come from. This was Hollywood after all. Bright-eyed, delusional hopefuls were a dime a dozen.

The one thing they all shared, the thing he thrived on that kept him young, was the easiest thing in the world to take from them—

Their dreams.

SICK IS THE NEW BLACK

BY ANDREW ROBERTSON

"OMG YOU ARE SOOOO LUCKY, Derek," Tyson drawled.

Shimmying a bit, he stepped through the clear zippered sheet stuck firmly to the door frame of Derek's hospital room in studded four- inch heels without a hint of hesitation. His shoes made him a towering six-foot-five and he had to duck to make it under the transom. "You should see how many people are waiting outside practically gagging that you're here! You've made it!"

Zipping the door shut, Tyson smoothed the plastic of his biohazard suit so anyone passing could better see his outfit underneath, which included a pink-satin lined long black cardigan that cost a fortune, then stared down at his friend in the hospital bed. It was a ridiculous and pointless exercise, he knew, but it was important to him. Artifice was like a little taste of religion.

"Take off that fucking plastic bag; you look like someone's dry cleaning!" Derek howled. "You clearly haven't told them yet, standing there in your shameful clingfilm cocoon. If you did, they would have stuck you in here like a prisoner with me instead of letting you parade around like a sad balloon. I should tell them the truth, force you to be honest for once so you can be a filthy pariah too. You always wanted to be me anyway, we could be twinsies. Why else would you have done *you know what?*"

Tyson felt a sting of embarrassment touch his cheeks, which was ridiculous. He knew Derek liked to be a bit fierce, but even after all this time, after everything they had been through, Derek's barbs could still get stuck in his more sensitive areas. They had both agreed to do this, Derek just had a head start.

He slowly and intentionally pulled down the zipper of the medical garment bag he wore and stepped out, turning his face to the side to hide the tender pink blossom of his cheeks. He dropped the offending husk on the floor and rubbed his hands against his hot cheeks. The two of them were as close as freaky bitches could be, but Derek thrived on the weakness of others and this close to the end Tyson didn't want that bitterness to flavor the air around them. After how close they had become in Derek's more tender moments, he didn't want to be the final target of Derek's razor-sharp tongue. They were besties, after all, and that would last forever.

Despite his sorry position on the bed, Tyson could see Derek's fashion sense was more than intact. He wore a pink and teal gown paired with a black veil, a bit askew, but perfectly tatty. Pink and black were the colors of the movement. His frail-looking body was propped up by pillows and few errant teddy bears. He was as unrealistically thin as he always wanted to be, but still so radiant and real, still living and on the edge of glory. He was covered by a hospital bedsheet up to the waist, but everything above the sternly pressed clinical grey cotton was bright and alive. There was no fear in Derek's icy blue eyes. That's what made this so exciting. There was nothing Derek wouldn't do for his art or to see his dreams come true.

A small and ancient television hung from the ceiling. From its speakers spilled muttered details of terrorism and weather as background noise. Derek's eyes strayed toward the screen as the stories changed.

"Waiting for something?" Tyson asked, knowing that the journalist had been here, the one trying to blow the lid off the whole movement. Derek had promised to wait 'til Tyson's arrival to do the interview, but now was not the time to inflame petty squabbles. And either way, she had no imagination that one. Joey the Journalist. The little idealist chasing something she could never understand.

"My story! You know that, cunt. How could you not?" Derek spat as he spoke, a symbolic but unintentional gesture as most of his functions were at this point. His voice dropped as he looked toward the window, lying to the gray sky beyond. "You never showed up, so I had to do it without you."

Derek never changed, but everything around the two of them had since Derek made global headlines. The whole way up in the elevator, Tyson was sure he was going to have a panic attack or hyperventilate. It was all so overwhelming. There was so much about the past week he couldn't tell Derek—it would destroy him —but there were so many things to celebrate. Derek's story was finally breaking on a major network. People had finally realized that the Exiters were part of a real movement, the first of their kind, and Derek was the figurehead. Tyson just needed to hold on a few more days, push through the pain.

The media coverage, the social campaign, the photoshoots, the fundraising pages... it had all happened so quickly, in a matter of months. And despite intentionally contracting multiple fatal diseases, some antique, Derek was still on top of his game. He would and could finally be *the first*. After so many fakers who quit before they made it, Derek had found a way. He was unstoppable just like always. That was what made Tyson's heart skip a beat. What Derek said, he did. It was reassuring as much as it was terrifying, but true art should be just that: a voyage into the unknown with a well-dressed guide.

"Omg I wish I could go out and see all my fans," Derek said with mock sadness in his voice, but of course he preferred to be called by his stage name, Miss D. That's how everyone online knew him too. The Notorious Miss D. "No one wants to ignore their fans, but they won't let me leave the room, even with a nurse and all that biohazard pap." His eyes lit up and flickered with purpose. "It's because I'm 'refusing treatment' so the fuzz say I gotta stay here 'til whatever happens happens. I mean, it's incurable, what the fuck do they think they could do even if I didn't 'refuse treatment?' Give me Advil and a suppository? A freakin' exorcism? That would be fun for sure, but it's incurable and so by definition, none of that other stuff matters. It's not like I set out to fake everyone like those other Exiter-wannabe Edgers. I'm Exiting and on top of the game, bitches! I mean, that's the whole point!" Derek let out a shrill laugh and then looked Tyson dead in the eye. "How many do you think there are out there?"

"Oh, shit girl, maybe fifty?" Tyson read Miss D's face and then amended his response, awkwardly brushing his platinum curls off his face with long black nails and looking sideways. "Probably closer to a hundred really, my math is trash and it was soooo hard to shove my way through them all... and then there's the security the hospital got to keep most of your fans out... well and the Anti-Vaxxers with their counter protest or whatever, which is such a fucking joke now!"

Both laughed a little too loud, like a maniac's stage whisper. Both could sense but not admit to the other that their reactions were practiced for an audience that wasn't in the room with them, but they were fully aware of a potential and ravenous audience just out of convenient earshot.

"I'm sure there would be more, but they won't let them in," Tyson confided softly, excitement betraying his cool demeanor and making his voice tremble. "The ones that are here refuse to leave, and I would swear by the smell that some are wearing diapers. It's a Lysol ad out there. Like, handle your own problems, am I right?"

"Handle your own shit!" Miss D screamed, not missing the opportunity to be on top of the punchline. "Fucking Edgers, they can't even commit!"

"And most are livestreaming anyway," Tyson

continued breathlessly, "crying, and screaming, and wishing they were you."

"Are any of them good-looking?"

"There were a few that were cute, I guess. One kind of jockish guy, kind of hot. He was standing with a straight-up goth Sicker. She was so Lolita there couldn't be any more lace or special effect maquillage left in the village. Probably thinks if he hangs for long enough, she'll suck him off in the handicapped bog. I mean, what's the point if you aren't going to catch anything, right?"

"Ha! Sickers. Those bitches are so lame, with their makeup and red eyeliner. I mean boo hoo! No one believes anything is wrong with you outside of bad cosmetics. And her boyfriend's probably a closet-case anyway. A power-bottom at the least," Miss D smiled, a bit brighter thinking of all the jealous bitches and fans he had outside, waiting to see or hear what would happen next, *literally* shitting themselves so they didn't miss a thing. A skein of drool appeared at the edge of his mouth, which he wiped away quickly with his good hand. *You always must be photo ready,* he reminded himself. *Doesn't matter about the neck down anymore, you're past that, but from the neck up, be dragulous! Final frame, girl!*

His gaze returned to the television, eyes popping Manga-style as his hand scrambled for the clicker and hit the volume button with a digit sparkling with sweat.

"I'm on!" He screamed, coughing a bit.

Bright on the screen above, Joey the Journalist appeared in a story preview with Derek projected behind her looking demented and glamorous, if not a bit tortured by his well-curated terminal illness.

"Up at eleven tonight, my investigative report on a social media movement that started as a look and has raced toward what obsessed adherents are calling the first Exiter," Joey relayed with a serious expression as the Channel 4 logo spiraled in the lower right corner. "What is an Exiter? In an exclusive interview with worldwide phenomenon Miss D, we find out. Does 'D' stand for disease? Is this a fad, a religion, or a social media death cult? Who is their mysterious leader? I'll tell you how the Sickers became the Edgers, and how one Edger is looking to become the first Exiter in a dramatic and deadly twist to this freakish and unusual online movement, implicating the Anti-Vaxxers. Join me later for the full story. Viewer discretion is strongly advised."

The room was, ironically, deathly silent for a beat.

"Tyson, I am on the edge of making history," he said, taking a deep breath through his nose and smoothing the gown over his outrageous breast implants. They had started to be rejected by his body, with tiny lesions spitting pus if they were pressed too hard, but Derek wouldn't let the doctors remove them. There was no point now anyway, the implants might as well stay and do their job. "No one will forget what I am doing. This is my purpose; I just know it! I feel so fucking excited I would dance in the halls if they would let me, but anyway. There are so many rules now. Maybe I should post..." he almost asked, his voice starting to rise before he caught it and stopped. "Tyson, they took away my phone. They think I'm a bad influence, couldn't you gag? It's censorship if you ask me, so I'll need to log into my accounts on yours."

Tyson felt his heart skip knowing how close he was to a true legend, a part of fucking history. And a necessary part because he brought the only tool that could tell the story. He reached into his designer shoulder bag, the bright pink logo of the Exiters stitched on to the side as a symbol of their movement. Fuck the Edgers and their desperate attempts at attention. Exiters were the true artists, the true celebutantes of the movement. Very deliberately he stepped back from the edge of the bed and pulled the large smartphone from the black canvas interior with a large arcing flourish, nails shining, relishing how he could finally make Miss D wait just like he had done to him. All those times he fell asleep waiting for Derek to greet fans or write a new post or come down from whatever drugs he was taking to prove how fearless he could be. All those hours watching Miss D puke on himself in the tub; before, Tyson was always waiting, always subservient, but not now. Now he was an accomplice, a right-hand man. He was *necessary*. Not a fucking sidekick or an unread footnote. He was on the right side of history. Why else would he have willingly injected himself with Derek's blood if they weren't meant to do this together? He stood with the phone at arm's length, but just out of reach before dangling it closer. Point made. Then his hand began to tremble uncontrollably, and he almost dropped the phone.

"Did you bring my make-up?" Derek asked warily, noticing the movement of Tyson's hand, wondering if it was nerves or something else causing the weakness. Snatching the phone away and smiling in a way that couldn't be said to be warm or cold, Derek hit the home button to get to work. There was no eye contact as his face was lit up by the screen and he began searching the networks to see what his public was saying.

"Yes, baby girl, most of it."

Derek winced, but as Tyson dumped out the bag on the bedside table, his wince turned into a glance and then into a huge and genuine smile with only a few teeth missing. For any posts they would have to put wax over the discolored ones if Derek's flipper wouldn't hold onto the gums that were rapidly turning to pink mush. The flipper was courtesy of crowd funding and had worked for the first few months after Miss D realized his teeth were not going to stick around for the grand finale.

"Tyson, you are the best girlfriend a guy could ask for!" he screeched. "I'm going to get into face and we can send out an update that will give these bitches a real bout of fucking diarrhea!"

"Baby, some of them look like one more shit could be their last!"

The boys laughed, ignoring the nurse that yelled at them to keep it down through the zippered plastic doorway.

"You know their parents will rush in soon, finally uncuff them from the stairs or railings and force some antibiotics in them, maybe some sedatives, try and get them to be good, normal, bullshit kids with no ambition."

"I know, right Miss D? That's why you're..." he paused and stopped dead before continuing. "...we're different. We have goals. We are going to be legends."

Miss D let out a huffy breath, barely perceptible, accompanied by a sideways glance that may have been a bit shady. Tyson was used to it. Derek didn't want anyone even getting close to what he did, but it was too late. They both had it. He just hadn't told Derek how far along he was. He hadn't told anyone. It seemed to be moving much faster for him than it did for Miss D. If Tyson had to admit it, he was scared. Every inch of his body that was affected was covered, and he'd been taking uppers and morphine just to be able to walk, but soon it wouldn't matter. As soon as Derek Exited, he could let go and they would be together forever on the Rainbow Bridge.

Pushing aside the veil so he could start fussing with his face, Derek began dabbing on concealer and contouring. Despite years of practice, he was fighting with skin that wanted to rip and split more than it wanted to shine. Sighing loudly, he regarded a bloody tear as it wept a small red ruby. Giving up for the moment, he went back to the borrowed phone.

"Did you bring any crazy glue?" He asked as he logged in and scrolled through his feed. "I might need it to finish my face."

"I don't think so babe, I'll bring some next time."

"Shit, I've made another ten grand! People are behind me. And here's a new fan page, the Miss D-Zeaserz!" He laughed a genuine laugh that descended into coughing and an odd, unaffected silence.

Tyson wobbled over to the bedside chair, a horrid

green fuzzy thing covered in plastic like everything else. The four-legged abortion looked like someone skinned a muppet from that retro kids show, but he needed to sit down. He felt the sweat breaking out all over his body, cold pin pricks on the back of his neck right down to his ankles. The pulse on the back of his thigh where the alarming hole hid was getting stronger. Still, he didn't want to pull focus from Derek's work, so he casually fell into it and pretended to be checking his slick, black claws.

Then he looked up, slowly, careful that Derek wasn't watching, and took in his friend's face as his skeletal fingers furiously tapped at the glass screen in his hands. Tyson felt like he had been looking at that face his whole life. Such perfection. Even when Derek was mean to him, it was still better that he was there with him than anywhere else in the world.

Before they met, things had been much different. Tyson had grown up in a small town, but despite his strong southern accent, and the town drinking more whiskey per capita than advisable, it was not the type of small-town unimaginative assholes use as an easy punchline. Everyone had their teeth, no one played banjo, there were never any confederate flags or black bodies hanging from the trees. No one ever called him a fag. No one ever asked him *why* he was gay. No one ever cared.

Then his family moved to the big city. Everyone in high school knew that Tyson was gay the moment he walked in, and for some reason, they all cared about that more than their own business. After decades and decades of gay liberation, in some places, none of that seemed to matter. You still had these big city dads that would tell their sons to be real men and 'beat the queer outta those fairies' while daddy and son were both going on apps so they could fuck boys like Tyson.

But the second week he was at that big city school with all its money and bored teenagers waiting for something new, in walked Derek. Actually, it wasn't a walk so much as a runway prowl. Here was this hundred-foot-tall Amazon in a bejeweled camouflage bodysuit striding past the other students with their shitty comments and basic barbs, but there weren't enough fucks in the world for Miss D to waste even one on what he called 'the city hicks'.

Tyson was standing by his locker in silver sky-high platform boots paired with a long, fuchsia velvet coat, jaw swinging as Derek rolled up to him and introduced himself. Derek's hair was long and dark, pulled back in cornrows that ended in small metal beads. They clacked together as the four-inch heels rolled his hips. His eyebrows arched like a supervillain above an unbelievable smoky eye.

"I'm Miss D darling, who are you?"

That was all it took for Tyson to be fully, completely smitten. Maybe a little too smitten, but high school is a bitch. And then they dropped out to become creatures of the night. Club kids and drag queens. Then Sickers. Then Edgers. And finally, Exiters.

"I told you we would be legends," Derek said, snapping Tyson out of his reverie. As he looked up, Tyson saw a smirk on Derek's face like he knew exactly what Tyson was thinking. He felt a bloom in his cheeks again, but this time, it was because Derek's attention was warmer, maybe even loving.

"How far along are you? Do you know?" Tyson cautiously asked, desperate to change the tone before he looked weak.

Derek eyed him sideways, picking up the makeup again. The moment was lost. "Enough time to become a true legend, a true performance artist, a true fucking Exiter 'cause I'll be the first to do it for real. I. Will. Be. The. First!" He tapped the eyeliner against the bed railing to punctuate the words fired from his mouth like warning shots as he held eye contact with Tyson. "The original. Not some faker claiming their parents stopped them from going all the way because they panicked, or the doctors wouldn't respect their religion and all that shit. Half those kids didn't even have anything serious, it was all Halloween greasepaint and refusing to eat. Or when they did eat, it was binging chocolate then running to their laptop and barfing on cam to gain sympathy. I don't want sympathy. I want to be a symbol. I will be eternal."

"When I was a kid," Tyson began, "my dog barfed up an entire piece of cat shit he had eaten and then after looking at it for a minute, ate the shit again! That's what those kids are."

There was a wheezing, wet sound, like bubbles rising from mud before another sound like a burp being held in. A vicious, animal smell rose from the bed. Miss D shifted slightly, eyeliner clutched in one hand, compact in the other.

"Sorry hun, I didn't toot. It's just that the hole in my leg is opening again. Do you want to look? The skin kind of moves on its own now, like there's something else in there. It's almost looks like a pair of lazy lips that can't quite stay shut. I call it Garfield because it doesn't seem to like mornings, just like that old cartoon cat, but makes a lot of noise in the afternoon and the night. Isn't that a riot? I don't know how it feels about lasagna but really babe, it looks just about the same. I know it... smells a bit odd. Just spray some perfume about."

Tyson paused for a moment to process that, recognizing that he had something similar on the back of his leg that followed him around all day leaking and spitting. That's why he had taken to wearing PVC pants. Less evidence. Sometimes he would cough out loud when he thought that the wound was going to 'fart'... cause that's what it sounded and smelled like. In truth, thinking about the hole made his bowels loosen.

He snapped back to reality and picked up a spritzer bottle from the side table beside the flowers Derek's parents had sent ages ago and gave the room a good soaking. The smell Garfield made was horrifying, but it was all a part of the process. All things couldn't be glamourous. You have to break a few eggs and all that tripe, breathe in and count to ten. In a moment the whole room smelt of strawberries, maybe a bit overripe, but better than before.

"How many likes do you think I will get when I finally Exit?" Derek asked dreamily, staring up at the collage of Edger celebrities he had made on the ceiling. He always wanted to be a global superstar, even before the movement began and his conviction and sense of purpose had practically offered him worldwide notoriety on a plate.

Tyson was lost in thought looking at the flowers. They were long dead, and the water only filled the bottom inch of the vase if that, green and brackish. Derek's parents had stopped visiting when they realized that he wouldn't accept any treatment outside of what would ensure he wasn't a threat to the rest of the population. The hospital's role was to keep him in a sterile environment, spray down any guests, and see that he stayed in one place. The nurses also made sure he wasn't in too much pain either, now or when the end came. No doubt Derek would want to go out screaming like Eartha Kitt to show his commitment to the Exiters, shouting dramatic embellishments and slightly derivative Balenciaga's 'til the last breath. Miss D's parents were also really pissed when they found out how he had gotten so ill, but this wasn't about them. It was about the movement! And they were Anti-Vaxxers so what did they expect? You can't ride your high horse and then get off when it doesn't suit your complexion anymore.

Tyson didn't want to tell Derek that he had stopped treatment entirely. They had agreed that he would continue until Derek Exited, but it wasn't practical. First of all, it barely did more than make him sicker, but second, he didn't want to be left behind to face his Exit alone, at least, not for too long. He also didn't want to tell Derek about the massive hole in the back of his leg that looked like a scorched cave the size of a grapefruit, or how he could see the bones of his spine where the skin had turned tight and red and dry on his lower back, or how his eyes felt like sandpaper under the lids and he had to sleep with them open.

He felt a wave of heat and sickness pass over him as the visiting hours bell went off. Relief. He could leave and deal with the next wave of illness before their next visit.

"Baby, I have to go now, but wait for me until tomorrow bitch, don't die yet!" Tyson cackled but they could both feel a bit of artifice in the goodbye. He lifted the biohazard suit off the floor where he had dropped it in embarrassed agony and forced his aching joints to bend into the legs, then arms, and then pulled the thick zipper up to his neck. "I'll bring the glue. What you don't use we can huff!"

"Come early, balloon baby," Miss D. commanded. "If anything new and noteworthy happens overnight you need to capture it for the record. Can't count on Joey to stop by *every* day."

"Will do," Tyson responded with an air kiss before striding painfully to the door and unzipping it in a series of awkward movements, like watching someone with back pain trying to retrieve a dropped quarter. "I'll be back at first light cunt, and you can..." But he never finished. As he started to step through the zippered plastic door, he felt a knife in his chest and his muscles contracted involuntarily causing him to fall, urine leaking down his leg and bile surging in his throat. Wetness pooled under him as his thin frame hit the floor, bouncing once as the smell of antibacterial cleanser filled his sinuses.

As he lay in the doorway choking on vomit, half in and half out of the room with the hazmat plastic underneath him, he could hear Miss D's fans shrieking and surging against the barrier that kept them in place. Security was shouting orders and it seemed to be a losing battle as the sound of heavy footsteps rushed toward him, and cellphones flashed, documenting his ordeal.

And worse, he could hear Derek.

"No, you fucking bitch, no you don't! Not before me! I always knew you were jealous. Get up Tyson! Get up, I'm the first Exiter, I made the deal with him, he said I would be the first! You stole my blood you cunt," he stopped, coughing on phlegm. "You won't take this from me you fucking Edger!"

But all Tyson could do was lie there, regretting how this had ended.

Regretting that it wasn't his fans rushing toward him, and seeing their faces drop as they realized the body shaking and choking in front of them was Tyson, always the B-list sidekick.

Watching as they stepped over his body as it evacuated itself so they could get to Miss D, more than one with a syringe in hand.

Hating that some of them came back to kick him as Miss D. shouted violent orders at them.

Somehow, after pushing down all the pain, his body was making tears.

And he was making history. 𝕏

ABOUT THE CONTRIBUTORS

~ ANDREW WOLTER ~

Andrew Wolter is the award-winning author of several books, including *Much of Madness, More of Sin* and *Nightfall*. His short stories have appeared in dozens of online and print publications. Under the name Tristan Wilde, Andrew writes homoerotic thrillers and has been a contributing columnist for several LGBTQ+ publications. A resident of Seattle, Washington, Andrew is an active member of Horror Writers Association and is currently working on several forthcoming projects.

~ JOE PHILLIPS ~

Joe Phillips is a 25 year veteran of the comics industry. After working on over 60 issues ranging from DC Comics Superman to Marvel Comics the Silver Surfer and creating his own character The Heretic, he began focusing his attention on the gay community. Along with illustrating, he also writes and directs animated films and videos including the award winning *House of Morecock* and *The Adventures of Stonewall and Riot*. joephillips.com

~ *John Peyton Cooke* ~

John Peyton Cooke is the author of *Out for Blood*, a gay vampire novel published in 1991. His third novel, *Torsos*, was a finalist for the Lambda Literary Award for Best Gay Men's Mystery in 1993. His other novels include *The Chimney Sweeper*, *The Rape of Ganymede*, *The Fall of Lucifer*, *Haven*, and *The Lake*. His "After You've Gone" was selected for Best American Mystery Stories 2003. His shorter works have appeared in magazines such as *Christopher Street*, *The Magazine of Fantasy & Science Fiction*, and *Weird Tales*, and in anthologies such as *The Valancourt Book of Horror Stories (Vol. 4)*, *The Pulp Horror Book of Phobias (Vol. II)*, *Stranger*, *Embracing the Dark*, and *Dark Love*. He was born in Texas and has lived in Wyoming, Wisconsin, New York City, Toronto, and London. He currently lives in Los Angeles with his husband and a whippet. You can find him at https://jpcooke.tripod.com.

~ *Robert Dunbar* ~

Robert Dunbar started life as a (bad) poet. Abandoning that, he eventually wrote for dozens of newspapers and magazines, everything from reviews to political interviews, then later wrote many episodes of television programs, mostly for PBS and Discovery. He's also written numerous plays (one pretty good). Plus he's authored a number of well-received novels. To learn more about his work, visit www.UninvitedBooks.com.

~ GREG HERREN ~

Greg Herren is an award-winning author/editor with over thirty novels, twenty anthologies, and fifty published short stories to his credit. He has won the Lambda Literary Award twice and the Anthony Award, and been shortlisted for numerous others, including the Shirley Jackson and Macavity awards.

~ RICK R REED ~

Rick R. Reed is an award-winning and bestselling author of more than fifty works of published fiction. He is a Lambda Literary Award finalist. Entertainment Weekly has described his work as "heartrending and sensitive." Lambda Literary has called him: "A writer that doesn't disappoint..." Find him at www.rickrreedreality.blogspot.com. Rick lives in Palm Springs, CA, with his husband, Bruce, and their two rescue dogs, Kodi and Joaquin.

~ RYAN FIELD ~

Ryan Field is the author of over 100 published modern gay romance novels and stories, including *An Officer And His Gentleman, Fangsters, The Rainbow Detective Agency* and best-selling *Virgin Billionaire Series*. He's also part of the Lambda Award winning book, *Best Gay Erotica 2009*, with one of his short stories that was published by LGBTQ publisher, Alyson Books. http://ryan-field.blogspot.com/ Social media @ryanfield.

~ *Norman Prentiss* ~

Norman Prentiss is the author of *Odd Adventures with your Other Father*, *Life in a Haunted House*, and *The Apocalypse-a-Day Desk Calendar*. He won a Bram Stoker Award for his first book, *Invisible Fences*. Other publications include *The Book of Baby Names*, *Four Legs in the Morning*, *The Fleshless Man*, *The Halloween Children* (with Brian James Freeman) and *The Narrator* (with Michael McBride), with story appearances in *Dark Screams*, *Postscripts*, *Black Static*, *Four Halloweens*, *Blood Lite 3*, *Best Horror of the Year*, *The Year's Best Dark Fantasy and Horror*, and five editions of the *Shivers* anthology series.
Visit him online at www.normanprentiss.com.

~ *Gregory :L Norris* ~

Gregory L Norris writes for national magazines, numerous fiction anthologies, novels, and the occasional episode for TV and Film. He once worked as a screenwriter on two episodes of Paramount's Star Trek: Voyager series and has had two feature films optioned by Snarkhunter LLC. Norris penned the novel *Ex Marks The Spot* (Woodhall Press) and the forthcoming *The Lost City of Books* (Van Velzer Press) and writes the *The Day After Tomorrow* novels for Anderson Entertainment in the U,K. based upon the classic Gerry Anderson made-for-TV NBC classic, which he watched and loved as a boy. He lives and writes with his gigantic rescue cat and emerald-eyed Muse in Xanadu, a century-old house located at the Outer Limits of New Hampshire's North Country.

~ DAVID GERROLD ~

David Gerrold has been writing professionally for half a century. He created the tribbles for "Star Trek" and Sleestaks for "Land Of The Lost." His most famous novel is *The Man Who Folded Himself.* His semi-autobiographical tale of his son's adoption, *The Martian Child* won both the Hugo and the Nebula awards, and was the basis for the 2007 movie starring John Cusack and Amanda Peet. Gerrold is the 2022 recipient of the Heinlein Award.

~ DARRELL Z GRIZZLE ~

Darrell Z Grizzle is a queer poet and horror and crime fiction author in shadow-haunted Kennesaw, Georgia, where he lives with two cats and way too many books. He is the author of *I Never Meant to Start a Murder Cult and Other Stories.* Darrell is a former parole officer who now works as a counselor in private practice. Visit him at www.ShadowHaunted.com or on Facebook, Goodreads, Twitter, and Instagram as @dzgrizzle.

~ ADRIK KEMP ~

Adrik Kemp is an award-winning writer and author of horror, speculative fiction and fantasy short stories and novels. He has short stories available with Aurealis Magazine, Third Flatiron, Transmundane Press, CSFG Press, Alban Lake Publishing and Pride Publishing. You can find him online @adrikkemp.

~ JACOB BUDENZ ~

Jacob Budenz is a queer writer, multi-disciplinary performer, educator, and witch with an MFA from University of New Orleans and a BA from Johns Hopkins. The author of *Pastel Witcheries* (Seven Kitchens 2018), Budenz has work published or forthcoming by Ghost City Review, Wussy Mag, Entropy Magazine, and Slipstream as well as anthologies by Mason Jar Press, Mad Scientist Journal, and Unbound Edition Press. You can follow Jake's work on Instagram @dreambabyjake, Twitter @jakebeearts, or www.jakebeearts.com.

~ COREY NILES ~

Corey Niles was born and raised in the Rust Belt, where he garnered his love of horror. His recent publications include *Demon Stump* in The Oddville Press and *The Crows Belonged to Me* in HWA Poetry Showcase Vol. VII. When he isn't nursing his caffeine addiction or tending to his graveyard of houseplants, he enjoys jogging on creepy, isolated hiking trails.

~ LEE THOMAS ~

Lee Thomas is the Bram Stoker Award- and two-time Lambda Literary Award-winning author of the books *Stained, The Dust of Wonderland, The German, Parish Damned, Like Light for Flies, Down on Your Knees,* and *Distortion* among others. His work has been translated into multiple languages and has been optioned for film. Lee lives in Austin, Texas with his husband, John.

~ *J Daniel Stone* ~

NYC born and raised J Daniel Stone writes urban horror with a queer focus. He sold his first story when he was 22-years-old and has since written three novels *(The Absence of Light, Blood Kiss* and *Stations of Shadow),* as well as a short story collection *(Lovebites & Razorlines)* and a novella *(I Can Taste The Blood).* He writes under a pseudonym to keep the wolves at bay. Visit him at www.SolitarySpiral.com

~ *Aaron Dries* ~

Author, artist, and filmmaker Aaron Dries was born and raised in New South Wales, Australia. His novels include *House of Sighs, The Fallen Boys, A Place for Sinners,* and *Where the Dead Go to Die,* which he co-wrote with Mark Allan Gunnells. His short fiction and illustration work has been published world-wide. Aaron's most recent release is the highly-acclaimed *Dirty Heads*: A novella of cosmic coming of age horror. Feel free to drop him a line at www.aarondries.com.

~ HAL BODNER ~

Hal Bodner is a multiple Bram Stoker Award nominated author whose freshman vampire novel, *Bite Club*, made him one of the top-selling LGBT authors in the country. Some twenty years later, the royalties continue to keep him in "cigarettes and nylons" – even though he quit smoking and never did drag. As a novelist, Hal is known for his biting wit, his realistic farce, and his completely and utterly irreverent comedy. His most recent release is a superhero urban fantasy from Crossroad Press, entitled *Fabulous in Tights*, followed by *A Study in Spandex*. Currently, Hal is working on a series of comic thrillers which paint classic noir fiction with a distinctly lavender glaze. Hal is married to a wonderful man, half his age, who never knew that Liza Minnelli was Judy Garland's daughter.

~ ANDREW ROBERTSON ~

Andrew Robertson is an award-winning queer writer. His fiction has appeared in magazines such as Stitched Smile Publications Magazine Vol 1, Deadman's Tome, and Sirens Call, and anthologies including *Alice Unbound: Beyond Wonderland*, *A Tribute Anthology to Deadworld*, *Group Hex* Vol. 1 and 2, and *O Unholy Night in Deathlehem*. He is also the editor of *Dark Rainbow: Queer Erotic Horror*, founder of The Great Lakes Horror Company Podcast, and a member of the HWA.

ALSO FROM LVP PUBLICATIONS:

The Pulp Horror Book
Of Phobias

The Pulp Horror Book
Of Phobias, Vol II

Revisiting the Undead

Subliminal Reality

Final Masquerade

Darkling's Beasts & Brews:
Poetry with a Drink on the Side

Available at LycanValley.com